MAGGIE GALLAGHER
LEGAL THRILLER

The Midwest Lawyer

The Bloodied Client

The Wrong Victim

This is a work of fiction. Names, characters, places and incidents either are the product of imagination or are used fictitiously. Any resemblance to actual persons, living or dead, events or locales, is entirely coincidental.

RELAY PUBLISHING EDITION, JANUARY 2026
Copyright © 2026 Relay Publishing Ltd.

All rights reserved. Published in the United Kingdom by Relay Publishing. This book or any portion thereof may not be reproduced or used in any manner whatsoever without the express written permission of the publisher except for the use of brief quotations in a book review.

Peter Kirkland is a pen name created by Relay Publishing for co-authored Legal Thriller projects. Relay Publishing works with incredible teams of writers and editors to collaboratively create the very best stories for our readers.

Cover Design by Deranged Doctor.

Print and ebook formatting by Lori Colbeck.

www.relaypub.com

THE BLOODIED CLIENT

PETER KIRKLAND

MAGGIE GALLAGHER LEGAL THRILLER SERIES
BOOK TWO

BLURB

A teenage girl is charged with the unthinkable…

The crime? The brutal murder of her own parents. The prosecution's argument seems airtight. But small town defense attorney Maggie Gallagher senses something isn't right…

Months earlier, Zoey Conrad had already faced her worst nightmare when two men broke into her room. In the terrifying struggle that followed, one intruder ended up dead. The judge declared it self-defense and dismissed the charges, allowing Zoey to rebuild her life in their small town. But now, with her parents found murdered under disturbingly similar circumstances, the evidence against Zoey quickly piles up.

Maggie knows Zoey and she wants to believe the girl is no killer. Yet the more she learns about the twisted life the Conrads led, the stronger her compassion for Zoey grows. But the deeper she digs, the worse things get. Especially since Maggie's own son has gotten personally involved.

As the prosecution builds an ironclad case and the clock ticks down, Maggie must race to expose the truth. If she fails, Zoey's fate is sealed —and an innocent life could be shattered forever.

CONTENTS

Chapter 1	1
Chapter 2	10
Chapter 3	20
Chapter 4	30
Chapter 5	43
Chapter 6	57
Chapter 7	69
Chapter 8	85
Chapter 9	94
Chapter 10	103
Chapter 11	111
Chapter 12	122
Chapter 13	129
Chapter 14	140
Chapter 15	154
Chapter 16	166
Chapter 17	176
Chapter 18	186
Chapter 19	193
Chapter 20	202
Chapter 21	210
Chapter 22	217
Chapter 23	224
Chapter 24	234
Chapter 25	243
Chapter 26	254
Chapter 27	266
Chapter 28	277
Chapter 29	284
Chapter 30	293
Chapter 31	300
Chapter 32	309
Chapter 33	324
Chapter 34	330

Chapter 35	335
Chapter 36	342
End of The Bloodied Client	347
About Peter Kirkland	349
Sneak Peek: The Wrong Victim	351
Sneak Peek: Small Town Conviction	357
Also by Peter Kirkland	369

1

You expect warning signs before a disaster. Sirens. Gunshots. Clouds rolling up on your perfect blue sky. But I was sure my sky was all blue, no clouds, no sirens. Nothing out of its place—at least, that I could see.

The Dunlaps were in for a quick probate issue—Emily Dunlap and her son Ken. Emily's husband George had passed on unexpectedly in a car crash, and I could see that her grief was still raw. She looked past me, not at me, as I talked through our business. My office had a nice view of the old courthouse, but I doubted she noticed it in her state.

"Mrs. Dunlap?"

She focused her gaze on me to show she was listening. Ken gave me the nod, so I went on.

"Most of the estate was in both of your names: the house, the business, your Atwood Lake cabin. There's no paperwork you need to worry about to transfer those assets. Same goes for—"

Ken cut in. "His retirement account?"

"Yes, that as well." Emily was back to staring past me, and I found myself frowning as I went on. "All his accounts were in both of your names, with the exception of this one." I held out the statement for her to see, but she didn't look at it. Ken reached out instead. Was he a little too eager? I thought back to an old case I'd once prosecuted, a son who had stolen his mother's estate. Sold it all out from under her while she stewed in her grief.

Ken smiled. "Uh, Ms. Gallagher?"

I realized I was holding on to the statement, clutching on tight as he tried to take it. But he wasn't the kid from that long-ago case, and Emily wasn't that sad, helpless mother. She had her sisters and cousins to lean on, and Ken was a good kid as far as I'd seen.

You're not a prosecutor anymore, I reminded myself. *And not everyone is a crime waiting to happen.*

I let go of the statement and cleared my throat. "It's an investment account, and it's just in your husband's name. Same goes for your Lexus, and your son's truck. I've prepared an order for the court to sign, to transfer those over. You should be through probate by the end of this month."

Ken let out a tight breath and sagged with relief.

"So we give this to the judge, and that's it? We're done?"

I could sense his fatigue, so I offered a smile. "I'll take care of that part. You're essentially done. All I need from your mom today is her signature here." I'd prepared applications to put the titles for the Dunlaps' two houses solely in Emily's name. Now I passed her a pen, and she signed them without reading.

"So that's all you need?" She seemed relieved too, glad to be done with this and with my office.

"That's all," I said, then searched for some words of comfort. "Your husband did a great job securing your future. He made this easy as easy could be."

Emily laughed then, a soft, broken sound. She blinked, then she stood. "Yeah. That was George."

The Dunlaps filed out and Auntie El bustled in, in one of her trademark loud floral blouses. I'd thought about asking her to tone down her wardrobe—we were a law office, not a car lot—but clients liked her. She put them at ease. And she cheered me up too, a bright splash of color to pep up my day.

"So sad," she said, when the Dunlaps were gone.

I sighed. "I know. How old was he? Sixty?"

"Sixty-one; far too young. Damn those drunk drivers." Auntie El set about straightening my desk. I winced, thinking back to Dad's drinking days, all the times I'd had to confiscate his car keys. There'd been a few times I hadn't caught him in time, and only by God's grace had he come home without hurting himself or anyone else.

Auntie El stepped back, done with her straightening. "You have Edie Endicott coming by later. She has some more questions about her 'divorce.'" She did bouncy air quotes, and we both groaned. Edie had been coming every week for a while, testing the waters on her maybe-divorce. "And you've got the Batchelder custody hearing, so you'll want to get down to the courthouse by four."

"Get me their file," I said.

Aunt Louise fetched the file, and she freshened my coffee. "You ever wish you'd get a splashier case? Like when Troy was charged with killing Coach Schafer?"

I shuddered at the memory. "That case was messy in a lot of ways. Don't forget, it started when his son almost died."

"But it was exciting. You live for a challenge. I've known you all your life, so don't act like you don't."

I thought again of the Dunlaps and their dull probate case, and how I'd flashed back to the Mulligan fraud. Had some part of me wished for a monster to fight? I did love a challenge, no doubt about that. But Troy's case had been awful. Folks had been hurt. I shuddered, remembering how hard it had been on Troy and his family.

"No one gets traumatized in probate court."

"But does it stir your soul?"

I swiveled my chair around to look out the window, at the old courthouse with its closely cropped lawn. No one heard cases there anymore, not since the new courthouse went up down the road. But still, when I looked at it, I always sat straighter. It reminded me why I did what I did.

"My soul's fine," I said. "Now, go on, get." I put on my "gruff sheriff" voice to show I was joking. Auntie El huffed, hands on her hips. Then, with a shake of her head, she went out, grumbling the whole way about stubborn people. I watched her go, smiling, then got back to work. I was fine with these types of workaday cases, and finer still with leaving at five. No long nights holed up in my office, desperately digging for contradictions in witness statements. No tossing and turning, losing sleep over whether I'd done everything I could to save my client's life. With these cases, I could rest easy—and have time to relax. I'd made it home every night last week to a hot dinner, and I expected this week to play out the same.

―――

I drove home through Kerry in a good mood. This was what I'd moved back for, the small-town quiet. The kids in the park in their letter jackets, tossing a football out by the pond. The moms with their strollers up by the swings. Mrs. Adler from the mini mart bringing in her displays: flats of fresh fruits and vegetables, buckets of flowers. She looked up and waved when I stopped for the light.

I drove on through the suburbs, past houses I knew. My cousin Liam's place. His neighbor Jim's. The Hensons', the Learys', the MacDougall place. Our own house was farther out, on the edge of town, big enough for the three of us but not so big we rattled. I pulled up behind Sean's car and headed inside. The good smell of tacos met me at the door.

"Tuesday already?" I stepped inside, stretching out the stiffness of the day.

"Don't yell through the house."

"That you yelling back?" I kicked off my shoes and stowed my briefcase with a grin, and went through to the kitchen to find my husband at the stove.

"I'm starving," I said, and stole a fried pepper. Sean pretended to smack me with his wooden spoon. Hot grease flew off it and spattered my sleeve.

"Shoot, just a minute."

"It's fine, don't fuss."

He got the vinegar anyway and mixed it with water, and dabbed my sleeve till the grease spot was out. Anyone else, it would've annoyed me, being fussed over when I'd said I was fine. But I loved when Sean cared for me. I always had. He did it in little ways that weren't intrusive. Little reminders he was here. He was mine. I pressed a kiss to his temple—my blue-eyed boy. His hair had grayed some since our move from Chicago, but he was still handsome, always would be to me.

"Ian home yet?"

"Yeah. You can get him. I'm about to dish up."

I called out for Ian, yelling through the house again. He yelled back he was coming. Sean rolled his eyes.

"Sit down and relax," he suggested. "I'll set the table."

I did as he said, stretching my legs out in front of me. The left one still got stiff at the end of the day, even after over a year of PT. I massaged my hip while Sean wasn't looking, but the pain just migrated down to my knee. Upstairs, Ian's door slammed, and I straightened up.

"Hey, Mom," he said, slouching into the kitchen, that hunched seventeen-year-old too-cool-for-school gait.

"Hey. How was school?"

"You can't ever ask about anything else?" He grabbed the placemats off the top of the fridge and set them out on the table, a little askew. He set out napkins too, and poured us all water. I watched him and tried to pinpoint his mood. Setting the table was a good sign, but the school snapback wasn't. His normal response was 'I don't know, fine?'

"Okay, how's your social life? Getting along with your friends?"

He snorted. "What am I, five?"

"When you *were* five, you wouldn't shut up. You'd go on and on while your—"

"Mom!"

"—nuggies got cold: *then my teacher did this. My best friend did that. We made paper turkeys*—"

"Dad, make her stop."

Sean set my plate down, loaded with tacos. He'd overstuffed them as usual, but I didn't care. I spooned on guacamole and pico de gallo, and leaned over my plate for a big, juicy bite. Beans squirted out and I spooned them up, and I sighed as I savored the sharpness of lime juice.

"How's soccer?" I tried when I'd swallowed at last.

Ian gulped water. "I quit the team."

I almost choked on my next bite. "You quit? Wha—"

Sean kicked my ankle and I shut my mouth. The last thing we needed was me "going red," as Sean called it when I lost my temper. A hilarious joke on my flaming red hair.

I breathed in through my nose and exhaled my feelings. Or tried to exhale them. Inside, I could feel my frustration rising. Soccer was Ian's thing. He'd always played soccer. And he was good at it, and it was a team sport, which meant it was gold for college applications. If he'd quit last year, when we'd moved to Kerry from Chicago, I might have understood. But he'd enjoyed playing last year. He'd gotten on great with his coach and his teammates. Why would he quit now?

"You quit soccer," I said again, more calmly this time. "I thought you were liking it."

Ian shrugged. "I liked it fine, but I'm too busy. I have too much homework to make it to practice."

I glanced over at Sean to see how he was taking this, and more importantly, if he'd already known. His look of bamboozlement told me he hadn't. I willed him to say something so I wouldn't have to, but he popped a forkful of rice in his mouth.

"College applications are coming up," I said, keeping my tone even. "After-school activities look good on those."

Ian took a page from Sean's book and bit into his taco. The two of them sat chewing, and I threw up my hands. "Okay, I get it. I'm not going to nag. Just tell me you'll think about adding another extracurricular. I'm sure you can find one that sucks up less time. How about debate club?"

Ian rolled his eyes at me. I rolled mine right back.

"Fine, not debate. Model UN. Mathletes?"

Ian covered his mouth so he wouldn't spray taco meat. Sean laughed too, *pfft* through his nose. I knew I wouldn't beat them, so I joined them instead. I laughed, and it felt pretty good. It felt normal.

That was my day. Normal. Boring. No sirens, no gunshots, no clouds in my sky. I did my normal work and came home to my family. We bickered over dinner, then came back together, same way we always did. Sean had brought lava cakes home for dessert, and I had two and crashed out from the sugar. I stretched out on the sofa with some contracts to review, and at some point, as normal, I fell asleep.

I half-woke when Ian yelled through the house, "Night, Mom!"

I half-woke again when Sean went up to bed, yelling through to remind me not to sleep on the couch.

I jolted awake to full dark, no stars, a pale spill of contracts across my lap. Something had woken me. A sound? A thump? I sat up, spine tingling, hairs stiff on my neck.

"Sean? Is that you?"

No answer. Silence. Then came the thunder of fists on the door, somebody banging. Had Ian locked himself out? But it was a school night. He wouldn't be out.

I squared up my contracts and set them aside, and squinted through the dark at the clock on the wall. Ten thirty. Who—

The banging came again, then the doorbell. Whoever was out there was mashing the bell, so its chimes ran together like *dingdingding-*

dong. I sprang off the couch and ran out to the hall, where I nearly crashed into Sean in his pajamas. He nudged me behind him and strode to the door.

"It's a girl," he said. "In her PJs."

Ian shuffled out to the top of the stairs. "Mom? What's going on?"

"Nothing. Go back to bed." I waved him back, but he didn't move. I pushed in to take Sean's place at the peephole. He was right—it was a kid out there in her pajamas. She looked sixteen, seventeen. Around Ian's age. I'd seen her before at Ian's school.

"Please let me in." Her voice was all ragged, like she'd been crying.

Sean nodded, and I opened the door. The girl stepped forward into the light. My breath caught in my throat as I saw the whole picture: the blood on her face and her pajama top. She looked like she'd been sprayed with it, or had it coughed on her. And in her hand, she was clutching a gun.

2

"Get upstairs," I yelled at both Ian and Sean.

The girl dropped her gun and started to cry.

"I need help," she said. "You're a lawyer, right?"

"I—"

Ian came hurtling down the stairs. "Zoey!" He lunged right at her, going in for a hug, and I barely got between them in time.

"No! No, don't touch her."

"Why, is she hurt?" Ian tried to push past me, but Sean held him back. I held my hands up for a time-out.

"What's happening, Mom? Zoey, you hurt?" Ian sounded frantic, but I couldn't focus on calming him down when I had a blood-covered, traumatized teen in front of me.

"What's happening is, we need to get her inside. Zoey, is that your name? Zoey, come in."

Zoey stared blankly, like she hadn't heard me. I glanced at the gun and realized she might not have. If she had fired it without wearing ear protection, she might've damaged her hearing.

"Zoey." I raised my voice. "Hey. Can you hear me?"

She put her hands to her head. "My ears are still ringing."

"Okay, come inside. You hear? *Come inside.*"

Ian tried once more to swoop in, but I headed him off. I dropped my voice to a low pitch so Zoey wouldn't hear.

"I get she's your friend and you want to be there for her, but she's just told me she needs a lawyer. I'm telling you, as her lawyer, her clothing is evidence. I can't let you touch her. Do you understand?"

Ian's scowl was thunderous, but he nodded yes. He followed me and Zoey into the living room, then hovered over us as I got her settled on the couch.

"Can I get her some water, or are her lips evidence?" Ian said, teenage sarcasm in full force. But I could hear his voice trembling. He was worried for his friend and trying to cover it with attitude.

"Get me my phone and then get upstairs. If you overhear what she tells me, that'll void privilege."

This wasn't the answer Ian wanted to hear, and he stood with his hands on his hips, glaring at me.

Sean got my phone and I set it aside, ready to call 911 once Zoey and I had talked.

"We should call her parents," Sean said. "Hey, Zoey? What's your home number? I need to talk to your parents."

Zoey jumped off the couch. "No! No, you can't!"

"They should know where you are."

Zoey's gaze darted to Ian, and then to me. She pressed her palms to her ears again and winced like they hurt. "Please don't. You can't. Did you call the police?"

"Not yet, but I'll have to," I told her. "After we've talked."

Zoey sat down again, though "sat" was the wrong word. It was more that she dropped down like her strings had been cut. I could see she was shaking, shock setting in, and I grabbed a quilt to drape over her shoulders. Ian snatched it from me and swaddled her himself. I let him do that, then I pulled him aside.

"Mom—"

"I need to talk to her now as her lawyer. That means you and Dad need to go wait upstairs."

Ian stared a long moment, and I thought he might fight me, then he nodded abruptly and went off with Sean. A sign of maturity? That would be nice. But I narrowed my eyes as I watched him head off. Maybe I was right, and he *was* growing up...or maybe he knew more than he was letting on. Was he somehow involved in this?

Upstairs, his door slammed, and my stomach turned. How well did he know this girl? Just from classes, or...?

Zoey sniffled. I shook my head. I couldn't dive down that rabbit hole, at least not now. What I had to do now was get Zoey to talk and gauge how much trouble this girl was in.

I caught Sean as he headed upstairs himself. "Track down her parents, okay? Ian has their last name. Call them."

Then they were gone, and it was just me and Zoey. I sat down across from her and leaned in, flashing what I hoped was a comforting smile. She recoiled slightly, not a good sign. I needed her to trust me and open up.

"So...bad day?" I tried, hoping a little humor would lighten the mood.

Zoey's lip twitched like she wanted to smile, but it only lasted a beat before fading. She looked down at her hands. The backs were all spattered with brown flecks of blood.

"Hey. Look at me."

Zoey looked through me, a thousand-yard stare. I kept my tone light, a hard thing to do when I had to half-shout.

"Why don't you tell me what brought you here?"

Zoey opened her mouth, then she closed it again. She licked her lips, and I tried not to grimace: she had blood there too, all over her face.

"I don't know," she said, almost too soft to hear.

"Whose gun were you carrying?"

"What?"

"*Whose gun was that?*"

Zoey's brow furrowed, but she didn't speak. I couldn't tell if she was trying to remember, or if she was testing her story for holes. Her manner felt off, though I couldn't say how. Too quiet, maybe. Too focused and thoughtful. If she'd showed up asking for help, that would have been one thing—but she'd specifically asked for a *lawyer* off the bat, and hadn't said a whole lot after that. But it was too soon to jump to conclusions. Maybe her silence was a symptom of shock. She was still shaking, her skin waxy-pale.

"Zoey? Whose gun did you have at the door?"

"Dad's gun," she said. "There were men. In our house."

Okay, that was something. "Men you knew? Or strangers?"

She took another few moments to think about that, then she rubbed at her ears again. "My ears are all stuffy. Like after a swim meet." She smacked on her head, as though to dislodge water. Definitely hearing loss, then—but that wasn't the most important thing right now.

"Zoey, who were the men? I need you to focus."

"They… I don't know. They had, like, uniforms? But they weren't cops. They were more like, uh..." She stared through me some more, her brow crinkled up. Then her expression cleared, and she sat straighter. "They had the same jackets, with the same logo. Sort of a star with a cross in the middle. I went to bed early, and when I woke up, they were there in my bedroom. They were grabbing me. Hurting me..." She rolled up her sleeve. "Can you see, are there marks?"

I switched on the table lamp, and yeah, there were marks. Faint and red still, but they'd darken, I knew. Deep fingermarks where someone had grabbed her.

"I fought them," she said. "I was screaming for Mom and Dad. But they just kept on dragging me up out of bed, and all I could think was, I once saw this ad. This PSA for stranger danger? It said there's two crime scenes: the one where they grab you, and the one after that where they find your body. I didn't want—didn't want—" Her voice rose and rose, and then cracked. She broke off. Bent almost double, hitching for breath.

"It's okay," I said. "Shh. Take your time."

She let out a sob, a rough, ragged sound. She grabbed at her hair and pulled it out to the sides. "I kicked one of them off me and then I ran downstairs. I got my dad's gun and I started shooting. I don't know if I, uh— I don't think— I wasn't aiming. My eyes were closed. I just… I wanted to scare them off. Make them go away. I think Mom was screaming, but I don't know. It could've been screams, or my ears, from the shots." She dropped her hair and tugged her ears instead. Rocked back and forth, then slumped on the couch.

"One of them, uh, he came at me again. I know I hit that one because he— He fell. I bent down to check on him, but his friend was still moving, so I ran off, and I ended up here."

"So, someone was hurt? You're saying you shot him?"

"Yeah, I think... Yeah? He was coughing up blood." She touched her face, all speckled with blood. My heart thumped at the thought of my old Army sidearm, nestled in its gun safe under my bed. Ian couldn't get to it, or I didn't *think* he could, but what if—

"Mrs. Gallagher?"

I reached for my phone and held it up so Zoey could see. "I need to call 911, now I know someone's hurt. They'll send an ambulance out to your house."

Zoey sat shaking as I made the call. I knew there was a good chance they'd send the cops out as well, not just to Zoey's place, but to my address. I'd have to move fast to get the rest of her statement.

"Will I, um..." Zoey sniffed. "Will I get arrested?"

"I don't know," I said. "But if you do, you have me. You don't have to say anything without me present."

"Yeah, I know. I watch *Law & Order*."

I frowned, trying to figure out what I was missing. Something with her story didn't add up. Then I remembered her reaction when I'd mentioned her parents. She'd freaked when I'd wanted to give them a call. But they weren't the ones who'd attacked her, so why that response? Did she think they'd be angry she'd used her dad's gun?

"Ian said you're the best. You found the coach's real killer and got Troy Weaver acquitted."

I coughed to hide my surprise. Ian had said that?

"I think they were both still alive when I left. They were both moving. The men, I mean."

Sirens rose a few blocks away, and I knew our time was short. I needed to make sure Zoey knew what to do.

"The police will be here in a couple of minutes, and they'll want to talk to you, but remember your rights. You don't have to talk to them, and I'm advising you not to. You have the right to have me present any time they question you, and not just tonight. Exercising that right won't make you look guilty. Is there anything I need to know that you haven't told me?"

The sirens cut out. The night flashed red and blue. Zoey turned to look, but I leaned into her sightline.

"This is important. Did you leave anything out? Anything I need to know as your lawyer?"

"I don't think so. No? I wasn't trying to hurt them. I only shot so they'd leave me alone."

"Okay," I said. "The police may take you with them, or they may not. But if they do, I'll be right behind you. And remember, not one word without me present."

Sean let the cops in, two older guys. I knew one of them slightly; he was a friend of my cousin Patrick's. The other, I hadn't met, but I could tell he knew me. His face went tight at the sight of me, and he glanced at his colleague. I ignored him and turned to Patrick's friend.

"O'Riordan, right?"

His face stayed blank. "Yeah."

"You should know I'm Zoey's lawyer."

"That's fine," he said. "But we just want to talk to her. She's not under arrest, at least not yet."

I moved to block him from Zoey, whose eyes had gone huge. "My client won't be making a statement at this time, but you should know there's at least one gunshot victim at her residence."

O'Riordan frowned past me, then he stepped back. He conferred with his colleague, then squared up to me.

"We're going to need her to come to the station. And my advice is, if this was self-defense, she should have nothing to hide. The best thing she can do here is cooperate."

Zoey started to say something, but I cut her off. "The only reason to take my client to the station would be to interrogate her, and she's invoking her right to remain silent. Unless she's under arrest, she's not going anywhere."

O'Riordan's face hardened. "Fine. She's under arrest." He went for his handcuffs. Zoey let out a yelp.

"It's okay," I told her. "I'll be right behind you."

Zoey bowed her head as he slapped on the cuffs. Then the cops guided her out to the car. She looked back at me as they helped her inside. Next to them, she looked smaller than she had in the house, and she seemed to dwindle even further as she got in the car. Hunched up in the back, she looked about child-sized, which I guessed was right. She was still a child. For a moment, I saw Ian huddled where she was. A chill ran through me, and I hugged myself.

"Maggie?" Sean said.

I turned. "Where's Ian?"

"Upstairs."

I exhaled, relieved, and went to follow Zoey, but Sean caught my arm.

"There's something else."

"I need to get to the station."

"I'll drive you. Come on."

"I'm coming too." Ian came stomping downstairs. "I need to be there for Zoey. She needs a friend."

I didn't want Ian anywhere near this mess. Didn't want anyone talking to him till I knew what he knew.

"They're not going to let you see her tonight. And this could take hours. You need to rest up for school."

"I'm not a kid, Mom."

"But I'm still your mother. And I'm telling you, they won't let you see her tonight. I need you to stay, and not fight me on this."

Ian looked like he had more to say, but Sean steered him inside before he could get started. Soon, Sean came back out and we got in the car.

"This was her parents' fault." Sean backed down the drive. He turned east on the darkened street, toward downtown. "Those men were from one of those, you know, those boot camps."

"What? Did they tell you that?"

"Yeah. When I called."

My stomach did a slow roll. "When you say 'those boot camps,' you mean...?"

"One of those ones like you see on TV, where they kidnap your troubled teen and put them through hell. Lorraine, that's her mom, said they'd hit a wall with her. They couldn't think of what else to do."

I watched the streetlights go by, a sour taste in my mouth. I'd heard of those camps all right, and what went on there. Kids tied to chairs.

Kids locked in cells. Kids fed spoiled food, then punished for puking. Kids *died* in those places, or so I'd heard.

"What, uh..." I cleared my throat. "What was your read on the mom?"

Sean's knuckles on the steering wheel had gone bloodless white. His mouth was a hard line, eyes fixed straight ahead.

"Not good," he said at last. "My read was, not good."

3

The police charged Zoey, as I'd thought they might. They'd got a statement from one of her attackers and booked her on assault with a deadly weapon.

Zoey seemed more puzzled than scared at first and sat picking her sleeve in the interview room.

"But those men were kidnapping me. Isn't that self-defense?"

I wasn't sure what her attacker had said, or her parents, for that matter. The cops had interviewed them on the scene. "If your statement was accurate, then yes. It should be. Is there anything you can think of you might have left out?"

Zoey looked at me like she hadn't heard me. Maybe she hadn't. I wasn't sure. "So, did my mom, did my parents post bail?"

I reminded myself she was still a kid, no criminal record, no prior arrests. Of course it made sense she had no clue how bail worked. But I didn't want to smack her upside the head with the truth. She'd had enough shocks for one night, and she still had more coming. Her second attacker was still in surgery, and word around the station was, it didn't look good.

"Not yet," I said carefully. "You need a judge to set bail."

"So where's the judge?"

I could feel Zoey fraying and starting to panic, and what I had to tell her wouldn't be comforting. But it was my job to be honest with her, and she needed to know what to expect.

"Once you're arrested, you'll have your arraignment, usually within twenty-four hours of arrest. That means tomorrow, you'll go to court—"

"What? So you're saying I'm stuck here all night?"

"You'll be spending tonight in juvenile detention, then you'll come back tomorrow for your arraignment."

"And that's when I get bail? I can go home?" Her eyes were enormous, brimming with tears. I wanted to tell her of course she'd get bail, but there was no "of course" here. Her hearing *might* go fine and she *might* be sent home, or she might get hit with additional charges that would make bail more complicated. I had no way of knowing, without all the facts.

"The judge will hear arguments on bail," I said. "Then in a week or so, since you're under eighteen, you'll have a second appearance in juvenile court, for what we call a probable cause hearing. It's to determine if the state's case is strong enough to prosecute, and if you'll be tried as an adult. Based on what you've told me, the state has no case. I'll argue you acted in self-defense, and if the judge agrees, we'll get your charges dismissed. But, Zoey, if there's anything you're holding back—"

"So I could be in jail a whole week?"

I could see she was exhausted and scared. And I wasn't sure how much she was hearing. She was pawing at her ears like they were still ringing—plus, panic had a way of blocking things out. But I had to try to comfort her as best I could.

"They'll set your hearing as fast as they can. And in the meantime, I'll be in close touch. If you need anything, you let me know, and if it's something I can do for you, I'll get it done."

Zoey didn't seem to notice my evasive answer. She was looking past me, at the closed door.

"Are my parents out there?"

"I think so, yes."

"Did you talk to them yet?"

"No, but I'm about to."

Zoey looked at her hands, now clean of blood. "Dad was yelling," she said. "When he saw what I did. That's why I ran, because, because..." She sniffled, blinked hard, and tried again. "Dad looked mad when he saw that I'd shot someone. Not mad at those guys, but mad at *me*. That's his big rule, don't touch his guns. Can you tell him I was only trying to protect us?"

My throat tightened up, and I went for my phone. I couldn't let Zoey hear my voice crack. I tapped on the screen till I felt I could trust myself, then I smiled and stood up.

"I'll tell him. Don't worry."

Out in the hall, I took a moment to steel myself. Zoey's parents were here, waiting out in the lobby. I could hear her dad yelling, muffled through the door. What I wanted to do was get up in his face, ask what was he thinking, having Zoey kidnapped. How could he treat his own daughter like that?

What kind of parent, of monster, *are you?*

I clenched my fists, hunched my shoulders, and breathed through my rage. Breathed till the red had gone out of my vision. What I needed to do here was win these folks' trust. Convince them I was the best choice to represent Zoey. Maybe then, I could mitigate the damage they'd done.

I straightened my hair in the window, then I strode out to greet them. They struck me as a typical PTA couple, Mr. Conrad still wearing his high school class ring, Mrs. Conrad demure in a tweed pencil skirt.

"Mr. and Mrs. Conrad? I'm Maggie Gallagher. I've been here acting as your daughter's attorney." I stuck out my hand, and Mr. Conrad shook it.

"Paul," he said. "And my wife, Lorraine."

I shook Lorraine's hand too, then got straight down to business. "First, I need to ask you, do you want to retain me to represent Zoey?"

Paul's brows drew together. "I thought you already were."

"She showed up on my doorstep saying she needed representation, and I've acted as her attorney up to this point. But when it comes to ongoing representation, as Zoey's parents, that decision is yours. Zoey's been charged with assault with a deadly weapon, but further charges may be forthcoming. Manslaughter is possible, or even murder, if the injured man doesn't pull through."

Lorraine clutched Paul's arm. "Murder? Zoey?"

"You defended Troy Weaver." Paul pointed at me. "Give us a second. We need to, uh..." He left the thought hanging and drew Lorraine aside. I pretended not to listen as they conferred. Lorraine wanted Hugh Barlow, their "usual" lawyer. I knew Hugh; he was a nice guy. He did mostly civil work. Paul wanted me, because I'd cleared Troy Weaver. He whispered to Lorraine that he thought Troy was guilty, as if I couldn't hear him in the cramped space. After a minute, he turned back to me.

"We'll take you," he said. He pointed at me again, and I tried not to bristle. Everything about him rubbed me the wrong way. I knew his type—big fish, small pond. They washed out quick-smart in the Army, crumbling when they realized they weren't in charge. I let myself picture that, and I felt better.

"I'll have my assistant send a contract tomorrow. In the meantime, let's talk. We have a lot to go over."

I went up to the desk sergeant and requested a place somewhere private, then led the Conrads to an interview room. Lorraine sat down, but Paul stayed standing.

"Sit down," I said. "This will take a while."

Paul scowled at me, but I ignored him. After a moment, he took a seat. I took my spot across from him and got out my notepad.

"I'd like to take notes, if you don't mind."

Lorraine didn't say anything. Paul narrowed his eyes.

"What for?"

"For my own records, so I'll know what was said."

Paul grunted, then shrugged. "I guess that's okay."

I wrote the date in my notepad and underlined it. Then I moved on to the big, burning question. "So, before anything else—Sean tells me what happened wasn't a kidnapping. Can you confirm that the kidnappers were in your home at your behest?"

"At my behest?" Paul said "behest" like he was testing its flavor, drawing it out in a broad, mocking tone. I stayed quiet and waited for him to go on.

"They're from Youth Rise," said Lorraine. She glanced at Paul.

"That's right," he said. "Youth Rise Rehabilitation. The Swoffords sent their kid there. He came out great."

I'd never heard of the Swoffords, or of Youth Rise, but I nodded anyway. "And, what goes on at Youth Rise?"

"Well, it's for—"

"The kids get—"

Paul and Lorraine both launched in at once, then stopped abruptly. Lorraine let out a high, nervous laugh. Then Paul cleared his throat and started again.

"It's a cross between summer camp and regular school. Kids there get exercise, discipline. Structure. They learn skills—"

"Skills schools don't teach. Not our schools nowadays. Here, look at this." Lorraine dug in her purse and pulled out a pamphlet. She slid it across to me and I picked it up. It was glossy, and printed on quality stock, showing photos of happy kids playing football and hoops. A girl in pigtails sat in a canoe, beaming up at the camera through gappy teeth. She couldn't have been more than eleven or twelve.

"Looks nice," I said, carefully neutral. "But why not just drive her there? Drop her off like a regular camp?"

Lorraine and Paul exchanged glances again.

"She needs help," said Lorraine.

"Youth Rise is, uh..." Paul took the pamphlet back and leafed through the pages. "It isn't a normal camp. It's for troubled teens." He found the passage he wanted and traced it with his finger. "'They need to be broken down and then built back up.' It's what's best for them. That's why they grab them. To lower their defenses. That way, the kids know they're not in control. They can't pull their usual sh—their usual tricks. Sulking won't work, or storming out. Kids learn how to show respect again, and how to take pride in themselves."

I found myself thinking again of the Army, how they'd ground us down in basic training. But we'd all been adults. We'd signed up for that. Zoey hadn't asked to be snatched in the night. I tried not to think what she must've imagined, waking up to a man dragging her out of bed.

"They get counseling," Lorraine said. "And they go to school. Most of their grades go up a whole letter."

"You mean while they're there, or when they get back home?"

Lorraine bit her lip. "I don't know. Both? I'd have to read through it again. There's a whole info pack."

I'd heard of that too, with these teen prison camps—fudged grades, useless classes. "Diplomas" no college would recognize. All so they could make their grandiose claims without technically lying. What kind of parent wouldn't at least take a school tour? At least verify its accreditation? I could feel my red rising, and I fought it back down.

"What made you decide Zoey needed a place like that? You say it's for troubled teens. Was she in trouble?"

Lorraine started to answer, but Paul cut in. "She was headed that way."

"Her friends were on drugs." Lorraine pursed her lips. "And that boy Ian, who yelled at his teacher."

Ian? My Ian? I gripped my notepad. The coil bit into the palm of my hand. Lorraine was still talking about kids on drugs.

"They're just a bad influence. A rough crowd, you know? We could see Zoey changing, starting down the wrong path."

I took a deep breath and kept my tone even. "Do you believe she was using drugs?"

"Not that we saw," said Paul. "But she might have at school, or at a friend's house. She did come home some days smelling of perfume, and we know kids can use that to hide they've been smoking."

"Personality changes!" Lorraine grabbed the pamphlet, searching through it herself now. "That's one of the warning signs, when they're on drugs. And Zoey was suddenly—she'd changed a lot. She had all these opinions on school. Politics. She called us 'regressive,' and when we'd try to talk to her, she'd go 'okay, boomer.'"

I had to bite my tongue to keep from laughing. This wasn't funny, but it was absurd. Zoey's crimes, as I counted them, were smelling of perfume, spending time with supposedly "rough" kids, and the odd *okay, boomer*. So, being a teenager, in other words.

I snapped my notepad shut. "I'll see Zoey tomorrow to prepare her for court, and we'll need to talk again before her hearing."

Lorraine stood up. "She'll be okay, right?"

"Of course she will." Paul stood as well. "Those idiots botched it, let her get to that gun."

I didn't comment on that, or on their jab at Ian. Nothing I had to say to them would be friendly or kind, so I let them walk out, and said nothing at all.

I headed out of the station in search of Sean, but our car was gone, Auntie El's in its place. She was down by the benches with a couple of cops, but she wrapped it up with them when she saw me come out.

"Sean needed to get home and check up on Ian. I said I'd come get you. How did it go?"

I didn't want to get into it in front of the cops, so I just groaned and got in the car. Auntie El got in too, and started the engine.

"Youth Rise, huh?"

I groaned again, deeper. Auntie El reached over and squeezed my arm.

"I brought you a lemon bar. It's in the glove box."

The last thing on my mind up till then had been food, but no one said no to Auntie El's lemon bars. I cracked open the Tupperware and set it in my lap, crumbs raining down as I nibbled my treat.

"You want to watch for those Conrads." She slowed for a light.

"Watch for them how?"

"They've sued a lot of folk here in town. Businesses, mostly. Some guy who punched Paul." She shook her head, tsking. "They always try to frame it so that they're the victim, but there's a pattern there that you can't ignore. You step one foot wrong with them, they'll take you to court."

"They think Ian's on drugs," I said. "Or a bad influence."

Auntie El laughed. "You don't believe that crap, do you?"

Ian *had* changed in the past few months, but no. No, I didn't. I wouldn't be surprised if he'd tried alcohol or marijuana, but anything more than that, no. Not a chance.

Or *was* there a chance, and I'd somehow missed it? I hadn't heard of Zoey until tonight, but they were friends? He was one of the "rough kids"?

And now I was going by Lorraine Conrad's judgment. I took a huge bite of lemon bar, chewed, and swallowed.

"I don't know what to make of any of this," I admitted. "They said Zoey's troubled, that she needs help, but the worst they accused her of was having opinions."

Auntie El snorted so hard she swerved. "I popped out of my mama with opinions to share."

"You and me both." I sighed. "You and me both."

"What do you do when you can't stand a client?"

I laughed. "Well, luckily, they're not my clients. Zoey is, and I feel for her, with those two for parents. What I'll do is my best for her. And hope they don't sue me for it."

4

Ian slept in the next morning and came late to breakfast. I studied him as he sat down. He was still in his PJs, his hair a hot mess. His eyes were red-rimmed, with bags underneath. I thought of Dad's eyes when he was deep in the bottle, red just like Ian's. Hollow and tired.

I grabbed Ian's hand as he reached for the milk and checked his nails for burns or stains. He snatched his hand back.

"What are you doing?"

"Sorry, I..." I couldn't tell him I'd been checking for drug use. Why *had* I been doing that? I didn't believe the Conrads' accusations. Ian wasn't a troubled kid, or no more than most, and I'd never suspected him of doing anything seriously wrong. Not till last night. "I thought I saw a cut," I said. "It was only a shadow." I could have told him I was scared. But I didn't.

He rolled his eyes. "You're such a mom."

"Yeah, and I'm your mom, so don't you forget it."

He poured milk on his cereal and took a bite. His appetite was still healthy. His color was good. He wasn't sniffing or picking his skin or losing weight like kids did on drugs.

I was so caught up in my thoughts that I startled when he spoke. "Can I come with you today?"

I blinked. "Come where?"

"Dad said you're going to take Zoey to court. I thought I could come with you to wish her good luck."

I glared up at Sean, who was making toast. He didn't see with his back turned, so I turned on Ian instead. "Zoey's in custody. They won't let you see her. And do I need to remind you it's a school day?"

"He's tired," said Sean. "He was up late last night. And with him so worried about Zoey, I doubt he'd be paying attention in class. Maybe if you take him, they can talk after court? She might get bail, and they could talk then."

I wanted to snap at him—tell him no. And, butt out. Sean had a point—Ian wouldn't focus at school today. But still. I needed him out of the way.

"We don't know if she'll get bail," I said. "And her hearing's not till eleven. I can't have you missing a whole day of school. But I'll tell her you're thinking of her. How's that for now?"

Ian hunched up his shoulders. "Fine. I guess."

I finished my breakfast and headed out to the car. The first thing I saw was that damn Youth Rise pamphlet. I'd taken it from the Conrads, meaning to read it, and now I grabbed it and flipped through the pages. I stopped when I got to SIGNS OF DRUG USE.

Personality changes

Is your child angry, rude, or defiant? Has your formerly friendly child become sullen and withdrawn? These may be signs—

"Signs your kid is a teenager." I slammed the pamphlet shut. I was not, was not, about to get into this. This was how these programs sucked parents in, convinced them their kids had problems, and they had the solution. I hated how that pamphlet got under my skin. Hated that part of me still looked for signs. My kid was fine, and if he ever wasn't, he had me and Sean. His family.

My phone buzzed. It was Liam. One of Auntie El's cop sons.

"Hey, Liam, what's up? I'm headed to juvie."

He cleared his throat. "That's why I'm calling. Your client's not at the zoo."

The zoo was a term I hated to hear, local slang for the Donahoe County Youth Detention Center. "Those kids aren't animals. And, okay, where is she?"

"She's here at the station."

"What's she doing there?" I was too confused to even be upset. "Don't tell me you kept her there all through the night?"

"Of course not," said Liam. "We took her down the street."

Down the street? To the adult jail by the courthouse? My whole face went hot, my neck, my shoulders. I could feel my red rising. "You threw a scared kid in with adult offenders? A kid who just woke up to... God knows what she thought? What were you thinking? Liam, I swear—"

"Okay, first of all—"

"She's only sixteen! And it's not like she's a frequent flyer. She's never been in trouble, and this is what you do?"

"If you'll let me speak—"

"That girl is traumatized. And you threw her in adult jail. What could you say that would make that okay?"

Liam waited a long moment to make sure I was done. Then he tried again, his voice tight with frustration.

"First, it was late last night when she came in, and after midnight by the time we were done. The Z—youth detention is an hour away, and county jail is only two minutes. Second, of course they had her in administrative segregation. She was nowhere near any adult offenders. I thought I was doing you a solid, keeping her close. So we could get her before a judge first thing today."

My anger faded, replaced by sheepishness. Liam was making sense. I drew a deep breath and let it out through my nose.

"Sorry," I said. "It's been a long night."

"So, you won't bite my head off when you get to the station?"

I laughed to vent tension. "No, we're good."

"Then, see you soon. And, hey, good luck. This must be hard for you, with her being Ian's friend."

My annoyance flared again, but not at Liam. At myself, this time, because I hadn't known. I tried to remember if Ian had mentioned her, if she'd been in any way on my radar. But all I could think of was one time at school, I'd dropped Ian off and she'd waved hello to him. Or waved him over? I wasn't sure. Who were his friends, other than Zoey?

I didn't have time to dwell on this now. Zoey was waiting, and she was scared. I needed to deal with her, then I'd worry about Ian.

———

The Conrads were waiting outside the station, Paul on his phone, Lorraine clutching a Whole Foods bag. She rushed toward me as I got out of my car.

"We brought court clothes for Zoey." She thrust her bag at me, right in my face. "Can we come in with you? They won't let us see her."

I took the bag and stepped back, shaking my head. "I need to talk to her first. Prepare her for court."

"But we need to see her," Paul insisted.

"She needs her mom," Lorraine added, as the couple pressed in on me.

I held them off with the bag. "As I said, I need to prepare her for court. Why don't the two of you wait in reception, and if there's time, I'll come out and get you?"

Paul turned bright red and started to bluster. I stepped around him and headed inside. He followed, still yapping, as far as the door, where the sergeant on duty frisked us. She gave us the once-over with a metal detector, then patted us down and went through my bag. When she finished, she nodded, and waved me inside.

"She's in Interview A."

I carried on, my bad leg throbbing. I'd leaned on it funny sidestepping Paul. Now I checked behind me and down the hall, then stopped to massage it till the pain ebbed away.

"Mags? You all right?"

I jolted upright, embarrassed that I'd missed Liam, half-hidden in the alcove by the evidence room.

"I'm fine," I said. "Just my bum hip."

Liam pursed his lips, but he let it go. "We've just had an update on that second kidnapper. He's still unconscious, in ICU. But they're saying he's stable, and he should pull through."

That was good news, at least. I squeezed Liam's arm. "Thanks. And, you know. Sorry for earlier."

I strode down the hall with a swing in my step, not wanting news of my limping to get back to Sean. Zoey cringed when I let myself into the room, then she relaxed when she saw it was me. She looked smaller than ever by the light of day, in the oversized police sweats she'd been given to wear.

"Whole Foods," she said, and her lip curled. "Is that from my mom?"

"Yeah. It's some court clothes. Want to get changed?"

I'd thought she might feel better with her own clothes to wear, but she scowled at the bag like it had offended her.

"Did you know the nearest Whole Foods is two towns away? And everything they have is cheaper at Adler's. Mom only shops there so she'll get those bags, so she can carry them and folks will know she shops there."

From what I'd seen of Lorraine, I didn't doubt it. But I hadn't come here to talk about that. I set the bag on the floor out of sight and took my seat across from Zoey.

"I'm here to prepare you for your arraignment, which will be happening in a couple of hours."

Zoey leaned forward. "And then I get bail?"

"Well, that'll depend on what happens in court. Before we get to that, we need to talk. Those men who attacked you, do you know who they were?"

I watched Zoey's face for the hint of a lie, but I believed her when she said no. Her expression showed fear, not guilt or defensiveness. That would be good when it came time to defend her, but it made what I had to say next a lot harder.

"This will be tough to hear, so I'll rip off the Band-Aid: your parents hired those men. They were from Youth Rise Rehabilitation. Do you know what that is?"

Zoey's eyes went wide. "You mean the boot camp?"

"Well, they market themselves as a boarding school, but yes. It's a center for troubled teens."

Zoey barked laughter. "You're kidding, right?"

I grimaced. "I wish I were, but—"

"No, really. You're *kidding*." She shook her head violently from side to side. "Joe Swofford went there. They go to our church. My mom's on the PTA with his mom. She knows Joe came back all—all messed up."

This was interesting, especially since it directly contradicted what the Conrads had told me the previous night. "All messed up how?"

Zoey scrubbed at her face. "No way. No *way*. My parents did this?" She was crying now, sniffling back snot. I let her get it out—better for it to happen now than in court.

"I'm sorry," I said, when her tears tapered off.

"Did they tell you this? Or was it the cops?"

"They told me last night, but Zoey—"

She screamed. It was a strangled scream, into her hands, but the effect was still startling and I flinched back. Someone banged on the door.

"She's fine, we're okay," I called.

Zoey sat for a while with her face in her hands, her breaths harsh and noisy as she fought for control. We had a lot still to get through, but I didn't rush her. I needed her to process this and be calm for court, but more than that, I knew she was hurting. My heart hurt for her, so small and alone.

"My parents," she said at last. She let her hands drop. I couldn't read her expression. Maybe fear. Maybe shock.

"They're waiting outside," I said. "They've asked to see you."

A flood of emotions raged across Zoey's face. Anger. Hurt. Outrage. She swallowed, throat working. When she spoke, her voice was thin. "Do I have to see them?"

"Not right now," I said. "But you'll want them in court with you to show their support."

"Their support." Zoey laughed, a low, bitter sound. "They tried to have me kidnapped."

"They did, but—"

"I don't want to see them. Can you make them leave?"

I weighed how the judge might view the Conrads' absence versus the impact of a courtroom meltdown. Zoey was calm for now, but I could see she was brittle, holding on by a thread and ready to snap. If that happened, what came out might be more tears. Or she might scream again. Cuss out her parents. I didn't know her well enough to guess how she'd break. Some reactions might get her sympathy from the judge—but others could be held against her.

"I'll talk to them," I said. "Why don't you get changed?"

I left Zoey to collect herself and change into her court clothes, and went out to reception to find the Conrads still there. Lorraine rushed me the moment I stepped into sight.

"Was that Zoey screaming? Is she okay?"

"She's upset," I said. "She, uh..." I trailed off, distracted, as I spotted Ian, standing outside with Liam's brother Patrick. Patrick was also a cop, which meant he knew damn well Ian belonged in school. Yet, there they were chatting away.

"There's that boy again." Lorraine pointed at Ian, sneering.

I bit my tongue hard. "You should go home. Zoey's scared and she's fragile, and she doesn't want you in court."

"But we're her parents!"

"You can't push us out." Paul jabbed his finger right in my face. I turned my back on him to talk to Lorraine.

"Lorraine, if you woke up with strange men standing over your bed, what would you think was happening?"

Paul was still arguing, making his case. But Lorraine's jaw had slackened, and her eyes went round as she took in what I was saying. I forced myself to speak gently, as far as I could.

"Zoey needs to be calm today for her arraignment. I don't think she will be if you two are there. She had a bad scare last night and she's been told you hired the kidnappers, so just for today, can you give her some space?"

Lorraine turned to Paul. "Maybe we should go?"

"Go? We just got here! We have a right to see Zoey."

Outside, Ian said something, and Patrick laughed. I clenched my teeth and turned back to Lorraine.

"I'll leave you to discuss this, but my advice is, go home. Let Zoey get through this, and then you can reach out when everyone's feeling calmer."

I left the Conrads to confer and hurried outside, and dragged Ian down the street, out of their sight.

"What are you doing here? You should be in school."

"Dad said I could come when we heard Zoey was here instead of at juvie."

I mentally cursed whoever had blabbed. Probably Liam or Auntie El.

"We're preparing for court right now. I can't let you see her."

"Auntie El made some lemon bars. Can you give her those? Pat said it's fine if the sergeant okays it."

Auntie El, then. Aunt Louise was the blabbermouth. I took the lemon bars from Ian, who craned to peer past me.

"What's going on? Is Zoey okay?"

"She'll be fine," I said. "Do you need a ride to school?"

"Pat said he'd take me, but can you give her a message? Tell her I'm here for her, whatever she needs."

"I'll tell her." I nudged him. "Now, go. Get to school."

Ian slouched back to Patrick as the Conrads stalked out. Paul shot me an angry look, which I chose to ignore. I headed back in and almost bumped into Liam, who caught me and steadied me as my bad leg gave way.

"You sure you're all right?"

"I told you, I'm fine." I moved to push past him, then stopped in my tracks. I knew there was more to this than Zoey had told me. More than I'd gleaned from my chats with her parents. I needed to know if I was about to get blindsided. "Were you here last night? Did you talk to the victim?"

Liam frowned. "You mean Zoey?"

"No, the kidnapper. The one who's awake."

Liam pulled a face. "Victim? Some victim. Snatching little girls in the dead of night."

"But did you talk to him? What did he say? He must've said something for you to arrest her."

Liam glanced around us, and then he shrugged. "Well, you'll find out anyway. What he said was, she knew who they were when she fired. Her parents were screaming they had invited them in."

A spasm shot through my leg. I stiffened and gasped. "I'm sorry. Did you say...she knew when she fired?"

"The second shot, yeah. She fired the first time, then she fired again, and between those two shots, her parents came clean."

I'd been positive, *positive*, Zoey hadn't known. Her shock had seemed real, her tears. That scream. Was she that good a liar, or had she not heard the full story? I thought of her last night, in my living room. How I'd had to half-yell so she could hear me. If her parents had warned her after that first shot was fired, would she have heard?

"You should get back in there. You don't have much time."

Zoey had changed by the time I headed back in, into what looked like a ten-year-old's church dress. She looked supremely uncomfortable and a little bit creepy, like Wednesday Addams at her confirmation. I must have been staring, because she pulled a face.

"I saw on TV that juries know when you're fake, like when you're trying to be someone you're not."

"There's no jury today, and the judge won't care." I tried to smile, even as the same question kept looping in my head. When had she known? Had she heard her parents and fired anyway? We didn't have time to get into that now.

"We'll be heading to the courthouse in just a few minutes, and we need to go over how that's going to go. What's going to happen is, they'll read out your charges, and you'll—"

"Plead not guilty!"

"Deny the charge," I corrected. "This is juvenile court, so you don't plead not guilty, but denying the charge has the same effect. And, after that, the judge will hear our arguments on bail."

"What if my parents, uh…what if they won't pay?"

I frowned. "You mean, if your parents can't pay your bail? They only have to come up with ten percent."

"No, I mean, what if they want me in jail? Those boot camp places are kind of like jail. What if they decide leaving me in there is like boot camp, but free?" Zoey scrunched up her shoulders and she looked like a child, small, sad, and scared in her Sunday school dress. I needed to distract her, so I pulled out the lemon bars.

"From Ian," I said. "For after court."

Zoey perked up. "Ian? He's here?" She peeled back the paper, and fresh tears sprang forth in messy wet floods down her tired face. "He thinks I love these." She choked on a sob. "I actually hate them. I hate all things lemon. But he's so sweet, I can't hurt his feelings."

I didn't have time to unpack that right now, but I made a note to quiz Ian later.

"Whatever happens in court today, you need to stay calm. No tears, no yelling, no making faces. If the judge denies bail, you need to remember, your probable cause hearing is coming right up. I'll fight hard for you there, so stay cool, okay? You're going to get through this, no matter what."

5

I knew walking in, the arraignment would be rough.

Oliver Altman, the Assistant County Prosecutor on Zoey's case, looked up when I entered. He didn't look nervous. He looked half-sick, but not in a bad way, like he thought I'd destroy him. More like a kid who'd snarfed half a Christmas cake and was trying to decide if he could fit one more slice. He looked *excited*, and that wasn't good.

I ignored him and kept my attention on Zoey.

"This won't take long," I said. "Remember, stay calm."

She gave a quick, jerky nod, but she was already shaking. Picking again at the sleeve of her dress. I put my hand over hers.

"Try not to fidget. If you're nervous, just focus on breathing, and you'll be okay."

The judge took her seat and the bailiff stood up.

"All rise. The Donahoe County Juvenile Court is now in session, the honorable Marcy Lowell, presiding."

I hadn't argued before in Judge Lowell's court, but I'd heard she was old school. She didn't like games. It wouldn't be smart to try to get cute with her, or to pull anything that might waste her time. She banged her gavel.

"All right. Who's up?"

Oliver called our case, and we headed up front, but he didn't hand over the charging document. Instead, he turned straight to the judge.

"Before we begin, I'd like to move that Margaret Gallagher be removed from Zoey Conrad's defense. She was a witness to the events of that night, and therefore cannot act as Miss Conrad's attorney."

Judge Lowell exhaled, then fixed me with a tired look. "Ms. Gallagher?"

"It's true Zoey came to me the night of the shooting, but the first words she said to me were 'I need a lawyer.' I acted as her attorney from that moment on." I glanced at Zoey beside me. She was picking at her sleeve. "I spoke briefly with Zoey, then I called 911 and accompanied her to the police station, where she was arrested. At no point did the police treat me as a witness. They didn't question me or request a statement. My only involvement has been as Zoey's attorney."

Judge Lowell frowned. She turned back to Oliver.

"I'd argue that was an error on the part of the police," he said. "Ms. Gallagher *is* a witness and should have been treated as such."

"But she wasn't." Judge Lowell scowled back at me. "I'm ruling Ms. Gallagher was acting as Miss Conrad's attorney. She wasn't a witness, and I don't see a conflict." She banged her gavel again. "All right. On to charges?"

Oliver deflated, but not as much as I'd hoped he would. Whatever ace he thought he had up his sleeve, conflicting me out wasn't it. He pulled out the charging document, but didn't hand it to me.

"We've just learned the victim has died. Therefore, we will be filing an amended complaint to include murder in the second degree."

Zoey gasped and choked on her spit. She bent over coughing and groped out for water. Her hand hit the glass and it tipped off the table. She shrieked as it smashed, breathless from coughing.

"Excuse me," I said. "Zoey. *Zoey.*" I crouched down to talk to her, but she was staring at Oliver. Retching into her hand with every hitched breath. When I reached out to touch her, she jerked away.

"Someone grab some more water," Judge Lowell said. "And clean up that mess before someone steps in it."

A bailiff moved in to clean up the spill. I sat next to Zoey and tried to catch her eye.

"Swallow," I said.

Zoey swallowed. Her jaw clenched.

"Now breathe in through your nose, and out through your mouth."

She sucked in a breath and coughed it out in my face.

"Try not to cough. You're okay. Just breathe."

Zoey closed her eyes and breathed in again. Someone set down a water glass at her elbow, a paper cup this time, just filled halfway. Zoey twitched at the sound of it being set down, but she didn't cough again. She opened her eyes.

"I'm okay," she said.

I could see she wasn't, but drawing this out wouldn't help her. I stood. "We're all right."

"Okay," said Judge Lowell. "Ms. Gallagher, can we proceed on the murder charge as well today, in order to avoid a second arraignment?"

I shot Oliver a black look. "We're fine with that."

"Then, Zoey Conrad, you have been charged with assault with a deadly weapon and murder in the second degree in the shootings of Michael Stanford and Harold Rooney. Do you admit or deny the charge of aggravated assault?"

Zoey glanced up at me. I gave her a nod.

"I deny it," she said.

"And as to the charge of murder in the second degree, do you admit or deny it?"

"I deny it," Zoey answered.

Judge Lowell frowned at me, then over at Oliver. She pushed up her glasses to squint at her calendar. "Then, I'm setting your probable cause hearing for October first. A week from today. Any motions you'd like to file in advance—"

Zoey grabbed at my arm. "What about bail?"

I nodded to indicate I was on it, but I could see she was close to her breaking point. Oliver didn't look at her. He drew himself up.

"I'd like to request that bail be denied. This is a serious offense, and not only that, but the defendant's parents were uncomfortable with her in their home. Releasing her to her family isn't a viable option."

My neck went hot, my anger mounting. Oliver had engineered this to blindside Zoey, thereby ensuring she freaked out in court. Now he'd implied she was unstable, a dangerous element in her parents' home. It was a move straight out of his boss's playbook—Carol Becker, the cutthroat chief prosecutor.

"Your Honor," I said, "my client is just sixteen years old. In juvenile cases, above all else, the court's responsibility is to act in the best interests of the child. My client has already been through a terrible trauma, being forced to defend herself from—"

"Objection!"

"I think we can all agree, the event was traumatic." I sucked back a breath, reminding myself to stay cool. "My client needs stability, not further upheaval. She needs to be home, where she can start to heal."

"We're in juvenile court." Oliver glanced at Zoey. "But it's the state's position that this isn't a juvenile case. Miss Conrad is sixteen, which means on a murder charge, she'll be tried in Ohio as an adult. Her own parents describe her as a troubled girl. That's why they hired her victims to remove her from their home. These factors demonstrate that state custody *is* her best interest, and it's the public's best interest as well."

I opened my mouth, but from the way Judge Lowell was scowling, I could see she'd already reached her decision.

"Bail is denied. I'm remanding Miss Conrad to Donahoe County Youth Detention pending her hearing." She rapped her gavel. "See you next week."

Court recessed for lunch then, and Oliver tried to book it. I caught him at the door and blocked his exit.

"That was ugly," I said. "You should be ashamed."

"If you mean the charges, I'd just heard myself." His ears turned pink, but he held my gaze. I stared him down hard.

"I mean, you could have warned me Harold was dead. Given me a minute to prepare my client. She's a child, and you told her in open court—you broke the news to her she'd taken a life. That's how you do it? You think that's okay?"

Oliver looked away, his ears now bright red. "I told you, there wasn't—I didn't have time."

"Bullshit," I hissed. "And this is your warning: I'd better see discovery as fast as you get it."

"Discovery? I just got—"

"*As fast as you get it*." I pushed past him roughly, back into the courtroom, and sat next to Zoey.

"You ready to go?"

She looked up at me with big, watery eyes. "Go where? I have to—I'm going to jail?"

I got back to my office right around seven, around the time I'd have normally been eating dinner. I'd had two more appearances in court after Zoey's: a DUI hearing, then a custody case. After that, I'd gone outside and just sat, not wanting to go home or back to the office.

Auntie El met me with a plate of cookies, and a super-sized mug of coffee. I had no taste for the cookies but I accepted the coffee, and took a big swig as I headed inside.

"I heard," said Auntie El.

I groaned. "It was bad. Not as bad as it could've been, but pretty bad." I gulped more coffee, scalding my tongue. It burned all the way down to my stomach. I'd have heartburn later, all through the night.

"Shall I get the whiteboard?"

I covered a burp. "Get it."

I didn't have much yet, and wouldn't for a while. Until Oliver turned over the files, there would be no crime scene photos. No interviews.

No medical records or ME's report. But I needed to figure out what I knew, and what I already had that I could use. Auntie El uncapped a dry-erase marker, then stopped to sniff it.

"I love the smell of these."

"I think that's benzene. Which, y'know, causes cancer."

She huffed. "So does everything. What have we got?"

I leaned back in my chair and stared up at the ceiling. Water stains had spread out from a leak in one corner. I'd have to paint over those, or have someone do it.

"Liam said the survivor, uh, Michael Stanford, said Zoey knew who they were when she fired. Not the first shot, but the second one. The fatal one."

"Okay." Auntie El drew a timeline. She put Zoey waking up at one end, then added the two shots with a space between. "Do we know how long there was between the shots?"

"Not yet, but Stanford said the Conrads were yelling. He said they told Zoey they were from Youth Rise."

Auntie El capped her marker and frowned at the board. "I'm trying to picture how many words that'd take. I mean, isn't that a lot to explain?" She rounded on me and started to yell. "They're from Youth Rise, don't shoot! We invited them here! They're not going to hurt you, just take you away!"

"You're right. That's a mouthful." I stood up. Started pacing. "But Zoey knew about Youth Rise. Her classmate had been there. Wouldn't just 'Youth Rise' have gotten the point across?"

Auntie El shrugged. "In the heat of the moment? That's a big pill to swallow. Not to mention the two burly guys in her face. She'd have been distracted. It might not have sunk in. Plus, didn't you mention she couldn't hear after firing the gun?"

I sat down again and reached for my laptop, and typed in *gunshot, confined space, hearing loss*. But how confined was the space? How loud was the gun? I scrolled past the AI crap and clicked on the first result that seemed legit, then on a couple more below that. "Looks like hearing loss is pretty likely. Her ears would've been ringing right off the bat, and she still couldn't hear too well when she got to my place. But Liam said her parents were *screaming*, and she heard me okay when I raised my voice."

"Has she seen a doctor yet?"

I shook my head. "I've called an otologist to set up an exam, but no one's got back to me, and it's past office hours. We might not get those results in time for her hearing. Still, I could call in an expert to testify about hearing loss in general. Argue she thought she was shooting intruders."

Auntie El took a cookie and munched happily. She offered me the plate again. "You sure you don't want one?"

I figured I'd better, to soak up the coffee. And I had to admit, it was delicious. Rich, sweet, and gooey with a gingery kick.

"I saw this thing on Facebook," Auntie El said. "About witnesses remembering things in reverse. Like, if a cop shoots a perp and *then* yells 'hands up,' witnesses remember the cop yelling first. Is it possible this Stanford guy is remembering it wrong?"

I Googled that, too, and turned up a tweet or two, plus an NIH article about memory and the courtroom. Not much there I didn't know from my own experience. "I might check with a memory expert," I said. "See if there's anything new I could run with. But could you find me some hearing experts? And maybe a couple who can testify on the unreliability of eyewitness testimony."

Auntie El added that to the whiteboard, under an underlined heading, TO DO. Then she passed me the plate again. I took another cookie.

"Put down under that, 'look into Youth Rise.' And not just them, but other youth programs. I need to know if it's normal, that kidnapping crap. And their reputation, look into that."

Auntie El pulled a face. "Depends who you ask. You'll find parents who swear by them, but the kids might feel differently."

"I meant more like, how's their safety record? How about academics, how are they there? Plus any police reports about investigations into their facilities or their management. If there's anything shady there, I need to know."

Auntie El capped her pen again and went to the window. She looked down the street, toward the new courthouse.

"The sunsets are gorgeous here, this time of year."

I grunted, half-listening, licking my teeth.

"What do you think of her? Did she hear it or not?"

The warm taste of butter went cold on my tongue. I massaged my temples. "I don't know."

"But you have an opinion." Auntie El sat. "Gun to your head, did she know they were Youth Rise?"

I winced at her phrasing, gun to my head. *Had* Zoey known? And if she had, had she fired in panic? I might've fired on them in her position, knowing if I didn't, I would be kidnapped and taken somewhere horrible. I looked out toward the new courthouse myself, at the smear of red sunset beyond its flat roof.

"I've been going back and forth," I said. "And not just on that. Zoey, she's..."

"What?"

I tried to marshal my thoughts. "On the one hand, I look at her and I see a scared kid. A kid who woke up to this absolute nightmare, and defended herself the best she knew how. But then, on the other hand..." I shook my head. "She never asked how her parents were. Or about the intruders. You've just shot two men, you'd ask how they are. I mean, you would, wouldn't you?"

Auntie El scratched her neck. "I think I would, yeah, but who knows in the moment?"

"But it *wasn't* a moment. It was two hours last night, then all this morning, and after court. All she ever asked me was about bail. And she ran from the scene straight to a lawyer's house. Or did she run to *Ian's* house? Was she looking for a lawyer or for a friend? Ugh, I don't know."

"You think you partly don't trust her because she's close with Ian?"

I laughed without meaning to. "I mean, duh? If she was friends with your kid, wouldn't you worry?"

"Did you talk to him yet? About all of this?"

I slid down in my chair. I'd been putting it off. "I haven't had time," I hedged.

Auntie El hummed, and went back to the window. The sunset was fading into deep purples and slate grays. "You should let him talk. Don't steamroll. Just listen."

"I don't steamroll."

"Since when?"

We both laughed at that. Truth was, I did steamroll. It was my default mode. But if I wanted Ian to talk to me, I'd need to show I could listen. I hadn't done that last year, and he'd bottled his feelings. Let them build up till he'd almost snapped.

"I should get home," I said.

"Yeah. Yeah, you should. Take the rest of those cookies. They'll soften him up."

I found Ian in the kitchen bent over his English notes. He stiffened as I walked in, braced for a fight.

"If you came to yell at me, can it wait?"

I exhaled my frustration. "I didn't come to yell at you. I came with snacks." I plunked the cookies down on the table. "Aunt Louise made these, so you know they're good."

Ian scoffed as I sat and shifted away. Still, he took a cookie and tried a bite. I noticed Sean in the living room glancing our way, then turning the TV down so he could eavesdrop. I let Ian munch his way through his first cookie, then I got up and poured him some milk. I set it in front of him and sat down again.

"Zoey had a hard day today, but she got through it. I won't lie, it was rough on her when the judge denied bail, but she knows her arraignment's in only a week. She's a strong girl, and she's going to get through this."

Ian sat forward, his standoffishness forgotten. "What did she say? Was she scared? What's it like in there?"

I didn't like to tell Ian the harder truths about how tough jail could be. How scared Zoey was, stuck behind bars. But I knew what he needed was my honesty, to know he could trust me when it came to Zoey's case. If I could win that trust, he might open up.

"That's a lot," he said, when I was done.

"I know." I took his hand. "Are you okay?"

He stiffened again, and then he slumped down. "It's not me in jail."

This was my chance to ask a few questions—while I had his trust, and he was willing to open up. "So, you're pretty close, huh?"

Ian stared at the crumbs scattered on his placemat.

"It's okay, you can tell me. How close are you two?"

"I guess we've been pretty close for a while now." He took a sip of his milk and I thought he'd say more, but he'd gone back to examining his placemat.

Don't steamroll, I reminded myself. This was a delicate subject. I needed Ian to open up to me, not shut down again.

"She's lucky," I said. "To have you as a friend. She has a tough fight ahead of her, and she'll need support."

Ian's face hardened, and I knew I'd stepped wrong. "What are you saying? You think she's guilty?"

"No, I'm not saying that, but the state might have a case." I stretched out my hand to take his again. Ian's hand twitched, but he didn't pull away.

"Kids at school are saying she did it. And on social media. They're calling her…"

"What?"

"All kinds of names. Psychopath. Freak. Even some kids I thought were her friends. So when you said that, I thought…"

I squeezed his hand. "I get it. She says thanks for the lemon bars. She really loved them."

"She got them." Ian smiled, shaky but genuine. "We met in art class, okay? She's smart. Talented. We've been hanging out, and she's, I don't know. Funny." His cheeks colored, and he looked away.

"So, she's your girlfriend?"

"We don't do labels."

I wanted to push further, to know everything. "Hanging out" to today's kids meant what, exactly? Dating? Sex? Experimentation? Were they serious about each other or just screwing around? And which of those options would I prefer? I felt suddenly old and out of touch, not just with dating slang, but with my son. Was Zoey his first...whatever you'd call her? Or had there been others? How didn't I know?

"I have homework," he said. He got up to go, then paused in the doorway. "You'll get her off, right? I mean, I know her. She got a bug in her tea one time, and she dried it out. Like, she pulled it out of there and took her napkin, and spent like five minutes blotting its wings. Nobody does that, but Zoey did. No way this was murder. Not Zoey. No way. You need to do your best for her, because she's a good person."

"I will," I said.

"You need to win." Ian walked off, and I watched him go. Sean shut off the TV and came ambling through.

"Not bad," he said. "You barely used your attorney voice."

I kicked him, not hard, and grabbed another cookie. "Did you know he and Zoey were an item?"

"I thought they might be. They sit together at lunch. But there's a whole group of them, so I wasn't sure."

I sat there breathing, taking that in. Sean hadn't said anything, but what was there to say? Ian had been sitting with some girl at lunch. That wasn't news. But this girl, *this* girl. Why'd it have to be Zoey?

"We need to stay on the same page with those two."

Sean sat down next to me and bumped his shoulder on mine. "I'd label them trouble. First love's a minefield."

I blew out a *pff* sound. He could say that again.

"How about some dinner? Give me those cookies."

I grabbed for the cookies, but he snatched them away. I could think of a label or two to fit him: eavesdropper, cookie thief, no help at all. *I'd have said something if I were him, like hey, I think our kid might be dating*. I'd have online stalked Zoey, at least the basics. But the last thing I needed was a fight with Sean.

"Dinner," I said. "Yeah. That sounds good."

6

I picked up my pace when I spotted Oliver heading back to the courthouse from his lunch break. He saw me too and jogged to catch up. I might still have beat him, bum leg and all, but he called my name and made it awkward.

"Hello, Oliver." I stepped to the side to let someone pass. Oliver strode up, and I knew what was coming. He wanted me to absolve him for last week's debacle, when he'd ambushed Zoey with her kidnapper's death. Well, he could forget about that.

"I'm glad I caught you." He grinned, too wide. "I've been feeling bad about last time. You got my discovery, didn't you? I sent it right as I got it. Zero delays."

Obviously I'd gotten it, or I'd have been on his case. I crossed my arms, waiting for him to finish.

"Well, anyway, uh..." He cleared his throat. "I *had* just heard. Literally, in court. I'd say about three seconds before you walked in. If I'd had time to warn you, you know I would, right?"

I could've told him he *had* had time, but he knew that already. His grin cracked and died. I reached for the door, then let my hand drop.

"You need to decide what kind of prosecutor you want to be. The kind who leans on cheap tricks and courtroom bombast, or—"

But Oliver wasn't listening. A small knot of press was swarming the Conrads, who'd just arrived in a town car. I willed them to keep walking and ignore the reporters, but they stopped on the court steps like they were posing. Paul held up his hand and Lorraine leaned against him.

"I have something to say," she said. "First of all, to the Rooneys, to Harold's family, I'm truly so sorry for the loss of your son. As parents, we can't fathom the depths of your grief." She dabbed at her eyes, which to me looked dry. "When we reached out to Youth Rise, they swore the intake procedure was safe. They promised us Zoey would..." She stifled a sob. "They promised they'd take her and bring her back healthy, with no harm to anyone involved. We took them at their word, and we're so sorry. That's all we have to say. We are so sorry."

The reporters pressed in, firing off questions, but Paul slung his arm over Lorraine's shoulders. He swept her into the courthouse and out of sight. I wanted to throttle her, throttle them both. They hadn't said anything to hurt Zoey's case, but they would soon enough if they kept pulling stunts like this.

"They're about to sue Youth Rise," Oliver said. "That's what all that was for, pointing the blame."

Annoyance flared in my guts—thanks, Captain Obvious—and I brushed past Oliver and headed inside. I wasn't sure if the Conrads intended to sue, but they'd done all they could to shift the blame off themselves. They'd barely mentioned Zoey, or her case, at all.

I avoided them and went straight to see Zoey. She was waiting in a holding room, dressed for court, this time in what looked like one of her mom's suits. She'd been twirling her hair, and it was mussed on one side. I sat down across from her.

"How are you feeling?"

"I don't know," she said. "Scared, I guess. They said no one ever gets charges dismissed. They said they don't charge you unless they've got a case."

I leaned forward. "Who's 'they'?"

"The other kids at the zoo." Zoey twirled her hair some more and stared at the table. "They were all like, 'see you back soon.'"

I'd advised Zoey to keep to herself, and this was exactly why. Kids giving her legal advice they had no business giving, sending her back to me pissed off and scared. I needed her calm today, and quiet. Remorseful. Not worked up and ready to rage at the court.

"Charges do get dismissed." I leaned over the table. "Hey. Look at me. I need you to listen. I can't guarantee that'll happen today, but we have a good case here. We have witnesses. Experts. I'm going to do all I can to get the charges dropped, but I need you to do your part. Do you know what to do?"

Zoey didn't say anything, just stared at her hands. She didn't look like she'd slept much, probably all week.

"I know you're tired and scared, but this is important. I need you to listen. Can you do that?"

She nodded, barely.

"Can you look at me?"

She looked up, and I reached for her hand.

"Now, I'm going to defend you, and I've got a great case. But you need to know, the State gets to go first. They're going to bring witnesses and all kinds of evidence. Some of it might sound bad, or it might not be true. But no matter what you hear, I need you to trust me. Don't try to argue, or speak for yourself."

"So they can say what they want about me, but I'm not allowed to defend myself."

"That's right, because I'm here, and it's *my* job to defend you."

I was having a tough time gauging Zoey's mood. She'd seemed scared at first, but now she seemed truculent. Like Ian when I tried to ask about school. Maybe resentment was what they had in common.

"Just stay calm," I said. "The judge needs to know you understand this is serious. A man lost his life, and—"

"The same man who did this?" She jerked up her sleeve and thrust out her arm, mottled with bruises, just starting to fade. I breathed in, then out, so Zoey could see.

"That's exactly the type of outburst you can't have in court. Do you see how I'm breathing, slow in and out?" I did it again, hoping she would breathe with me. "I need you to do that whenever you want to yell out. Then, if it's something urgent, you whisper. To me. Not to the whole court. Can you handle that?"

Zoey gave me that look again, so like Ian. "I'm not stupid," she said. "I'll be quiet in court. But I don't think it's fair that they get to paint me like some kind of ruthless killer. I didn't ask for this. I was asleep."

It was a child's argument, talking about what was "fair"—but she wasn't wrong.

"You can do this." I reached out and patted her arm. "You're unbelievably strong to have done what you did, defended yourself like that. Defended your parents. I'm going to go in there and fight like hell for you, and I need you to trust me. You trust Ian, right?"

Zoey pursed her lips. "Yeah. I trust Ian."

"So trust what he said about how I'm the best, and you just sit back and let me do my job."

Zoey thought for a moment, then her lip quirked up. "He also said you're a nag, and can't cook."

I laughed, though it hurt a little to hear Ian thought that way. What mattered was, I'd got through to Zoey. At least, I hoped I had. All I needed from her was for her to be quiet, and I thought maybe now, she might manage that.

I studied Judge Lowell through Oliver's opening statement. She was a hard one to get a read on, though she struck me as a thoughtful jurist. Some judges, you could fit into easy boxes—tough on drugs. Lenient. Harsh sentencer. Judge Marcy Lowell was none of these, at least all the time. She seemed to take each case on its individual merits. She also seemed never to smile or relax, and scowled the same way whatever was said. Lawyers around juvie court called her "Resting Judge Face," but I'd never heard one word suggesting bad practice. She glowered all through both of our opening statements, only relaxing when I sat down.

Oliver called Michael Stanford, Zoey's surviving attacker. He was a big man, tall and broad, and his seat creaked as he sat down. Judge Lowell's scowl didn't shift one iota, but I heard a murmur from the gallery. Oliver hurried to cover it with his questioning.

"Mr. Stanford, could you describe for the court your role with Youth Rise?"

Stanford smiled. "I'm a counselor, and Director of Sports and Games. I handle the outbound trips—hikes and all that—and also PE classes, including our team sports."

"And what qualifications do you have for that role?"

"I have a BS in PE and health, and I'm CPR certified, and a certified OhioMHAS Peer Recovery Supporter."

Zoey made a huffing sound. I nudged her arm to remind her to keep her reactions under control. Stanford was coming off friendly for now, a gentle giant with a disarming smile. But I'd have my turn soon to cut through all that. If Zoey could hang on, she'd see for herself.

"And what were you doing the night of the shooting?"

"Well, we were doing what we call an extraction, picking up Zoey for orientation. There are a couple different ways we do that. Sometimes, we'll pick the kids up from school, have them called to the office and take them from there. Or sometimes, for privacy, we'll go to their home to pick them up and drive them to camp."

Oliver nodded like that made sense. He matched the rhythm of his speech to how Stanford talked, all low and soothing. Hypnotic, almost.

"And what happened when you tried to extract Zoey?"

Zoey elbowed me hard. "Aren't you going to object?"

I shushed her, but her whispers grew louder.

"But he's lying. That's not how it happened at all. They weren't just picking me up. They were—"

"Ms. Gallagher. Is your client all right?" Judge Lowell had turned her sour face on us. I squeezed Zoey's shoulder.

"Yes, Your Honor. We're fine." I leaned in and whispered in Zoey's ear, "Remember, I'll get my chance."

"She resisted," said Stanford, not looking at Zoey. "We woke up the subject. Normally at that point, we'd tell her who we were and what we'd come to do. And Harold got started, but she began screaming. She kicked Harold off and I went to secure her, but she wiggled out of the sweatshirt she was wearing over her pajamas and ran down the hall. We gave chase, and that's when I saw the gun. I yelled out, 'Don't shoot' and I put up my hands, but I was too late. She shot me in the arm." He touched his arm where his sleeve bulged from the bandage.

"Could you describe the injury you suffered?"

He straightened his sleeve. "Well, the doc at the ER called it a graze. But to my eye, it was more like a furrow. It took twenty stitches to close it up."

Oliver paused to let that sink in. "Did she know who you were at that point?"

"Not by that first shot, but she found out right after. Her parents were there, and they were screaming as well, begging her not to shoot. Then we laid it all on her while she held the gun on us. We all tried to talk her down. Me and Harold. Her folks. We told her, she knew she wasn't in danger, and Harold said, 'Okay, can I take the gun?' And I swear she nodded, so we thought it was safe, but then Harold stepped forward, and bang. Through his chest."

Zoey was practically vibrating in her seat, but she held her tongue. The moment I was up, I got straight to the point.

"When you entered Zoey's bedroom, was she asleep?"

"Yes, but—"

"And how did you wake her?"

"We pulled off her covers."

"You restrained her, didn't you?"

Stanford made a huffing sound, his face turning red. "Yes, we restrained her for her own safety. Kids try to run, and they crash into—"

"You took hold of both of her arms."

His voice had gone rough. "Yeah, but she—"

"And you grabbed her so hard, you left severe bruising."

"Yeah, but—wait, no! I never saw—"

"And you didn't attempt to identify yourselves?"

"Yes! I mean, no. I mean, she was screaming."

"You had never met her before?"

"No, but I don't see—"

"So you burst into a young girl's bedroom, found her asleep, and dragged her out of bed. She didn't know you, and you didn't identify yourselves. Is that correct?"

"Yeah, but that doesn't give her the right to shoot us." He threw his hands up and let them drop down again. His control was in tatters, and I kept up my barrage. I asked where she'd kicked Harold, when, and how hard. How long it took her to break away. I waited till Oliver objected—badgering—then I let Stanford breathe, just for a second.

"This wasn't your first extraction, was it, Mr. Stanford?"

He shook his head. "No."

"In fact, you've done twenty-three just like Zoey's."

Stanford glowered down at me. "I guess. If you say so."

"Your employer says so. And on how many of these extractions has a child been hurt?"

He puffed his chest up. "We've had no serious injuries."

"And how about minor ones? How many of those?"

Stanford hesitated. He glanced at Oliver. "I mean, bumps and bruises. A broken toe. They lash out and hit furniture, or they thrash around. They injure themselves, but we minimize that. That's why we restrain them, as I said before."

"So you restrain them, but they're still breaking bones. How many children have broken their bones?"

"Uh, I think two. A toe and a finger."

If there'd been a jury, I might have cracked my knuckles. But I doubted Judge Lowell would appreciate that.

"So a ten percent rate of broken bone injuries. I just have one more question: after Zoey shot you, why didn't you run?"

Stanford stared. "Run?"

"She had a gun. She'd shown she'd use it. So why didn't you run from her?"

"Because—because..." He looked at Oliver. "I can't speak for Harold. But I've been trying to get on with Kerry PD. They wouldn't take me because I have type 1 diabetes. But I thought if we could talk her down, maybe they'd see I could still do the job."

"So you thought by bullying a scared teenage girl, you'd be a hero, and you'd get the job you wanted?"

"When you say it like *that*, you make it sound stupid. But I thought it would work."

I stood a moment to let that sink in, how stupid it *did* sound. How stupid it was. How that stupidity had cost Harold's life. Then I shook my head. "That's all for this witness."

Oliver redirected and got some details, how one kid had hurt himself punching the wall, and the other had stubbed his toe on a dresser. But I'd got what I needed, at least for now. The rest, I'd tear down with my own experts.

Next up, Oliver called the ME, whose report didn't say much we didn't all know. But she kept on repeating "point-blank gunshot wound," reinforcing that Zoey had fired from close up. She'd been within one foot of Harold when she took her shot, close enough to leave stippling around the entry wound. Close enough to lock eyes with Harold and fire off the shot that had taken his life.

On cross, I got the ME to admit she couldn't rule out self-defense, and that such a close shot was consistent with a shooter in fear of imminent injury. Zoey leaned into me.

"That was good, right?"

I nodded, but it was only a start. The ME's admission created some doubt, but enough to tank Oliver? Not on its own.

After that came an officer who'd attended the crime scene, then a neighbor, Dean Schneider, who'd heard the shots.

"Mr. Schneider, you were home the night of the shooting." Oliver made a show of checking his watch. "Would you mind describing what you saw and heard?"

Schneider scratched his cheek, nails scraping on stubble. "I didn't see much. Not anything, really. I was giving Freckle, that's my cat, his mite and tick treatment. He hates how it smells, so I have to distract him. So I was tickling him, and that's when I heard the gunshots. The first one went off, and Freckle went flying. He ran out of the room and straight up the stairs, into my bedroom and under my dresser. He was just coming out, when *boom* came the second one."

"The second…?"

"The second gunshot."

"And do you know how long exactly was between those two shots?"

"Yeah, from my doorbell cam. I thought it might've caught it. But it didn't show anything, only the sounds."

"And how long was it between those two shots?"

"Thirty-two seconds. It's on the clip."

Oliver checked his watch again and waited a few seconds. "About the same length of time it took you to testify. To tell that whole story, with seconds to spare."

I stood. "Objection. Counsel is testifying." And wasting the court's time, but I left that part out.

Judge Lowell sipped her water. "Sustained. Move on."

Oliver did, and then he called Zoey's father. I knew right away we were in trouble. Zoey gasped at the sight of him and bolted up in her seat.

"He's testifying? Against me?"

"He has no choice."

"But—"

"Breathe, remember? Slow, in and out."

Zoey breathed gustily, loud through her nose. Paul Conrad glanced at her, then looked away. He had a scowl on to rival Judge Lowell's, his lips drawn down as if by two weights. I could see he was angry, but it was less clear with whom. The night of the shooting, Zoey had thought he'd been mad at her, when she'd looked for his help after she'd shot Harold. He was breathing like she was, short, plosive breaths. Refusing to look at her or at Oliver.

"You'll be fine," I told Zoey.

I prayed I was right.

7

Oliver started with a few simple questions. Where was his gun kept? Why was it loaded? How did Zoey get to it if it was locked away? Paul answered with short, clipped statements, sticking to the facts. He kept his gun in his study, in a locked drawer. And of course it was loaded. It was for self-defense. Zoey had gotten to it by breaking the lock. Jamming a letter-opener into the drawer.

"Can you tell us what happened during Zoey's extraction?"

Paul tugged at his tie. "Well, we were watching. To make sure it went right. We didn't want them to hurt her, or—the whole reason we did this was to keep her safe. We were scared. At that school of hers—"

"Mr. Conrad."

"Some of those kids are a bad influence. We were scared *she'd* get hurt, and they promised they'd help her."

"Mr. Conrad, if you could please answer the question."

Paul's gaze again darted over to Zoey.

"We didn't see much. It was late. It was dark."

"So, your hall light was out?"

"Well, no, it was on, but it isn't that bright."

Oliver stepped forward. "What did you see?"

Zoey leaned into me. "Does he have to say?"

"Shh. Yes, he does. And then it's our turn."

Zoey subsided, but she was picking her sleeve. Picking the seam apart right at the table. I thought about stopping her, but she stilled by herself. The moment her father spoke, she froze where she sat.

"We were waiting downstairs," he said. "By the front door. That's what they told us, to wait by the door, so on her way out, we could reassure her. Tell her we loved her and she'd be okay."

Zoey made a strangled sound. I squeezed her arm.

"Then there just came, uh, a whole lot of banging. Banging and yelling, then Zoey ran out. She ran down the upstairs hall, into my study, and those men were chasing her. Stanford and…Rooney." His voice cracked on the dead man's name and he cleared his throat. "Zoey slammed the door on them. We heard the door slam. Stanford, uh, tripped on the rug in the hall. He'd just gotten up, when—or, no. Wait."

"What happened?" said Oliver.

"Stanford tripped on the rug. Rooney helped him up. Then Stanford opened the door. That's when the gun went off."

"And who fired the gun?"

Paul had gone a meaty brick red, and I wondered if he might stroke out right there. "Well, Zoey did, but—"

"How many shots?"

"There was one shot, and then another."

"And what did you do in between those two shots?"

This time, Paul didn't look down at Zoey. He looked back, instead, at Lorraine in the gallery. Oliver moved closer.

"What did you do?"

"We ran up the stairs. To talk to Zoey."

"And what did you say to her between those two shots?"

Paul cast a nervous glance at the judge. "I don't... It was chaos. I can't quote exactly—"

"But what was the gist of it? What did you say?"

Paul gripped the witness stand, still addressing the judge. "Wouldn't that be perjury, if I testify to what I said when I can't remember? If I swore to tell nothing but the truth and I'm just guessing?"

Judge Lowell turned her scowl on him. "Answer the question."

Oliver rose up on the tips of his toes, a gesture so ludicrous I nearly laughed. He looked like a kid who could hardly sit still, so excited to answer a question in class. I knew what was coming, what he'd been waiting for. "Permission to treat this witness as hostile?"

"Go ahead," said Judge Lowell.

Zoey grabbed my arm. "What does that mean?"

Oliver was advancing on the witness stand. I had no time to explain, so I gripped Zoey's arm.

"Sit tight, okay? It's my turn next."

Oliver squared up to Mr. Conrad. "Did you advise Zoey she was in no danger, and the victims were in your home at your invitation?"

Paul made a *buh* sound. A bitten-off stutter. He was still staring straight at Judge Lowell. "But isn't it perjury, if I don't—"

"I just need the gist, sir," Oliver pressed. "Not your exact words. Now, *did you advise Zoey she was in no danger?*"

Paul sat as stiff as if he'd turned to stone. Oliver waited, poised for the kill. The courtroom was quiet and still as the grave, and in all that silence, one word rang out.

"Dad," Zoey gasped.

A murmur ran through the courtroom. Paul jerked where he sat.

"Ms. Gallagher, do you need a moment to confer with your client?" Judge Lowell was giving us her *actual* judge face, not just her resting one, and I swallowed hard.

"One moment, Your Honor." I took both Zoey's hands to get her full attention. "I know it's hard watching Oliver go after your dad. And I know you might be scared to hear what comes next. But the State's almost done, and then it's my turn. Five minutes, okay? Can you hold on for five minutes?"

Zoey was still staring up at her dad. She wasn't moving at all—didn't seem to be breathing.

"Hey, Zoey. Breathe."

She sucked a quick breath. "Can my dad go to jail? If he says the wrong thing?"

I gripped her hands tighter, hoping the pressure would ground her. "All he needs to do here is tell the truth. And all *you* need to do is trust me. Can you do that?"

She drew another quick breath, and then a deeper one. Then she sagged in her seat and let her head hang. I stood.

"Thank you, Judge. We're fine to continue."

Oliver puffed up like a frog in a pond. I wanted to pop him, but this was all he had. Soon it'd be my turn, and I would destroy him.

"Mr. Conrad, did you advise Zoey she was in no danger?"

"I think so," said Paul. "We, uh, tried to explain." He twisted his wedding ring, then folded his hands. "I can't tell you exactly what we said or didn't say, but the gist would've been that they were from Youth Rise. I think I told her to drop the gun, but I'm not certain."

Zoey was crying beside me, not making a sound, huge silent tears rolling down her cheeks. Paul hadn't looked once at her since her outburst. He didn't look as Oliver wrapped up his questioning, either. He looked only at me as I stood for cross, his glassy, shocked eyes fixed on my lapel pin.

"Mr. Conrad," I said, "I know this is hard for you. I'll keep it short, just a few questions." I'd prepped him ahead of time and he'd been solid, but Oliver had rattled him. I needed to keep this straightforward and simple. "First, can you describe for me, between those two shots, what was Zoey doing?"

"She was, uh…" Paul's voice caught and broke. He grabbed his water, drained it, and tried again. "We ran upstairs, like I said to the other lawyer. Zoey was pushed up against my desk."

"What do you mean, pushed up?"

"Cringing, sort of, with her back to the desk. Sort of half sitting on it, pointing the gun. Or, not really pointing it, she was shaking so hard. She kept looking at us and then at the Youth Rise guys."

"How did she look to you?"

"Scared. She looked scared."

"Did she seem to understand what was going on?"

"No, she kept screaming 'get out, get away from me.' The one guy, uh, Harold kept reaching toward her. We were trying to explain to her, but I don't think she heard."

"Why didn't she hear?"

"Because those guys were yelling. We all were. Lorraine and me, Zoey, the Youth Rise guys. We were all trying to tell her—"

"You were all shouting at once?"

Paul took a ragged breath. "Yeah, all at once."

"Had you prepared her at all for what was going to happen?"

His voice jumped an octave, thin with frustration. "No, because those guys said we didn't need to. They said they'd come in and handle it all."

"What did they tell you was going to happen?"

"They said they'd come in, and it would be simple. Like they were arresting her, like the police." He scratched his neck and repeated, "Like the police."

"In hindsight, having seen how they handled themselves, and Zoey's terror when they barged in, would you say this approach was a good idea?"

He bowed his head. "No. I would not."

"Thank you, Mr. Conrad. That will be all."

We took a brief recess then, and when we came back, I saw that Lorraine was no longer in court. Paul wasn't either. They'd left Zoey alone. I hoped she wouldn't notice, but her eyes went straight to the gallery. Straight to the spot where her mother had been. She wilted when she saw those empty seats. I felt for her, but this was my shot. I gave her shoulder a quick squeeze, then called my first witness.

"Defense calls Dr. Sandra Chung, AuD—Doctor of Audiology."

A small, neat woman took the stand. Sandra's testimony wouldn't be flashy, but it would make Swiss cheese of Oliver's case. His argument was, Zoey knew who her victims were. She knew she wasn't in danger, so she couldn't claim she acted in self-defense.

"Dr. Chung, how harmful is gunfire to a person's hearing?"

She looked at her notes, then pushed them aside. "Extremely," she said. "In a case like your client's, an unprotected shooter, a gun going off in an enclosed space less than two feet from her ears, hearing loss isn't just possible. It's virtually inevitable, at least in the short-term."

"Can you explain that? Why is it inevitable?"

"Well, first of all, gunshots are impulse noise, generated in this case by the rapid expansion of gases. Impulse noise tends to be short in duration, but extremely high in amplitude. A gunshot can reach intensities over 140 decibels, with anything over 120 being considered intolerable."

"And how would a sound like that affect the human ear?"

"Without protection, the effect could be catastrophic. The cochlea—the inner ear—contains thousands of hair cells, whose job is to convert sound vibrations into electrical signals the brain can interpret. An extremely loud sound such as a gunshot can damage those cells, impeding their ability to function. This damage may further lead to inflammation, which can further harm inner ear structures. This type of damage may be reversible, but most cases result in some permanent hearing loss."

"Can you describe for the court what the immediate effect would be? What you'd feel and hear in the minutes after the gunshot?"

Dr. Chung took a deep breath. She straightened her notes. "That would depend on where the damage was concentrated, which areas of your inner ear were most affected. But essentially, you'd experience what's called acute tinnitus. You might hear a ringing sound, or a low hum, or hissing or buzzing sounds in your ears. Physically, your ears might feel sore or stopped up."

"And is it possible you'd have trouble hearing or understanding speech?"

"Absolutely, it's possible." Dr. Chung sat up straighter. "As I mentioned before, tinnitus is likely. Loud sounds damage hair cells, whose function is translating sound into electrical impulses your brain can interpret. When they can't do that job, sounds get hard to interpret. Patients with gunshot-related hearing loss, even when they pass acuity tests, often still find it difficult to distinguish one sound from another."

"Like if several people were talking at once?"

Oliver stood. "Objection—leading the witness."

"Fine, I'll rephrase. Could you describe what you meant by difficulty distinguishing one sound from another?"

"What you just said *would* be a common example—confusion when several people are talking at once. Or when there's background noise. Patients often have trouble distinguishing one stimulus from another. They often describe it like being in a room with an echo: there's too many sounds one on top of another, and the more they pile up, the less they make sense."

I could've pressed further, but I'd gotten what I needed. Dr. Chung couldn't say to a medical certainty whether Zoey had heard the warning or not. But I'd managed to establish she might've had trouble, and I would circle back to that later. But first, I had another witness to call.

"Could you state your name for the court?"

"John Willis, ma'am."

I'd picked Willis for his Army background. He radiated wholesome hometown GI Joe. "And, can you describe what you do for a living?"

"I'm in security, ma'am, but six weeks every summer, I take off to do backwoods retreats."

"And what's a backwoods retreat?"

He glanced at Zoey. "They're for troubled teens. We take them out camping and hiking, canoeing. Teach them survival and leadership skills."

"And how do you get them out to the woods?"

Willis smiled. "Well, ma'am, their parents drive them, or we have our own bus if they need a ride."

"So, you don't kidnap them from their beds at night?"

Oliver stood again. "Leading the witness."

Judge Lowell glowered at me. "Sustained. Rein it in."

"Why don't you use the tactics used by Youth Rise?"

"Well, because, ma'am, our programs are fun. And kids can't have fun if they don't feel safe. We don't want to scare them or cause any trauma, or God forbid hurt them, or get hurt ourselves."

"And what made you want to get involved with backwoods retreats?"

Willis thrust his jaw out, big, Army-square. "Because I was at Youth Rise. When I was fifteen."

"So you were kidnapped?"

"*Objection!*"

Judge Lowell's frown deepened. "No, I want to hear this. But Ms. Gallagher, tread lightly."

Willis sat straight. "I was kidnapped, yes."

"And what was that like?"

"It was like a nightmare. I was asleep. I woke up to two men grabbing me by my arms, yelling at me to get my ass out of bed. They were screaming and swearing. Punching me in my belly. When I tried to fight back, they broke my nose."

"And did they tell you where you were going?"

Willis chuckled. "Yeah. They said I was going to hell."

I stood quiet a moment, letting that sink in. Then I was done with him, and Oliver took his turn. He tried to pick holes, to shake Willis on the details, but he was unshakeable. He'd survived hell. He smiled at Zoey on his way out, and miracle of miracles, she seemed to relax. I, on the other hand, was tense as I'd ever been.

"At this time, I'd like to call Officer O'Riordan." He was one of the officers who'd arrested Zoey, and he glared at me as he took the stand. But his attitude didn't matter, only his testimony. I wasn't interested in his thoughts on Zoey's involvement, just in one tidbit I'd picked up from Liam.

"Officer O'Riordan, do you wear hearing aids?"

He blinked, surprised. "I'm sorry. Do I—?"

"Do you wear hearing aids?"

"I— Yes."

"And are you required to wear those when you're on the job?"

"Yes, to comply with department standards."

"And what are those standards?"

He rubbed his left ear. "Uh, it's been a while since I read the guidelines. But I need to be able to hear between five hundred and three thousand Hertz. I can't have more than 30 decibels of hearing loss at any of the tested frequencies. I need my hearing aids to bring me into compliance."

"Officer O'Riordan, can you explain how you came by that hearing damage?"

He rubbed his ear again, and his lips tightened. "Firearms training, ma'am, from my time in the Army. We didn't know then what we know now about hearing protection."

"So you're saying your hearing was damaged by gunfire."

"Yes, ma'am."

I paused to let him relax, and then I changed tack. I plucked a folder off the defense table and strode up to O'Riordan. "I am now showing you what's been marked as Defense Exhibit 101. Did you take this picture?"

He squinted down at it. "Yes."

"What does it show?"

"It shows the defendant the night of the murders."

"And does it accurately depict the bruising to her arms?"

O'Riordan's frown deepened. "Yes, it does."

"Your Honor, I would offer Defense Exhibit 101." I took back the folder and walked it over to Oliver, who examined the picture and said, "No objection." Then I passed it to Judge Lowell, who took it and looked at it.

"It is received."

I turned to Zoey. "I would now ask the court to take note of my client's arms today. Zoey, would you hold them up for the court?"

Zoey held up her arms. Her sleeves slid down. A couple of gasps went up at the sight of the mottled black bruises. Judge Lowell rapped her gavel.

"We get the idea."

Zoey lowered her arms and pulled down her sleeves.

"For the record, my client has shown the court the bruises still present on her arms from Harold Rooney's attempts to restrain her."

I sat down then. Oliver stood, and got O'Riordan to describe the sustained nature of the gunfire he'd experienced during long hours and days of firearms training. I wasn't worried, because I had more to come. First, I called the sergeant who'd done Zoey's booking, who confirmed he'd had to yell so she'd hear him. I called a guard in as well from the jail where she'd been held that night, to testify that Zoey had had trouble hearing. All that remained now were closing arguments.

Oliver went heavy on the time between shots. Thirty-two seconds didn't sound long. But it was long enough to watch a TV ad. To brush your teeth or nuke a cold cup of coffee in the microwave. He demonstrated how long it was, standing in silence, watching the second hand sweep round his watch. Zoey's ears might well have been ringing, but was it believable *nothing* got through? Not even *don't shoot*, or even just *don't*?

The first shot might well have been self-defense, a wild shot fired off in the heat of the moment. But that moment was over by the second shot. Zoey'd had thirty-two seconds to see the men were unarmed. One was incapacitated, with a shot in his bicep. She had no reason to fear imminent injury or death. Shot two was murder, simple as that.

"This was self-defense," I said, when it was my turn. "Zoey Conrad woke up to two men in her room, dragging her bodily out of bed. Grabbing her hard enough to leave bruises. They had already harmed her by the time she went for that gun. She had every reason to fear for her life. But that first shot she took wasn't the fatal one. Thirty-two seconds later, she fired again. So the question comes down to that second shot."

I took a deep breath and drew my back straight. "Two large men burst in, in the dead of night. Dragged a young girl out of her bed. Didn't back down when she fired her first shot. Instead, they yelled at her for half a minute, while her parents, behind them, yelled over them. Stanford wasn't incapacitated; his arm was grazed. He was still shouting at my terrified client.

"We've heard testimony from multiple witnesses that Zoey couldn't hear clearly hours after the shooting. They had to yell at her to get her through booking, and to process her into and out of jail. That was *hours* after—and she fired that second shot in under a minute. Between those two shots, as we heard from her father, she begged them to leave. To get out of her house. When they failed to do that, she finally fired, and she only did that when Harold got close. When he got within one foot of her, close enough to leave stippling. In approaching her, he forced the issue: she fired when she believed she had no other recourse.

"If she hadn't fired again, what would have happened? She *would* have been kidnapped. Possibly hurt. Zoey Conrad fired two shots in self-defense, in reasonable fear for her life and her safety."

I stood down, and Oliver made his rebuttal: Zoey had choices other than shooting. When Rooney came at her, she could have run. She could have fired a warning shot. Instead, she went for the most extreme option, resulting in a man losing his life.

He sat, and Judge Lowell called another recess, this time to deliberate in her chambers. "We'll reconvene in an hour, when I've reached my decision."

Time seemed to drag as I sat with Zoey, and I could only imagine how it felt for her.

"I *didn't* hear," she said. "Or, I don't think I did. It was like they were yelling through a concrete wall."

"I believe you," I said, unsure if I did.

"I—I think I maybe, I did understand, not their exact words, but that they meant 'don't shoot.'" My parents, I mean. They kept shaking their heads. Does that mean I'm guilty, if I, if I—"

I put my hand on her arm. "No. No, it doesn't. That's not how it works."

She sniffled, and I wished I knew how to comfort her. She'd taken a life, and that had to weigh heavily, even without Oliver trying to paint it as murder. Of course she would doubt herself. Anyone would.

I cleared my throat. "I believed what I said up there. You went through something terrifying. You did what you had to do to feel safe."

Zoey opened her mouth to say something else, but the bailiff stood up just then.

"All rise!"

Judge Lowell swept in and took her seat at the bench, and waved us all back down with a sigh.

"I'll keep this brief." She reached for her gavel. "There's no question that first shot was self-defense. As for the second shot, I've weighed all the evidence. The state has shown the Conrads explained the situation, as did Mr. Stanford and Mr. Rooney. But they've failed to show the defendant heard any of it, or that she fired out of anything but fear for her life. She'd just woken up to a violent attack. She was terrified, and her hearing was damaged. For thirty seconds, she begged her assailants to leave. She gave them plenty of time to back off, and they didn't. I'm ruling this self-defense. Charges dismissed."

She brought down her gavel and Zoey squeaked. I sat down to talk to her.

"Hey. You okay?"

She was staring at Judge Lowell, or at her gavel. "Does this mean... What does this mean?"

"It means we won," I said. "You get to go home."

"Home." She peered up again, to where Lorraine had been. "Did my parents leave?"

"I don't know. I'll go check."

I went to get up, but she threw her arms around me. I could feel her sweating through her mom's jacket.

"Thank you," she whispered. "I thought—I was sure..."

"It's over," I told her. "Ready to go?"

"I can go straight from here? I don't have to go back?"

"Just give me a second, and I'll find out." I went and found the corrections officer who'd brought Zoey to court, hoping against hope she was one of the good ones.

"Listen, my client's had a rough day, and she'd as soon not go back for processing. Any chance I could take her straight home for court? I'll swing by later for her personal effects."

The officer frowned, but she agreed, and I took Zoey to look for her parents. I wasn't sure how I felt about sending her home with them, but she wanted to go, and it wasn't my business. I'd done my part, and Zoey was free.

Paul and Lorraine were waiting out in the hall, and they crowded in on us when we stepped out.

"We heard, we just heard!" Lorraine rushed at Zoey. She enveloped her in a bone-crushing hug. Zoey hugged back, and then she hugged her dad. He whispered he was sorry, and she shook her head.

"We're really so grateful." Lorraine turned to me. "We couldn't watch. We were sure she, uh…"

"You worked a miracle." Paul's voice was rough. He'd let go of Zoey, and was straightening his tie. "Do we have to sign anything, or pay any fees?"

"I'll send you my bill," I said. "But you're all done here."

Paul jogged Zoey's arm. "Did you hear that? We're done."

"It's over," Lorraine said. "Come on, let's go."

Zoey looked back at me on their way out, just a quick glance on her way out the door. Maybe it was the light, or just my misgivings, but I thought she looked worried. I thought she looked…scared. Then she was gone, and the door shut behind her, and it was over.

Nothing left but the paperwork.

8

My Wi-Fi was out again. I yelled through the office. "Could you wiggle the thing again?"

Auntie El laughed. "Could I wiggle my thing?" She danced past my door, old-lady twerking. I waved her off.

"You know what I mean."

She futzed with the router and my signal came back. The Batchelder custody case was dragging on—Loni Batchelder was an airline pilot, and initially claimed she wasn't home enough to take the kids full time. Bert Batchelder, my client, had agreed she could have them on weekends, but now she'd changed her mind and wanted full custody. My hunch was, things were about to get messy.

"You should leave that," Auntie El said. "Get home for dinner."

"I still have work to do."

"So take it with you. And I'll get someone in to look at that Wi-Fi."

I looked out at the street, warm in the golden hour. It would be nice to sit down with Sean and Ian. Maybe watch something before I got back to work.

"Okay. You're right. And thanks, Auntie El."

"Aw, you're welcome. You need a hug?"

I really did, and Aunt Louise gave the best ones, but I didn't want to admit I felt fragile now my distractions were gone. Zoey's case had cut too close to the bone, and not just because she was friends with Ian. Cases with kids involved made me nervous, particularly the idea I might let one of them down. I'd been prosecuting a kid back in Chicago, when his dad had assaulted me outside the courthouse. I fended him off okay, but in the process, I scared the kid's brother, who slid into the driver's seat of his dad's station wagon. He ran me down and damn near killed me, and part of me still wondered, had I deserved it? My case against his big brother hadn't been strong, almost as flimsy as Oliver's against Zoey. Had I railroaded him? Maybe I had.

"You need a hug." Auntie El came bustling around my desk, and she leaned over me and gathered me up. I sank into her, relieved, and inhaled her perfume. She smelled good underneath, like cinnamon. Baking. I closed my eyes and slid my arms around her, letting her warmth melt my worries. For now, anyway.

―――――

Sean's car was gone when I got home, and when I headed inside, the house felt deserted. I yelled out, "Anyone home?" but nobody answered. We needed a dog, I thought. Ian would love one. A big cuddly shepherd or a retriever.

Lonely, I drifted through to the kitchen and saw that Sean had left a note on the table.

Subbing in for debate team. Mind starting dinner?

He'd drawn a heart underneath. I smiled, then I grimaced. Ian had told Zoey I couldn't cook. If he only knew how unfair that was. How helpless Sean had once been in the kitchen. I'd taught him the recipes Ian had grown up on, like grilled mac and cheese and Irish stew. Though, now I thought of it, we hadn't had those much lately. Over time, Sean had spiced up the rotation. We had taco Tuesdays now, and homemade pizza. Calzones. Frittatas. Who'd taught him *that*?

I got out a cabbage to start some colcannon—warm, hearty Irish food after a long day. I'd just started washing it when I heard the front door slam. Ian slouched in and curled his lip at my cabbage. He didn't say anything, but I was tired and on edge, my hurt still fresh from Zoey's comment. I knew Ian had likely been blowing off steam, grousing about some uninspired dinner, but damn it, *he* should try cooking sometime. *He* should try pleasing three different palates. I scowled back at him.

"Why are you home so late?"

Ian stiffened, defensive. "What do you mean, late? It's not even seven."

"I mean school ends at three and you quit soccer. So where have you been?"

He shrugged. "Studying."

"Yeah? Who with? And where did you go?"

Ian opened the fridge with a huff of displeasure. He glowered at its contents, then slammed it shut again. "With Zoey, okay? We went to the library."

I knew *that* wasn't true, as they were repainting, and the study rooms had been closed off all week. I'd seen them roped off when I'd dropped by.

"The library's closed," I said.

"What? No, it's not."

"The study rooms are, which you'd know if you'd been there." I could hear my voice rising, and I reined myself in. "Don't lie to me."

"Then don't pry. Zoey's my friend, and if you don't like that, tough. You don't get to dictate—"

"Honey, I'm home!"

We both shut up at Sean's cheery greeting, but we were still in standoff mode when he came breezing in. He took in my red face and Ian's jutting elbows, and his face fell.

"Uh-oh. What's up?"

I glowered at Ian. "You want to tell him?"

"Mom's all in her feelings that I hung out with Zoey." Ian rolled his eyes, and for a second, I wanted to throttle him. I took a deep breath, trying to settle my temper. Still, it wasn't okay that he had lied.

"I'm all in my feelings that you weren't honest. Is she why you quit soccer? Is that what's going on?"

"Mom—"

"Okay, okay." Sean got between us, his arms stretched out. "I've got some groceries out in the car," he told Ian. "Why don't you get them and put them away?"

Ian sloped off, muttering something about cabbage. I yelled after him, "Colcannon's a side dish!" It wasn't as if he had to eat it or starve. But he kept moving, rolling his eyes. Sean pulled me into my second hug of the day, but I was too irritated to want to be touched. I squirmed free, bristling like a hedgehog.

"Cool down," said Sean. He massaged my shoulders. I stiffened at first, then slowly relaxed.

"He lied," I said.

"I know. Not good."

Ian came back, seeming calmer, and plunked the groceries on the table. "I know you're mad," he said. "But could we let this one go? Zoey's been through a lot, and she needed a friend."

"We get that," said Sean. "But our problem's the lying." He pulled out a chair, but Ian didn't sit. He set to work rage-unpacking the groceries, his pique back in force now Sean had pressed the issue. My urge to nag rose, and I didn't resist it.

"We need to know where you are, or we don't know you're safe."

Ian shoved canned tomatoes into the cupboard. "I'll be eighteen next year, and I'll be moving out. What'll you do then, chip me like a dog?"

"You'll be in college," said Sean. "We'll know where you are."

Ian tossed a cucumber into the fridge. "That's all you talk about, you and Mom both. College this, college that, all about college. You ever think maybe I don't want to go? Not everyone does. There *are* other options."

I made the same sound I'd made getting hit by a car, somewhere between a whoof and a whimper. I couldn't breathe. Had he just said...?

"And don't look like that." He flung in the peppers. "Not everyone has to be a lawyer or a teacher."

"All right," Sean said. He took the veggies from Ian. "You're going to bruise those, so give them to me. And go on and wash up, and I'll order some dinner."

Fresh irritation spiked hot in my chest. Had he not seen my cabbage? But, fine, okay. Screw it. Might as well reward Ian with a big bag of fast food. It'd be all he'd afford if he skipped out on college.

"He's working you," said Sean, as Ian flounced out. "You know he just said that to distract you from his lying."

I knew, but I *didn't* know. Not a hundred percent. What if he did want to opt out of college? Of course he'd have options. I knew that as well. But at his age, I'd have done anything to get into college. I'd joined the Army to get my tuition paid for. It didn't make sense to me, not wanting that chance.

"He needs boundaries," I said. "He's testing our limits."

"He is," agreed Sean, packing the broccoli away. "I'm not thrilled he lied to us, or with his attitude. But I think on this one, we need to tread lightly."

I massaged my temples. "Tread lightly? Why?"

"Because there's another conversation we need to have here. They might not do labels, but Zoey's his girlfriend. We need to talk rules with him, and we need him to listen. The more worked up he gets, the more he's going to fight us."

"Zoey." I exhaled, trying to stay cool. How many girls went to that damn school? And Ian had picked out the one with the murder charge. Not only that, but those awful parents...

Sean let the fridge swing shut and moved behind me. He started massaging my shoulders again. "Let's say no school night dates. And what else?"

I leaned into his hands in spite of myself. The massage felt amazing, but I resented that Sean was playing me too. Pushing my buttons as surely as Ian had. They knew all my weaknesses and weren't afraid to exploit them.

"No calls after ten." My voice came out half a moan, and I shrugged Sean's hands off. "And if they're studying, I need to know where. It needs to be somewhere safe, not..."

"Not Zoey's house." Sean pulled a face, and I sighed with relief. He saw it too, that the Conrads were bad news. The last thing I wanted was Ian at their place.

"They can study here," I said.

"But no closed doors."

"And the lying?"

"I'll drive him to your aunt's place tomorrow after school. She'll have some chores for him. That ought to teach him a lesson."

"Not just tomorrow. The rest of the week." I narrowed my eyes. "And he'll wash my car."

"I'm okay with that." Ian walked in again. He'd scrubbed his face, and I could see he'd calmed down. "I'm sorry I lied. I thought you'd get mad."

"Where did you go?" I asked.

"Out to the farmer's pond. But we just sat and talked. We weren't... y'know."

I knew, all right. The farmer's pond was a fair walk out of town, off on its own, hidden by forest. When I'd been Ian's age, it'd been a make-out spot. I thought back to four years ago, when I'd sat him down for "the talk." It had been awkward, but I'd got through it all—condoms, consent, hygiene, the lot. Did he need a refresher now, or better to leave it?

"We have some rules," said Sean. "If you want to see Zoey. No school night dates. No calls after ten. If you want to spend time with her, we need to know where you are."

"And never at her house." I shook my head. "If you want to study, you can come here, or the library's fine, but—

"I knew it. You hate her."

"No, we do not." I touched Ian's arm. "But we don't know her parents, so we don't want you over there."

"You don't know my other friends' parents either, and you don't care if I go to their houses."

"Maybe we should care." I drew myself up. "You want us to go stricter? Because we can. An 8 p.m. curfew, I'll track your phone—"

"Okay, I get it! We won't go to Zoey's." Ian got up again and stretched till his back cracked. "Can I go call her and tell her the rules?"

"Yeah, fine, go on." Sean waved him away and Ian headed off. Sean bumped his shoulder up against mine.

"That could have gone worse."

I closed my eyes and pictured a river running through me, carrying off all my tension and stress. Auntie El had suggested I try meditation, but my attempts so far had just left me frustrated.

Sean let out a sigh. "Are we screwing up?"

I snorted laughter. "Aren't we always?"

Sean laughed as well, then sobered up. "I mean, letting Ian see Zoey at all. She took a man's life, and I know the judge, ugh…" He buried his face in his hands and groaned. "I know it was self-defense, and she might be a decent person, but her parents sure aren't. And a thing like that— You can't take a life and have it not leave a mark. It's a lot to put on a kid, trying to deal with that trauma. On Ian, I mean, trying to help her through it."

I stared for a long time at the empty fireplace, at the old dried-out log that had come with the house. "I don't know," I said at last. "I have no idea. But if we tell him no, we'll push them together. We'll put him in a spot where he feels like he *has* to lie because it'll be the only way he can be with her. At least if we support him, he might still be honest."

"Do you think—" Sean broke off and pulled a sour face. "I hate even thinking this. She's just a kid. And what her parents did was deeply wrong. But do you think she *did* know what she was doing when she fired that shot?"

I wanted to reassure Sean that Zoey wasn't that kind of person. To reassure myself—but I'd asked myself the same thing. I swallowed, tasted acid, and swallowed again.

"We're Ian's parents," I said. "Let's focus on that."

Sean slid his arm around me and pulled me close. I leaned my head on his shoulder, savoring the simple comfort. Still, I wished I knew—had Zoey known? And more than that, I wished I could look forward and see if, one day, she'd hurt Ian.

"He's a good kid," said Sean."

I closed my eyes. "I love you."

9

I was thinking about dogs again on my way to the office, like the big hairy Newfie the Adlers had. It hung out in their yard all day, just up the street from us, and jammed its nose through the front fence for pets when I passed. A dog like that could be good, a big cuddlebug.

I almost didn't notice the car parked out front of the office building, a souped-up classic with a flashy paint job. Whoever's car it was had parked in my space, leaving me to nose up under the bird tree. That'd mean a stop by the town car wash later, one more item on my to-do list.

Heading into the office, I called up the stairs, "Hey, Aunt Louise, did you see..."

The words died on my lips as I pushed through the door, and the face behind the reception desk was not Auntie El's. Instead, I was looking at a short, stocky woman, with a purple-streaked black bob shaved down one side. Her arms were bare and heavily inked. When she saw me, she grinned.

"Morning, boss. She went to get coffee."

My hackles rose. "Boss? And you would be?"

She pulled out the front of her T-shirt to show me the logo. "I'm Alia, your Rent-A-Nerd. And, *whoof*, do you need one."

I narrowed my eyes at her. She didn't look like a nerd. And her tattoos were bugging me—well, one tattoo. A skull in a red beret, half scribbled out. I pointed at it.

"What's going on there?"

Her grin disappeared, and she pulled down her sleeve. "Sorry," she said. "I know you were Army. So was I, and I loved it, but they tossed me out."

A dishonorable discharge. Who had Auntie El hired?

Alia smoothed down her sleeve, and now she looked embarrassed. "I'm getting it covered. That's why it's crossed out. They've just done the outline, so..."

I couldn't think what to say to that, and I didn't have to. The door banged open and Auntie El bustled in. She plopped a big, fancy coffee drink down on the desk, with sprinkles and whipped cream and even a cherry. Alia grabbed it and took a big slurp.

"Thank you so much. You're a lifesaver."

"It's the least I could do. Oh, you've met Alia?" Auntie El turned to me, but I barely noticed. How much had that coffee cost? Eight bucks? Or ten?

"You sent my aunt out for coffee?"

Alia's face fell. She wiped cream off her lip. "Stuck my foot in it, huh?"

"Oh, don't be silly." Auntie El handed me my usual black coffee, but not from our office stash. From the bakery downstairs. "Our machine's on the fritz. I was going anyway."

"It's actually not," Alia said. "It's your power bar, or rather, it's your old wiring. You'll need an electrician to come look at that, but for now, I've plugged it straight into the wall."

"See? She's a genius. She's fixing our Wi-Fi." Auntie El went to our snacks cabinet, rummaged around, and came out with some muffins. I went to reach for one, but she swept right past me, offering the plate to Alia instead.

"Ooh, did you bake these?"

"Still warm from the oven. Go on, take two. One for the road."

Alia did, and I felt like a five-year-old, seething as another kid stole all my treats. Stole my aunt too, and my parking spot. Who did she think she was coming in here, with her crossed-out tattoos and her streaky hair?

"I need to take this," she said, and pointed at our router. "It's so old, it's killing your Internet speed. You literally can't use the bandwidth you're paying for, so I'll grab you a new one and bring that by tomorrow. In the meantime, I've cleaned out all of that malware and installed browser extensions that'll protect you from more."

"So we can't get online for the rest of the day?"

Alia smiled. "Oh, no, you can. Your modem has Wi-Fi. The router just gives you a better signal. I'll circle back to you first thing tomorrow." She grabbed her coffee and muffins to go, and I heard her peel out in her silly flashy car. I glowered at Auntie El.

"Where'd she come from?"

"Rent-A-Nerd sent her. Isn't she sweet? You know, she used to be such a shy kid." Auntie El beamed, but I was still fuming. *Sweet* wasn't close to how I'd describe Alia. Edgy, maybe. Pushy as hell. I could see why she hadn't done well in the Army.

"Do you know her well?"

"I know her family," said Auntie El. "The Daltons, you know them. From out by the Pines."

I knew the Daltons all right, and their place outside Kerry. All three of the Dalton boys had done time in county, and Liam and Patrick had stories galore.

Auntie El smacked me. "Oh, don't look like that. She's not like her uncles."

"What do you know about her and the Army?"

"Not a lot, and I hope you're not rushing to judgment." She fixed me with a stern look, and I felt myself wilt. "I don't know what happened there, but I do know people, and from what I heard, she's someone who's trying. Maybe she screwed up, but who hasn't? You?"

My hip twinged and I thought of Chicago again, of that terrified twelve-year-old behind the wheel. His brother hadn't been all that much older, and now he was locked up doing five to ten. *Had* I screwed up there? I might never know.

"I should get to court," I said. "Lunch around noon?"

"I'll swing by Adler's and grab us some food."

I nodded and was about to head out the door when my desk phone rang. I strode back to answer.

"The law office of Maggie Gallagher, Maggie Gallagher speaking."

Silence down the line. Then I heard breathing.

"Hello, can you hear me? Maggie Gallagher speaking."

"Mags?"

My annoyance from earlier surged up again, bitter this time with the tang of old grief. I closed my eyes and breathed out.

"Yeah. Hi, Dad."

"You sound good," he said.

"Thanks. So do you." I wasn't sure if he did or not. He hadn't said much. I should've let Auntie El answer the phone. Let her take a message I'd never return. Now I was stuck with whatever this was, whatever had prompted him to pick up the phone. Or maybe I wasn't. "Listen, it's good to hear from you, but I've got court, so—"

"This'll be quick."

"Well—"

"I'm coming home," he said before I could protest. "Just for a visit, but I'd like to catch up. I'd love to see Ian, and how are things with Sean?"

I couldn't think. Dad was coming to Kerry? I'd thought of all places, he'd never come here again, back to the place where it all fell apart. He'd lost Mom here—and then his sobriety, and his job. And me, he'd lost me, or let me go.

"Maggie? You there?"

I grunted. "I'm here."

"So, what do you think? You got time for a visit? I'd love to take the whole family to dinner." *The* family, not *your* family, like it was his as well. But he hadn't seen Ian since he was little, and last time I'd seen him, he'd been drunk off his ass.

"I'm sober," he said. "Just got my five-year chip."

I should've been relieved to hear that, but instead what I felt was the prick of resentment. So, I hadn't been worth getting sober for, but his new life selling life insurance was? I knew that wasn't fair, and I bit back a sigh.

"I need to go," I said. "But it'll be good to see you. Call me when you're in town and we'll set something up."

I hung up and hurried out before Auntie El could accost me, already pushing Dad from my mind. He was my past, and my present was here. Arguing motions in the Batchelder divorce.

———

I came home again that night to a quiet house, Sean heating up leftover casserole in the oven.

"You're late," he said. His tone was even, but I could tell from his posture he was annoyed. I'd stayed late at the office drafting more motions, and going over the Conrads' invoice. They'd sent it back, wanting it itemized, as if I'd bilk them with some hidden expense.

I leaned down the hallway and peered up the stairs: no line of light in Ian's doorway. No music either. "Ian's out on a school night?"

"Don't overreact," said Sean.

I tensed. "Overreact to what?"

"I said he could go. They have a test."

They? They, who? Sean was being cagey.

"He's at Zoey's, isn't he?"

"*No!* Of course not. They're at the library. I drove them myself." Sean checked his casserole, then straightened up. "Listen, we agreed the library's fine. And they *do* have a Spanish test. I talked to their teacher."

"You're right. We did say that." I took a breath to relax, then I spotted the oven clock. "But not till past ten. It's five past already."

Sean frowned. "Crap. I hadn't noticed that."

"I'm calling him," I said, and pulled out my phone. Halfway through the second ring, his voicemail picked up. That was another rule, and a long-standing one: his phone must be on if he went out at night. I called again, and again it went to voicemail. "The library closes at, what? Eight thirty?"

"Nine, but he was walking home. Still, he should be back by now." Sean went to the front room and pressed his face to the window, shading his eyes to peer past the streetlights. "I don't see him."

"Did he try to push for a later curfew? To go out to eat after, or anything like that?"

"No, no, he didn't. He knows the rules. And I'd have talked to you first if I was going to change them." Sean came back to the kitchen and poked a fork in his casserole. It smelled delicious, cheesy and hot, but all I could focus on was the oven clock. It ticked over from 10:09 to 10:10, which put Ian ten minutes past his curfew.

"I'm calling the Conrads." I jabbed at my screen. The line rang four times, then voicemail again. "Do you have Zoey's number?"

"I don't," Sean said. "Try her socials, maybe?"

I searched for Zoey, but came up with nothing. Next, I tried scrolling through Ian's Insta—at least the one I knew about. I knew kids today always had fake accounts, ones they put up as a front for their parents. But Zoey was on his, and I clicked through to hers, and…nothing. No posts since before her arrest.

Sean came up behind me. "He'll be home any minute."

I nodded, but my stomach was tied up in knots. All I could think about was Zoey in court. Zoey in my living room, spattered with blood. Zoey's first words to me, *you're a lawyer, right?* I didn't trust her or her cheapskate parents, trying to shave pennies off their legal fees.

We sat at the table with the casserole cooling, watching the minutes tick by on the clock. Fifteen minutes late, seventeen. Twenty. I stood up with a clatter and pulled my jacket back on.

"What are you doing?"

"I'm going to drive up the street and try to catch Ian."

"I'll come with you."

"No, you wait, in case I miss him."

Sean hugged me, but quickly, and told me to find him. I nodded and kissed him and then hurried out. Ian had missed curfew a few times before, but never by more than five or ten minutes. Twenty minutes wasn't like him, but maybe it was like Zoey.

I drove up the street with no sign of Ian, and past the library, and then the diner. Maybe Zoey had convinced him to go for a bite, just a quick bite before he went home. I'd done that a few times when I was his age—missed curfew to go out and hang with my friends. But when I stopped at the diner, the tables were empty. A lone server was making the rounds, cleaning up. I tapped on the window but she shook her head.

"Ian, damn it!" I pulled out my phone again. His number went straight to voicemail. The Conrads' did too this time, and I jumped back in my car. Where else could they be, if not at Zoey's? Not at the farmer's pond. It was pitch-dark this late. Not at a party on a school night.

I sped to the Conrads' house ten miles over the limit, only slowing when I caught my first glimpse of the lights. Bright police lights flashing red, white, and blue.

My stomach flipped over.

It couldn't be.

But I turned the corner, and it was. It was. The Conrads' house was surrounded by cop cars, the whole front yard full of police.

Whatever had happened here, it was bad.

Very bad.

10

Calm settled over me as I lurched from my car, not the cool-water calm that came with no worries, but the enforced calm of crisis mode.

First thing I did was scan for Ian. I didn't see him, or Zoey either. I couldn't see anyone up by the house, except the police spread out over the lawn. The only civilians on-scene were Zoey's neighbors, including Dean Schneider, whom I knew from court. They'd all grouped up at the foot of the drive, right at the yellow line of the police tape.

"Did you see what happened?"

I addressed my question to all of them, but it was Dean who took the bait.

"More gunshots," he said. "A whole lot this time. The ambulance left, so we're waiting to see—" He broke off as headlights flared through the trees, and then a white van pulled into view. I read the word CORONER over its windshield, and I went cold inside.

Ian. Oh God.

Someone bumped up on me. "You think she did it again?"

More voices came, hushed, overlapping.

"I saw her, she—"

"—just so sad—"

"—no other cars?"

My phone buzzed in my pocket. I scrambled it out.

"Sean?"

"Ian's home."

My knees went weak and nearly buckled. Specks danced in my vision, and I leaned on my car. Sean was still talking, filling me in on the details.

"His phone died. That's why he wasn't answering. But don't worry, he's home now, and he's okay. I've tightened his curfew to nine for two weeks, and no more study dates, at least on school nights. You heading home?"

"Zoey," I croaked. "Is she there as well?"

"No, Ian walked her back to her RV. That's why he was late, because—"

Whatever he said next, I didn't hear it, because the Conrads' front door swung open at last. Two men came out with a bag on a stretcher, and then two more, with a second body bag. I watched, cold with horror, as they loaded the bodies up—limp bags of meat that once had been people. Had Zoey done this? But, no, she couldn't. She'd been with Ian.

Or had she? Had *they*?

I clenched my jaw, stilling the whirl of my thoughts. No point speculating till I had more to go on. Right now, I needed to stay in control.

I spotted Liam up by the door and waved to catch his attention. "Liam! Hey, Liam. Sean, I need to go."

"Liam's there? What's happening?"

"I'll call you back."

I hung up and waved again and shouted to Liam. His mouth drew down at the sound of his name. He looked around, checking if his colleagues had noticed me, then hustled over and ducked under the tape.

"What are you doing here?"

I bit my tongue on the truth. I didn't need the cops knowing Ian had been with Zoey. Not till I'd talked to him and knew what he knew. "I heard on the grapevine there'd been gunshots. Were those Paul and Lorraine in the black bags just now?"

Liam didn't answer as a news van pulled up, disgorging its crew with their cams and boom mics. I could hear them bitching as they set up, how they'd been across town on some other job. They'd missed the bags rolling out, and of that I was glad. Now they called out to Liam, but he turned away. One of them spotted Dean, and they grabbed him instead.

"Liam." I followed him up to the tape. "What can you tell me? Is Zoey in there?"

"You're still her lawyer," he said, half to himself.

"Are you saying she needs one?"

"I'm saying I don't know. Your client's not here. And I need to get back, so go home, okay?" He was walking away from me, back to the house. I called after him.

"Wait! Do you know where she is?"

Liam kept walking, waving over his shoulder. I swiveled around, searching for someone to talk to. Dean was still speaking to the reporters, holding court as he counted off the number of shots he'd heard.

"It was just one shot first. One loud bam. Then I got up to look for my cat. The last shooting scared him, so I went upstairs. I got maybe halfway, and they fired four more shots. And I think I heard glass shatter, like they shot out a window."

I edged up on a man who was standing apart, watching the scene through Coke-bottle glasses.

"How about you? You see anything?"

His eyes were fish-huge behind his thick lenses, giving him a cartoonish wide-eyed expression. But he narrowed them at the sight of me. "You're that lawyer from TV."

"Maggie Gallagher." I stuck out my hand. He didn't shake it, but he didn't walk away either. He turned back to the Conrad house, all lit with police lights.

"I heard the cops talking," he said, after a while. "They were saying Paul's Rolex was still on his wrist. Nothing was taken from what they could see. How's it feel knowing you put a killer back out there, and three weeks later she kills again?"

I chose to ignore that last part. But I had to admit, the thought had crossed my mind. I knew Auntie El had said the Conrads weren't popular thanks to all their lawsuits, but it was still a fact that Zoey had motive to take out her parents.

My phone buzzed again, and I pulled it out. Sean.

"Sorry, I'm leaving now. I'm on my way."

"You're there, aren't you? It's all over the news." Sean's voice was low, almost a whisper. I guessed Ian was still up, and maybe in earshot.

"I thought Ian might be here. How did he seem?"

"Totally fine. He scarfed your dinner."

"And he didn't say anything?"

"He said he walked Zoey home when they were done. Not to her house, though. To the RV."

I frowned. I couldn't see an RV, not in the driveway or in the street. But that didn't matter now, not next to Ian.

"I'm on my way," I said. "You're *sure* he's okay?"

"Well, he's on your dessert now, so I'd say probably. Yeah."

"Keep the TV off. Keep him away from the news."

I hung up with a sigh of not-quite-relief: I wouldn't be sure till I'd seen for myself, but from what Sean was saying, Ian sounded all right. Whatever had happened, he'd had the sense to steer clear.

I got in my car and sped off, heading home.

Auntie El had my coffee on deck the next morning, strong, black, and hot as I took my first sip.

"I figured you'd need that." Auntie El grimaced. "Is it true she's missing? Zoey, I mean?"

I'd talked to Liam first thing before heading out, and yeah, it was true. No sign of Zoey. The police had tracked down the RV she'd been squatting in, at a campsite on the outskirts of town. She wasn't there or at the houses of any of the friends they'd checked with. They were waiting to see if she'd show up at school.

"I keep thinking, what if this is a kidnapping? If everyone's assuming Zoey's the killer, and meanwhile she's out there somewhere, vulnerable. It could be revenge, or... Or, I don't know."

Auntie El stroked my arm, like petting a dog. "Did they put out an Amber Alert?"

"I asked Liam, but he said it's not time for that yet. But he said they put out an APB."

"And now, I've got that DUI to prep for. And could you check for me, for the Batchelder case, on that psychologist's report for the younger kid? I was expecting it yesterday, but I don't have it yet."

I headed for my office, but halfway, my phone buzzed. When I saw it was Sean calling, my mouth went dry. He had first period English, so if he wasn't in class—

"Is Ian okay?"

"They just paged me. He isn't in school."

"Didn't you drive him there?"

"He must have left."

I bit my tongue hard to hold back my questions. What did he *mean* Ian had left? Why wasn't Sean watching him? Where did he go? But Ian was seventeen, not five years old. And Sean had his work to do. This wasn't his fault. I took a deep breath and let it out.

"I'm on it," I said. "I'll try his phone."

"I tried it already. He's not picking up."

I felt my red rising. "We'll see about that."

I hung up, and Auntie El reached for my coffee. "Give me that," she said. "You're burning your hand."

I handed over the coffee and saw that my whole palm was red, moist from my sweat and the steam off my mug. It stung and I winced, but my attention was elsewhere, on Ian's voicemail. I hung up on it, hissing, and tapped out a text.

Pick up your phone NOW or lose it for 1 month.

The next call I make will be to Patrick.

"Put this on your hand," said Auntie El. She splodged buttery hand cream onto my palm. It felt cool and soothing on the tender skin, but all I could focus on was my phone's blank screen. I counted ten seconds, then twelve. Fifteen. Then the screen lit up, and I grabbed the call.

"Ian!"

"You'd call the cops on me? For skipping school?" His voice fairly dripped with teenage outrage, but underneath that, I could tell he was nervous.

"Put Zoey on," I said.

"What? She's not—"

"Drop the BS." I cut him off sharply. "Listen, I know you care about Zoey. But the longer she runs from this, the worse it'll get. She needs to come forward with whatever she knows. Let me talk to her now, no more games. This is serious."

I heard Ian's breath catch, then static. A cough. Then Zoey's rings clacked as she took the phone.

"Ms. Gallagher?"

"Yes. First off, are you okay?"

Zoey took in a shuddering breath. "I—I don't know. Is it true they're both dead?"

I ignored the question. We'd get to that later. First, I needed to assess her situation. "When's the last time you spoke to them? Do you remember?"

She hesitated. "Um... Last night?"

"What time last night?"

"I don't know, early? Before the library. They were fine then."

"The police need to talk to you. There's an APB out. If they think you're hiding, that's going to look bad. Where are you? I'll swing by and drive you to the station."

I heard Zoey swallow.

"I can get there myself."

"That's not a good idea. We need to talk first. Where are you, Zoey?"

Silence stretched out, thick with tension. Then came two beeps, and I knew she'd hung up. I called back, then texted, but she didn't reply. Neither did Ian, and I wanted to scream. I wanted to throw a full-on toddler tantrum, but I didn't have time for that, and neither did Zoey.

11

I just about exploded when the front door slammed open, so hard it made the spring doorstop buzz. Every nerve in my body fired at the sound, a full-body shock that made me throw my phone. Auntie El tried to catch it, but she still had my coffee, and it sloshed down her arm and onto her skirt. My phone hit the floor and bounced in its rubber case and came to rest between Alia's feet. I jabbed a finger at her.

"What the—what the hell?"

"Sorry," she said, and stooped to rescue my phone. She dusted it off. "Screen looks okay."

"What are you doing here, slamming doors, scaring the daylights out of everyone?"

"I brought your new router." She held up the box. "And your door, it's a wind tunnel, with your back window open." Alia pointed past me, at my office. Sure enough, the top window was cracked, as I'd left it.

My anger drained out of me and I stood feeling silly. "I'm sorry. I shouldn't have snapped at you. We're having a day, but that's not your fault."

"Anything I can help with?"

I shook my head. "Just work stuff." But Auntie El stuck her oar in, as she loved to do.

"Maybe she *can* help. You need to find those kids, right? Well, Alia was in intelligence, same as you were. But she's just fresh out, not some grizzled old vet. She might know some up-to-date..." She twiddled her fingers. "Phone tricks? Maybe she can find them if you give her your phone."

I didn't know what to be more pissed off about, Auntie El's meddling or referring to me as a "grizzled old vet."

"I don't want to butt in," Alia said, showing some self-awareness for the first time. "But if you mean your kid, you could track his phone. Or I could check socials, see what's happening there."

I started to snap that I could do that myself, but I'd left Find My iPhone off as a gesture of trust. And as for Ian's socials, what were they these days? I knew about TikTok and Bluesky and... Mammoth? But he had others. A whole colony.

"Would they even be posting now?" I glanced at my screen.

Alia grinned. "Trust me, they're talking. Maybe not *your* kid, if he's with Zoey, but the rest of them, whoo boy. They won't shut up."

My jaw dropped. "How did you—"

"Know they're together? The whole school suspects, and they love the drama." She pulled out her own phone and swiped it awake. "Here, check this out."

Alia thrust her phone in my face, and I found myself gaping at a WhatsApp exchange.

they r like fully bonny & clyde ☠

no way shes innocent twice in a row

don't you have class right now????? telling aunt june. ;-P

"My cousin's in their Spanish class," Alia said.

I could think of a few words for Alia's cousin, some of them Spanish, none of them nice, but I bit them all back and threw up my hands. "Fine. Do your thing."

Alia was quick. I had to hand her that. She drifted toward my chair already scrolling.

"Got a couple of kids here who saw Ian in town, just down the street from here, by the diner. But that was a while ago. Just let me—oh! ShortKing08 saw your kid about an hour ago, heading out past the puke can toward the creek."

I tried to make sense of that, but it wouldn't compute. "I'm sorry, the puke can? And what creek?"

"The trash by the White Castle by Crescent Park? Everyone pukes there after bush parties. And the creek's Mill Creek, out by the campground."

Okay, that made sense. "Zoey was squatting there," I explained. "In an RV. But the cops checked, and she's not there this morning."

"She might be in the woods behind the park. There's an old cabin there where the kids go to party."

I stared at Alia, at her streaky hair. At her many earrings and her tattoos. To me she looked barely older than Ian.

"Alia."

"What?"

"How old are you?"

She winked. "Twenty-five, but I know what I'm doing."

Was I really doing this, putting my trust in Alia? A snarky twenty-five-year-old, tossed out of the Army? But she was a local. She knew local kids. She'd been one herself just a few years back.

"I'm heading out to the park," I said. "Can you keep looking? I know you've most likely got places to be, but I'll pay for your time. And I'd be grateful."

"No worries." Alia held up her phone. "I'll text you if I find anything else."

Ten minutes later, I was rolling up on the park. Another five, and I was lost in the woods. I called Auntie El and she passed me to Alia.

"Okay, I've got you. Where are you right now?"

"I don't know, lost? On a trail. In the woods."

"Yeah, but, like, look around. What can you see?"

I swallowed my annoyance and took a good look around. "I see trees, and…more trees. The trail forks up ahead."

"Is there a pile of rocks there?"

"No."

"Then you've gone too far." She guided me back to the previous fork, then down a different trail littered with garbage. It struck me she must've come out here herself, to drink cheap beer and puke in the puke can. Had Ian been doing that? With Zoey, maybe?

I heard their voices before I saw the cabin, and I paused outside to eavesdrop a moment.

"I can't," Zoey said. "They'll think I did it."

"How could they think that? You were with me."

"They hate me. They think I'm, like, a 'troubled teen.' Even your mom does. You said so yourself."

"Wait, wait, shut up. Somebody's out there."

My phone was buzzing, a text from Alia. I stowed it and picked my way to the cabin.

"It's me," I called, though I was sure they could see me. The "cabin" was roofless and half tumbled down, light slanting in through the cracks in its walls. Bottles glinted inside, and less savory items, like discarded condoms. An old pair of jeans. "I'm not going in there. You two come out."

They came to the door, but didn't step out. Zoey was hiding half behind Ian.

"You can't run from this," I said. "But I can protect you. Why don't you come out here, and we can talk?"

Zoey stood for a moment, chewing her lip, then she took Ian's arm and they came out together. They stood elbow-to-elbow, scared but defiant.

"Give me your phone." I held my hand out to Ian.

"Mom—"

"Give it here."

Ian handed it over and I put it away.

"I was just telling her she needs to go in. The same thing you told her, so—"

I held my hand up for silence. Now wasn't the time. I had plenty of questions stored up for Ian, and a long lecture, but it could wait. And Zoey had already waited too long.

"Zoey," I said. "Do you want me to continue representing you, as your attorney?"

Zoey glanced at Ian. He squeezed her hand.

"Yes."

"Good, then come on. We're going to talk, then we'll head for the station."

"Wait, the police station? Will they arrest me?"

"I can't promise they won't. That depends on what they have on you. But if they do, I'll be right there with you. And it'll look better if you come in yourself. If you make them come looking, that won't play in your favor."

Zoey's face scrunched up, and I thought she might argue. "I didn't do this," she said. "You believe me, right?"

I didn't know what I believed, but I knew that I needed Zoey to come with me. "We'll go somewhere and talk, and you can tell me what happened."

Zoey frowned, but she followed me to my car. Ian got in the back with her, and I drove back to town. I parked in the lot behind the police station, but I didn't get out right away.

"You kids don't say anything to the police. Not till I tell you it's okay. Ian, that goes for your cousins as well. If you see Liam or Patrick, say hi and that's it. In fact, why don't you head for my office and wait? I think Auntie El baked some muffins today."

Ian hugged Zoey, and then he went. I motioned for her to join me up front.

"I didn't do this," she said.

"Okay, first things first." I pulled out my notepad and held it up. "I'll be making some notes, but for my eyes only. Now, I need you to tell me what happened last night."

Zoey scanned the parking lot and scrunched down in her seat. She stared at her hands, her lips a tight line. I was reminded of the first night we met, when I'd asked her what happened and she'd looked at her hands. She'd sat for a moment, not speaking, just thinking, and I'd wondered whether she was trying to remember...or if she was testing her story for holes. Now she was doing the same thing again, breathing hard through her nose as she stared at her knuckles.

"I met Ian around five," she said. "At the library. We have a Spanish test, so we needed to study. They closed at nine, so then..."

"So then, what?"

Her expression was furtive. She wouldn't meet my eye.

"The library closed, and then where did you go?"

"Well, I've been staying in the Nelsons' RV. It's in winter storage out at Mill Creek. They aren't using it, and I needed some space, and my parents don't care, so I figured where's the harm?" She tilted her chin up, defiant, and our eyes met. Hers shone with tears—of anger? Grief?

"You're saying you and Ian went to Mill Creek?"

Zoey nodded.

"Did anyone see you there?"

"No. I don't know. There were a few people out there, but down by the campground. Not by the parking lot, where the RV is."

"How about at the library? Anyone see you there?"

Zoey picked at a hangnail on her left thumb. "Mrs. Lachlan saw us when we came in. She told us the study rooms just got repainted, and not to get fingerprints on the clean walls." She brightened. "Oh, but we did make some prints to spite her. With graphite we crushed up from our pencils. Those would prove we were there, right?"

I made a mental note to scold Ian later—what was he, five, leaving fingerprints? But for Zoey, I dredged up an encouraging smile. "That might help, yeah. Did anyone see when you left?"

Zoey paused again, thinking. "I'm not sure? Mrs. Lachlan was somewhere in back, but maybe somebody saw from the diner?"

I made another note, this time in my notepad, to check with the diner staff and any patrons I could find.

"Ian told us he walked you back to the RV. Did he leave right after, or did he stay a while?"

"Um..." Zoey tugged at her hangnail again.

"Just tell the truth. You won't get him in trouble."

"He stayed a little while and we played on his Switch. Then he saw he'd missed curfew and he ran off."

"And what time was that?"

"Around ten, ten thirty? I'm not sure exactly, but not that late."

Her definition of *not that late* needed some work, but her account matched up so far with what I knew to be true.

"And then, what did you do for the rest of the night? Did anyone see you?"

She shook her head. "I just stayed in the RV. Messed around on my phone. I went to sleep around, I don't know, 2 a.m.. I've had trouble sleeping since—since what happened."

"When did you find out about your parents?"

"My phone woke me. It was blowing up. I texted Ian, and you know the rest."

"All right," I said. "I need to go tell them I've found you, and you're safe. You sit tight, and I'll be right back."

I circled around front to find Patrick sitting with Ian, but Ian had taken my advice to heart. He was chatting with Patrick about fantasy football, and what he thought of Patrick's draft picks.

"Not to cut in on the fun—Ian?" I beckoned him to me and he shuffled over. Patrick gave us some space, but I walked Ian off to the side.

"What did you do last night? And I mean the whole truth."

Ian launched straight in without stopping to think. "We went to the library. Dad dropped me off, so he'd know the exact time, but I'd say five or so. And we stayed till they closed. Then I walked Zoey home, and she wanted to play Dead Cells, you know, on my Switch. So I stayed a while, then I saw I missed curfew, and I ran home, and that's about that."

I narrowed my eyes at Ian's account. It matched up with Zoey's, but did it match too closely? It struck me as rehearsed, the way they mentioned the times. The Switch. The details lined up, but they all felt too pat. Then again, they'd spent most of this morning together. I doubted they'd talked about anything else.

"Wait out here," I said. "I need to talk to Liam."

Liam was still in reception when I headed back in, swigging a Coke from the machine. I bought one too and took a long swallow, letting the caffeine kick wake me up.

"I have Zoey out back, waiting in my car. But she's not up for an interview. She's had a rough morning."

"We will need to talk to her. If not today, then soon. She could be a witness, or..." He left the thought hanging, but I caught his drift well enough.

"Is she free to go today?"

Liam shrugged. "She's not under arrest, if that's what you're asking. But she's only sixteen, and she's lost her parents. We can't let her roam around by herself. She'll need a guardian, or she'll go into foster care."

I turned to go, but Liam called after me.

"How about Ian? We'll want to talk to him too."

I didn't want either of them talking to the police just yet, not till I'd had a chance to verify their statements. "I don't want him involved any more than he has to be. And right now, he needs to get back to school."

I called Auntie El to come and get Ian, then I headed back to my car to talk to Zoey.

"My parents," she said, as I opened the door. "When can I, uh... Right now, where are they?"

Right now, I expected they were in the morgue, waiting in drawers to be examined. I didn't want to put that image in Zoey's head, so I skirted the truth. "Right now, they'll be with the ME. Once she signs off on them, they'll be released. You can make your arrangements then, with your family. Speaking of whom—"

"I don't have any family." Zoey dashed at her eyes and gave a wet sniff. "I mean, I think maybe I have an aunt in Tacoma? But I barely know her. She and Mom weren't close."

"Which brings me to my next point. You're still a minor. What that means is..." A lump rose in my throat and I broke off mid-sentence.

Zoey was trying to hold it together, but her eyes were streaming like they'd sprung a leak. Her chest was hitching and she looked halfway sick, sore, red-rimmed eyes and dry, cracked lips. I could guess how she'd been living in that RV, because I'd lived much the same when Dad had checked out. Junk food for meals. Gallons of soda. Long nights up worrying, *what happens next?*

I cleared my throat. "What that means is, I'll need to call your family's lawyer and see if your parents made custody arrangements. But for today, if the police sign off, you can come home with me."

I'd be Ian's hero, but Sean might just kill me. But Zoey was sixteen, and she was alone. And this would be one night, two at the most. And it *was* the right thing, or the kind thing at least. A peaceful night or two, somewhere familiar, before the storm came.

And, it was coming.

12

I met Hugh Barlow, the Conrads' lawyer, for lunch at Lefty's. That was his MO, suggest a lunch meeting, then head for the restroom right as the bill came. I wouldn't have minded, but Barlow was loaded, old family money plus a booming practice.

He was already seated when I came in, sipping a glass of what I hoped was the house red.

"I ordered us the pork chops," he said as I sat. "I hope you don't mind, but I skipped breakfast."

Maybe I ought to have minded, but I didn't. It was Thursday at Lefty's. Everyone got the special: flattened pork chops with a side of sweet slaw. I thanked him and helped myself to some wine, seeing as he'd ordered a whole carafe. The waiter came over and set out our meals like he'd been waiting for me to arrive. Hugh dug into his slaw, and I went for my pork chop, loading my first bite with applesauce.

"So the Conrads," said Hugh, when he'd done chewing. He shook his head and his heavy jowls quivered. "A nasty business. And you're defending the daughter?"

"Representing her, yes." I smiled to hide my annoyance. Zoey hadn't been arrested, at least not yet, but even Hugh was assuming she'd done it. "You handled their will."

"Uh-huh, that's right." He reached for the vinegar and sprinkled it on his coleslaw, and took another big bite, which he chewed at length. "Lorraine's sister Joyce will get custody of Zoey, but that might get complicated if she does get arrested. Joyce is in Tacoma, but I'll reach out."

"Appreciate it," I said. And I did appreciate him saying *if* and not *when*. I'd talked to Alia after the station, and she'd warned me the vibe around town wasn't good. She'd seen on a Nextdoor group a band of parents, wanting to know if Zoey would be at school. They didn't want her near their kids.

"There's also this." Hugh set down his fork and reached into his briefcase, which he'd left out on the seat next to his. "This is a copy of their funeral arrangements. They had a pre-need with First Memorial."

I took it and glanced at it, but it seemed pretty standard.

Hugh leaned in. "Between us, you'll want to watch yourself. The Conrads were well-liked in their church, and that congregation's all movers and shakers. The mayor and his wife go there. A lot of big business types. And Zoey, the feeling is she's a lost soul. She doesn't have many friends, but she's been seen drinking. Going to those parties out in the woods."

I wondered again if Ian had gone to those. He'd never come home reeking of booze, so far as I knew. But what of those nights he'd stayed over with friends? He could've gone then, and I'd have been none the wiser.

I frowned. I was getting distracted. I hadn't come here to brood over Ian. "What about enemies? Anyone couldn't stand them?"

Hugh cocked his head, either thinking or pretending to. "Not that I'd know off the top of my head."

"I heard they'd been involved in quite a few lawsuits."

"Those are all settled now." Hugh speared a pork chop. "And they weren't the type of thing you'd shoot someone over. Product liability, all that sort of thing."

I got the sense Hugh was skirting the truth, or at least dressing it up some on his clients' behalf. But for now, it didn't seem like a good idea to prod too hard. I needed him cooperative until the estate details were hammered out. As for the lawsuits, eventually I'd have to dig deeper into the Conrads' personal lives—but not today. Still, my frustration rose as we kept eating, and when we finished, I got up from the table.

"Nature calls," I sang, and sailed off to the restroom, and I took my time fixing my makeup and smoothing my hair. By the time I came out, Hugh had paid the bill and was gathering his briefcase with a cloud over his head.

"Oh, the bill came? Next time, my treat!" I flashed him my sweetest, most innocent smile, and floated out to my car feeling smug as a cat.

By the time I got home that night, I'd missed dinner, and Sean was waiting outside on the porch. He stood at the sight of me and came down to the driveway.

"I'm supposed to be subbing tomorrow for debate club."

I bristled a little. "Well, hello to you too."

"This is serious, Maggie. I'd be at school till five. And I don't feel right leaving those two home alone."

"So keep Ian with you. Have him try out debate club. He needs extracurriculars now he's quit soccer."

Sean blocked my way as I tried to skirt past him. "This is serious, Maggie. And I feel like you're—you're... Like you're deliberately missing my point."

I could tell he was mad by the breaks in his speech, those pauses where he'd stop himself from saying worse. I set down my briefcase in the driveway.

"Okay, lay it on me."

Sean peered past me, up at the house. When I followed his gaze, I saw Zoey and Ian sitting together in the living room bay window. He was checking on them, I realized. Worried about Ian. Fair enough, so was I.

"It's one thing you defending her, but having her in our house? You didn't even talk to me, and..." Another pause.

"And what?"

"And I've been hearing things. Around the school. You know I don't gossip or set much stock by it, but how sure are you she didn't do it? If she did, that's three people she's killed. I don't want her home with him, not on their own."

A breeze blew up the driveway and through my thin jacket. The chill made me shiver, and I rubbed my cold arms. At the time, it had felt like the right thing to do, letting Zoey come home with us. But the truth was, I couldn't say she wasn't the killer, or that she wouldn't do it again. On the other hand, the Conrad gun was in an evidence locker, my gun was locked up secure in its safe, and I kept my ammo in a separate safe. And Zoey would be out in two, three days max. Still, Sean was right. I should've involved him.

"I'm sorry," I said. "It's just, I thought..."

Sean stood hard-faced, waiting for me to finish.

"No, no excuses. I should've discussed it with you first."

Sean's expression softened, and he picked up my briefcase. He steered me up the walkway toward the house. When we got to the doorway, he set my briefcase down, and he turned me to face him.

"It's your dad, isn't it?"

I'd almost forgotten about Dad's call. Put it out of my mind, more like, hoping he'd forget the whole notion. But I hadn't had time yet to mention it to Sean.

"How did you know—"

"Auntie El told me."

Of course. She'd have checked the caller ID. I pushed my hair off my face. "He wants to come visit."

"And, do you want him to?"

"No. Maybe. I don't know." I blew out a frustrated breath and it fogged white, the chill in the air deepening with sunset. "He seems better now. Says he's five years sober. But when I was Zoey and Ian's age—"

"I know. Come here." Sean pulled me into a long, too-tight hug, and it hurt to lean into him, my weight on my hip. But I did anyway, wanting the comfort. Sean might have his faults, but he was rock-steady. Whatever happened, he'd be there for Ian and me. I could count on that, and I loved him for it.

"You're freezing," he said. "Let's get inside."

We headed in, and Sean went to the kitchen. I went to the living room and sat next to Zoey.

"Mind if we chat a minute?"

She nodded but didn't speak, and I could see she was tired. In a little bit of shock maybe, as reality sank in. Ian didn't move, and I shot him a meaningful look.

"Fine, I'll get out. Let you do your lawyer thing."

I waited till I heard Ian talking to Sean, then I turned to Zoey. "So, I talked to your parents' lawyer, Hugh Barlow, and he's calling your Aunt Joyce out in Tacoma. Your parents left custody to her in their will."

I watched Zoey closely, but she didn't react. She was staring past me at the fireplace.

"Zoey? How are you doing?"

She closed her eyes. "Tired. And I can't believe this is real. My parents..." She broke off and rubbed her dry eyes. "Can I go to bed?"

"Yeah, of course you can. Go on upstairs. There's extra blankets in the cupboard by the stairs."

She went, and Ian came charging back in.

"Did I hear you say they're shipping her off to Tacoma?"

Of course he'd been eavesdropping. "One step at a time."

"But her aunt could take her away? Just like that? Away from everything, everyone, even her friends? That isn't fair. She's going to have no one." Ian's voice shook, and I held out my hand to him.

"Come on, come sit."

Ian hunched up his shoulders, but he sat in the window, the last of the sunset reddening his hair.

"It's not fair," he said again. "She doesn't deserve this."

"How are you holding up?"

Ian seemed to shrink in on himself. "I know what everyone's thinking. What you must think. But she's a good person, like *deeply* kind, and it's killing me that she's hurting right now and I can't fix it. So I'm not good. I won't be till she is. How would you feel if it were me in trouble?"

I swallowed painfully. "I'd be devastated."

"Because you'd know I didn't deserve it. And I know with her. She didn't do this."

Because he'd been with her, or because he had faith in her? I wanted to pry, but now wasn't the time. Instead, I moved next to him and put my arm around him, and after a minute, he leaned his head against mine.

13

Zoey's Aunt Joyce called first thing Monday morning, while the kids were getting ready for school. Well, Ian was ready. Zoey was balking, but with Joyce in my ear, I couldn't hear why.

"I'm not saying no," Joyce was saying. A baby was squalling into the phone. "Of course I'll take Zoey, no question there, but I'm a single mom with a newborn. I can't travel right now, you understand. But if she can get out here, my door is open. Could you tell her from me I'm just so sorry? I'd tell her myself, but Elle just spit up."

I guessed Elle was the one howling to bring down the house. "You go," I said. "I'll let her know. And I'll be in touch once we've made arrangements."

I put down the phone and hurried out to the living room. "What's going on here, what's the holdup?"

"I can't go," said Zoey, and held out her phone. "Look, they're protesting me outside the school."

I took her phone, and sure enough, some parents had posted a notice on Nextdoor: **SHOW KERRY HIGH ADMIN THIS IS NOT OK –**

NO KILLERS IN CLASSES NEXT TO OUR KIDS! Meet at the FRONT gates Mon 8:15, bring signs if you got 'em or just bring yourself!

"There's nobody out there," Sean was assuring her. "The school called the cops and they shut that all down. No one will bother you—"

Ian laughed aloud. "You know how kids can be, protest or not. Can't we stay home till they find the real killer?"

Even if I was fine with the idea of Zoey staying home—which I wasn't—the thought of her alone with Ian in the house all day? "I don't think—" I started, but a knock cut me off. A sharp, aggressive knock, three hard bangs. I didn't need to look out to guess who it was. Sean did, and he immediately herded the kids back from the window. But he was too late. They'd already spotted the black-and-white.

"No way." Ian pushed himself in front of Zoey. "They can't take her, right? You can stop them. Right, Mom?"

The cops knocked again, and I went to answer. My stomach felt heavy, full of sick dread. I'd been half expecting this, but that didn't help.

"*Mom*! I was with her! She didn't do anything wrong. They can't take her, right?" Ian's voice cracked, panicked.

I turned. Held my hands up. "Everyone, quiet. Not a word out of any of you, do you understand?"

Ian started to say something. Sean smacked his arm. Zoey stood cringing with her back to the wall. I swept them all with a withering glare, then I opened the door on two uniforms and Liam. Liam had his fist raised to knock again. He lowered it at the sight of me and thrust out his chest.

"Ms. Gallagher, we're here to arrest your client for the murders of her parents."

My stomach lurched again when he said *murders*, but I kept my face stony. Crisis-mode cool. Zoey whimpered behind me. Ian let out a shout. I turned quickly, hushing them both.

"Give us a minute," I said to the cops.

"Sorry," said Liam. "We have a warrant." He stepped in past me, and I called out to Zoey.

"Listen, just go with them. I'll be right behind you. Liam, I'm invoking her Fifth Amendment rights."

Ian lurched forward, but Sean pulled him back. Zoey's face went blank as the cops slapped the cuffs on her, staring at nothing, not blinking at all. I caught up to Liam as they marched her out the door.

"What's happening?"

"Your client is under arrest."

I resisted the impulse to punch his big arm. "I get that, but why now? What have you got?"

Liam waited till his colleagues got to their car and opened the door to push Zoey inside. Then he glanced at Ian and pulled the door shut.

"A neighbor's dog walker saw Zoey go in there, into her parents' house around half-past nine. She heard yelling from inside around ten o'clock. Right after that, everyone heard the gunshots. Seems cut-and-dried, if you ask me."

So Ian *had* lied. He'd lied straight to my face. Not only that, but he'd kept the lie going, every time I'd asked to go over his story. He would have lied to the police if I'd let him. My neck went hot, prickly with the sting of betrayal.

I'd deal with him when I got home.

For now, Zoey needed me at the station. I got in my car and followed Liam downtown. Zoey didn't speak as they took her for booking, and stared resolutely at the ground at her feet. Liam came out and got me when they were done.

"They took my phone," she said.

"You're under arrest."

She jumped a little at my sharp tone, and I turned my back on her and breathed to calm down. I was still fuming, furious with Ian, and furious with Zoey for drawing him in. He was involved with this, all thanks to her, and who had he talked to other than me? I tried to remember if he'd seen Liam or Patrick lately. How about Auntie El? Had he lied to her?

"I need your password," Liam was saying. Holding Zoey's phone out. She shook her head.

"We're going to get a court order, so you might as well. Show us you can co-operate, and—"

"*Liam.*" I called out loudly and he turned around.

"Tell her it's true," he said. "Help her help herself."

I fixed him with a hard look. "No warrant, no password. And even if you do go and get that warrant, giving a password is testimonial. Demanding she do so violates her Fifth Amendment rights."

Liam rolled his eyes. "Fine. Suit yourself." He stalked off, leaving me to my million questions: why *had* Ian lied for her? What did he know? What had gone on between those two at the party cabin? Dear God, would she need a pregnancy test?

I stepped forward when I saw Liam heading back over. "I need to talk to my client before you take her in."

"All right," said Liam. "But make it quick."

I tried to catch Zoey's eyes, but they were fixed on her shoes again. "Now you've been arrested, I need to ask, do you want me to represent you in this matter too?"

Zoey didn't answer. Was she sulking? Or maybe having some kind of panic attack?

"Zoey, I'm your lawyer," I said. "You're right you don't have to talk to the police, but if you don't talk to me, that's a problem."

"I'm tired," Zoey said. Her voice cracked and she coughed.

"I know that." I forced myself to gentle my tone. "I can't imagine how hard this is, or how you feel. But, Zoey, I need you to talk to me now. Do you still want my representation?"

"I want to go home," she said, barely a whisper. "If I say yes, can you get me home?"

"I'll do all I can for you, same as last time." This time would be harder, but I guessed she knew that. Whatever else she might be, she wasn't stupid. She looked up at me, her tired eyes red-rimmed.

"Fine, yeah. I want you. I'm going to jail now?"

"To youth detention, same as before. I'll see you tomorrow first thing in court."

She didn't look back as Liam led her out and pulled her knees to her chest in the back of his car. I'd have felt bad for her, if not for Ian.

"And where do you think you're going, young man?"

I'd nearly bumped into Ian heading out of the house, his bag over his shoulder, his winter coat on.

"School," he said. "That's what you want, right?"

I snatched his bag from him and yanked on the zip. Not one textbook or notebook, just like I'd thought. "Let's see, your PJs. A book. *Throne of Glass*? I know that's not for English class, so—"

"It's for Zoey, okay? The PJs are because the zoo is an icebox. And she was bored in there, so she needs a book."

I pulled out a wax fold of Auntie El's cookies. "You can't take her this. Any of this. They won't let it in. That's not how it works. And how were you planning on getting out there?"

Ian snatched his bag back and flung it on the floor. "Then how *does* it work? She has to freeze?"

Rather than answering, I pulled him inside. I was the adult here, and I had to act like it, at least until Sean got home and could play good cop.

"Mom—"

I sat Ian down on the couch. "You lied to me again, and that's not okay." Ian opened his mouth, but I held up my hand. "You're not talking. I'm talking. You lied to me, and you'd have lied to the police if I let you. What I need to know now is what you knew when."

Ian thrust his chin out. "I didn't know anything, and I still don't. There's nothing *to* know, because she didn't do it."

"Maybe, maybe not," I shot back. "But how can I believe you when we both know you lied to your father the night of the murders?"

Ian's eyes widened. Genuine surprise. "I didn't— What?"

"You told your father you walked Zoey back to her RV. But she was seen entering her parents' house at half-past nine."

Ian's surprise faded, and he drew in on himself. Closed body language. What was he hiding?

"The best thing you can do for her *and* for yourself is tell me the truth. I need to know what happened if I'm going to defend her."

Ian picked at his sleeve like I'd seen Zoey do. Just how much time had they been spending together? He pressed his lips together and sat up straight.

"I thought she might get in trouble," he said. "But not for murder. There's no way."

"In trouble for what, then?"

Ian reached for his sleeve again and I took his hand. Watching him display Zoey's tics disturbed me to no end. I hadn't noticed him changing, but somehow he had. He'd closed himself off to me but opened his heart to Zoey, to the point he would lie for her. Jeopardize his own future. I squeezed his hand to show him I was still there. However far he strayed from me, that would stay true.

"Her parents were supposed to be at their Bible study. She was going to sneak in and grab a few things."

"A few things like what?"

"Like some clothes. Money."

"So you lied to your father because she was stealing?"

Ian scowled. "Not *stealing*. They owed her that stuff. All I really lied about was where I took her. The rest is all true. I know she didn't do it. I thought if the cops knew she had an alibi, they'd keep on looking and not fix on her. They stopped looking in the Weaver case because they knew it was Troy. Only, it *wasn't* Troy. It was that kid. So I thought if I told them—"

I grabbed him by both arms, startling a yelp from him. "You talked to the cops? Who did you tell?"

Ian tried to jerk free. I shook him hard.

"*Who did you talk to?* I'm not kidding!"

"Pat."

All the air went out of me in a rush. He'd gone to his cousin. To the police. Made a statement he knew was false, behind my back. And Patrick, *damn* it! Why hadn't he told me?

I realized I was still gripping Ian, my nails digging into his thick winter coat. I let him go and smoothed down his sleeves. "I'm sorry," I said. "I'm scared, is all."

Ian's expression softened. "Yeah. I am too."

"Did you go to the station? Make an official statement?"

"No, we just talked. On the bench by the station."

My head spun. "All right. Go on up to your room for now."

Ian rose stiffly and grabbed his bag. He'd made it halfway upstairs before I remembered.

"Ian?"

He stopped, but didn't turn around.

"Give me your phone."

"Mom—"

"Your phone. Now."

Ian stood so long I thought he'd refuse, and I realized if he did, there wasn't much I could do. He was bigger than me now, and in better shape. But he reached into his pocket, pulled out his phone, and tossed it down the stairs to me. He didn't throw it hard, but it stung when I caught it. I tucked it away.

"Now, go to your room."

I waited till I heard Ian's door slam, and then I made my way to the couch. I collapsed into it, my legs turned to rubber, and Sean found me still there when he came home that night. He jumped when he saw me, then flicked the light on.

"You scared me, sitting there in the dark."

"I'm scaring myself lately."

"What do you mean?" Sean came over and sat down beside me, the November cold pocketed into his clothes. When he took my hand, his skin was cold too. I rubbed his hands between mine to warm them up.

"I think I've made a mistake agreeing to represent Zoey."

I waited for Sean to tell me I hadn't. That every defendant deserved a fair trial, and I would get her that because I was the best. Instead, he pulled his hands out from mine and took off his cold coat and tossed it away. He pulled me in for a long hug, and I breathed him in, his faint smell of classrooms and burning fall leaves.

"She needs you," he said, when he pulled back. "But we need you too. We need you healthy. If this is too much for you—"

"You can't leave her hanging!" Ian came charging downstairs, and I winced. I hadn't heard him come out of his room, and I definitely hadn't meant for him to overhear us.

"We're just talking," I started.

"Well, stop talking about that!" He barged into the living room, his face pale and stricken. "You can't be thinking of ditching her when she's stuck in jail, and her parents are dead—and do you know how sad she is? She's totally broken, and she's alone. All her friends have just bailed on her, and you're bailing too? How can you do that? What's wrong with you?"

Ian was looming over us. I stood, and then Sean did.

"Calm down, son," he said. "Your mother wouldn't do that."

"But she just said—"

"She wouldn't just bail. If she had to step aside, she'd find someone good to take over the case."

Ian's hands flew up, grabbing the sides of his head like he was on the verge of tearing his hair out. "Someone good? Someone good? Who's *that*, way out here, out in the ass end of nowhere?"

"Language," Sean said. Ian made an *ugh* sound. My eyes prickled harshly, and I wanted to cry. Instead, I dug in my pocket and fished out Ian's phone.

"What's your password?" I asked him.

Ian glared at me. "Why?"

"Because if I'm going to do this, I need to know everything. I need all your texts, and anything else you sent. Full access, Ian. Now, your password."

He pinched his lips for a moment, then slumped, giving in. "Good-LuckZoey, all one word, and the o's are all zeroes. Oh, and capital G, L, and Z."

I keyed in the password and pulled up their texts, but the history was empty.

"Where are your texts?"

Ian hunched up his shoulders. "I, uh, deleted them. But please don't abandon her because of that. She didn't tell me to. It was all me."

One thing after another. Would the hits never stop? I breathed in through my nose like I'd had Zoey do, but the promised calm never came. "What was in them that you didn't want anyone to see?"

"Nothing, just normal stuff, but it was private."

I wanted to facepalm, but I held myself still. "Ian, no matter what, the police will get those texts. I might be able to stall them, but they *will* get a warrant. What will they find on there that I need to know about?"

I thought I saw panic flash in Ian's eyes. He raked his hands through his hair. "I don't know."

"Don't panic. Think. You must have some idea."

I watched Ian's struggle play out on his face. To tell or not to tell. To betray Zoey?

"She vented sometimes," he said. "About her parents. But I swear it was normal stuff, not, like, 'I'll kill them.' But everyone will get that, right? Her parents were *evil*. They tried to get rid of her. That isn't right."

I knew whatever Ian said, the truth would be worse, not because he was lying to me, but because he loved Zoey. He'd see the best in her, downplay her flaws, look for the kindest interpretation of anything she said. Much like I did with Sean and with Ian himself. Like anyone would for someone they loved. But the state would do the opposite, and it would be bad.

"All right," I said. "All right, thanks, Ian. I'll need you to write down whatever you remember. Any little snippets that you can recall."

His face lit up, hopeful. "So, you'll still defend her?"

I looked at Sean, then at Ian. "Yeah, kid. I will."

Ian lunged at me and wrapped me in a bear hug. As my bones creaked, all I could think was, I needed to get those texts before the police did.

14

I called Alia on my way into court. She picked up on the first ring.

"You've got Alia!"

I coughed, unused to that level of pep, especially at eight o'clock in the morning. "This is Maggie. Uh, Maggie Gallagher."

"Hey, good to hear from you! How are things with Zoey?"

I frowned, suspicious. She sounded…happy to hear from me? She had to want something—but *I* had called *her*.

"Ms. Gallagher? You there?"

I shook my head. "Sorry. I'm calling because you're good with phones, right? Do you know how to recover deleted texts?"

Alia hummed. "What kind of phone?"

"An iPhone. My son's phone."

"Oh, yeah, that's easy! All you do is, you go in your Messages app, and in your conversation list, you—"

"Hold on, hold on." I dug in my pocket in search of my notebook. "Sorry, I'm just on my way into court, but if you'd repeat that, I'll write it down."

"Or you could drop off your phone at your office, with a note on which contact you want the messages restored from, and I'll have it done for you when you get out of court. I'm going your way anyway, so it's no big deal." She paused, and I felt it, the other shoe dropping. "Also, I was wondering…"

Yeah, here it came. She wanted something, all right.

"I need a job." Her voice jumped up an octave. "I mean, I have Rent-A-Nerd, but that's strictly part time. They don't have much work for me, but I feel like you might. Zoey's case is a lot of work, right? If you need an investigator, I can work hard. I'm good with tech, as you know, and I'm good with people, and if you hire me, I won't let you down."

I covered my phone so she wouldn't hear me sigh. Auntie El would be thrilled if I did choose to hire her. The two of them got on like a house on fire. And she seemed energetic and competent, and she'd been a big help tracking down Ian. But her Army history. That dishonorable discharge. I needed to know who I'd be getting in bed with.

"I'd need to do a background check," I said at last. "Is there anything you can think of I should hear from you first?"

It was Alia's turn to exhale a harsh breath. "You mean my discharge."

"Yeah. I mean that."

"My CO grabbed my ass. I punched his lights out."

I let out a whistle. "That's what I'll find?"

"I reported him a bunch of times, y'know, for harassment. And someone from CID talked to me once. But they never did anything because he hadn't touched me—and then he did, and I touched him back. And apparently, they felt that what *he* did was totally fine, because he got promoted and I'm back at home, sleeping in a hammock in my uncle's garage. Which, don't get me wrong, I love a good hammock, but how is that fair? How the hell is that right?"

I could hear the anger trembling in her voice. She reminded me a little bit of Zoey in court—*I don't think it's fair*, she'd said. And she was right. It wasn't. She and Alia were both still young enough to expect life to be fair, maybe not in their heads, but at least in their hearts.

"That's rough," I said. "And, okay. I'll consider you. But I can't bring you on as a full-time employee. It'll be contract work, and you'll bill your hours to the clients. And work might be—"

"*Yes!*"

I winced at her shriek, but I couldn't help smiling. "As I was saying, work might be sporadic."

"That's fine, Ms. Gallagher. That's totally fine. Any work you can throw me, I'm here. I've got you."

"Then we'll talk later, and we'll hash out the details. And thanks again for helping with Ian's phone. I'll leave the password with Aunt Louise so you can get in. Oh, and Alia?"

"Yeah?"

"Call me Maggie." I hung up and headed back to the office, dropped off Ian's phone, and hurried to court. Zoey's arraignment was quick, nothing unexpected. We denied the allegation, and the judge denied bail. Zoey shrank in her seat as the police started toward her.

"It feels like déjà vu," she said. "But it won't stop. How do I wake up from this? How do I—"

"You need to come with us," said one of the officers.

Zoey stood up. She looked tired. Resigned.

"Stay strong," I called after her as they led her away. She gave no sign she'd heard.

I was worried. I wasn't sure she'd quite grasped yet that this was all real, that she was in for the fight of her life. In her shock, she was pushing away what had happened, clinging to the idea she might somehow wake up. *It feels like a dream. Like déjà vu.*

What wasn't a dream was the week that awaited me, getting my ducks in a row for her probable cause hearing. I headed from court straight back to the office and set to work digging through what I had.

"So, this dog walker." I scanned through her police statement. "She left with the doggos around half-past nine, and saw Zoey—just Zoey—enter the house. But Ian told me he walked her home. Why didn't she see...?" I shook my head to clear out the cobwebs. Ian's not being there was important to me, but not so much for Zoey's defense.

Auntie El set her marker down. "Are you okay?"

"Yeah, I'm good." I stood to get my blood flowing. "So she saw Zoey enter, then she walked the dogs. When she returned, she heard shouting. It was right about ten. She said she didn't see Zoey, or hear what was said."

"So the Conrads could've been arguing with somebody else?"

I shrugged. "In theory, but it's not likely. That street's full of doorbell cams and nosy neighbors. If someone else *did* go in, they would've caught it. At least, if they went in through the front door."

"Anything to suggest someone might have come in some other way?"

"Not so far."

We ran through what we had, which was precious little. The dog walker's statement. Zoey's mystery texts, which were bound to hurt us, not help us. Oliver didn't have them yet, but I had to assume he'd get them, though maybe not in time for Zoey's hearing. I assigned Alia to deep-dive her socials, and Auntie El to dig into the Conrads—who had they sued? Any festering grudges? Any possible chance someone else might've done it?

That night was tense at home. Ian was subdued. Sean didn't make dinner because I'd promised I would, but I forgot and came home to cold takeout.

"Think she did it?" said Sean, as we cleaned up the kitchen.

I swept crumbs off the counter. "I have no idea."

"But your gut feeling?"

"She's hard to read. Still in denial. I don't think she's even processed what happened. But if I had to guess…" I pushed my hair back. "You know what? No. I don't know if she did it, but my role here is to make the State prove she did, beyond a reasonable doubt. That's my job, to make the State do theirs."

The next morning, the trickle of discovery started, and over the next five days, it became a flood. Auntie El kept her ear to the ground for fresh gossip, and Alia kept me up on the word around school. I called Zoey's aunt Joyce in Tacoma in hopes she might make it out to support her, but her baby was colicky. She couldn't come.

"I'll try to make it out later," she said. "I mean, if you can't get the charges dismissed. But I don't know about—you don't think she did this, do you? I can't have her near Elle if it ends up she's guilty."

My stomach felt sour heading into the hearing, knowing how alone Zoey really was. Her case was up first on the docket, and she'd been woken at dawn, brought out half-asleep with bags under her eyes. At her previous hearing, she'd seemed scared but alert. Now she seemed checked out, her tired eyes dull. I'd brought her a dress from her own closet, and it hung loose on her like she'd lost weight.

We all rose for Judge Lowell and she sat down heavily, fixing Zoey with a long look. I thought she might say something, but she just banged her gavel.

"All right, let's get started. Mr. Altman?"

Oliver called our case, and I nudged Zoey forward. She took her seat glassy-eyed and sat picking her cuff.

"Try to relax," I told her.

She coughed and stopped picking, but just for a moment. She started again as Oliver stood. I'd done my best to prepare Zoey for today's proceedings, and for their likely outcome—that she'd be headed for trial. But I was less confident than ever she'd handle this well.

"I'll illustrate today that this was a brutal crime, and that probable cause exists to move this case to adult court for trial. I will present evidence that demonstrates that not only did Zoey Conrad kill both her parents, but she took active and immediate steps to hide her involvement. Nor did she hesitate to involve others in her deception.

"On the night of the murders, Zoey Conrad came home. She fought with her parents—a physical fight. I'll show crime scene evidence portraying their struggle, a struggle that led to the nuclear option: Zoey went for her father's gun, in his study. She pursued him downstairs into the living room, where she shot him at close range through his throat. Her mother tried to escape, running out through the laundry, and Zoey Conrad shot her through the back of her head."

I watched Zoey as Oliver ran through his opening. Her gaze was blank, stony, and she kept picking at her sleeves. She'd need a psych eval. And therapy. Whatever had happened, it had left its mark.

Then it was my turn, and I stood up. "The State will present a lot of evidence today. Evidence showing the Conrads were killed. But what they won't show you is who did the killing, beyond conjecture based on circumstantial evidence. They have a witness who'll testify to seeing my client, and another who'll testify to having heard gunshots, but beyond that, the rest is all guesswork. They *will not* show evidence of my client firing a weapon, or being involved in a physical struggle, and the reason for this is, no such evidence exists. Therefore, the State cannot establish probable cause that Ms. Conrad committed these crimes."

Oliver called his first witness, the responding officer, who described what he'd found at the Conrads' crime scene. He called Patrick as well, who testified to Ian's statement—that he'd been with Zoey at the time of the shootings. Then, he called up a forensic expert, who came armed with a series of slides.

"Could you state your name for the court, and your occupation?"

"I'm Geri Rice," the forensic tech said. She was a large woman, around Auntie El's age, but without Auntie El's deep-channeled smile lines. "I'm a senior crime scene analyst with the Donahoe County crime lab, a job I've held for twenty-three years."

"Thank you, Ms. Rice." Oliver pointed at the projection screen. "I'd like to introduce into evidence State's Exhibits 1 through 10. Ms. Gallagher has seen them and stipulated to their admissibility."

Judge Lowell frowned at me. "Is this true, Ms. Gallagher?"

I stood. "Yes, Your Honor."

"Then you may proceed."

Oliver tapped on the edge of the screen. "Can you explain for us what's on these slides?"

Geri leaned forward. "These are our photos of the Conrad crime scene. It's our job to go in and document evidence, which can be used to determine what happened."

"And what are we looking at, here on this first slide?"

Geri cleared her throat. "This is the Conrads' upstairs hallway, between the stairs and Mr. Conrad's study. You can see there's a lamp down here… Actually, do you mind?" She didn't wait for permission and went up to the screen. "You see a lamp's been knocked over, and some books are off the shelf. One of the books, you see this one right here? We found a stain on the cover, which we determined was blood, and we sent that out for DNA analysis. We were also able to determine that the stain was a contact transfer, not the result of drips or spatter."

"What does that mean, a contact transfer?"

"It means the blood was transferred directly, via the book coming into contact with a source of blood."

"Like, for example, someone being hit with it?"

"Yes, that could potentially cause a contact transfer." She skipped to the next slide, showing the book, the end of its leather spine stained deeper brown. "We found hair on the cover, along with the blood, which has also been sent for DNA matching." She clicked to the next slide. "This is Mr. Conrad's study, and his desk drawer is open. The lock's been snapped off, and we found this nearby." She clicked to a close-up of a bent letter opener.

Oliver stepped up, and he took back his clicker. "I want to take a beat before this next slide. Its contents may be disturbing to some people present." He waited to see if anyone left, and when nobody did, he clicked to the next slide. Someone gasped in the gallery, and a murmur went up. The judge called for order. Geri stood stolidly. I turned to Zoey, but she hadn't looked up. Had she known already what she would see? Paul's blood all over, a wild splurge of red?

"What are we looking at?"

Geri pointed at the coffee table where Paul had landed, shattering it as he fell through the glass. "What we're looking at here is a pool of blood. This is where Mr. Conrad was found."

"And how about on the walls, all this blood over here?"

"That's what we call arterial spray. Explosive exsanguination from a ruptured artery."

Zoey winced at "explosive," and pinched her own wrist. I laid my hand over hers to stop her picking.

"Can you describe for us anything else you found at the scene?" Oliver went on.

"We found urine pooled in the upstairs bathroom." Gina clicked to the next slide and tapped on the screen. "Here by the door is the main pool of urine, then a trail leading out to the top of the stairs." She moved to the next slide, showing the banister, a smear of blood on its outer edge. "We found blood here, and drops on the stairs, leading down through the laundry to the side door, where Mrs. Conrad was found shot in the back of her head. We also found shots through the window and in the wall."

She had fibers as well, found on Paul Conrad's shirt, which she had matched to fibers from Zoey's. Zoey's hair in his study. Her prints on the book. A print of the shoe she'd been wearing that night, captured in dust on the laundry room floor.

I whispered to Zoey, "Don't pick," then I stood.

"Ms. Rice, when you talk about fiber transfer, can you say for sure how those fibers were transferred? The fibers, for instance, on Paul Conrad's shirt?"

"Not for sure, no, but it would involve contact."

"Between my client's shirt and Mr. Conrad's?"

"Yes."

"So, in the laundry? Contact would happen there, right?"

A chuckle from the gallery. Geri's lips tightened. "That's possible, yes."

"In other words, the fibers could've been transferred well before the murders occurred, correct?"

"Yes."

"And how about other fibers? Did you find other fibers on Paul Conrad's clothing other than the one that matched my client's shirt?"

"Yes, quite a lot of them."

"All identified?"

"No, not all yet, but we're still running tests."

"So, it's entirely possible that these other fibers on Mr. Conrad's shirt match someone other than my client?"

"Yes, that's possible."

"And my client's hair and her fingerprints and her shoe print, can you determine when those were left?"

"No."

"So let me make sure I understand your testimony correctly. You found evidence Zoey lived in that house?"

"Yes."

"That her shirt came in contact with her father's?"

"Correct."

"But we don't know when or how, right?"

"That's right."

"And she'd read a book from her own shelf, and stepped in dust in her own laundry room. Do I have that all correct?"

"Yes, that's correct."

"That's the sum total of the evidence you gathered from the scene that connects to Zoey?"

"Yes."

"However, you found *no* evidence whatsoever that conclusively places my client at the scene at the time of the murders?"

"Not directly, no."

"Thank you, Ms. Rice."

Oliver stood again. "Redirect, Your Honor. Ms. Rice, did you find any evidence of anyone *other* than Zoey Conrad and the victims at that crime scene?"

"No."

"Anyone else's prints on that book?"

"Just Lorraine Conrad's."

"And the revolver?"

"Just Paul Conrad's prints, and Zoey Conrad's."

"Thank you, Ms. Rice."

Oliver called the ME up next. He had her describe her training and expertise, then run the court through her autopsy procedure.

"Can you describe for the court Paul Conrad's injuries?"

The ME was a small woman, with short white-blonde hair. She projected an air of no-nonsense calm. "Paul Conrad's cause of death was a single ballistic wound to his throat, with a .38 bullet lodged in his spine. He also had bruising to his arms, hands, and face, and damage to his right eye, including a ruptured eyeball, and tearing of the muscle and ligaments supporting that eye. He had a hairline fracture of his left patella."

"How would you describe the injuries to his arms and face?"

"I'd describe most of the bruising as fairly minor, with one severe contusion to his right eye and eyelid, and the skin over the orbital bone."

"Consistent with somebody being attacked?"

"Consistent with a physical altercation."

"And how fresh were these injuries, these contusions?"

"They would have happened that day, quite soon before death. The blood was still pumping, leading to bruising, but the bruises were fresh at the time of his death."

Oliver nodded, apparently satisfied. "Thank you. That's all."

I stood and took a breath, centering myself. I couldn't dispute the ME's evidence, but I could reframe it to introduce doubt. Not only that, but this was a chance for me—a chance to feel out the witness, how effective she'd be in court, and maybe even learn something I could use later.

"You said Paul Conrad had bruising on his arms and face, bruising consistent with a physical altercation. Could you describe the injuries to his hands, in particular, in more detail?"

The ME checked her notes, but I doubted she needed to. She projected an air of unruffled calm: just doing her job, no horse in this race. "His knuckles were bruised," she said. "Minor contusions."

"So, bruising to his knuckles—that would indicate he threw a few punches?"

"His injuries were consistent with a physical altercation."

"Well, they weren't consistent with mere defensive wounds, isn't that right?"

"No, they were more consistent with injuries that occur from hitting someone or something, not just shielding blows."

"So, he struck his assailant hard enough to leave bruises on his own knuckles, but my client was photographed by the police. She had no matching injuries. How would you explain that?"

"Objection—the witness didn't examine the defendant."

"She's a medical expert. She can have an opinion. How probable is it to bruise your own knuckles, but not leave a mark on the person you've punched?"

The judge banged her gavel. "Objection sustained. Move on."

I took another deep breath, and looked over at Zoey, tiny and fragile in the defendant's chair. I knew Judge Lowell was looking as well. "How much force does it take to cause bruising?"

"That depends on the age and health of the subject, their skin condition, any medical issues."

"And in your examination of Paul Conrad, did you note any physical conditions that would have caused easy bruising?"

"No."

"So, you'd describe him as a healthy adult?"

"Yes. Paul Conrad was in good health."

"How much force would it have taken to cause the bruising you found on his knuckles?"

"Again, I can't answer that. It would depend what he hit. If he struck a hard surface, not very much. If he struck something yielding, a fair amount."

"If he struck a person?"

"A moderate blow."

I looked over at Zoey, tiny and hunched. A moderate blow from someone Paul Conrad's size should have left marks on her. Should have knocked her flat. Maybe he'd missed her, punched the bookshelf instead. Maybe he'd punched it on purpose to scare her, hoping she'd run. Or maybe he *had* punched somebody else, punched the real killer, who'd gotten away. I couldn't say *that*, so I stood quietly, giving Judge Lowell a moment to think it.

"All right," I said at last. "That will be all."

I couldn't tell, when the ME stood down, if the doubt I'd introduced played in my favor or not. Or if Judge Lowell would disregard it entirely. What I'd wanted was to reinforce the point I'd made with the forensic tech: that the State had no direct evidence Zoey had been there. They had no blood, no gunshot residue, not a mark on her person.

I sat down feeling I'd made some headway, but then Oliver called his next witness to the stand. Zoey stiffened beside me, and I took her hand. This would be rough, and not just for Zoey.

"The State calls Ian Gallagher to the stand."

15

"Could you state your name for the court?"

Ian looked at me. I nodded minutely. He'd been subpoenaed. He had no choice. I'd prepared him for this, but I knew he was scared, and his voice shook as he stated his name.

"Ian Gallagher."

Oliver shifted so his back was to me, likely not wanting my reaction to distract him. I hoped he could feel me staring holes in his back.

"And what is your relationship to the defendant?"

"She's my, um…" Ian cleared his throat and spoke more loudly. "She's my girlfriend."

"So your relationship was close. She confided in you?"

"Confided? I don't know. Like, about what?"

"Did she ever speak with you about personal matters? About her relationship with her parents?"

Ian hunched up his shoulders. "Sometimes. I guess."

"Could you look at this document and tell me what it is?" He passed Ian a printout and Ian went red.

"It's a chat transcript," he said. "Between me and Zoey. From when we were playing Bluefish online."

"This is an accurate record of your conversation?"

Ian read through it. "I think so. Yes."

"And it hasn't been altered in any way?"

"No."

"Your Honor, I'd like to enter this transcript as State's Exhibit 23."

Judge Lowell nodded. "So entered."

I'd known this was coming, the gaming transcript—the game company had turned it over without protest. It wasn't as bad as the texts from their phones, but it was bad enough, and Ian's guilty expression wasn't helping. Oliver pushed the transcript toward him.

"Would you mind reading this for the court?"

Ian smoothed out the printout. His Adam's apple bobbed. "Zoey hopped on and messaged me, um, wyd. That means 'what you doing?' I said, nm, u? That's 'not much, you,' then she said 'in my room. Mom just yelled at me for that B in Spanish. Wish she would…' Um."

"Please continue."

"'Wish she would fly up her own ass and die.'"

A few scattered titters rose from the gallery. Judge Lowell gave her gavel a quick warning tap.

"Keep reading," said Oliver.

Ian's face reddened further. He stared at the printout. "'I wish both of them would just disappear.'"

Another murmur went up, and Judge Lowell banged louder.

Oliver kept going, coolly unruffled. "Now, Mr. Gallagher, let me ask you this: did you see Miss Conrad the night of the murders?"

Ian's throat clicked as he swallowed hard, thrown off the change in Oliver's line of questioning. "I, uh, we... Um. We went to the library. My dad dropped us off and we stayed there till closing time. It was dark by then, so I walked her home."

"You walked her to her parents' home at 2220 Spruce Street?"

"Yeah. Uh, well, almost. I was about to miss curfew, so I turned back at her street."

"And what time was that?"

Ian's shoulders bunched up. He sucked air through his nose. "I guess it was probably around nine thirty? But—"

"But you told police you were with her till almost ten thirty, and that the two of you were at the RV park, not at her home."

I half-stood. "Objection. Counsel is impeaching his own witness."

"Your Honor, I've called this witness to show he conspired with the defendant to provide a false alibi. I'm not impeaching him. I'm establishing facts."

Judge Lowell shot Oliver a long-suffering look. "Overruled, but tread carefully. This is your witness."

Oliver turned back to Ian. "The morning after the murders, did you see the defendant?"

Ian nodded.

"Answer verbally, please."

"Yeah, I saw her. She texted me."

"And what did her text say?"

"She asked me to meet her."

"And what did you talk about, when you went to see her?"

"About, uh…" He glanced at me. I couldn't help him. I kept my face neutral, and he looked away. "We talked about her parents. About them getting killed. She was scared the police would think she had something to do with it."

"Did *you* think she did?"

"*No!*"

"Did you think it was possible?"

"No. I know Zoey. She'd never— She wouldn't."

Oliver nodded like he understood, and changed tack again, keeping Ian off-balance. "What did you tell police about Zoey's movements that night?"

Ian's lip curled. "Nothing."

"You didn't talk to police?"

Ian shook his head. "Mom told me not to."

"So you didn't speak to Officer Patrick O'Brien, and tell him—"

"Objection—leading the witness!" I was on my feet before I could think, in full mama bear mode despite my best efforts. I tried to rein it in, but it was too late. Oliver half smiled, and I knew I'd screwed up.

"Permission to treat this witness as hostile?"

Judge Lowell's brows twitched. "Granted," she said.

"So you're saying you didn't tell Officer O'Brien you were with the defendant the night of the murders?"

Ian glared back, defiant. "I talked to my cousin while he was off duty. My cousin Pat, not Officer O'Brien."

"But your cousin *is* Patrick O'Brien, a patrol officer with Kerry PD?"

"Yeah, but I didn't talk to him *as* a patrol officer. I talked to him as my cousin, on his own time." Ian's gaze flicked to me again, but I had nothing for him. He was on his own up there, beyond my help. Watching him, I was furious—I'd taught him better than to get involved—but oddly proud. Ian was scared, but he'd kept his cool so far. He'd kept his answers short, to the point, like we'd practiced. A little bit longer, and he'd be home free.

Oliver stepped forward, moving in for the kill. "What did you tell your cousin about the defendant's movements?"

Ian looked Oliver square in the eye. "I told him I was with her at the RV. I said we played Switch till just after ten, then I saw I'd missed curfew and I ran home. But I only said that because—"

"Did you discuss your statement with the defendant before you spoke with your cousin?"

"Yeah, but I—"

"And did it occur to you your off-duty cousin might later mention your story while he was on duty?"

"Uh…" Ian's eyes darted, panicked, to me.

"Don't look at your mother. Look at me. Did you intend for your chat with your cousin to serve as an unofficial statement to police?"

Ian swallowed again. "Uh… Maybe? Yeah?"

"Did you or didn't you?"

"Yeah, but if—"

"Were you hoping your statement would divert suspicion from the defendant?"

"She didn't do it."

"Yes or no, were you hoping—"

"*Yes*! Yes, okay? If I didn't—"

"Thank you. That's all for this witness." Oliver spun away, leaving Ian to sputter. He'd gone so pale I thought he might puke. I stood up quickly, before he could make this worse.

"Mr. Gallagher, could you state for the record, what's our relationship outside this courtroom?"

Ian gulped a huge breath. Let it out in a whoosh. "You—you're my mom."

"Now, I just have two questions. I'm speaking now as Zoey's attorney, not as your mother, and I need you to remember you're still under oath. Why did you give a false statement to Officer O'Brien?"

Ian took another breath. Closed his eyes for a moment. When he opened them, he seemed calmer, and his voice came out steady. "You defended another murder case last year. The Troy Weaver case. He didn't do it. But the cops were so sure he did, they stopped looking for the real killer. He almost went to prison because the cops were too—" He stopped talking abruptly and ran his hand through his hair. "Because the cops didn't *look*. I didn't want the same thing to happen to Zoey."

"And whose idea was this? Yours or Zoey's?"

"Mine," Ian said. "She didn't want me to lie. She wanted to tell the truth, but I said we couldn't."

"Thank you." I stepped back. Oliver stood.

"Redirect, Your Honor?"

"Go ahead."

Oliver stepped up again. "Did you force the defendant to go along with your lie?"

"No, but—"

"Thank you."

Oliver called one last witness once Ian stepped down.

"Can you state for the court your occupation?"

The witness pulled himself up to his full height. "I'm a detective with Kerry PD, and I'm the head of our cybercrimes unit. Well, I'm the whole unit. We're a small shop." That got him a couple of halfhearted chuckles. Oliver smiled.

"I'm going to show you what's been marked as State's Exhibit 25. Do you recognize this exhibit?" And can you describe for me what's in this photo?"

"That's a photograph posted to a Threads account."

"Who does the account belong to?"

"The profile picture matches the Defendant, the username matches the Defendant's first and last name, with no space between them, and there are photographs of the Defendant posted on the account."

Oliver nodded "Is this photo in the same condition as it was when you viewed it on the account?"

"Yes."

"Your Honor, I'd like to admit this photograph as State's Exhibit 25."

I had no objection, and the judge admitted it. Oliver turned over the next photo on his easel, a shot of a pair of feet in rainbow-toed socks.

"Can you describe the photograph to the court, Detective?"

"The subject of the photograph is what appear to be the defendant's feet, with the kitchen of the RV she'd broken into in the background. The caption underneath it reads 'home bored.' And the time and date on it is ten forty-two the night of the murders. Exactly eight minutes after the last shot was fired."

"Was the photo actually taken on that date at that time?"

"No. The EXIF data shows that it was taken on November tenth."

"So, several days before the murders occurred?"

"Yes."

I had nothing on cross, not for this witness. The photo was damaging, and hard to explain. When I'd asked Zoey about it, she'd said she *was* home by then, and she couldn't explain why she'd chosen that photo. "It just *felt* bored," she'd said, which wasn't much help.

Oliver called up the neighbor's dog walker, and one of the neighbors who'd heard the shots. The dog walker had seen Zoey enter the house, but couldn't be sure she was still inside later, when she passed again. She'd heard two people shouting, a man and a woman. The neighbor had heard the shots, and that was all. Then it was my turn to call witnesses, and I didn't have much. But I did have one possible card up my sleeve.

"Thank you for being here, Dr. Chung. Would you explain for the court what you do?"

Dr. Chung leaned forward, into her mic. "I'm a doctor of audiology. I diagnose, assess, and treat hearing, balance, and related neurological issues."

"And did you examine the defendant back in October, after she fired the revolver used in this crime?"

"I did."

"And what were the results of that examination?"

Dr. Chung checked her notes, but only briefly. "Miss Conrad had mild noise-induced hearing loss, due to acute acoustic trauma." She went on to explain the extent of the damage, and the tests she'd used to measure it.

"And did you repeat these tests at any time?"

"Yes, I did. Two days ago."

"And what were the results?"

"Zoey was showing some signs of recovery." She smiled. "Some of that damage is going to be permanent, but her ability to detect high-frequency sounds had improved."

"Improved..." I stood for a moment, to let that sink in. "Assuming Zoey fired the same weapon a second time, less than eight weeks later, in the same enclosed space, what would you expect to see with respect to the damage to her hearing?"

"I'd expect that she'd exhibit further damage. Further hearing loss, or damage to auditory processing."

Oliver steamed straight in on cross. "What would you expect to see if the defendant wore hearing protection?"

"I'd expect to see little or no further damage to her hearing."

"And did you warn the defendant to wear protection in future?"

Dr. Chung blinked. "I'm sorry?"

"Did you warn Miss Conrad to wear hearing protection if she chose to discharge a firearm again?"

"Yes. Yes, I did. I'd warn any patient in her situation that further damage could be severe."

I recalled the responding officer to the stand, and got him to admit no hearing protection had been found on the scene, or in their search of the surrounding area, but Oliver had done a good job of neutralizing my witness. All I had left was picking holes in the police investigation. Establishing they hadn't investigated anyone else, just as Ian had said.

"But our investigation's still open," said the officer. "If new leads come in, we'll investigate them."

Oliver's closing painted Zoey harshly, as a brutal killer. She'd shot her father through his throat at point-blank range. Chased her urine-soaked, bloodied mom through the house, then shot her straight through the back of her head. Not only that, but she'd been calm enough only eight minutes later to post a false alibi photo to her Threads account. She'd tricked her naïve boyfriend into trying to protect her. The evidence revealed a calculated crime, one that Zoey Conrad had motive, means, and opportunity to commit. The standard of probable cause had been met to put Zoey's case in front of a jury.

"This may well have been a calculated crime," I said. "And it was certainly a brutal one. But a crime committed by my client? The State has established *someone* killed the Conrads, and laid out in detail how they did it. But all they have to suggest my client's guilt is that she was seen entering the house half an hour prior, and *someone* was shouting in the moments before the shooting. But the voices the witness heard were a man and a woman. She couldn't identify either one. The State has not shown my client was present, and her improved hearing and lack of injuries suggests she wasn't.

"As for this alleged coverup... Teenagers often use photos to make a point—funny GIFS, for example. Memes. Celeb pics. These don't necessarily relate to the time or place where the post was made, but to the poster's emotional state. The State has not shown my client *wasn't* home bored. She had half an hour from the time she was spotted to walk half a mile to the RV park—a walk that would've taken her maybe ten minutes.

"Since the State cannot place her at the scene of the crime, what have they shown, except that a crime took place? Not one single neighbor spotted her fleeing. Not one doorbell cam. She could have left at any point after nine thirty, and the State has failed utterly to show she didn't. I'd argue they've shown a crime was committed, but have failed to connect my client to it. I'm asking at this time that the case be dismissed."

"You're good at this," Zoey said, when I sat down. "But I don't think it worked this time. I think it's like you said, and they'll—"

Judge Lowell rapped her gavel. "I've made my decision. The State has shown probable cause to proceed to trial. The defendant, being sixteen years old and charged with a category 1 offense, will be removed to the Donahoe Court of Common Pleas for trial."

Zoey exhaled. "Is that adult court?"

"Yes, it is."

Oliver stood. "The State moves at this time that bail be denied. The defendant fled the scene following the murders, and hid overnight in a local park. She has few ties to the community with her parents gone, and we have reason to believe she is a flight risk."

Judge Lowell turned to me. "Ms. Gallagher?"

"My client is a sixteen-year-old child with no income, no passport, and no resources. She has nowhere to flee to. I request bail be set at a reasonable amount."

Judge Lowell set her gavel down. I thought she looked tired. "A sixteen-year-old murder defendant with no supervision? No. I'm denying bail for now, but I suggest you make arrangements for her care and supervision, then raise the issue at her arraignment in adult court."

Oliver hadn't sat down, and he stepped up again. "Your Honor, the State would further like to request that you order the defendant to comply with the police's warrant for her phone password. Her phone contains evidence pertinent to the crime, and it's essential to their investigation."

"Your Honor," I argued, "that warrant is unconstitutional. Providing her password would be testimonial, and—"

"Nice try, Ms. Gallagher." She reached for her gavel. "So ordered: the defendant will comply with the warrant."

To his credit, Oliver didn't gloat this time. "We'll make it our priority to download that data, and get you discovery ASAP."

"Thank you," I said, though it stuck in my throat. The texts were in now, in their tens of thousands, hundreds of digs and jibes at the Conrads.

However I spun it, this would be bad.

16

I knew something was wrong, pulling into my driveway. I'd headed home after court to change and grab lunch, and a car I'd never seen before was parked in the street. The house's front door flew open as I made my way up the steps, and Sean bolted out, blocking my path. He pulled the door shut behind him, and I felt my heart sink.

"What's going on?"

"It's nothing bad," he insisted, hands up in a "don't shoot" pose. "I just wanted to warn you—"

Damn. It had to be something serious if he felt the need to come out here and warn me. I felt my stomach twist into a knot.

"Who's in the house?"

Sean squeezed my shoulder. "It's your dad."

I expected a surge of anger. Outrage. Hadn't he promised he'd call ahead? But all I felt was tired. Dad? Here and now? I sighed deep from my gut.

"Thanks for the warning."

Sean pulled me into a quick, hard side-hug. "He seems good. You've got this."

We headed inside and into the kitchen, and Dad was at the table sipping a Coke. He looked good, healthy. Ruddy and tanned. I could've said something to that effect, but I couldn't find it in me.

"Dad. What a surprise."

"Sorry I didn't call."

I sort of grunted, not much of an answer. Sean poured me a Coke, and I sat down and started sipping it. It felt strange, awkward, being in the same room with Dad. I couldn't think what to say, unusual for me.

"I've missed you," he said.

"I—" The words stuck in my throat. Should I say *I've missed you too*? I had, but I hadn't. I'd hoped he'd stay gone. I couldn't watch him again spiral down into hell. But people recovered, and for some, it stuck. Maybe Dad would be one of the lucky few.

"I'm moving back here," he said. "Or thinking about it." Color rose in his face, and he scratched at his cheek. "Shoot. Didn't mean to just blurt it like that. But I'm thinking with you guys here, it might be time. Family's important, and… What do you think?"

Resentment rose up—he was asking *me*? After all he had put me through, he'd placed me on the spot like this, pretend that my opinion mattered? Why hadn't it mattered when I was a kid, and all our money for groceries ended up being spent on booze? But my resentment died away as fast as it sparked. I didn't have the energy to dig into All That.

"It's not as cheap as it used to be, property here."

Dad nodded. "I know. But I'm doing well. And you look good too. How's the, uh…?" He made a vague gesture at his own hip. Mine twinged in response, but I chose to ignore it.

"Everything's good, Dad." *No thanks to you.* "And if you want to look at some places, I know an agent."

His face lit up. "So you'd be on board?"

I was spared having to answer by the front door banging open. I heard Ian's book bag thump on the floor.

"Who's car's in the road?" he called.

"Come see for yourself."

He shuffled in, suspicious, then he caught sight of Dad and his expression shifted to cautiously pleased. "Grandpa? Is that—"

"Kiddo! Come here!" Dad flung his arms out. Ian stepped into the hug, and even returned it after a moment. Dad patted his back. Touched his tousled hair. "Could do with a haircut."

"So could your nose."

Dad burst out laughing, and so did Sean. After a minute, I chuckled as well. Dad pulled back from Ian, his eyes slightly damp.

"Let me take you for ice cream. Like the old days. Come on, the whole family. Grandpa's treat." He stretched his arms back out, as though to embrace all of us. Sean glanced at me, and I sucked a deep breath. Ice cream. Just ice cream. How bad could it be? Experience screamed *really bad*, if I let him in. He'd win Ian's heart with his warmth and his joking, but then he'd break it when he fell off the wagon. Because he always fell off the wagon. *No* hung on my lips, but I couldn't say it.

"All right, why not? Let's get ice cream. But then, I need to get back to the office."

Dad whooped, and he drained the last of his Coke. They all trooped off—him, Sean, and Ian. I leaned on the counter and exhaled, harsh and ragged. My eyes felt too dry, like I'd been up all night. Dad was back in town. How would that—

"Mom?"

I jumped. "Ian? I thought you went out."

"I came back to check on you. Are you okay?"

My eyes prickled, and I had to blink hard. When I spoke, my voice came out raspy. "I'm good. Thanks, kid. How are you holding up?"

"Good with Grandpa," he said. "Less good with Zoey." He looked down at his feet. "Mom?"

"Yeah? What is it?"

"Are you still mad at me? You know, for lying? And for in court? Do you think it's my fault that you lost today?"

The breath went out of me like I'd been gut punched. "Oh, Ian, no. That wasn't your fault. Oliver presented a whole lot of evidence. No matter what you said, we were going to trial." I hugged him hard. "I don't love that you lied to me. But I understand why you did it. And family forgives."

Ian's lips twisted into a wry smile. "Like you're doing with Grandpa?"

"Like I'm trying to do." I shoved him lightly. "Now, go get your coat."

I dragged myself back into work after ice cream, drained emotionally and physically now my court high had faded. A hard day in court was a lot like a fistfight: you walked out of it battered but filled with adrenaline and feeling no pain. Punch-drunk, still flying. Then, you came down, and it all hit you at once.

Alia struck the next blow as I walked in the office.

"The DA's office shared Zoey's phone dump. It's a lot more than those texts we got. You need to see."

Auntie El bustled up with a big mug of coffee and a chocolate croissant from the bakery downstairs. I eyed the pastry, suspicious.

"Just how bad *is* this?"

"Here. Have some chocolate." She thrust the croissant at my face, and I took a bite. Sure, I'd just had ice cream twenty minutes ago, but I *always* had room for a chocolate croissant. Chocolatey goodness flooded my mouth and I groaned.

"I've done her TikTok, and now I'm on Insta." Alia was on her computer, scrolling away, and she gestured at a thick pile of printouts. "I'm printing out anything you need to see. Any violent-type imagery, any hate on her parents."

"Hate…" I groaned in frustration around my croissant and took a big gulp of coffee to wash it down. "Would you say there's a lot of that? Hate on her parents?"

"I'd say homegirl's mad. And with good reason."

I massaged my temples against my impending headache and reached for a folder marked SIGNAL – 2025-2026. "This is all from one app? I've read thinner novels."

Alia rattled a bottle of aspirin. "If you need one, just holler."

"I might later. Thanks."

I dove into the transcripts. At first it was boring—no, not just boring. Mind-numbingly dull. A glimpse into the minutiae of some kid's random chit-chat.

lol yeah?

ha lol

@ mill creek now u get the hummus??

thout u wer getting it???? mom forgot my allowance

shit be right there give me 5 mins

At least they were snacking healthy. Unless hummus was code for drugs. But, no, Zoey's friend had stolen the hummus, and texted a pic of it as she fled the scene. Great—accessory after the fact, to add to her rap sheet.

I skimmed the next few pages, till Ian's screen name popped up, the same one I'd seen him using on Insta. At first, I smiled, seeing how sweet he was with her. Then I read on, and my smile faded.

so how was your mom?

she's such a bitch.
like she never got a B in her entire life? I would bet money she failed home ec
her ambrosia salad looks AND tastes like dog barf
wish she'd just drown in it and leave me alone. 💩

I scanned through the next page, and the ten after that, and the farther I read, the worse it got. Not that she said anything gruesomely awful, but there was a grinding repetition of the same sentiment—*I wish she'd just die. I wish they were dead. Life would be SO GOOD if they just disappeared. Can't aliens like come and abduct them or something???????* Poop emoji. Troll emoji. Chef's knife emoji. I pushed my chair back so hard it hit the wall.

"You okay, boss?" Alia squinted up from her reading.

"I'm fine," I said. "I'll be back later. Could you sticky-tab any time Zoey says something like 'I wish they were dead' about her parents?"

Alia winced. "I might need more sticky tabs."

I stomped out to my car, my headache now throbbing, and drove out through Kerry, to the woods beyond the town limits. Normally, I loved a drive out through the back roads—the forested calm of it, the fresh country air. But today I just wanted to get where I was going, and I drove fast, blowing past the speed limit.

Zoey was waiting when I arrived at Youth Detention, already set up in an interview room. She barely looked up when I sat down.

"How are you doing?" I asked. She might not be my favorite person at the moment, but she was still my client. My responsibility.

She snorted. "Look around you. How do you think?" She didn't sound angry, or even upset. Her tone was resigned, like she thought this was it for her. That she'd have this grim, chilly backdrop for the rest of her life.

"Zoey." I leaned forward. "This isn't over. I'm going to fight for you when it comes to your trial."

"I know," she said. "But you think I did it, right?"

Yeah, maybe.

I wasn't certain of her guilt, but I damn sure wasn't certain of her innocence either.

I didn't want to lie to her, so I deflected the question. "It doesn't matter what I think, or what anyone thinks. What matters is what can be proven in court. I got disclosure from the DA of the data on your phone. It includes a whole lot of texts here, a lot of DMs..." I broke off, trying to think how best to phrase this. Too harsh, and she'd withdraw into herself. "You talk a lot about wishing your parents were dead. A lot about wishing they'd disappear. The State's going to see those and take them as motive, and the jury might see them that way as well. I need to hear your side. What were you thinking when you said those things?"

Zoey chewed her lip. Picked at her sleeve.

"Zoey, please. I know this is hard. But I need to understand—"

"I just thought it'd be easier..." Her voice cracked and broke. She closed her eyes, sniffled, and wiped her nose on her sleeve. "I had these books as a kid, *The Boxcar Children*. The kids in them... they didn't have parents, but that was okay. They solved mysteries. Went on vacation. Figured things out for themselves. I know that's not real life, but I used to think, wouldn't it be easier without all the..."

"What?"

She shrugged. "They were never there anyway—except to yell at me when they thought I'd screwed up. Like this one time, when I was seven? They went out to church bingo and left me alone, and I ate a whole pound cake and puked in my bed. And then they got mad at me because I made a mess. They always do stuff like that, like they won't help with my homework, but then they get mad at me if I get a B."

I got the sense there was more to this she wasn't saying, but parental neglect at least was a start. Emotional abuse. Abandonment. It gave some context to the text messages, made them seem less cold-blooded. "Did you discuss this with anyone other than Ian?"

Zoey shook her head. "My therapist, sort of? My mom made me go to her a while ago. But everything I said, she told my parents, and you can guess how that went."

I slid my hand toward her. "Tell me—how did it go?"

She stared at my hand, her eyes wet and red-rimmed. "I wanted to go back to how it was before. At least then they sometimes—" Her face crumpled, and she buried it in the crook of her arm.

"They sometimes what?"

"It sometimes felt like they loved me," she mumbled into her arm. "I just wanted parents like everyone else. I didn't want them to really go away."

I felt my own throat close and my eyes well up, and I checked myself quickly. I couldn't fall apart in front of a client, no matter how peeled open I felt from her words. Because I'd been where she was with my own dad, fending for myself. Eating spoiled leftovers. Getting sick on the carpet—though I'd told Dad he did it. All I'd wanted was the same thing Zoey said she did: a dad who loved me enough to put me first.

"I want you to think hard before our next meeting." I swallowed to clear the thickness in my voice. "Think about how your parents treated you, and how that made you feel."

She laughed, not a merry sound. "So, easy homework?"

"I know this is hard." I patted her hand. "But anything you can think of, I need to know. Any evidence of mistreatment or neglect by your parents. Especially anything you can prove."

Zoey asked then if she could go back to her cell. I had no more questions, so I called for a guard. I left feeling sick, and worse, unsure: was Zoey a lonely kid aching for her parents' love, or was she an angry one who'd finally snapped? Were her tears from heartbreak, or from being caught?

I wasn't sure if what she'd told me helped Oliver, or if I could spin it to help Zoey's case.

17

I was pleased to find Judge Yost presiding over Zoey's arraignment. He was a former family court judge, which I felt might work to our advantage. He was younger himself, still in his thirties—young enough, I hoped, to see himself in Zoey.

Oliver charged two counts of aggravated murder, as I'd expected. Zoey pleaded not guilty without incident. Then, it came time to argue for bail. As soon as she heard the word "bail," Zoey sat up straight for the first time all day, her pale face alight with desperate hope.

"Your Honor, the State moves that bail be denied." Oliver glowered down at Zoey and her face fell. "The defendant stands accused of two brutal murders. She presents significant danger to the community, and add to that, I believe she's a flight risk. At the time of the murders, she wasn't living at home, but in an RV she had broken into. She has significant survival skills, and a propensity to run."

Judge Yost nodded. He turned to me. "Ms. Gallagher?"

"Ms. Conrad is hardly a flight risk, Your Honor. She's a sixteen year old with no passport, no car, and no driver's license. Nor does she have resources to allow her to flee. She has no money, no credit cards, and no family support. Her bail would be secured by her parents' estate, funds she would forfeit if she were to flee.

"In addition, Ms. Conrad has no history of juvenile delinquency. She's a good student with no disciplinary record. Not only that, but her custody—" I hesitated. I didn't want Zoey back in my house, under the same roof with Ian. With my family. But if I couldn't demonstrate she had a safe place to go, I could fight all I liked for her and she'd never get bail. "She doesn't have family here, so she's been staying with me. With an officer of the court. I'm willing to continue that arrangement until new, court-approved accommodations can be found.

"Finally, my client is a minor. In family court, the welfare of the child must take priority over all other considerations. This is a serious matter, and we're not in family court, but my client *is* a child, and her welfare still matters. I'd ask that Your Honor set reasonable bail."

Oliver started to say something else, but Judge Yost waved him down.

"Mr. Altman's correct: these are serious charges. But I don't buy his argument she's a flight risk, especially supervised by her attorney. A couple of sleepovers in a nearby RV park do not constitute 'significant survival skills.' Nor does the defendant have access to funds. I'm granting bail in the amount of two million dollars, and the defendant will wear an ankle monitor."

Zoey bit back a cry. Squinched her eyes against tears. I touched her arm.

"Hey. This is good news."

"Good news? *Good news*? Two million dollars? I haven't got that, or anywhere close!"

I could see her spiraling, getting ready to crack. I gripped her arm tightly and turned her to face me. "Listen to me: this is a win. You only have to put up a ten percent bond. That's two hundred thousand."

"I don't have that either!"

"No, but your parents' estate does. I'll talk to their lawyer and work something out."

"I thought—didn't you say I couldn't inherit? Because of, uh, slayer laws or whatever? And that's why the judge had to appoint you my public defender?"

"If you're convicted, then that's right—you couldn't inherit anything from your parents. But you haven't been convicted yet. You can use those funds for bail, and if you're found guilty, the money will be returned to your parents' estate."

"So, you'll get me out? Promise?"

"I can only promise that I'll do my best, but I think we have a good chance. You'll have to go back to detention for now, but I'll put in a call today to Hugh Barlow."

"Thank you," she whispered. "But hurry. Please."

I made my way back up the street after court, grabbing bakery coffees on my way to the office. We had a long afternoon planned, reviewing the evidence, and I wanted Auntie El and Alia pumped full of pep.

"Coffee lady," I sang, heading inside. Both Auntie El and Alia already had coffees, but they came running anyway when they saw what I'd brought: a tall almond mocha for Auntie El; a cream-topped monstrosity for Alia.

"You know what this means," said Auntie El. "She's buttering us up for a trip to the salt mines."

Alia sucked whipped cream and let out a moan. "Bring me my pickaxe, if it comes with hazelnut syrup."

"I'll buy dinner too," I said. "Whatever you want. But first, clear the whiteboard. I want to start fresh, look at this through a trial lens. What will the jury see? What don't we know yet? What *doesn't* the State have that we can dig into?"

"Oliver sent over a 3D reconstruction of the crime scene," said Auntie El. "And photos as well. They're pretty grim. I'd say if you can, you'll want to get those excluded. What is it they always say on TV: more prejudicial than probative? Does that apply here?"

"Rule 403 of the evidence code." I frowned. "It might apply. Let me see that reconstruction."

Alia turned her laptop around and hit PLAY. Two figures ran out—faceless 3D mannequins—and tussled by the bookcase in the upstairs hall. The smaller one grabbed the gun. Chased the other figure downstairs. Shot out his throat. Arterial spray shot out, and I'd seen enough.

"Yeah, that's disturbing. That's not coming in. But there won't be a lot I can do about the photos. I can argue they're prejudicial, but it's hard to make that case. This reconstruction, on the other hand—if we can get our own expert to dispute the details, it shouldn't be too hard to get that tossed out."

"But the State will still have the evidence they used to construct it." Alia reached for the ME's report. "They'll still have their expert up on the stand, going through the sequence of events piece by piece. Showing Lorraine's blood, and that pool of piss."

"Language," I snapped, then cringed at my tone. "Sorry, I just—you're so close to Ian's age."

"I'm sure he knows that word too."

"I'm sure he does." I pulled a wry face, and Alia winked. Auntie El rolled her eyes at the both of us.

"If you kids are done bickering, I had a thought." She took a swig of her coffee. "*Mm.* Hits the spot. But what I was thinking was, Oliver's got his story, and it's a good one. Riveting. So what about our side? What's our narrative, and how can we make it more convincing than his?"

"It's not so much about telling our story as poking holes into Oliver's. That's how we create reasonable doubt."

"But they don't know Zoey's side," said Alia.

"That's true. They don't. And anything we know that they don't *is* an advantage." I stood up, unconsciously sliding into court mode. Slowing my speech to a persuasive cadence. "Zoey came home to collect a few things, her clothes. Some money. Maybe some snacks. She was expecting to find the house empty, her parents at their regular Thursday church group. Instead, she found them in her bedroom, packing her bags. They'd decided to send her away after all, to a church-run boarding school out in Utah."

"I looked the place up," Alia said. "It's a regular school, not one of those camps."

I sighed, sliding back into regular mode. "She was pretty upset. Zoey, I mean. And who wouldn't be, coming home to that? What would you think, if you were in her shoes?"

"I'd think my folks didn't want me." Alia touched a locket I hadn't noticed before, a little gold heart on a fine chain. It didn't match with her general punky aesthetic. "My heart would break if I ever thought that. My folks aren't perfect, God only knows—well, *everyone* knows the length of Dad's rap sheet. But I never once had to ask if they love me."

I'd had to ask, more times than I could count, and Alia was right. "Our narrative doesn't do much to make Zoey look innocent. Maybe if she claimed temporary insanity—that she was too upset to think straight...but that's not the story she's telling. What Zoey says happened is she ran out crying. Ran out the back and straight to Mill Creek. But nobody saw her, at least nobody who has come forward. And that 'home bored' post looks pretty bad."

"Someone could still have seen her," Alia said. "Mill Creek's not busy this time of year, but there's still guys that sleep out there under the awning. One of them could've seen her. I could go out and ask."

I nodded. "That's good. And maybe check in with your cousin? She might have heard some rumors going round school."

Alia grimaced. "No helpful ones so far. And a few that might hurt us if they grow legs. Like, kids are saying Zoey liked Burzum—and they're just a band, but their frontman's a killer. I mean, convicted, did time, the whole bit. That sort of thing won't play well with a jury."

I scowled: killer rockers. Just what we needed. "I think our next step needs to be a deep dive on the parents. I'm pissed Ian lied, but he was right. The cops aren't looking too hard into them and who else might have had a grudge against them."

"Way ahead of you." Alia jumped up. She went to my desk and retrieved a folder. "Printouts of anyone who posted an angry or threatening message on the Conrads' Insta account. And a couple of police reports about harassing phone calls, but I don't know how seriously I would take those. Seems like one call, and they'd run to the cops."

I leafed through the folder, which was surprisingly thick.

"Kharper, who's that?"

"Oh, I know this one," said Auntie El. "That's got to be Karen—remember Dr. Karen?" She smiled at Alia, who nodded. "Sweet girl, grew up in town. Started a dermatology practice, and she was doing well. But she left a few years ago, for Columbus, I think."

"Karen Harper," said Alia. "Her details are in there, but I couldn't get much. The Conrads sued her for malpractice, but the records are sealed. She had to sell her house to pay for the judgment, and she moved in with her parents right after that."

I pointed at the whiteboard. "Auntie El? Do the honors?"

She wrote up the details as I skimmed through the file.

"How about this one, ODINSVENGEANCE?" He'd posted on Insta in screaming all-caps, *YOU ARE A PARACITE AND A BLOODSUCKER! YOU ARE TO LAZY TO MAKE A HONEST LIVING SO YOU LEATCH OFF HARDWORKING AMERICANS LIKE ME AND MY DAD. BUT KARMA IS A BITCH AND YOUR A BITCH BABY AND SHE WILL SNAP YOU BY YOUR SCRUFF NECK.*

"Leo Ackers," said Alia. "The Conrads sued his dad. He had to close his contracting business. But he was close to retirement, and this was years back. Leo could've stayed mad, but if we're looking for the likeliest suspect, my money's on this guy." She leaned over my shoulder to shuffle the pages. "Barry Robeson, owns the Budget car lot. He thought Paul was having an affair with his wife, and he cold-cocked him outside Pam's Chicken."

"I remember that," said Auntie El. "Knocked the Big Bumper Bucket right out of his hands."

"Paul sued him, of course. Won 50K. But the worst part for Barry was everyone knowing. And his wife left him too, so there was that."

I leafed through the rest of the file as they gossiped, debating the merits of Pam's versus Krunch Chicken. Alia had included not just the

Insta stuff, but a list of lawsuits the Conrads had filed, along with win/loss checks, and their rewards. "Jesus. Who sues this much, besides a law firm?"

Auntie El rolled her eyes. "It's a joke around town, because Paul was a day trader. People used to say that you had to watch yourself when the market was down, because that was when he'd sue you. It was sort of a backup income for them."

I'd never say a crime victim had it coming, but Paul sure hadn't tried too hard to make friends. It didn't jibe with what Hugh Barlow had told me about how the Conrads were respected. Well-liked around town. I flicked through the list of defendants again.

"Who were these people? I mean, were they... How the hell did the Conrads have any friends, if they went around suing everybody in sight?"

Auntie El laughed. "Oh, you *are* new in town. I keep on forgetting that, because you grew up here."

Alia smirked too and shrugged one shoulder. "They went after working folks, or out-of-towners."

"What about Dr. Karen? She was from here."

"She was a Buddhist. Not one of them. You check that defendant list against who goes to First Baptist, I guarantee you won't match one single name."

I snapped the folder shut, feeling disgusted. "Well, that gives us—"

"Mags?"

I jumped. How had I not heard Dad come in? He was leaning in the doorway, a brown bag in hand, and now he smiled crookedly and held it up.

"I brought treats," he said. "Pain-au-chocolat."

"We already have treats."

His face fell, and I felt instantly bad. He was making an effort. The least I could do was meet him halfway.

"Sorry," I said. "We're just really busy. We have a ton to get through, but could we meet up later?"

Dad's smile was back, cautious. He set the bag on my desk. "Sure, Mags. No problem. I just stopped in to say, I checked out a house today here in Kerry that I think might suit me. I've given my notice, so it's happening. My move."

I was spared having to respond to that by my phone ringing: Hugh Barlow returning my call about pulling together the money for Zoey's bail.

"You're all set," he said. "As soon as you've fixed the custody issue, you can go on and get her."

I thanked him and engaged him in a bit of small talk, waiting for Dad to leave before I hung up. The second he did, I flopped down in my seat. Auntie El frowned at me.

"That was Barlow, right? Bad news?"

I massaged my temples, my headache coming back. "Good news on bail, but arranging custody could be a challenge. Not many foster homes want a kid accused of murder. I'd take her again, but..." I groaned deeply. "Ian."

"I wouldn't mind having her," said Auntie El.

I straightened up. "What?"

"Yeah. Why not? I've got plenty of space for her with my kids all grown. And there's not much trouble she can find on the farm."

Auntie El's house *had* once been my happy place, when Dad was drunk or when he was gone. I'd always felt wanted there, peaceful and safe. Maybe a dose of that was what Zoey needed.

I scrunched up my face. "Doesn't Uncle Carl have guns?"

"Yeah, and they're locked. No way she gets near 'em."

I couldn't think of a reason Auntie El shouldn't take her. If Zoey hadn't killed her parents, then she was just a kid who'd had some seriously awful things happen to her. She deserved a place where she felt safe and cared for while she tried to process everything going on. And even if she *had* shot her parents, it was looking like she'd had a strong motive. There was no reason to believe she was a thrill killer or a psychopath.

"All right," I said. "Thanks, Auntie El. The court will have to agree to it, but either way, thanks."

18

Alia drove us out to the Budget car lot, arguing her ride would buy us goodwill.

"Come on, he's a car guy. And isn't she sweet?" She patted the hood of her souped-up Camaro. "Restored her myself. Who wouldn't love her?"

I kind of hated her—the car, not Alia. Too flashy by half. Undignified. But I knew enough about car guys to know she was likely right about Barry Robeson. So we piled in, and she drove us over. I expected her to drive like a kid on a joyride, but she drove cautiously and got us there safe. Then she ruined it all with a big, cheeky grin.

"We should take her out someday on the back roads. Let me show you what she can do when I open her up."

"Yeah, I'll pass. Is that our guy?" I pointed at a stocky man bustling to greet us. Alia nodded.

"That's Robeson."

Robeson was what you'd picture if someone said "car salesman": red-faced and slick-haired, dressed in a cheap shiny suit. He slapped on a smile as he approached.

"Good morning, ladies, a beautiful day! Aren't you loving this weather we're having? Winter's the best season, if you ask me."

"Gorgeous," I agreed, though I hated cold weather. It played havoc with my joints since my injury.

"That's a nice ride you've got," he said, addressing Alia. "Helping your mom pick out a new ride?"

Alia and I exchanged glances. He thought we were family. I considered whether playing along might get him talking, but the Conrad case was all over the news. The minute we mentioned it, he'd guess who we were.

"I'm Maggie Gallagher," I said. "I'm a lawyer representing Zoey Conrad. I am *not* the police," I assured him. "I'm not here to hassle you or air your dirty laundry. I'm trying to build a picture of the Conrads' home life, and—"

Barry's smile vanished faster than a plate of Pam's chicken. "I've got nothing to say to you." He turned to go.

"Just a couple of questions—did you know them before that? Before the lawsuit, did you—"

"No comment." He strode off at a fair clip. I winced and followed.

"Look, I'm on your side here. Some of those lawsuits—Paul Conrad ruined a whole lot of lives. If we could just talk, even—"

"Nope. Go away." He picked up his pace and I shouted after him.

"Do you remember where you were the night of the murders?"

"Ask my lawyer," he yelled, and headed inside. The door swung shut behind him, and I huffed in frustration. Alia cocked her head.

"Should we go after him?"

I sighed. "No point. And I doubt he's our guy."

"I don't know," said Alia. "He seems to still be pretty angry with Paul."

"Yeah, but he didn't know who I was. If he'd killed the Conrads, I'd expect him to know me. He'd have kept up with the case, would have seen me on TV. Guilty men *always* check to make sure they're not suspects."

We got back in the car and drove into town, to Adler's Mini Mart, where Leo Ackers worked. He was stocking shelves when we walked in—a pinched and wiry man with a bald pate. His deeply lined face made him look older, but I knew from Alia's file he was forty-two. He didn't look up as we made our way in, just kept on stacking cans of baked beans.

I cleared my throat. "Leo Ackers?"

He craned to look at me. "Yeah?"

"I'm Maggie Gallagher, and this is Alia. We're looking into some suits filed by Paul and Lorraine Conrad. Would you have a minute, so we could chat?"

His shoulders slumped down, and he looked tired. He set down his last can of beans and stood up. "You're that lawyer, aren't you? If you ask me, their girl did it. Don't blame her at all, stuck living with those two." He hawked, then glanced over at Mrs. Adler, and swallowed his spit instead of fouling her floor. Still, I got the point. He hated the Conrads.

"You're not alone in that view." I smiled, wide and chummy. "We just met Barry Robeson. He had some nice things to say."

Leo laughed. "I guess he would, right? Sleep with a guy's wife, that's one thing. Whatever. But sue him right after? Take his nest egg? That's a next-level bastard, is what that is."

"I guess you've experienced that for yourself."

Leo's face clouded. "You don't think *I* did it? I don't know what you heard, but they never sued me. They sued my dad."

"Oh, no. I didn't come here to accuse you." I chuckled a little, like the idea was ludicrous. Like Leo's potential guilt hadn't crossed my mind. "Actually, we're here today to try to get a picture of the Conrads' home life. What Paul and Lorraine were like, you know? The real stuff, not just what they put on display. We're talking to you because you worked for them, right? How did that go, before the lawsuit? Did you happen to see them interacting with Zoey?"

"I don't know," he said. "I guess they were fine? The kid wasn't home much, as it was summer. She was off with her friends, so we didn't see much of her."

"And what did you do for them, what kind of job?"

"It was up at their lake house, you know, Trout Lake? Not one of the mansions, but the ones past Shell Beach. They'd had a storm, and a tree came through their roof. We pretty much rebuilt the place, me and my dad."

"And the lawsuit was…?"

Leo's brows gathered into a rage unibrow. "Those assholes burned their own place down, and they blamed us—said we screwed up their wiring. They made out twice, first from insurance, then they looped back and took a chunk out of us. But I swear to you, the wiring was fine. Dad was a stickler, and me, I'm no slouch. And we checked and double-checked, both of us did. But the judge found us liable, so that was it. Dad lost the business. We lost the house. I wanted to appeal it, but Dad was done." He shrugged, relaxing. "He was planning on retiring anyway. But the house was a blow. Dad loved that house."

His story lined up with Alia's case file: the wiring, the lawsuit, the business, the house. And Leo seemed upset, but no more than I would be if some client sued me and gutted my life. I decided to poke a bit to see what would happen.

"I'm sorry," I said. "Must've been tough."

Leo's eyes narrowed. "It was worse than tough. And I popped off online some. Guess you saw that?"

I saw no point denying it, so I nodded. "Yeah."

"Well, that's all I did. Posted some warnings. So other contractors would know what they did, and they would steer clear—the way I wish Dad and I had."

"All right," I said. "Thanks, that's—"

"They did have a fight one time."

I frowned. "A fight?"

"I mean, just the parents. Not with the kid."

This was new information. I kept my tone casual. "Do you remember what it was about?"

He shrugged. "Not sure, but she threw a plate at him. It flew out the window and smashed on Dad's truck. You think there's a chance they killed each other?"

I laughed. "No, there's not. Thanks for that, Leo. If you think of anything else, call my office." I left him with my card, and we headed back out. It was getting to lunchtime, so we stopped for burgers. Alia ordered a kids' meal, and I felt a stab of worry. Was she not making enough for a real meal? I'd given her as many hours as I could, and I knew she was still working for Rent-A-Nerd.

"I order them for the toys," she said, like she'd read my mind. She fished out a plastic car and waggled it at me. "My cousins love these —the twins, I mean. It's their birthday next week and I want to finish their set."

"How many cousins do you have?"

She smirked. "I have tons. If you count second cousins, we could fill our own town."

I bit into my juicy adult-sized burger. Alia dipped one of her dinosaur nuggies.

"What did you think?" she said. "I mean, of Leo."

I chewed my food, thinking that over. "He has an alibi, or claims he does. And I didn't get rage from him, but you never know. I thought that was weird, him suggesting that they might have killed each other."

Alia sipped her Coke. "Yeah. That was strange. But what was stranger was, he never once said their names."

I blinked. "He didn't?"

"Nope. Not once. Not Paul's, not Lorraine's, and he called Zoey 'the kid.' Think he was trying to distance himself?"

"Could be. Never noticed that. That's a good catch."

We finished our meals and threw out our trash. Alia went back to the counter and got a cookie to go.

"I'll keep digging," she said, as we headed out. "Do a deep dive on the rest of those lawsuits."

"And get a full background check on Ackers and Robeson. I doubt either one of them did it, but you never know."

Alia grinned. "Should I check if they knew each other, Ackers and Robeson? Or what about all of them, all the defendants? What if this was, like, a class-action murder? You know, like *Murder on the Orient Express*?"

I snorted, but I'd heard stranger theories. Had stranger theories ended up being right. "Go for it," I said. "But don't spend too much time on it. I need you focused on what seems most likely, not chasing down every stray hunch."

Of course, what seemed most likely was that Zoey did it. I'd chase down just about any lead suggesting she didn't.

19

I spotted Alia on my way to the courthouse, in her bright red Rent-A-Nerd jacket. It was almost Christmas now, winter in full swing, and she'd switched from her flimsy summer windbreaker to a thick winter one with a high collar. She waved hello and jogged up to join me.

"Pretrial hearing today?"

I grimaced. "Yeah."

"Well, you can thank me when your hearing's on time. I just got done updating their scheduling software."

It surprised me to hear they *had* any software and weren't just running on paper and ink. Alia laughed.

"Kidding! The look on your face. I was just fixing Judge Levinson's laptop."

Now, that I believed. I glanced back at the bakery. "You have time for a coffee? I've got a few minutes."

"I wish." She held up her phone. "I've got three more gigs lined up, all before noon. But good luck in court today. Go defense, right?"

This wasn't a ball game, but I had to smile. Alia's enthusiasm was easy to catch. I headed into the courthouse feeling energized, going over my arguments in my head. My mission today was to winnow down the State's witness list, and get as much of their evidence tossed as I could.

Any local jury would already know this trial wouldn't be Zoey's first rodeo. They'd all have been following media coverage of her boot camp shooting, her arrest, her hearing, the dismissal of charges. But that didn't mean I wanted Oliver bringing it in, trying to cast Zoey as some kind of serial killer. And he'd do exactly that, given the chance.

Judge Yost looked down at me, then at his docket. "I'll now hear arguments on pretrial motions, starting with the defense motion to exclude evidence related to the Rooney shooting. Ms. Gallagher, if you would?"

"Your Honor, the Rooney shooting was ruled self-defense, and all charges were dismissed against my client. It's not evidence of a pattern or prior bad acts, nor does it have any bearing on this case. Furthermore, the Rooney case is emotionally fraught, involving the death of a young man by shooting. Including facts or testimony pertaining to this case would only serve to prejudice the jury."

Oliver glared at Judge Yost, and then at me. "The fact is, Miss Conrad's parents paid to have her kidnapped. She was injured in that attempt and traumatized. That trauma is evidence supporting motive, and therefore relevant to this case."

Judge Yost scratched his ear. "Then, as of now, I'm excluding any evidence related to Miss Conrad's actions surrounding that shooting, but *not* any evidence pointing to motive, as long as that evidence doesn't presume guilt."

My neck went hot. I'd anticipated Judge Yost ruling this way, but I'd hoped to keep the Rooney case out entirely. Still, today's battle was far from done. I took a moment and pretended to consult my notes, giving me a moment to gather myself. That 3D reconstruction *couldn't* come in, and it was my job to make sure it didn't.

"Your Honor, per my motion to exclude State's Exhibit D, a 3D reconstruction of the Conrad crime scene, I have here a detailed report from Dr. Mark Gillies, a forensic team lead from TBH Labs." I held up the folder. "I'd like to call Dr. Gillies to the stand."

Dr. Gillies stepped up, a whipgrass-thin man, with a sharp nose like the tip of a pencil. He took a seat and pushed up his glasses.

I had Dr. Gillies run through his credentials, then I asked him about his lab. He rattled off his answer, bright like ad copy.

"TBH is an independent forensic lab with a decades-long history of cooperation with law enforcement. We are experts on crime scene evidence, and highly experienced in crime scene reconstruction."

"And, have you reviewed the State's reconstruction?"

Dr. Gillies pulled a face. "I have."

"What's your professional opinion of that reconstruction?"

"I found it, ah…" He paused for a moment, maybe self-censoring. "The State's reconstruction is quite flawed. It makes a lot of assumptions based on missing, incomplete, or misinterpreted evidence. For example, the reconstruction shows a fight happening here, two figures struggling in the upstairs hall, then one of them breaks off and runs for the study. There's no physical evidence to support that theory of events. No evidence the killer made the first move to retrieve the revolver. All we know from the evidence is a disturbance took place, not who was involved or what it looked like, or at what point the killer went for the gun.

"In my opinion, the State's reconstruction is strongly biased, and implies levels of violence and premeditation on the part of the attacker that is not supported by the evidence."

I ran Dr. Gillies through his whole report, every detail, every movement where assumptions were made that were not explicitly supported by the evidence. By the time I was done, Judge Yost looked bored, and Oliver looked like he'd swallowed a bug. Still, he stood gamely, ready for cross.

"Dr. Gillies, have you ever made a mistake?"

"Yes, I have."

"Have you ever been sued for a mistake made in court?"

"Yes, I have."

"Could you describe the nature of that mistake?"

"This was long ago, when I worked for the State. I made an error and mislabeled fingerprint evidence, resulting in the appellate court sending the matter back for retrial. But that was—"

"Thank you, Dr. Gillies. Is it possible your report on this case contains similar errors?"

"No, it is not. The State's reconstruction contains no blood spatter evidence."

Oliver's face darkened, but he went on. "Let me rephrase that. Is it possible your report on this case contains *any* errors?"

"I don't believe it does, but yes. It is possible."

"Thank you, Dr. Gillies. That will be all."

Dr. Gillies stepped down, and Oliver called *his* expert, who was as long-winded as Dr. Gillies. By the time he was done, I was glazing over, myself. I had only one question for him on cross, to establish his relative lack of experience—seven years compared to my guy's thirty. He stepped down, and I stood up again.

"Your Honor, we've heard from two experts, and they can't agree on what this crime looked like, or whether it's even possible to tell from the evidence. I can argue all that again in front of a jury, but I believe the point is made: this recreation is just one possible interpretation of events. Additionally, it's violent. Deliberately disturbing. It adds nothing not covered by forensic evidence and serves no purpose but to prejudice the jury."

Oliver gulped from his water glass, then he stood up. "Your Honor, our reconstruction comes from a reputable lab, and I would argue it *does* add value. Forensic testimony can be very dry, and it can be difficult for a jury to visualize. What our reconstruction does is, it lets them see what they're hearing. It condenses hours of testimony into a visual format, easier to remember and to digest."

I snorted without meaning to and covered it with a sneeze. "Easier to remember"—it was that, all right, with its red fans of arterial blood.

Judge Yost's lips tightened as Oliver sat. He pushed Oliver's lab report to one side.

"Have you got this video? I want to see it."

Oliver pulled out a USB stick. "Do you have a projector?"

"Just give it here."

The bailiff took the stick and passed it to Yost. He plugged it into the laptop, found the file, and pressed play. Oliver leaned up, trying to see.

"Right from the start, Paul's caught off guard. The killer—"

"I can see for myself." The judge waved him to silence. His glasses reflected the crime scene in stereo, flickers of movement. Red sprays of blood. Then it went dark, and he closed his laptop.

"I am ruling this video assumes certain facts which are in dispute, and the presentation in video format carries a high probability of unfair prejudice. Therefore, its doubtful probative value is easily outweighed. If you would like, I will enter your thumb drive into evidence for appellate purposes."

"Thank you," said Oliver. "Please do."

"Then, moving on." Yost rapped his gavel. "Next, the motion to exclude, ah, Dr. Granger."

I swelled with my victory, but I wasn't done yet. "Your Honor, my client's former therapist, Dr. Julia Granger, is on the State's witness list. But she cannot testify, because such testimony would violate doctor-patient confidentiality."

"I'm inclined to agree," said Judge Yost. "Mr. Altman?"

Oliver puffed himself up like he always did when he thought he had a trump card. The annoying thing was, he was frequently right. "Your Honor, I have here a release form signed by the defendant, showing Dr. Granger disclosed that she would be sharing the content of her sessions with her parents. Thus, confidentiality has already been pierced, and Dr. Granger can testify."

I bristled, annoyed—I'd spoken with Dr. Granger. She hadn't mentioned a signed release. She'd been in a hurry, and I'd meant to get back to her, but since that first meeting she'd been dodging my calls.

"So ruled," said Judge Yost. "Anything further?"

I didn't have anything else. I hadn't gotten everything I'd wanted, but I wasn't unsatisfied. The reconstruction was out, and that was a win.

Oliver caught up to me on our way out of court. "I wanted to give you the heads-up before I send you my witness list. I'll be calling Ian again, to testify to Zoey's coverup and her texts."

I nodded. "I expected that. And I'll be calling him myself."

"So, it's no problem?"

"No problem at all." Still, I left the courthouse with a sour belly, and a sense of foreboding I couldn't shake. If Oliver's objective had been to rattle me, he had succeeded, and I wasn't sure why. I *had* been planning on calling Ian. He was my best shot at defanging Zoey's texts. Putting him on the stand opened him up to questioning from Oliver—I'd known that all along. So it shouldn't bother me. But…it did.

I dug out my phone as I headed back for my car.

"Maggie?"

"Hey, Sean. Can you do lunch?"

"Sure, I'd like that. Everything okay?"

I sat on one of the benches outside the courthouse, more tired than I should've been at not quite noon. "I'm fine," I said. "Just want to see you."

"All right. Let's get burgers. See you in ten?"

I sat another minute breathing the wintry air. Main Street smelled of snow, though it hadn't snowed yet. But the forecasts all promised a perfect white Christmas.

"Merry Christmas," I muttered, and I got up. I walked to the diner and arrived just as Sean did. He came up and hugged me, and we headed inside. I found a table while he got our burgers, and I sighed as he ordered mine—mustard, no onions. One thing I could count on was Sean's memory: a year ago, I'd have gotten extra onions. But recently, onions had started giving me heartburn, so my doctor had banned them. I'd halfway hoped Sean might forget, and I could indulge in the forbidden treats.

Our burgers were done in five minutes flat, and we both took big bites of them and groaned in sync, satisfied. Sean pointed a finger-gun at his head.

"Just shoot me when we start dressing alike."

"You shoot me first." I rolled my eyes. I knew there was a part of Sean that liked the idea of us as an old married couple. I liked it too, the idea we'd make it that far. Even if that dream *did* include matching sweaters.

"So, what's up?" He reached for my hand. I twined my fingers with his and closed my eyes.

"I'm worried about Ian, when he testifies. If Zoey's convicted, he might blame himself."

"You think that'll happen?"

"I don't know." I gripped Sean's hand tighter, then let him go. "How's he been in school? I mean, with his friends? Alia's been showing me what those kids are saying online about him and Zoey. Does he still have— Is he okay?"

Sean had picked up his burger. Now he set it back down. "He still sits with the same core group at lunch. Not *all* of them, though. A few have peeled off."

I licked my teeth. Tasted mustard. "Do you think they'd bully him? Those kids that bailed?"

Sean took his time thinking about that. When he finally spoke, he didn't sound sure. "I don't see everything. They know I'm his dad. They're not going to go for him when I'm in the lunchroom, but in the halls, on the schoolyard, it's harder to say. He's a jock, or he was. That buys him some capital. But his closeness to Zoey..."

I pushed my tray away, no longer hungry.

"I'm keeping an eye out as far as I can. And he knows if he needs to talk, he can come to us."

"It's Christmas soon," I said. "Let's give him a good one. Let's get Auntie El in on it and make it special."

"How's that going? With Zoey staying with Auntie El, I mean."

"I think pretty well, from what Auntie El's saying. She says she's been helpful around the house. But she's heard her crying some in the night."

"Then a nice Christmas ought to be good for her." Sean took my hand again. "But, Maggie?"

"Yeah?"

"Let her do the work. You need a break too."

I took a slurp of my milkshake, thinking *from his lips to God's ears*. A day off for Christmas, I would take that.

20

Stepping into the farmhouse was like an assault: sounds, smells, and heat like a wave from the kitchen. It hit me so hard I fell back a step, bonking into Ian, who bonked into Sean.

"Ow, that's my foot!"

"Mm, I smell pie."

They pushed on in past me, kicking snow off their boots, and that was when the second wave struck: not heat, not cooking smells, but an onslaught of puppies. They charged out of the sitting room in a blur of black and tan, and arrowed straight for me, ignoring the men.

"No! Shoo! Get off!"

The puppies jumped up on me, big-pawed and goofy. They hung out their tongues and nosed at my crotch. I didn't have enough hands to fend them all off, so I settled for petting whichever heads I could reach.

"Auntie El? Help? Come get your hellhounds."

Auntie El only laughed from the depths of the kitchen, but Zoey came out, bringing the scent of pie with her. She pulled two of the pups off and the rest flocked right to her, fighting each other to climb in her lap. Ian crouched down with her, and they climbed on him too, cramming their noses into his ears.

"They like you," said Zoey.

"What kind are they?"

"Farm dogs," yelled Patrick from the TV room. I could hear him and Carl watching a game, and a bunch of kids screaming out back. Shrugging my coat off, I peered down the hall.

"Is Dad here yet?"

"Yeah, with the kids, helping them build a snow fort."

I couldn't help it. I pulled a lemon-suck face. Where was that Dad when I was a kid? At work was where, till Mom passed away. Then in a bottle. Passed out on the couch. Still, begrudging the kiddos their fun would be petty. Denying them that wouldn't bring back my childhood.

"How about Liam? He here somewhere?"

"At his in-laws," called Carl. "Their turn this year."

I wondered if it truly was their turn, or if he'd begged off because Zoey would be here. He'd hit the roof when he found out she'd be staying here, and he'd been keeping his distance ever since.

"I'm going to go see if Auntie El needs help."

No one responded or seemed to hear. Sean had drifted toward the TV. Zoey and Ian were tickling the dogs. Zoey was laughing as they pawed at her legs, lifting and kissing them. Ruffling their ears. Maybe this was the girl Ian had fallen for, not the scared, shut-down kid from the courtroom, but this silly, sweet kid who loved a good pup.

"I taught them a trick," she said. "Check it out." She pulled a squeaky toy out of her pocket, held it over her head, and yelled out, "Jump." All the dogs jumped for it and bowled her over. She shrieked breathless laughter from under the pile.

"That's not a trick," Ian said, groaning. "You hold up a toy for them, they're going to jump."

I left the kids to the dogs and made my way to the kitchen. Auntie El was bent over basting the turkey, and when she stood, her face was bright red. She fanned herself.

"Oh, that oven! Would you check on the pies?"

I hadn't baked a pie in who-knows-how-many years, but I crouched down to peer into the second oven. The pies were browning up nicely, bubbling sweet juice.

"No, you have to get in there, not just look through the window."

I found a pair of oven gloves and opened the oven. A wave of infernal heat hit me in the face. Wincing, I leaned into it, and yeah. Those were pies. Just about done, from the looks of their crusts.

"Set them out on the counter," Auntie El said.

I set them to cool, all in a row, leaning over to smell each one in turn: apple-cinnamon, cherry, and butter pecan.

"No pumpkin?"

"I would have, but those bloomin' dogs…" She chuckled, not really mad, and stirred her gravy. "I had the pumpkin cracked open, all ready to scoop, and those mutts all got into it and chewed it to bits. You don't want one of them, do you?"

"Hell, no. No way."

"Wait, we can have one?" Ian had snuck up and was leaning in the doorway, Zoey behind him with a dog at each side. I opened my mouth to say no, we could not, but hadn't I been thinking a dog might be good for him? Not one of *these* ones, all scruffy and loud, but—

"They're good boys and girls," said Auntie El, not helping. "Their dad's our Scratchy, dug under the fence. Their mama's this gorgeous retriever-mastiff mix. Good dogs for kids, and guard dogs as well."

"I want this one," said Ian, scratching the biggest one. "You're my guy, aren't you? Who's a good boy?"

I huffed. "Oh, great. Now, he's falling in love."

The back door slammed, and the dogs all ran off again. Next thing I heard was Dad fending them off.

"I'll get them," said Zoey.

"Don't." I smirked, spiteful. "Grandpa *loves* dogs."

"Right, all you all get out of my kitchen." Auntie El flapped her apron, shooing us out. Zoey and Ian headed out to the hall. I stole someone's jacket and slipped out back, not in the mood yet to deal with Dad. The kids had made teams for a snowball fight, Pat's kids on one side with his sister Bridget's, and on the other side, the neighbor kids. One of them spotted me and yelled out *invader*, and next thing I knew, the snowballs came flying. I batted them off me and they broke up, scattering snow all down my collar.

"You made her mad!"

"Get to the castle!"

The kids all scurried back into their snow fort. I packed a ball anyway and flung it over their ramparts. They giggled and shrieked as it exploded, taking a good chunk of battlement with it.

I stayed out a while to help beef up the snow fort, then when my fingers went numb, I went in. Sean pushed a hot toddy into my hands, and I looked around for Ian and Zoey. They'd curled up on the couch to watch *A Charlie Brown Christmas*, under a pile of half-snoozing dogs.

"Cute," I said, turning to Sean…or at least, to where Sean had been. At some point, he'd peeled off and Dad had taken his place. Dad frowned at the backs of the kids' scruffy heads.

"If he wants my advice, he should stay single."

I stiffened, offended, though I wasn't sure why. I'd thought the same thing: that Ian should focus on school and not on a relationship with a girl who might be trouble. But I was his parent. Dad was just Grandpa, and he barely knew Ian, through his own fault. He had no place coming in and passing judgment.

"He's setting himself up for a whole lot of heartbreak. And I'm not even talking about the trial. You'll get her acquitted, and then what's next? Ian's a smart kid. He's going to college. She'll be stuck here, going nowhere."

My hackles rose. "Aren't *you* moving here?"

"Yeah, but that's different. My family's here. She's a dead-end girl, no matter what."

Ian shifted, and I thought he'd heard. But he only leaned over and put his arm around Zoey. She leaned on his shoulder with a quiet sigh. Dad made a *tch* sound, and I wanted to smack him. Did I love Zoey for Ian? No, I did not. But she cared for him—I'd seen that from her texts. She helped with his math homework. Kept him on track. She'd even defended me to him after her first case, when Ian was pissed I hadn't taken him to see her.

"Keep your eyes on your own fries," I said, keeping my tone even.

"Why? I'm just saying—"

I snapped. "Well, don't. Your parenting credentials—"

"Whoa, whoa, whoa, whoa." Sean stepped between us. Pressed a kiss to my temple. "It's Christmas Eve. Goodwill to all men."

"Goodwill to *some* men." I glared daggers at Dad. "Other men think they can sashay back into town like they only just left, but it's been half my life, Dad. It's been—"

"Dinner's served!" Auntie El barged in, loud and in charge. She grabbed me and dragged me with her to the kitchen, where dinner *wasn't* served, but was about to be. Auntie El shoved me toward the turkey. "Take that out. You're carving. Carl's hands are all…" She made claws with her hands, meaning arthritis.

"You sure you want me with a knife in my hand right now?"

"You gonna screw up this fine Christmas dinner?" Auntie El was still smiling, but her voice was pure steel. "I didn't get up at zero stupid thirty and slave the whole day over a hot oven for you to spend dinner trading barbs with your dad. I get it, he hurt you, but now's not the time to get into it. You got the rest of the year to chew on your beef, but this is our one night to feast on this turkey."

She made a good point, I had to admit. I carried the turkey out and set it up center stage, and Ian and Zoey brought out the sides. We all took our places and Carl said grace. By the time we all called out *amen*, my good mood was returning. Dinner smelled great, and the family was here, the little ones giggling at the kids' table.

"Right, Mags, I'm starving." Dad held out his plate. I took it from him and set it aside, and served Carl first, then Auntie El. I piled Ian's plate and Sean's, and then I filled Zoey's, and Patrick's and Bridget's —every plate I could find. Then I carved white meat for the kids' table. Only then did I slice off some thigh meat for Dad, and I smirked as I passed his plate down the table. But by that time, he was talking football with Sean, and Patrick was piling his plate high with Brussels sprouts. Ian and Zoey were feeding the dogs, sneaking them morsels under the table. My mean little gesture had gone unnoticed, and maybe that was how it should be. If Patrick, a cop, could eat dinner with an accused murderer and not make a big deal of it, I could be civil with Dad. At least for tonight.

I sat and filled my own plate and dug in at last, and moaned at the richness of Auntie El's gravy. Sean nudged me and winked.

"Pretty good, right?"

"Delicious."

"No, I mean…" He gestured around us. "We'll be empty-nesters soon. We've got to savor these times while we can."

I frowned at that term, empty-nesters. It made us sound old, but I guessed we were getting there.

"Ian asked me to take one of those dogs home." Sean leaned in closer so our shoulders bumped. "I thought maybe we'd let him. What do you say?"

"You know it'll end up being our dog when he goes off to college."

"I wouldn't mind that." Sean reached under the table, and I realized he, too, was feeding the pups.

"We'll have to roll it out of here if you keep doing that."

"So, that's a yes?"

I smiled down the table at Ian and Zoey, deep in some absorbing teenage discussion. A dog would give Ian something to take care of. Something to focus on if Zoey's trial got rough. If the worst happened, and she was convicted… Well, at least a dog would be some comfort to him.

"Yeah. That's a yes. Why not, right?"

"Ian! Hey, Ian!" Sean waved down the table. "We're getting a dog."

Ian gave out a cheer, and so did Zoey. So did the little kids, though I doubted they'd heard us. Ian leaned down to pet his new buddy.

"You hear that, big boy? You're coming home."

The puppy yipped and wagged its tail. Dad held his plate out, wanting more carrots. Patrick passed him some, and I sipped my wine.

It was starting to feel a whole lot like Christmas. At least until Monday came rolling around, and with it more motions and more witness interviews, more Internet rabbit holes chasing down leads.

21

I walked into the office to find my desk occupied, Ian and Zoey with their heads together. They had their books spread out, tackling what looked like math homework, and Zoey was explaining her answers to Ian. Judge Yost had ordered her to stay home from school pending the trial's outcome, and she was doing remote learning so she wouldn't fall behind. Seeing her now with Ian, my first thought was, *here? Why not the library?* But I guessed I could answer that: Zoey was gun-shy. Just a few days earlier, Auntie El had taken her out for a burger, and the diner's manager had asked them to leave. On their way out, some kid had yelled, "Killer!" and Zoey had wilted like a flower in a storm.

"Hey, kids," I said. "How's the homework?"

Zoey sang out "Good," but Ian just groaned. I was about to go over and check on his work when my phone buzzed. Saved by the bell.

"Alia, hello. Give me one second." I stepped into the hallway. If she was calling, it was probably trial business, and I didn't need Zoey overhearing our call. "What have you got for me?"

"Karen Harper," she said. The dermatologist the Conrads had sued for malpractice. "I finally got in touch with her. She's been on vacation. But she's happy to talk to me, so I'm heading out now."

I grunted my approval, but I wasn't too hopeful that the woman would have anything useful to share. The Harper suit had settled a long time ago. She made for a highly unlikely suspect, and any info she had about the family would be very dated by this point.

"I'll give you a call when I'm on my way back." Alia hung up, and I headed back in. Auntie El pointed at my phone.

"Anything good?"

"No, just Alia. She's found Karen Harper."

Zoey made a strangled sound. She dropped her pencil. Ian bent to get it and I glimpsed her face, in the instant before she pressed both hands to it.

I started toward her. "Zoey? You all right?"

She sucked air through her fingers. Let her hands drop. "I should get back. Auntie El? Can we go?"

Aunt Louise was bent over the file cabinet and hadn't noticed Zoey's change in mood. "Didn't you kids want to finish your homework? There's pie in the fridge if you're getting hungry."

"No! I'm not, uh—" Zoey stood up. "I left the dog door locked, and the puppies inside. They'll pee all over. I need to get back." Her voice cracked, thin with panic, and she hugged herself. "Please, Auntie El? Please take me back?"

Ian grabbed Zoey's books and shoved them back in her book bag. "I'll take you," he said. "We can borrow Mom's car."

Zoey half-ran out, Ian hot on her tail. Auntie El started after them.

"I'll see what that's about."

"And would you give them a ride? The roads are still icy. I don't like Ian driving with ice on the roads."

Auntie El flashed me a quick mock-salute, then she hustled off, calling for Zoey. I drifted over to where she'd been sitting and found Ian's workbook still open on my desk. They'd been doing calculus, and Zoey's neat writing sat alongside Ian's, where she'd written out problems for him to solve.

I figured I'd better stop home myself, and make sure our pup hadn't peed on the floor.

———

Our pup—Zombie, so named by Ian because he bit heads, or at least licked them profusely—*had* peed. He watched me clean up, hunched and ashamed, then jumped all over me when I broke out the dog treats.

"Good boy, Zombie. Ugh, what a name. He couldn't have called you anything else?"

Zombie snuffled my empty palm, and then he licked it, hoovering up the last crumbs of his bacon treat. I took him out in the back yard for a quick number two, then cleaned up after him and brought him back in. He raced for the TV, wanting to watch with me, but it was time I got back to the office.

"Later, bud. Now, 'bud,' *there's* a name. Who's my good buddy? No, sit. No, stay."

I managed to slip out without Zombie escaping and was heading for my car when Auntie El called.

"How's Zoey?"

"Upset, but she's ready to talk to you. And, Maggie? Come quickly. You need to hear this."

I couldn't speed with the roads as slick as they were, but I wasted no time getting out to the farm. Auntie El's tone had been like nothing I'd heard from her, vibrating with what sounded like barely contained rage. I tried to remember when I'd last seen her angry. Not peeved, not offended, but properly *mad*. What could Zoey have said to her to get her stirred up like that? And would it help us, or make things worse?

I pulled up to the farmhouse and half ran up the steps. Auntie El stepped out on the porch to meet me. She pulled the door shut behind her so Zoey wouldn't hear.

"You need to be gentle. Don't push her, okay?"

"I will, but what happened? Is she all right?"

Auntie El's face did some angry gymnastics. She shook her head side to side and looked up at the sky. "Those people," she spat. "You can't call them parents. They don't deserve that name, or anything close."

"You mean the Conrads?"

"Just talk to her." She went and sat in the creaky porch swing, and toed it back and forth in quick, jerky movements. I went in and found Zoey installed on the couch, the dogs all around her and one in her lap. She was staring, red-eyed, at the powered-down TV.

"Sorry," she said. "I didn't mean to run out like that."

"No, it's okay." I sat down across from her. One of the pups came to sniff at my shoe, then went right back to Zoey and snuggled into her side. She petted the dog and took a few long, deep breaths, then she looked away from me and started to speak.

"Dr. Karen… My parents… What they did wasn't right. She was so nice, and they just, they…"

I put my hand on her arm. "Take your time."

Zoey scratched the pup's scruff, seeking comfort. "I got this rash when I was six, this gross red rash all over my back. My pediatrician thought it was allergies, but it kept coming back, so we went to Dr. Karen." She shuddered, and one of the dogs licked her hand. "She gave me this cream, and at first it was working, but one night right after my mom put it on, it felt as if it was…burning. Like, the worst pain. I was screaming, and my skin started peeling away."

My own skin crawled. "You mean like a sunburn?"

"No, like a *burn* burn." She turned her back on me and pulled up her shirt, and the skin there was puckered with old, twisted scars, all the way from her waistband to the line of her bra strap.

"The cream Dr. Harper prescribed did that?"

Zoey tugged her shirt down. She let out a bitter laugh. "No. It didn't. It was something my mom had. Some kind of chemical. I don't know what."

I stared at Zoey, unsure what to think. Her story sounded paranoid, too evil to be true. Her *mother* had done this? On purpose?

"What makes you think—"

"Because I heard them talking." Zoey shuddered, refocusing on the dogs, avoiding eye contact. "I *heard* them," she muttered. "They didn't think I was home. They were talking about maybe doing it again—with Dad's meds this time. With his GI doc. But Mom was like, no, because they almost got caught last time. They almost got caught when they sued Dr. Karen."

I couldn't believe what I was hearing. "You're saying your parents gave you those burns so they could sue?"

"*Yes*, they did, and I can prove it. Or, I can't, but I'll show you, I..." She pulled out her phone and scrolled through her e-mails. "After I heard them, I went to the Clerk's Office, and I got the trial transcript. My parents claimed I had an allergic reaction to the cream, and that it was Dr. K.'s fault for not checking my allergy list before writing the prescription, but Dr. K. had an expert come on to defend her, and the expert said no allergic reaction could have done that and that they were chemical burns. Only, my parents' expert was more convincing, I guess, so Dr. K. lost. But I heard them. They *lied*. They fucked up her life, for money."

I took Zoey's phone and forwarded the email she'd pulled up to myself. If her parents had done this, that made them monsters. They'd destroyed Dr. Harper's life, and worse than that, they'd scarred Zoey for life. The pain she must have gone through for, how much had it been?

"They were doing it again," she said. "They were going to sue Youth Rise, and when that didn't work, that new place in Utah. They wanted me to get hurt so they could sue. That's why I was living in the RV park."

Through my horror, it hit me, Zoey had left a paper trail. She'd requested court transcripts. If Oliver learned that, he might connect two and two. A story like this would speak strongly to motive—so strongly a jury might never see past it.

I swallowed hard. "Who knows about this?"

"Just you so far, and Auntie El."

"Not Ian?"

"No. Or, not the whole story. I told him about the rash, but not what my parents did. Dr. Karen deserved to know, and I *was* going to tell her, but I was scared if I did, she'd get my parents arrested. And I know they deserved it, but—I *was* going to tell."

"Don't tell anyone now. Not while your trial's happening."

Zoey gathered the puppies close to her chest and buried her face in their shaggy fur. "I didn't do it," she said. "I know how it sounds. They messed up my back, and I was scared of them sending me to one of those messed-up camps, so I lashed out. But I'm not like them. I— I'm *not*. Whenever I don't know the right thing to do, I think what would they do, then I do the opposite. *They* always hurt people. I never would."

I believed her when she said she didn't want to be like them. And I wanted to believe she wasn't the killer. But I doubted a jury would, if they heard that story.

22

Zoey's trial began on a cold day in February, with a dusting of snow over Kerry's main street. Two press vans sat parked across from the courthouse, a local crew and one from Columbus, but I ignored them as I headed inside. I had nothing to say to them, and no time to waste.

Jury selection had gone pretty well, with no more than the usual push and pull. Oliver went for the linear thinkers—accountants, engineers, A + B = C types. I wanted jurors with imagination, ones who'd take a small doubt and blow it up in their heads. I was especially looking for individualists, likely to distrust authority and the police. A lot of my case would hinge on the investigation, and whether the police had cast their net wide enough. For law-and-order types, that would be a hard sell.

One thing that bugged me was Oliver's questioning: he polled the jury on child abuse. Had they been victims? Did they know anyone who had? Questions like that meant he knew something, but how much did he know? Had he found the court documents?

I saved most of my challenges for anyone who seemed too knowledgeable, like they'd been actively following the case. Of course, being locals, they all knew who Zoey was, but I didn't want jurors who'd been using her as entertainment, and doubtless prejudging her in the process.

I touched Zoey's arm as the courtroom filled up. "Remember what we talked about."

Zoey had been picking at the hem of her cuff, and now she stopped. "I know. No picking."

"Try to relax."

"I'm trying. But I'm scared."

I gave her arm a squeeze. "It's okay if they see that. It shows them you're human. But you can't be *too* human, if you see what I mean."

Zoey half-laughed at that, an exhaled *ha*. I hoped she'd remember everything we'd gone over—no outbursts, no picking, no matter what. She'd already be on thin ice with this jury. She needed to show them the girl I'd seen at Christmas, and in quiet moments at Auntie El's—the girl who helped Ian with his math homework.

Judge Yost made his entrance and we all rose. He surveyed the courtroom and nodded.

"Be seated."

We sat.

"Are we ready to proceed?"

"Yes, Your Honor," said Oliver.

"Then, you may begin, Mr. Altman."

Oliver stood, raring to go. I could see it in his posture and the set of his shoulders: he was determined, and he'd come to win. "Your

Honor, ladies and gentlemen of the jury, we're here today because Paul and Lorraine Conrad can't be. They can't tell us what happened the night they were killed, but the State will present evidence to prove that the person who killed them was their daughter. It's your job as the jury to see they get justice. You'll hear all the evidence against Zoey Conrad, then return a verdict, which I'm going to demonstrate can only be 'guilty.'"

He then described the facts of the crime—how the bodies were found, how Paul and Lorraine had died. He'd refined his delivery since the probable cause hearing, giving more weight to the saddest details. Leaving pauses to let the full horror sink in. The jury sat riveted as he plucked at their heartstrings, making sure to describe the Conrads not just by their names, but as *mother* and *father*. Loaded words.

Then he turned his focus to Zoey herself. "I will be calling Dr. Granger, the defendant's therapist. Her testimony will show that Zoey is troubled, and that she harbored deep resentment toward her parents. She's an angry young lady with a violent past, and that night, she—"

I was up on my feet quick as greased lightning. "Objection, Your Honor! We dealt with this pretrial, and there is nothing in Dr. Granger's testimony to support the idea my client is violent."

"Sustained," said Judge Yost, but it wasn't a victory. Oliver had done what he'd set out to do: with the words "violent past," he'd evoked the Rooney case. It would now be fresh in the minds of the jury, not just the Conrads' deaths, but Rooney's as well. Yost went on anyway, instructing the jury. "The jury is instructed to disregard the prosecutor's statement about Ms. Conrad's past and not draw any inferences from it." Yost turned to Oliver. "Counsel, I'll warn you once. Let's not have it happen again. Are we clear?" he admonished.

"Yes, Your Honor."

I sat back down, fuming. Oliver fixed the jury with a grave expression.

"Aggravated murder in the state of Ohio is defined as purposely causing the death of another, under one of a number of aggravating circumstances. The relevant one here is premeditation: these murders were committed with prior calculation and design."

He outlined his evidence, and what each witness would show, keeping his language florid throughout. Every time he said *mother*, one juror—a middle-aged mother of three—flinched. When he described the murders as *grisly* or *brutal*, two of the older ones tightened their lips. One younger man kept looking at Zoey. I recalled that he was father to a three-month-old. I could guess what he was thinking: where had her parents gone wrong, raising Zoey? How could he avoid the same mistakes?

Oliver smiled at the jury as he wrapped up, as though to say *you've got this. I trust you.* "At the end of these proceedings, once you've heard all the evidence, I'm going to ask you to return a verdict of guilty. You'll see, beyond any reasonable doubt, that these callous, premeditated crimes were committed by none other than the defendant." He swept his gaze Zoey's way on the word *defendant*, and every head on the jury turned to look. She wilted, but managed to keep her hands still.

I squeezed her shoulder so the jury could see—it was good for them to see me being kind to her. Treating her as a person deserving of kindness. I leaned in and whispered, "You're doing great." Then I stood, my smile fading as I approached the jury. They needed to see Zoey as human, sympathetic. They needed to see me as a fellow parent, chilled by the deaths of a mother and father but convinced, all the same, of Zoey's innocence. Sickened at the idea she might pay the price for someone else's crime.

"Ladies and gentlemen of the jury, my colleague was right. We are here today in pursuit of justice. And in this courtroom, justice means only one thing: weighing the evidence and answering one question. Has the State established, beyond a reasonable doubt, that my client is guilty?

"The State's evidence is thin, and it's circumstantial. You've heard their witness list—it's quite a mouthful—but when you look closer, it's a lot of hot air." That got me a chuckle or two from the jury, but I kept my face stony, no hint of a smile. This wasn't a joke to me, and they needed to know that. "The evidence will show my client went home that night, entering the Conrad house around nine thirty. But Paul Conrad was shot thirty-five minutes later, and Lorraine Conrad two minutes after him. You'll hear neighbors testify they ran to their windows, but not a single one will testify they saw my client.

"Forensic evidence will show my client was there at some point, proven by her hair and her fingerprints, fibers from her clothing. But this was her *home*. The undisputed evidence will show she'd lived there all her life. But what you won't hear, and what you won't see, is *any* evidence she was home at the time in question. The State *cannot* place her there at the time of the murders.

"And timing isn't the only issue they'll ask you to ignore. You're going to hear evidence Paul Conrad was injured. That he was involved in a hand-to-hand altercation. My client was examined upon her arrest, and she didn't have one single bruise on her person. Not one cut or scrape. Not even a broken nail. The evidence will show she—"

I broke off as I spotted movement, someone behind me shuffling into the gallery. When I glanced up, I saw Dad had snuck in, and he winked at me when he saw me looking.

"Ms. Gallagher?" Judge Yost raised his brows at me. I faked a cough, trying to regroup.

"Sorry, Your Honor. Frog in my throat." I coughed again, swallowed, and turned back to the jury, mentally kicking myself for getting distracted. Every fresh law school grad knew better than that.

"The State will present evidence of my client entering the house, but what they can't tell you is when she left. She could have walked out at any time prior to the murders, and her lack of injuries suggests she did." I'd said that already. I changed gear quickly, working to regain my rhythm.

"The State's case will focus heavily on motive. But a lot of people had motive to commit these murders, as the evidence will show. The Conrads ran a cottage industry based on lawsuits. Nearly half of their income was from litigation. They left a swath of destruction in their wake. Businesses shuttered. Multiple bankruptcies. At least one divorce. These defendants had motives as strong as my client's, perhaps even stronger."

I noticed one of the jurors was nodding, one of the older men in the back row. Oliver had challenged anyone who'd personally been hit with a lawsuit, or worked at a business that had been hit, but maybe this man had known someone, or heard something.

"What happened that night was a tragedy—but was it one caused by my client? The State cannot place her at the scene of the crime, nor can they tie her to a physical altercation. Their case hangs on motive and motive alone, and in a town full of motives, that spells reasonable doubt."

I stepped down feeling good about my opening statement, in spite of Dad throwing me off. The jury had been with me, I thought, by the end. Though, that might not last when they saw the crime scene photos.

"Let's recess for lunch," said Judge Yost. "We'll be back at twelve thirty."

I was gathering my briefcase when I noticed Liam. He headed straight past me toward the counsel table, and before I could call to him, he pulled Oliver aside. I watched, throat gone tight, as the two of them spoke, and Oliver's brows shot up. He started after Judge Yost, who was headed for his chambers, then turned back toward Liam.

"You're sure?"

Liam nodded. "Positive."

Oliver took off in pursuit of Judge Yost, who was already halfway out the door. "Your Honor, a moment!"

I heard Judge Yost exhale. "What is it, counsel?"

"I'm requesting a conference in your chambers, to discuss new evidence that's just come to light."

My stomach did a swan dive. I felt suddenly sick. New evidence, *what* evidence? What fresh hell was this? I supposed there was *some* chance it might be exculpatory, but that didn't seem likely, given Oliver's avid expression. Judge Yost heaved another long-suffering sigh.

"All right, let's talk. Counsel, in chambers."

Zoey blinked up at me. "What's going on?"

I shook my head. "I don't know."

"Is it bad? Wait—Ms. Gallagher! Is it bad?"

But I had no answers, nothing to tell her. I turned, guts churning, toward Judge Yost's chambers.

23

Judge Yost frowned as Oliver passed him a USB stick. "This isn't that reconstruction again, is it?"

"No, Your Honor." Oliver, to my eye, was practically vibrating, his excitement palpable. I wanted to pierce a hole in his smugness, but I had no idea yet what I'd be picking holes in. I contented myself with a subtle-ish huff.

Judge Yost plugged the stick in and pulled up a video.

"This is from the Tulleys' Ring cam," said Oliver. "They live on Spruce Street across from the Conrads, and two houses down, on the bend in the road. Their home faces the Conrads' on a forty-five degree angle, allowing a view of the Conrads' side door."

Judge Yost took his glasses off, polished them on his robe, then put them back on. "Why is this just coming in now?"

"Because the Tulleys have been traveling in Europe, and they got home a few days ago. They arrived to discover the police had been trying to contact them and immediately turned over their Ring cam archive."

Oliver leaned over and pressed play on the video. I didn't want to see what came next, because I knew in my guts it was about to destroy me. To blast a hole through my opening statement, and through my entire defense.

"This is nine twenty-eight." Oliver scrolled forward. Zoey came into the frame and let herself in through the Conrads' front door. She looked back down the street just before she went in, maybe seeing if Ian was watching her go.

"And now, we fast-forward to just after ten." He scrolled forward again. Nothing happened at first, and Judge Yost leaned forward.

"What am I looking at?"

"Wait just a second."

We waited, the judge frowning down at the screen, Oliver leaning over him, almost bouncing. I tasted acid in the back of my throat.

Bang came the first shot, and the windows flashed white. Then a period of silence, maybe a minute. More shots rang out, and more bright white flashes. Then Oliver skipped forward five minutes more. The side door burst open, and Zoey flew out, sprinting for the woods, a duffel bag swinging from her flailing arm.

"This establishes her presence inside the house at the time of the murders."

I barely heard Oliver through the ringing in my ears. It was worse than he'd said, worse than he'd grasped so far—but he would see it. And the jury would too, and it would destroy us.

Because Zoey hadn't just been in the house. She'd left through the side door, through the laundry room, which meant she'd have had to step over her mother's still-warm corpse. She could have run out through any door, but she'd picked that one—the one with no light outside from the neighbors' houses. The one shielded, or so she'd thought, from view of the street. The level of coldness implied by that choice, the sheer calculation... I thought I might throw up.

"This is a discovery violation," I croaked. "This evidence should be excluded. The defense has had no opportunity to examine the evidence or—"

Judge Yost closed his laptop. "Why *is* this footage so late coming in?"

"As I said, the Tulleys were traveling. And—just a minute..." He consulted his phone. "I have a police report, they *did* try to contact them, but they were on some kind of silent retreat. The camera's access logs show when the footage was accessed, and that it hadn't been viewed until now. The timing's unfortunate, but this is essential evidence."

"I agree," said Judge Yost. "This evidence is coming in very late, but under the circumstances, I'm going to allow it."

"Then I need a continuance." I drew myself up. "To evaluate the authenticity of this footage."

"Two days," said Judge Yost. "And that'll give you the weekend."

I nodded numbly, still reeling. If this was as it looked, we were in trouble. And I didn't see how it could be otherwise. It was all there in stark black and white, complete with time stamps. Zoey's face clear as day. I'd argued for form's sake that it might not be authentic, but even I didn't believe the Tulleys had faked or doctored this.

Judge Yost shooed us out so he could eat his lunch, and I hurried out through the deserted courtroom. Ian was waiting with Dad near the door, and they both hurried to meet me when they saw me coming.

"What's going on?" Ian grabbed for my arm. "Mom? What was—"

"Not here."

"I thought you were great," said Dad, as I tried to skirt past him. "Your opening statement, is that what that's called? I believed you a lot more than that other guy. He's kind of smug, isn't he? Kind of—"

"Yeah, thanks." I barged past him and straight out the door, tossing a half-assed apology over my shoulder. "I need to get to my office. Talk later, okay?"

Dad sloped off somewhere before I could smooth over my brushoff, but Ian followed me back to the office. Zoey was already there, helping Auntie El with some filing. Ian went straight to her, and I let them hug. Then I cleared my throat.

"Ian, we'll need the room."

He spun around, outraged, then saw my expression. "Is this a privilege thing?"

"Yeah. It is."

I waited till Ian left, then gestured Zoey to my office. Auntie El and Alia came in with her.

"So, the new evidence was this video." I plugged in the stick and played it back for them, then rounded on Zoey. "You want to explain?"

She cringed, going white. Shook her head side to side.

"This is serious, Zoey. I need to know why you lied."

Zoey bit her lip hard. Auntie El moved to comfort her, hugging her close.

"You're okay," she said.

"I can't."

"Yes, you can."

Zoey covered her face. She was shaking all over. Auntie El helped her sit in my new Aeron chair.

"It was mostly true, what I told you before." Her voice hitched and she sniffled and wiped at her eyes. "I went home, I went in, and my parents were home. They were packing my room up to send me to Utah. We had this huge fight, and I said—I said— The last thing I said to them was…" She broke off, crying too hard to speak. Her breath came in a long whine through her tight throat. Alia knelt next to her and took her hand.

"Shh. It's okay."

She let out a wail, then. "It's not. No, it's not. The last thing I said to them was, I fu— I fu— 'I fucking hate you.' And sometimes I did, but not all the time. They were still Mom and Dad."

"I get it," I said, thinking of my own dad. I'd hated him plenty when I was her age, when he'd check out and leave me to fend for myself. When he'd get drunk and yell at me. When he wasn't himself. "Listen," I said, "my dad was a drinker. Life wasn't good with him. It was awful sometimes. I don't have scars that you can see, but he hurt me in other ways, and I hated him for it. But I wouldn't have wanted that to be the last thing I said to him."

Zoey looked up at me, red-eyed and snotty. "I can't take it back."

"I'm sorry. I know."

Auntie El handed her a wad of Kleenex. Zoey blew her nose and she dabbed at her eyes. She sniffed and composed herself, then tried again.

"Mom got upset and she went to the bathroom. That's when I heard— when Dad heard downstairs… He told me to wait, and to stay in my room."

"What did he hear?" I asked.

"The back door," said Zoey. "Someone inside."

"You're saying there was somebody else in the house? Someone broke in?"

"Not *broke* in, exactly. The door was unlocked, so I guess more like walked in?" Zoey had stopped crying, but her trembling was worse. Her teeth were chattering as if she were cold. Alia squeezed her hand and she grabbed it in both of hers, clinging to it as she went on.

"I wasn't that scared at first. I could hear them talking. They sounded okay, not yelling or anything."

"Who was it? Could you tell?"

Zoey shook her head. She closed her eyes tightly. "I didn't hear much. They were talking at first, just normal voices, then Mom went downstairs, and they started to yell. This guy was like, 'asshole, you ruined my life,' then Mom started screaming at him to get out, and next thing I knew, they were running upstairs. They were running, and—"

"Who was?" I needed to get this straight.

"All of them. This guy ran up first. I only caught a glimpse of him— he was in, like, a hoodie? He didn't see me, just ran past my room. Then they were fighting."

"Your dad and the stranger?"

"Yeah. They were fighting, and my mom was yelling, and— I was afraid to look. I just…I just stood there, in my room. But I could hear scuffling, and he hit my dad, I guess, because he yelled, but in pain? Then, the next thing was like…" She went quiet.

I nudged her, but gently. "What happened next?"

"Dad was yelling at Mom to call the police. Hoodie guy must've gone in the study. He came out, and Dad was like, 'no, no, no,' like he was trying to talk him off the ledge. I saw them go by again, Dad with his hands up. This guy had his gun. Dad made a break for downstairs, and then—then—" Fresh tears streaked down her cheeks. She wiped them away with the back of her arm. "I hid under my bed. Mom yelled out 'Paul.' It was the worst thing I've ever heard, the sound of her voice. Like she knew he was dead, and then *she* ran downstairs. I don't remember, um…"

"Take your time."

Zoey bent over, head in her hands. Her chest hitched, and Auntie El rubbed her back gently.

"It felt like forever," she said in a whisper. "Like it took a really long time. Mom was screaming for Dad, then just, like, screaming. This guy shouted 'stop' and that's when he shot her, and everything went quiet. I just waited like…I guess a few minutes? But it felt like hours with this killer downstairs. Finally, I heard him run out." She was shaking so hard now, I thought she'd come apart. Alia got my coat and draped it over her shoulders.

Zoey was shaken. That much, I could see. Tears could be faked, but the pallor, the trembling—I'd never seen anyone fabricate that. The mom in me wanted to rock her and comfort her, as I'd done for Ian when he was little. But I was her lawyer first, and I still had a job to do.

"What did you do next? After you heard him run out?"

"I, um…" Zoey shivered. Pulled my coat close. "I grabbed my bag. The one they had packed for me. I ran downstairs, toward the laundry room. I saw her, my mom. I tried to—to help her. But when I looked, the back of her head was … It was all blood. And I ran away."

I wanted to stop there and let her recover, but I still had questions I needed to ask. "How about the post you made to your Instagram? The 'home bored' post. Why'd you do that?"

Zoey wiped at her eyes again and shook her head slowly. "I don't really know," she said. "I ran into the woods. I pulled out my phone, and I guess I was thinking… I was going to text Ian, or call the police. But when I opened my phone, that picture was open, and that's when it hit me, what if they thought *I* did it? So I put it up, like an alibi."

It made sense, for teenager logic—especially a teenager in a panic. But that didn't mean the jury would buy it. I needed to get to the bottom of this. "I can see, in the moment, you weren't thinking clearly. But how about later? Why not tell the police you saw the attacker? Why not give a description?"

"Because…" Zoey wiped at her nose again. "I'd already lied. My alibi post. I thought if I told them, they wouldn't believe me. But *he'd* know I told, and he might— Might come back."

"The man in the hoodie? You thought he'd come back?"

She nodded slowly. "If he finds out I told, I'm a witness, right? What if he comes back to shut me up?"

I could see her fear rising, her eyes going glassy. I had a whole lot of things I wanted to say to her. For starters, did she realize how dumb it had been to lie? She'd trashed any credibility she might have had right out of the gate. Not to mention letting the real killer off the hook. And she'd dragged Ian into it, right from the start.

But I reminded myself that she was a kid. They were both still just kids. Expecting smart choices in the face of a crisis—

"I'm sorry," said Zoey, her voice gone small. "I'm so sorry I lied to you. And to Ian."

I sat down and rolled my chair close to Zoey's. "Did you see anything else, besides the hoodie? Hair color? Size? Did you see his face at all? Or was there anything distinctive about his voice that you noticed?"

Zoey balled herself up in my office chair. "He and Dad were yelling over each other, and Mom was crying... I couldn't hear his voice that well. And I just caught a flash of him as he ran by. He had his hood up. I couldn't see much."

"Was he as tall as your father?"

She shook her head. "No. He was more around your height and pretty skinny."

"And how about his hoodie? What was that like?"

"Black," she said, and rubbed at her eyes. "Or, the front was black, but the back had a logo. A lightning bolt, like a superhero."

"Did you see—"

"I think that's enough for now." Auntie El had been quiet, but now she stepped forward. "It's been a rough day. I'd best take her home."

I wanted to argue, to keep pushing Zoey, but when I took a good look at her, I knew Auntie El was right. Zoey was sweating and pale as milk, shivers running through her. She was clearly in shock. I still wasn't certain I believed her story, but her trauma was definitely real. Pushing her now would only be cruel.

"All right," I said. "We'll pick this up later."

Auntie El helped her up and they headed out. Zoey stopped at the door and turned to face me.

"I didn't kill them," she said quietly. "I hated my parents, but I loved them too."

I didn't know what to say, so I only nodded. The two of them left, and I heard Auntie El's truck start. Alia poured me an extra-large coffee.

"Drink up," she said.

I took a gulp.

"What do you think? What's your play here?"

I had no idea, so I gulped more coffee. Maybe now was the time to try for a plea deal, before Oliver sewed us up even tighter. But Zoey would resist that. Ian would, too. One thing was certain: I had a long night ahead.

24

I met Liam on his lunch break, at the diner.

"I'm paying," he said.

"No, it's my treat."

Liam narrowed his eyes at me. "Nope. Not this time. You've got that look like you're here for a favor, and I can't be seen accepting bribes."

"Accepting a burger."

"A bribe's a bribe."

I shrugged, giving in, and ordered my burger with extra onions. I needed the comfort food, heartburn be damned. Liam got the fish filet, perhaps to annoy me. He knew damn well I hated the smell. I guessed I deserved it, the way I'd been lately, too busy to socialize outside the case. When had I last just sat down with Liam, with no agenda?

"How have you been?" I said.

He raised a brow. "That's why you called me? To see how I'm doing?"

"No," I admitted. "But I've missed you and Pat. I haven't seen much of you outside of work."

"We're good," said Liam, softening a little. He unwrapped his pickle and held it out. "Want this?"

"Hell, yeah." I loved a good pickle. "Auntie El said you took one of the puppies."

"Uh-huh, the little one. Brownie, we're calling her. She's great with the kids, a total sweetheart."

"Ian named ours Zombie."

Liam laughed. "Braaaaains."

"Speaking of brains…the Conrad case is breaking mine."

Liam sat straighter, his expression souring. "Zoey, huh? I have a bone to pick with you there. You had to set her up at the farmhouse? Really? You couldn't have found her a nice foster home somewhere else?"

"Taking her in was your mom's idea."

"Oh, I know that. We've had it out, too. And listen, I'm not thinking Zoey's a danger. If I did, I'd have stopped this straight out the gate. She's a hurt kid who snapped and killed her abusers. She's no threat at all to anyone else. But she doesn't have to shoot Mom to hurt her. Mom takes in strays. She gets attached. When that girl goes down for this, it'll break her heart."

"So, you think she did it?"

"Who else? We've placed her there now at the time of the murders. Far as I figure, we've got her dead to rights."

Hearing Liam say it, it sounded right. People *could* snap when they were pushed too far. And what were the odds of some random intruder going straight for the gun in Paul Conrad's desk? It sounded preposterous. But what if it wasn't? What if what Zoey said was exactly what happened?

I took a bite of my burger and washed it down with my Coke. "This will sound far-fetched, but hear me out. What if there was another shooter?"

"*Another* shooter. Working with Zoey?"

"No, hypothetically, working alone. Someone who broke in, maybe, and surprised the Conrads."

Liam had been chewing, and now he swallowed. "So, a burglar? Unlikely. We didn't find any sign of forced entry."

"What if the Conrads left their back door unlocked?"

Liam narrowed his eyes. "Did Zoey say something? Is this coming from her?"

"It's a hypothetical. It's, uh…" I tried to think how to frame this so he'd take it seriously, without violating attorney-client privilege. "I was on Lorraine's Facebook, digging for clues. Anything I could use to win points with the jury. And I happened to notice a post she made, back when the mayor ran for reelection. She said he'd made the town so safe that people didn't lock their doors at night anymore, and that got me thinking, did she lock hers?"

I could tell from his face Liam wasn't buying it. "You want to know what I think?"

"Sure. Go ahead."

"I think Zoey Conrad's a good girl who snapped, and now she can't face what she did. It's easier to paint someone else as the killer than admit it was you, that you killed your own parents."

"I never said this was coming from Zoey."

Liam gave me a *yeah, right* look, but he didn't argue. He took a bite of his sandwich, chewed, and swallowed. "You want me to look into him. This mystery shooter."

"I want to be sure," I said. "Don't you want that?"

Liam sipped from his Coke and leaned back in his chair. "Thing is, we *are* sure, or as sure as sure gets. We found nothing to indicate anyone else in the house, or anyone with motive—"

"Motive? Are you kidding?" I did a facepalm. "Paul and Lorraine Conrad sued half the town. That's dozens of motives. Did you not check on them?"

Liam's sullen silence told me he hadn't, at least not beyond a cursory look.

"I've made up a list. I'd appreciate—"

Liam held up both hands. "Maggie, I love you, but I have other cases. And not every client's unjustly accused. Sometimes they did it, and this one… She did it."

"That's your verdict, is it? As judge and jury?"

He cupped his forehead like he had a headache. "Look, I'm not saying she's a bad person. And you're right that her parents weren't angels. That boot camp they wanted to send her to was a horror show. I don't think anyone wants to see her do life for this. But I'm not going to waste my time or the department's time looking for some lone-wolf shooter who doesn't exist."

"You can't make a few calls? Check a few traffic cams? How about other Ring cams in the neighborhood? If he came through the woods to get to the door, maybe someone spotted him by Poplar or Finch. You could check the cams there, or—"

"You think we haven't done that?"

"What about back roads? Roads out of town? Plenty of people have home security—something might pop."

"You want me to check every camera in town?" Liam laughed. "Do you have *any* idea how long that would take?"

"Less than the life sentence Zoey is likely to get."

"It would take *hours* to track down all those cams, then days to sift through the footage. And this list of yours, we have it, too." He snatched up my lawsuit list and did an eyeroll. "It would take weeks to deep-dive on all these suspects, on the off chance one of them snuck in the back. Even if I wanted to, I'm not my own boss."

"But think about—"

"I'm telling you no, Mags. This is me saying no. I'd help if I thought there was something to find, but I'll be honest. I truly don't."

I could see from his stance he was done arguing, straight-backed, chin up, arms crossed tight. If I kept pushing, I'd just get his back up, and that would get Auntie El on my case.

"All right," I said. "But if you hear anything…?"

He softened as well, and his shoulders relaxed. "I'll keep my ear to the ground. You never know."

That was better than nothing, and I would take it. "Thanks, Liam," I said.

"Now, can we eat our lunch?"

We finished lunch with casual conversation, then he walked me most of the way to the office.

"I admire you," he said, as we passed by the courthouse. "You really go balls-to-the-wall for your clients. But take care, okay? Don't wear yourself out."

On impulse, I turned and pulled him into a hug. "You too. Stay safe out there."

"I always do."

Back at the office, I called Alia in. I knew she'd been nerding all day and would be tired, so I stopped downstairs for coffees on my way in. A shot of hazelnut syrup seemed to revive her, but sipping on mine didn't touch my exhaustion. Maybe Liam had a point about wearing myself out.

"The cops are a no-go." I flopped in my chair. "Liam said it'd take days to find all those Ring cams, and get the right footage, and then go through it."

Alia shrugged. "In detail, maybe. But those door cams flag when they pick up movement, so we'd check the flags first, and that would go quicker."

"Doesn't solve the issue of the lawsuits." I groaned. "We can't check out all these names."

"There has to be some way to narrow them down."

"We could start with the ones with criminal records, and anyone slapped with a restraining order." Liam was right to say that anyone could snap if they were pushed hard enough, but it happened a lot easier with someone who had a history of violence.

"That's still quite a lot of them," Alia said. "It's kind of gross, actually, how many of their victims had already been dealt a bad hand. A lot of them had dealt with previous lawsuits, or they had mental health issues, or they were old. They had just enough left to make them worth suing, but not enough to defend what they had."

I frowned. "Barry Robeson does pretty well for himself. And Dr. Karen doesn't fit that profile, either."

"I think Barry Robeson was just Paul seizing an opportunity when it came up. You know, take the pissed off, jealous husband and goad him into taking a swing—then cash in. But Dr. Karen's the interesting one, because it looks like it was after the case with her that they decided to narrow their victim pool. Which fits with what Zoey said about how they almost got caught. They wouldn't want to sue anyone who could afford to hire experts after an expert nearly blew up their game."

My jaw had gone tight, and I rubbed at my face. "We'll start with the ones who took the worst losses. Lost homes, lost businesses, that sort of thing."

Alia finished her coffee and licked the rim of her cup, getting the last of the chocolate whipped cream. "What about that lightning bolt hoodie?"

I shrugged. "It might be worth looking. If Zoey could draw what she saw on his hoodie, we might be able to match it to some brand or group." Exhaustion swept through me, a sick, wilting wave. I drained my coffee and felt even sicker. "If this is all nonsense, I swear to God —if she's sending us down some damn rabbit hole…"

"You should go," said Alia. "Go home, get some rest. I'll get started on this and let you know if I find anything."

I thought about arguing—I had so much to do still—but Liam had also picked up on my tiredness. I could go, take a nap, then get back to work after. An hour, maybe two, what could it hurt?

I woke to full dark, the smell of cooked cabbage, and Ian flicking my forehead.

"She's up," he called.

I squinched my eyes shut again. "What's going on?"

"We made dinner," he said. "All your favorite foods. Even that cabbage goo."

I sat up. "Colcannon?"

"Yeah, we made that, and your beef stew. And Auntie El dropped off a loaf of her soda bread."

I rubbed my eyes, still woozy from sleep. "How long was I out? Did I sleep straight through to my birthday?"

Ian laughed. "No. We just wanted to spoil you a little. You've been working so hard trying to do right by Zoey, we thought you deserved kind of a treat. And to keep your strength up. Are you okay?"

My eyes prickled suddenly, and my throat went tight. Ian hated colcannon, and cabbage in general. He'd described my cooking as *aggressively bland*. But here he was now making all of my faves, at a time when I'd hardly been my most present.

"Mom? You okay?"

I was spared trying to answer by Zombie barging between us, licking all over my sleep-swollen face.

"Ugh, get him off! Zombie! *Bad* Zombie."

Ian pulled him off, laughing, and Zombie jumped him instead, big messy licks to his hair and his face. That dog was well-named, I had to admit.

"Shoo, boy," said Ian, and pushed Zombie off. "Go on, get your dinner. Get dinner! Go on."

Zombie might not have understood much, but *dinner* was one word he knew by heart. He charged off to the kitchen, and I grabbed Ian. I dragged him into an embarrassing hug—a smothering mom hug, so tight he gasped.

"I love you," I said. "And thank you for dinner."

25

Monday rolled around, and I felt like a kid again, praying for a snow day to shut us out of court. Even one day's delay would mean I'd have one more day for digging. One more day for running down Ring cams and logos. With a storm warning out for the whole region, I had reason to hope the court would shut down, but Monday dawned clear, not a snowflake in sight.

I shared a quick, somber breakfast with Sean and Ian, and Ian made noises about coming to court again. But I didn't want him there today of all days. Oliver would be busting out his crime scene photos, and I didn't need Ian seeing all that.

"You've missed too much school," I said. "But you can come for my closing."

Ian started to argue, but Sean shot him a warning look. He subsided and went back to stirring his oatmeal. None of us had much appetite.

I made it to court with a coffee-sour stomach and did my best to brace Zoey for the day ahead. If she crumpled in court like she'd done in my office, sweating and shaking and hitching with sobs, that wouldn't play at all well with the jury. They'd see it as theater. Pandering. I didn't want Zoey to seem like an ice sculpture, but at the same time, I needed her to hold it together.

"Do I have to look? When he shows the—the photos?"

"No, you don't."

"It won't make me seem guilty?"

Truth was, she'd seem guilty either way. "Don't look," I said. "Just breathe and stay calm."

I took some deep breaths myself as Oliver took his place and set up the projector for his crime scene photos. I'd seen them already as part of discovery, and even on my laptop screen, they were bad. Blown up full size, they'd be a nightmare. But I could spin that, I thought, to work against Oliver—the mismatch between the violence of the crime scene and the small, frightened girl he was accusing. The more I could play on Zoey's youth and her size, the harder it would be for the jury to buy that she was responsible for what they'd see in Oliver's photos.

Oliver called Liam first to the stand.

"Would you state for the court your name, occupation, and connection to this case?"

Liam didn't look at me, or at Zoey. "I'm Liam O'Brien, and I'm a detective with Kerry PD. I responded to the scene of the Conrads' deaths."

"How long have you held this job?"

"Eighteen years."

"And in that time, you've investigated how many cases?"

"Almost four hundred."

Zoey shifted beside me, chewing her lip. I put my hand on her arm and she went still.

"Could you walk us through the Conrad crime scene?"

"We were called out for shots fired on Spruce Street, multiple 911 calls to the same address. We took two cars to investigate and another for crowd control. Due to the prior fatal shooting at that address, we had concerns the neighbors might—"

"Objection—move to strike."

Judge Yost looked annoyed. "Sustained," he said. "Jury will disregard the witness's last statement. You're on thin ice, Counsel," he added, shooting Oliver a look that no lawyer ever wants to see from the presiding judge.

Liam had reddened slightly at my objection, but he'd recomposed himself by the time I sat down.

"Detective, without referencing anything in the past, what did you do when you arrived on the scene?"

"We first cleared the scene," he said.

"What does that mean?"

"It means we swept the property in search of the shooter: the house, the garage, the trees out back. We determined the killer was no longer present. I put out a BOLO for anyone fleeing the scene and sent some patrol officers to canvass the area. Then, with the place secured, we documented the crime scene, took photos, bagged evidence, collected statements from witnesses."

"Detective, I'm showing you what's been marked as State's Exhibits 15 through 22. Do you recognize these photographs?"

Liam flipped through each one before answering, "Yes, I do."

"Did you take these photos?"

"No, but I was present at the scene when our evidence tech took them."

"Do these photographs fairly and accurately depict the scene as it existed when you observed it the night of the murders?"

"Yes, they do."

Oliver turned to Judge Yost. "Your Honor, we'd ask the Court to admit State's Exhibits 15 through 22 at this time.

Judge Yost looked at me, and I gave a slight nod.

"Hearing no objection from the defense, State's Exhibits 15 through 22 will be admitted," Yost announced.

Oliver strode over and fired up his projector, revealing the photo I'd guessed he'd show first: Paul Conrad sprawled in a scatter of glass, his eyes wide open and fixed on the ceiling. He'd been shot through the throat, and his blood had sprayed the walls. Judge Yost didn't blink, but the rest of the courtroom did. Assorted gasps went up, and a strangled cry. Zoey herself didn't look up, but she tore at her lower lip with her front teeth. Dead skin came away, and a drop of blood welled up.

"Zoey. Your lip." I passed her a tissue. She took it and stared at it like she'd never seen one before. She licked the blood off her lip instead.

Oliver faced Liam. "How did you assess the crime scene?"

To his credit, Liam didn't dwell on the horror. He kept his eyes on Oliver, not on Paul's photo. "The first thing we did was a perimeter sweep. We checked all the entry points to the house, and the grass and the flowerbeds, for anything unusual."

"Unusual, like what?"

"Like disturbed grass or earth where someone was lurking, or signs of forced entry."

"And did you find any?"

"No."

"And what about in the house, was anything missing?"

"No," Liam answered. "We found some displaced items. Furniture knocked over. Signs of a struggle. But a whole lot of valuables were still in plain view. A wide-screen TV. Jewelry. Electronics. Paul Conrad's Rolex was still on his wrist."

Oliver gestured up at the screen, at Paul Conrad's watch sprayed red with blood. "Is that his wedding ring still on his hand?"

Zoey made an unhappy sound. "He's making them look."

I shushed her. She was right, but there wasn't much I could do about it. Oliver was being showy, but he was allowed. After what seemed like forever, he switched to the next slide, an overview of the living room, with only Paul's legs showing. It should've been better, but it was worse, with the close-up blood spray.

"Did you conclude, from what you observed, that this was a robbery?"

"We couldn't rule out a robbery gone wrong. It's not unheard of for a perp to get spooked and run out with nothing. But robbery wasn't our first thought, no."

"Why not?"

I stood. "Objection—calls for speculation."

"Sustained," said Judge Yost.

Oliver switched to his next slide, showing the study, the desk drawer forced open, the bent letter opener. "What room is depicted here?"

"That room appeared to be Paul Conrad's study."

"Did you look through that room?"

"We did."

"What, if anything, did you find?"

"We found an open desk drawer with the lock broken and several boxes of ammo inside. We also found a gun-cleaning kit."

Oliver ran through all the photos, not just the bloody ones, and had Liam catalogue all that they'd found, what conclusions he'd drawn, and where those had led him. Every road led to Zoey, and the jurors were buying it, nodding along like twelve bobbleheads. Rather, fourteen of them, including the alternates.

I stood up on cross and approached Liam, reminding myself not to go too hard. The jury had liked him. They liked the police. I'd alienate them if they saw me bully him—but I still needed to make my point.

"Would you say, when you investigate the scene of a crime, part of your job is to interpret evidence?"

Liam tensed minutely, sensing a trap. "Partly," he said. "But it doesn't end with us. Forensics, the crime lab—"

"But you look at the evidence and come to conclusions. Narrow your suspect pool. Would you say you do that?" I realized, too late, I'd cut him off. Two jurors were frowning, one shaking her head. I wanted to kick myself, but I took a step back instead. Smiled slightly to make myself seem less aggressive.

"We investigate all the evidence and all viable suspects."

"And how many suspects did you investigate?"

"All the evidence led to Miss Conrad."

"So you didn't investigate Bobby Ray Brown?"

Liam's expression stayed neutral. He checked his notes. "We didn't speak to him, but yes, we looked into him."

"What about Sarah Patterson? Johnny Hill?"

"Johnny Hill's name came up in our investigation. He's the plumber the Conrads sued for bad copper pipes."

"Would it surprise you to know they sued all three of them—and that they had been in the Conrads' home before?"

"No," Liam said. "We were aware of the Conrads' lawsuits."

"Were you aware of Mary Griffith, or Lester Pierce, or the four other people who'd been sued by the Conrads and expressed hard feelings?"

Liam glanced at his notes again. "Yes—Carrie Wood, Joe Brattigan, Sam Myles, and Jennifer O'Toole."

"Did you interview any of them?"

"No, we did not."

"Did you interview *any* suspect, besides my client?"

"No, we did not."

"Are you currently investigating any other suspect?"

"No, we have no other suspects."

"So, no. You're not."

"Not at this time."

I'd milked all I could out of the shallow suspect pool, and I could see the jury's patience nearing its limit. I changed tack, pivoting back to his testimony.

"You mentioned earlier, you've investigated almost four hundred cases over the course of your career. How many cases have you investigated specifically for the robbery-homicide unit?"

"I'd say about half of those."

"And how many cases as lead detective?"

"Thirty-two," Liam said, more sure this time.

"And of those thirty-two, how many were homicides?"

"One. Just this one."

"So this was your first time taking lead on a homicide?"

To his credit, Liam stayed steady, though a small muscle jumped in the side of his neck. "I treated the investigation like any other, according to my training and experience."

"So you talked to witnesses, collected evidence. You had your men sweep the area for anyone fleeing. Did they find any evidence, any trace of the killer?"

"No."

"Did they find anything connected to Zoey?"

"No."

"So you arrested my client when the dog walker came forward, saying she'd seen her enter the house?"

Liam shifted, uncomfortable. I snuck a glance at the jury. They were listening with interest, but I sensed their tension. I hadn't won them over yet.

"We arrested her following the dog walker's statement, which discredited her alibi. But we—"

I had no choice but to cut him off this time, before he could get into other evidence. "So based on that statement, you arrested my client. Did you continue investigating anyone else?"

"No."

"At any time following the dog walker's statement, did you investigate anyone else?"

Liam didn't show it, but I knew he was fuming. "No."

"You found signs of a struggle at the crime scene?"

"We did."

"Furniture overturned? A book stained with blood?"

"Yes."

I kept pushing. "You saw the injuries to Mr. Conrad's knuckles, right?"

"Yes."

"So, between the broken glass, overturned furniture, and Mr. Conrad's injuries, you naturally concluded there was some altercation between Mr. Conrad and his assailant, correct?"

"We thought that was the likely scenario."

"And you arrested my client how many days after?"

"Two days."

"Did you see any signs she'd been involved in a struggle? Any physical injury to her person?"

Liam hesitated, then forged on. "I didn't conduct her physical exam."

"At this time, I'd like to show the witness what's been previously marked as Defense Exhibit 4." I held out the photo for Liam to take. "Did you take this photograph?"

"Yes, I did."

"And it accurately reflects the defendant's condition as it existed at the time of her arrest?"

"Yes."

"Can you point to any injuries to Miss Conrad's person?"

"Not in this photograph."

"And did you observe any?"

"No."

I took the photograph back and glanced over at Zoey, knowing the jury would follow my gaze. "How tall is my client?"

"Around five foot six."

"And how tall was Paul Conrad?"

"Six foot three."

"Thank you," I said. "That's all for this witness."

Oliver stood up. "Redirect, Your Honor. Detective O'Brien, have you seen this before? An altercation where one party's injured, but the other walks off unscathed?"

"I have," Liam confirmed. "It's unusual, but it's certainly possible."

"And did you arrest Miss Conrad solely based on the dog walker's statement?"

"No. She was just the last piece of the puzzle."

Oliver thanked him and stepped down, satisfied. Liam had held up well, and the jury had liked him, but I'd noticed a few of them checking out Zoey, especially once I brought up her uninjured state. She'd never been a big girl, and after the weight she'd lost from stress, she looked like a stiff breeze might blow her away. I could tell they were picturing her in a fight with her father, and realizing how unlikely it seemed. I thought I'd scored some points there and established the first hints of doubt.

Oliver called up the dog walker next, and a ballistics expert to match the bullet to Paul Conrad's gun. He called the Taskrabbit who'd repaired the drawer where the gun was stored—to establish, he claimed, Zoey knew where it was. That it was in the same place it had always been. That particular witness had me silently raging, knowing for the jury, the broken drawer would remind them of the Rooney shooting. Oliver had seamlessly backdoored it in, in a way too subtle for me to object to.

"How are we doing?" Zoey asked me, as I drove her back out to Auntie El's. "I tried not to look at them, I mean the jury, but whenever I did look, they were staring at me."

I could see how to her, it might feel that way, but in fact, I'd have liked them to look at her more. A jury that didn't look much at the defendant was often a jury that thought they were guilty.

"We're doing all right," I said. "But this is just the beginning. Tomorrow, your texts come in, and those won't look good for us."

"But you'll have your chance to defend me, right?"

I knew what she needed was reassurance, so I told her I would. She'd get my best defense. All she had to focus on was staying calm.

"Thank you," she said, when I dropped her off. She paused with one hand still on my car door. "I know you still think I probably did it, but I see you in there. Fighting your hardest. I've never had anyone fight like that for me." Her pale face crumpled, and she ran away, up the steps to the farmhouse and then inside. I heard the pups yipping and hoped they could comfort her, because she had a hard fight still ahead.

26

Oliver started his second day strong. He called the ME first to the stand, and she once again testified to Paul Conrad's injuries—but this time, she did it with autopsy photos, showing the damage in all its red glory. At first, I hoped this was a miscalculation, a chance for me to harp on Zoey's small stature. The improbability of her besting her father. But the jury's reaction to Paul Conrad's throat wound, and to the entry wound in Lorraine's fresh-shaved head, told me the gruesome photos had found their mark.

Worst of all, Paul Conrad's eye injury didn't look that bad. He looked like he'd died with a bad case of pinkeye, and some slight swelling around the orbit. He hadn't lived long enough to bruise very badly. It wasn't the kind of injury that only a heavyweight could inflict. The truly horrible injuries were the ones inflicted by the gun—and I could tap dance around it from here to eternity, but anyone could fire a gun, no matter their size.

On cross, my first move was to request Oliver take down the photos. I needed the shot of Lorraine's head out of sight. Her shaved skull looked sad, and worse than that, vulnerable. A reminder she'd been terrified, trying to flee. I didn't want that in the heads of the jury, at least no more than it needed to be.

I crossed on Paul Conrad's eye injury, and how severe it had been: how long did bruising take to develop? How did death affect that process? The ME explained that once blood flow stops, so does bruising.

"So if Paul Conrad had lived, that bruise could have darkened?"

"Yes."

"And did he have other injuries, besides gunshot wounds?"

I had her run through his injuries, their type, and severity, focusing on their number and variety. I wanted the jury to contrast that with Zoey's lack of injury and wonder how she could've tussled with a man Paul Conrad's size long enough to inflict all these cuts and bruises without sustaining so much as a scrape.

Next up, Oliver called Dr. Granger, Zoey's therapist.

"Dr. Granger, would you explain your profession and qualifications for the court?"

Dr. Granger seemed nervous, and kept touching her hair, then remembering not to and folding her hands. I got the sense this was new to her, testifying in court. "I'm a child psychologist," she said. "I have dual PhDs in psychology and school psychology, and I've passed all licensing requirements for the state of Ohio. I have almost six years of clinical experience, mostly with children between twelve and eighteen."

"And the defendant was one of those children?"

"She was, between January 2023 and September 2024."

"Could you describe why she came to you, and her parents' concerns?"

"Objection." I went to stand, but my knee locked. I banged my bad hip hard on the table, and yelled without meaning to, clutching my leg in pain. Judge Yost half-rose.

"Are you all right?"

I took a series of quick breaths and swallowed hard, hoping my voice wouldn't crack when I used it. My eyes were watering, my neck damp with sweat. "I'm all right, Your Honor. Just bumped my hip." My voice seemed okay, so I risked straightening up, in spite of the pain screaming down my sciatic nerve. "The Conrads' concerns are hearsay, Your Honor. Dr. Granger can't testify to what they might have said."

"Sustained," said Judge Yost. "And, please sit down. Do we need a recess?"

I shook my head. "Thank you, Your Honor, but no."

Zoey leaned close to me, eyes big with concern. "Are you sure? That looked like it hurt."

It *had* hurt, still did, but taking a break wouldn't help with that. What I needed was ice, Sean taking care of me, and TV to distract me from the throbbing pain.

"I'm good," I said, and managed a smile, hoping the jury had seen her lean into me. Hoping they'd picked up on her empathy and concern. As silver linings went, it wouldn't be much, but I wasn't too proud to take what I could get.

Oliver looked irritated starting back up, like my banging my hip had been some kind of stunt. I sat sweating, my leg and my ass on fire, my hip a furnace hot as the sun. I pinched the web between finger and thumb, a trick I'd once learned for quieting headaches. It didn't do much for the ache in my hip, but it did help me focus in spite of my pain.

"Did you ask the defendant why she'd come to see you?"

Dr. Granger was fiddling with her long hair. She stopped, clasped her hands, and brought them down to her lap. "She wasn't the defendant then. She was my patient. And I did ask her, yes, what she hoped to get out of therapy."

"What was her response, do you recall?"

"She said her parents sent her. She said they were worried."

I didn't stand to object this time, just jerked in my seat. "Objection, Your Honor. This is double hearsay."

"Sustained," said Judge Yost. "Jury will disregard."

"Why did Miss Conrad tell you she was in therapy?"

Dr. Granger looked flustered. "This was some time ago. I can't recall verbatim."

"Would it refresh your memory to review your session notes?" Oliver had already picked up his copy, and now he leafed through it, finding the page. "Does this help refresh your recollection about what Miss Conrad told you concerning therapy?"

Dr. Granger's lips tightened as she scanned the page, and then she looked up. "Kids Zoey's age, they need to test you. They say things, outrageous things, to—"

"Excuse me, Dr. Granger. Would you answer the question?"

She shook her head. "What was the question?"

I swallowed back the urge to huff in frustration. I could see she was trying to protect Zoey, but despite her intentions, she was making it worse. By refusing to answer, she was priming the jury for something shocking. Almost as bad, she was annoying Judge Yost, who now cleared his throat. Oliver squared his shoulders.

"Why did Miss Conrad say she was in therapy?"

Dr. Granger glanced over at me and Zoey, then pursed her lips and went back to her notes. "I asked her why she was there, to establish a starting point. It's useful to get the patient's perspective, not jump to conclusions based on what I've heard from her teachers or parents. She said to me, ah…" She read from the page. "'I want to kill my parents. Can you help with that?'"

A couple of gasps went up from the jury box. Zoey slouched down like she wanted to disappear.

"I didn't say it like *that*," she said. "I said it like, joking."

"Your Honor," I said, "I have to object to this. Out of context, these statements are prejudicial, and offer little or no evidentiary value. I move this response be stricken from the record."

"I disagree," said Oliver. "It speaks to the defendant's state of mind."

Judge Yost pushed his glasses up. "Overruled. Counsel, you may cross-examine to establish context."

Oliver's lips twitched, almost a smile. I knew he was new to this, still high on the thrill of it, but if he didn't quit smirking like a smug frog, one day somebody would smack that smirk off him.

"What else did she say about her reasons for coming?"

Dr. Granger looked dazed. She stared at her notes. "I asked if she was serious. She laughed. Rolled her eyes. She said, 'if I was going to shoot someone, I'd start with them.'"

"Thank you, Dr. Granger. Did the defendant describe any other violent fantasies?"

"That wasn't a fantasy. It was—"

Oliver stepped forward, looming over her. He wasn't a large man, but Dr. Granger was small, and she shifted back as he got in her space. "Did Miss Conrad report any violent fantasies?"

Dr. Granger coughed. "Yes. A few times. I suspected, uh…"

"Did you describe these fantasies there in your notes?"

She leafed through her notes, breathing hard through her nose. "Well, in one case, her mother had slapped her. Zoey reports wishing she'd slapped her back."

"Just slapped her?" Oliver moved closer, almost standing on top of her. Dr. Granger was back to fiddling with her hair.

"No, she described, ah, breaking her nose."

"You said this happened a few times, a few fantasies. What were some of the other ones, if you recall?"

"She described putting laxatives in her father's coffee. She thought it'd be funny if he, ah… At church. That was the main one, the one she'd go back to. He was, as she put it, 'full of it.'"

"Did you warn her parents of these threats by Miss Conrad?"

"I discussed Zoey's statements with her parents, yes. But neither they nor I—"

"Thank you, Dr. Granger. That will be all."

Standing, my first move was to dial back the tension. It wasn't easy with my hip and leg screaming, but I conjured what I hoped was a friendly smile, half for the doctor and half for the jury.

"Dr. Granger, I'll start with an easy question. Did my client ever tell you she loved her parents?"

"Yes. Many times."

"Did she talk about good times they'd had together?"

"Yes—yes, she did. How she wished there were more of them. She said she felt bad because she sometimes wished her dad would sue someone, because he'd be in a good mood after he won. They used to go out for victory dinners, and she talked about those a lot. How they felt like a family during those times."

"You said you discussed Zoey's more extreme fantasies with her parents. Did you do that to warn them of an imminent threat?"

"No." Dr. Granger leaned forward, eager, looking relieved to have a chance to speak freely at last. "I didn't consider these fantasies threats, nor did her parents. Zoey knew I'd be sharing what we discussed. I gave her a safe setting to vent her feelings. Her hope and mine was that by sharing her frustrations, her parents would take the steps to try to reach reconciliation. She often said things she knew I'd repeat, and even asked me, 'will you tell my parents?' Like she wanted to make sure her message got through."

"To the best of your knowledge, did my client put laxatives in her father's coffee?"

"No. Never."

"Did she slap her mother?"

"No."

"Did she ever, to your knowledge, act on any violent fantasy she discussed with you in therapy?"

"No. She did not."

"When she told you she wanted to kill her parents and asked for your help with that, were you alarmed?"

"No, not at all."

"Why not?"

Dr. Granger stopped fidgeting. "Well, she was smiling. It was a joke. A lot of patients start out with jokes to defuse the tension."

"Did she ever make credible threats of serious violence?"

"Never."

"Thank you, Dr. Granger." I felt like I'd missed something, some pressing question, but my sweat was soaking the pits of my blouse. The pain was so intense that I felt sick, and if I didn't sit down soon, I thought I'd keel over. Oliver stood again.

"Redirect, Your Honor."

"Go ahead," the judge told him.

Oliver moved closer to the witness. "Dr. Granger, just a couple more questions: you've described your sessions with the defendant as a safe setting. Are you saying she felt *unsafe* speaking directly to her parents?"

"Objection—calls for speculation." I half-rose again.

Judge Yost exhaled hard. "Rephrase the question."

"Did the defendant ever mention feeling unsafe, or disclose abuse going on in her home?"

Dr. Granger sat quiet for a long moment, then took a deep breath and started to talk. "I can't testify to physical abuse in the home, beyond the few slaps Zoey brought up in sessions. But Zoey was a victim of emotional abuse. Her parents withheld love and affection, contingent on factors like her performance in school. And Zoey's whole affect changed when they were present. She became quieter and more cautious, wary. She stopped making jokes or trying to be funny. She displayed a lot of behaviors that sent up red flags—not that she was dangerous, but that she felt threatened."

"Under Ohio state law, you are a mandatory reporter, in cases of abuse, isn't that correct?".

"Yes, that's correct."

"Did you ever make such a report about Zoey?"

Dr. Granger looked down. "No. I did not."

"Why not?"

"Because the abuse she disclosed to me was primarily emotional in nature, which doesn't trigger mandatory reporter laws. Maybe I should have reported the slaps. But we're talking about two or three open-palmed slaps, and a report of abuse triggers an investigation. Child services gets involved. Parents lose custody. I didn't feel that was in Zoey's best interest."

"But she disclosed abuse to you?"

"Emotional abuse. Yes."

"Thank you," said Oliver, and he sat down. I bit back my groan, but a hiss still escaped me.

Judge Yost broke for lunch and I sped home, and took two Aleve and a hot shower. I changed into a fresh suit and sped back to court, arriving last minute as the judge took his place. I wasn't back to one hundred percent, but the sick edge had gone off the pain in my hip, and I was ready for Oliver's next witness.

He called on an expert to go through Zoey's texts, a professor of linguistics with a degree in psychology. He'd written a paper on teen communication, with a focus on digital media, which he'd later expanded into a popular book. Oliver cherry-picked Zoey's worst moments—colorful insults, gore-splattered memes. Moments of her wishing death on the Conrads. The professor leaned heavily on his own book to finger some statements as predictors of violence, so when it came my turn, I turned the same text—which I'd spent hours reading and annotating—against him.

"Here on page 132 of your book, you mention periods in texts can be seen as aggressive by teens, so they're mainly used when there's a need for clarity, or sometimes to indicate real aggression."

"That's true."

"Would you be surprised to learn, in nearly a hundred thousand messages analyzed and admitted into evidence, my client used periods in only three thousand—and that three quarters of those had to do with homework?"

"It's not a hard and fast rule, that periods must be used to indicate aggression. Teens *do* express anger without punctuation, and use punctuation without being angry."

"Right, but if you'd look at State's Exhibit 36, page 934—" I handed him a printout. "Would you mind reading that exchange, with punctuation?"

The professor made a show of adjusting his glasses. "Ian, all lowercase: didn't mean you looked bad, no period. Zoey, uppercase T: Then why would you say that, question mark. You're an asshole sometimes, period. I'm going to bed, period. Ian, uppercase W: Wait, exclamation point. Zoey, uppercase S: screw you, period."

"Would you characterize this exchange as aggressive?"

"It's certainly…heated," he admitted, looking uncomfortable.

I made him read out three more exchanges, all using periods, all spats with friends.

"Would you say my client used periods to indicate aggression?"

"In those texts, she did. But in other exchanges with aggressive content—"

"If Miss Conrad used periods in fifty-eight out of sixty exchanges involving personal conflict, what conclusion would you draw from that?"

The professor pulled a sour face, but he answered my question. "I'd conclude she used them in situations of conflict, as a means of expressing her anger. But her threats weren't—"

"My client's 'threats,' right. Let's look at those. Would you mind reading this one, from page 806 of State's Exhibit 36, about Paul Conrad?" I passed him another sheet, and he read aloud.

"Zoey, all lowercase: like yosemite sam lol when bugs bunny shoots him, no period. Zoey, all lowercase: all burnt up with those blinking eyes lol no period. Zoey, all lowercase: hed deserve it lol, no period. Ian: laughing emoji."

"What does LOL mean?"

"It means 'laughing out loud,' but it doesn't always mean literal laughter. As I said in my book—"

"Right, LOL has multiple uses: punctuation, irony, expressing contempt, is that right?"

"Yes."

"But Ian's response was a laughing emoji. What does that suggest to you?"

"…That he was laughing."

"So, like a joke. Like he thought she was joking?"

"The subject matter hardly seems like something to joke about."

"But she *was* joking?"

"Perhaps Ian thought she was, but—"

"Objection," said Oliver. "This witness's expertise does not extend to state of mind."

"Sustained," said Judge Yost. "Please don't speculate. Confine your opinion to subjects that are within your area of expertise."

"Thank you," I said. "That's all I have." I risked a glance at the jury, and they looked pretty skeptical, not of me, but of Oliver's witness. Judge Yost looked severely unimpressed. My hip was throbbing, but I felt light as air. This round, at least, I'd scored a small victory. Taken the teeth out of Zoey's texts.

Tomorrow, Ian would once again take the stand, and the jury would see the Ring cam video. But today had gone our way, and I told Zoey so. She'd been doing well so far, but tomorrow would test her, watching her boyfriend testify against her. I needed her in the best spirits she could be in, ready to power through no matter what.

27

Ian sat at breakfast, not eating his oatmeal. I'd done my best to prepare him for what he would face, but even so, this would be rough. All I could do now was be his mom.

"Ian, I'm proud of you."

He didn't respond. I wasn't sure he'd heard me at all.

"Ian?"

He blinked. "Sorry, what? I was practicing what I'd say on the stand."

"You don't want to sound too rehearsed," I reminded him. "Just be sincere, and be honest. You're a good kid, and the jury will see that." I hoped that was true, but I was worried. Ian had lied, and that would come up again, which would undermine him in the eyes of the jury. Would they see my sweet son up there, who'd tried to protect Zoey because he genuinely believed in her, or would they see a delinquent who'd helped hide a murder?

Oliver called John Tulley before he called Ian—the owner of the Ring cam that'd blown up Zoey's alibi. I could see he was enjoying his moment in court, the thrill, the attention. The chance to be part of things.

"I live two down and across from the Conrads," he said. "Well, *lived*. They were good neighbors."

"And where were you on the night of the shooting?"

"On vacation in Europe, with my wife. It was our second honeymoon, so we vacationed for three months. We'd had our phones off most of the time, so it wasn't till we got home I found out what happened."

"What made you decide to check your cam footage?"

"I turned my phone back on when we got home, and we had all these messages from the police. They wanted to see if our cam caught anything."

"I'm showing you what's been previously marked as State's Exhibit 37. Can you please tell us what this is?"

"It's footage from my Ring cam at 2260 Spruce Street."

"Was the camera working properly on November thirteenth?"

"Yes. We have other footage from that date and there's no indication the camera was interrupted or malfunctioned or anything like that."

"So it accurately depicts what was recorded?"

"Yes, I didn't notice any problems."

"How did you save this particular footage?"

Tulley appeared thoughtful. "I opened my Ring app, went into history, and saved the file I wanted to download."

"When did you do that? What was the date and approximate time, if you have that information?"

He made a humming sound. "The same day we got home from our vacation. So, I think that was February fourth."

"What did you do with it after you downloaded it?"

Tulley smiled, now on solid ground. "I brought it straight to the police and gave it to Detective O'Brien."

"Did you alter the footage in any way?"

"No." He half-scowled. "I wanted the police to have accurate information."

"Your Honor, at this time, I'd like to offer State's Exhibit 37 into evidence."

"Objection, Your Honor. Lack of foundation. The State hasn't established chain of custody." I rose halfway and then returned to my seat.

"Your Honor, we request that the exhibit be admitted *de bene*. The state will call Detective O'Brien to establish chain of custody."

"The objection is overruled. State's Exhibit 37 will be admitted subject to the condition that the prosecution establishes chain of custody."

Oliver started up his projector and played the video.

"Mr. Tulley, can you please describe for us what was on that video?"

Tulley's chest swelled. "Yes. You can't see a lot of their house on our camera, but it's the one where you jus saw those flashes. You can see their side door because of the angle. Our cam caught the flashes, you know, from the gunshots, and five minutes later, someone ran out that side door. And I recognized that person as the defendant."

Oliver was done with him, and Tulley stepped down. The jury had barely reacted to the video. They seemed unsurprised, which wasn't good. They'd assumed all along Zoey had been in the house during the shooting, and this evidence was just confirmation. And Ian would be the cherry on top, admitting she'd conspired with him to lie to police.

Oliver called Liam back to establish chain of custody, then it was Ian's turn, and he stepped up. He made it okay through the first half of questioning, where Oliver established he'd lied to Patrick. He'd learned from his first time facing these questions, and he answered calmly, not trying to hide anything or justify himself. He came across as a kid who knew he'd made a mistake and was sorry and owning up to it. The jury was nodding, eating it up, but I couldn't relax yet. Not till he was done.

"How would you describe your relationship with the defendant?" Oliver flashed Ian his best chummy smile.

"Zoey's my girlfriend, as I said before."

"Permission to treat the witness as hostile, Your Honor?"

"Granted."

"So, she's still your girlfriend? You're still together?"

Ian colored slightly. "Yes, we are."

"And would you say you trust her? That she's honest with you?"

"Yeah—yeah, I trust her. I still believe—" Ian caught himself. We were venturing into dangerous territory because Zoey had told Ian, against my advice, about the stranger who'd snuck in the back. If Oliver asked him directly what Zoey had told him about the night of the murders, he'd have to answer honestly. I didn't want Hoodie Guy coming onto the record unless I could prove he had been on the scene. Without proof, it would sound like a desperate lie.

"You still believe what?"

"I believe she didn't do it."

"But you deleted your texts the morning after the murders, isn't that true?"

"Uh, I think… Yes."

"Following a conversation you had with the defendant?"

"Yes."

"But not all the texts on your phone, yes? Just the ones between you and Miss Conrad?"

Ian coughed. "Yes."

Oliver's eyes narrowed. "Why did you do that?"

"Because people might read them."

"And why did you think that might be a problem?"

"Because—because…" Ian's tongue darted out, wetting his lips. "We talked about lots of things. Those texts were private."

"Texts like…okay, hold on a second." Oliver reached for a fat stack of printouts, and shuffled through it, pure theater. He could have printed out just the quotes he would need, but he wanted the jury to see the thick stack of papers. To wonder what else was lurking in there. "'I wish they'd just die,'" he read, and skipped to a new page. "'Why can't aliens abduct them and not bring them back?' 'I hate my dad worse than anyone, except for my mom.'" He'd dogeared the pages to find the right quotes, but from where the jury was sitting, they wouldn't see that. All they'd see was him turning to random pages and finding angry, hateful messages on every last one. In reality, most of her texts were quite boring.

Now, Oliver strode up to loom over Ian. "Did you delete those texts because you thought she looked guilty?"

"I know she's not."

"That's not what I asked you. Did you think those texts made the defendant look guilty?"

"Out of context, maybe, but—"

I stood. "Objection—relevance. It doesn't matter what the witness thought."

"Sustained," said Judge Yost. "Move on, counsel."

Oliver stepped back, giving Ian some breathing space—a show of compassion meant to appease the jury.

"When you spoke to the defendant the morning after the murders, what did she tell you about when she left the house?"

"She told me, uh…" Ian cleared his throat. He reached for his water and took a big gulp. "She told me she left pretty much right away. She got home and found her parents packing her room, and she ran off so they couldn't send her away."

"But that wasn't true, as we've seen on the doorbell cam. Did the defendant mention anyone else in the house while she was there?"

Ian went quiet. Oliver pressed on.

"The defendant was in the house at the time of the murders. Did she mention seeing anyone else?"

"Not…not—" Ian's gaze flicked to me. I could see him panicking, and willed him to breathe. We'd been over this, and he knew what to do, but panic could often trump preparation.

"That would be a great alibi, seeing someone else do it. Did she ever mention anyone else?"

Ian reached for his water, then put it back down again. "She did," he said.

"And did she— Wait." Oliver stopped cold as his brain caught up to his mouth. He'd been expecting a "no" there. So had the jury. Now he blinked quickly, recovering himself. "Sidebar, Your Honor. May we approach?"

"I think you'd better," said Judge Yost. He looked as unimpressed as I'd ever seen him. I felt like a kid being sent to the principal's office as I stood and the two of us approached the bench. Oliver glared at me, then at Judge Yost.

"If the defense has evidence they intend to offer, they need to disclose it."

"We understand that, Your Honor, and we've complied with our obligations. This is the *State's* witness, and the witness is directly responding to Mr. Altman's question. In fact, he should be allowed to complete his answer."

Judge Yost frowned at Oliver. "Anything further, Mr. Altman?"

Oliver was fuming, but he had no leg to stand on. "No, Your Honor. I'm ready to proceed."

"Defense?"

"No, Your Honor." I'd known this might happen, and I'd come prepared for it. Introducing evidence this way was by no means ideal, but now it was out there, I'd make the most of it.

"Then, let's get back to it."

Oliver waited till I'd sat and the courtroom had quieted, then turned his attention back to Ian. "I just have one more question, about this new alibi: when did the defendant tell you this story?"

"Tuesday."

"That was after the Tulleys' tape was discovered, right?"

"I wouldn't know about the timing of all that."

"No further questions."

On cross, I couldn't ignore Ian's revelation. Oliver had tripped up and brought the possibility of another shooter into evidence. Not jumping on that would look bad to the jury—like I didn't believe the story, myself.

"My client told you she witnessed the shooter?"

Ian looked hesitant, but I'd prepared him to deal with this. Now I gave him the slightest nod, and he swallowed hard. "Yeah. She was hiding. He ran by her room."

"What did she tell you about what she saw?"

"Objection—hearsay." Oliver had gone red and was almost shouting. "Defense can't introduce hearsay statements from her own client."

I stood. "Your Honor, the State opened the door to this. The jury has the right to hear the whole story."

Judge Yost blew out a frustrated breath. "Approach," he said.

We approached the bench again, and Judge Yost glowered at us. "Ms. Gallagher, this is highly unusual. Your own son has revealed your client's case theory, without you having to put her on the stand?"

"I know how it looks, but—"

"How it *looks* is like you trapped counsel into opening the door. I am inclined to sustain the objection."

I'd lost this scuffle, but in a sense, I'd still won. I'd got Hoodie Guy in through Oliver's screwup, and made a show for the jury that I'd wanted him in. That, in my view, he was real evidence. Now, I set to work undoing the rest of the damage.

"Ian, you're a senior at Kerry High, right?"

"Right."

"How's that going for you, you getting good grades?"

"Yeah, mostly As, maybe a B or two. Zoey's been helping me with AP calc. She took it last year. She's really smart."

A couple of jurors were smiling a little, and I took that as a sign my strategy was working. I needed to show Ian was a good kid—a smart kid, hardworking, in AP classes. First I'd show that, then I'd show a harder truth: that even good kids resented their folks sometimes.

"Ian, do you know me outside this courtroom?"

He chuckled a little. "Yeah. You're my mom."

"I'm going to show you something, another text chat." I pulled it up on a slide so the jury could see it. "This is State's Exhibit 36. We've seen it before—a transcript of text chats between the witness and my client." Ian winced at the sight of it. One juror laughed. I read it out for the court.

hey wyd

about 2 sit down 2 moms cabbage surprise 🤢

she does this 2 torture me

ew lol

like this is fully a crime against humanity

if they put her on trial for this shed get the ☠️

"Sorry," said Ian, when I was done reading.

"That's okay. We can't all love cabbage. But do you really think mine should get me the death penalty?"

"No! Of course not. That would be stupid."

"Do you think I'm…hold on." I clicked to the next slide. "A raging, hormonal, menopause-addled…bee emoji?"

Ian's ears turned red. "No, you're not that."

"Then why did you say I was in your chat with Zoey?"

"Because I was mad, you know? We'd just had a fight, and I was blowing off steam. But I'd never have said those things if I knew you would see them. I never wanted to hurt you…I'm sorry, Mom."

I didn't want to keep pushing him—he was embarrassed enough. And I could see he felt bad, knowing he'd hurt me. Knowing I'd read through six months of his venting. But I couldn't stop till I saw the jury was with me.

"Zoey said she wished her parents would disappear. Have you ever wished I would?"

Ian glanced at the screen with his text on display, maybe wondering if he'd said that in some forgotten conversation, and if I'd seen it. He hadn't, at least not in so many words, but his expression said it all.

"Not really," he said. "I mean, when we fight sometimes, I've probably said it. I told Zoey I was applying to Moscow State University. She said she'd come with me and we'd both be free."

"And *do* you intend to go study in Russia?"

"No way. Of course not. It was a joke."

"Thanks, Ian," I said. "That's all from me."

Ian sat looking thoroughly miserable, and I knew the jury was taking him in: a good kid, a kind kid, clean, all-American, who'd called his own mother a menopausal monster. Who'd likened her cooking to a war crime. A good kid who'd said some things he didn't mean, and who'd never had any harmful intent. He felt awful, knowing I'd seen what he said, and was beating himself up for hurting my feelings. I knew they were seeing Zoey in him, her texts, which weren't much worse than his were.

For Zoey's case, this was a small victory, but in my mouth, it tasted like—like my cabbage did to Ian. I sat glum and stony through Oliver's redirect, and watched, my heart breaking, as Ian stepped down.

"The prosecution rests," Oliver said.

I drew a deep breath, because time was up. Come Monday, I'd have to put on my case, whether Alia tracked down Hoodie Guy or not.

28

We ordered in from the new little Greek place, which had taken over from the old little sandwich place, which had before that been a French café.

"Mm, this is tasty," said Auntie El, dipping her pita in her tzatziki. "Fingers crossed this one stays open a while."

"It won't," said Alia. "That place is cursed."

Auntie El shook her head. "No, its only problem is that it's two doors down from Pam's Chicken. Whenever a new place opens, she drops her prices and undercuts them right out of the market."

I grabbed a stuffed grape leaf while the grabbing was good, though I didn't have much appetite after today in court. Ian had hugged me and said we were fine, and that he knew I'd done it for Zoey. But all I could picture was his red face, his stricken expression when I'd pulled up his texts. When this case was done, I'd make it up to him. Take him out for a special meal somewhere, without a single cabbage leaf in sight.

I turned to Alia, shifting back into work mode. "So, anything yet, with the black hoodie?"

She frowned, and I knew the answer was no. "Nobody saw him, at least not so far. But there's still a few people I need to talk to. Oh, and the judge came through on your subpoena. They're sending over the traffic cam footage. The cams near the scene, the cops already went through, but there's a couple they didn't check from the outskirts of town, and I'm still chasing down some private security cams."

It was a long shot, going through traffic cams. They didn't record constantly—they only fired up when they caught a speeder. For our mystery shooter to appear on a traffic cam, he'd need to be in a car, and he'd need to be speeding through one of six intersections equipped with traffic cams within Kerry town limits. My current theory was that he'd fled through the woods in back of Spruce Street, which only left us two intersections, unless he had looped back to drive through town.

"We need to find this guy, if he exists." I reached for my coffee and found it all gone. "Ian was under oath. I don't blame him for blabbing. But the way it stands now, Zoey looks like a liar, with this alibi out there she can't back up."

Alia nodded. "I've been thinking about that. If I were on the jury, I'd be asking myself, if she saw the shooter, why wouldn't she say so right from the start?"

"They need to hear from her," said Auntie El. "If she told that story, like she told us…"

I dug in my purse and found my aspirin, dry-swallowing two capsules. I didn't have a headache, but I could feel one brewing. The last thing I needed was Zoey on the stand, fair game for Oliver. He'd tear her apart. But with her claims of seeing the shooter out there, what choice did I have? The jury could hear it from Zoey's own lips, or they could *not* hear it and draw their own conclusions.

"Get on those cameras," I told Alia. "Especially the private ones. Those record all the time, not just for speeders."

She nodded. "Got it."

"And how about that lightning bolt? Any luck there?"

"I sent you an email a few hours ago, with a Google Drive link to a bunch of symbols and logos. You can show them to Zoey and see if anything clicks."

"I should go see her," I said, and swallowed a burp. "Ugh, this Greek salad's giving me heartburn."

Alia dug in her purse and pulled out some Tums. "It's probably the stress more than the salad. You should get home early. Give yourself a break."

I took the Tums and ignored the advice. Zoey's trial would be over in a few days. I could take a break then, and not one moment sooner. I would go hard for her till the bitter end, defend her with all I had. That was the job.

When Zoey answered the door, I thought she'd been crying. Her eyes were all red, her face pink and puffy. Then she rubbed her eyes and covered a yawn.

"Sorry," she said. "I was taking a nap."

It hit me she had to be as tired as I was, maybe more tired, with her future hanging in the balance. If she were convicted, she'd be doing real time. Death was off the table for a minor defendant, even one charged as an adult, but she could end up with a life sentence if worse came to worst.

"I won't take too much time." I steered her toward the kitchen. "You want something to eat? Maybe a coffee?"

She plopped down at the table. "No, I'm okay." The puppies had followed us, and now they nosed up to her, sniffing her pockets for hidden treats. She petted them absently. "Is this about Ian?"

"It's about his testimony, and your alibi. He's brought it up now, and it's part of the record. And as it stands…"

"It sounds like a lie."

I nodded. "As far as your defense goes, that leaves us two choices. First, I can go on with what I have. I can point the jury to your lack of injuries, and the long list of other people with motives who were never investigated. I can bring up the lack of physical evidence—but it's going to look bad that you were on scene, and even worse that you initially lied about it, making it seem like you had something to hide."

Zoey stared at the table. "And my other choice?"

"Your other choice is, you can take the stand. You can tell your story in your own words. What you saw. What you heard."

"But then, doesn't the other side get to go at me?"

"Yes, the State would have the right to cross-examine."

"So he could ask me about—about everything, and no matter what he asked, I'd have to tell the truth?"

"Yes. And he likely knows you asked for court documents, so your parents' abuse would come on the record. What they did to Dr. Harper, and what they did to you."

"Won't that make it look even more like I did it?"

I sucked air through my teeth. "I'll be honest, it might. It'll probably build sympathy for you from the jurors, but it does add to your motive."

One of the puppies was nose-bumping Zoey, and now she lifted it into her lap. She wrapped her arms around it like a child with a teddy bear.

"I don't know if I can get through it without breaking down. When I think about—about—" Her voice cracked, and she sniffled. "When I think about hearing my parents get killed, seeing Mom's body, her blood on the floor..." A shiver ran through her. The pup licked her face. She pressed her forehead to its snout and ruffled its ears. "Can I bring the dog with me?"

I chuckled. "No. But it's not the worst thing if you show some emotion. Breaking down completely might look insincere—like a performance. But no one expects you to be a robot."

"I'm scared I'll throw up, or freak out, or something."

"You can take something for nausea if that's a problem. Auntie El can take you to get a prescription."

Zoey set the pup down again and brushed hair off her sweater. "You think I should do this, get up there and testify. Don't you?"

"I'll be honest: it's almost always a mistake for a defendant to take the stand. But in this case, it *might* help, if the jury wants to believe you. But that will be a challenge, given the facts of the case. I'll prep you thoroughly, but it'll be a risk."

"But if I don't, they won't hear my side."

"They won't."

"Then everyone will know what my parents did. They'll all find out what kind of people they were." Her voice had gone quiet, her gaze faraway, as if she were no longer speaking to me. "I never wanted that. I really did love them. Like Ian said in court today. He called you those names and stuff, but that was just venting. You're still his mom, and—I mean, I'm not saying you're anything like my parents. You're not. You're a good mom. But they *are* still my parents."

I sat quietly, letting her work through what she needed to work through. This was her decision, not one I could make for her. It took a whole lot of strength to stand up to a parent, even one who was no longer present.

Zoey looked up at me. "They were bad parents, weren't they?"

"They weren't the greatest."

"They hurt a whole lot of people who didn't deserve it. Would I be able to give some of that back?"

"What?"

"The money they stole with their fake lawsuits." She wiped her eyes on the back of her hand. "If I win, and I get—if I get their estate, could I pay back the people they screwed over?"

She wouldn't have nearly enough to do that. The Conrads really did treat the lawsuits like an income stream—and it was one they weren't slow to spend. They'd had some money in savings, but not a ton, and a chunk of it would go to paying my fees. "Maybe some of them," I hedged. "But those were a lot of suits."

Zoey sat thinking, picking her shirt sleeve. After a while, she stopped and sat straight. "I want to," she said.

"You want to pay back the victims?"

"No—well, *yes*. But I meant, I want to take the stand. If I'd spoken up sooner, like with Dr. Granger, she might have reported it. And then maybe the police would have looked into what they'd done, and the whole cycle would have ended years ago. They never would have contacted Youth Rise. That man wouldn't have died. And maybe they wouldn't have died either. All keeping quiet does is get people hurt."

"So, you're sure?"

"Yes. I need to do this."

Sadness washed over me, because she was right. She needed to get up there and put herself through the wringer—to hurt herself again by laying out all the ways her parents had hurt her over the years. Whether Zoey had murdered her parents or not, this crime, this nightmare, had started with them.

"You're a strong girl," I said. "I'm proud of you."

She blinked. "You are?"

I told her I was, because it was true, and somebody had to, with her parents gone.

They'd never been there for her much at all.

29

I drove to Auntie El's farm first thing Saturday, wanting to catch Zoey while she was still fresh. But when she came out to meet me, she looked exhausted, like she hadn't slept much, or maybe at all. Her eyes were red-rimmed, her skin pale and greasy, a spray of new zits across her forehead.

I guided her through to Auntie El's living room and let her get comfortable on the couch. But when she called the dogs to her, I shooed them away.

"I need you focused wholly on trial prep."

Zoey twisted her lank hair around her fingers. "The pups help me focus. They keep me calm."

"But you won't have them when you take the stand."

She made an unhappy sound, and I took her in, her pallor, her chewed lip, the way she kept fidgeting. "You can still change your mind," I said. "You don't have to testify."

"Yeah, I do."

I leaned forward. "You really don't. And if you can't concentrate, it'll hurt more than help. If you think—"

"I can do this." She straightened up. "I was nervous last night, so I didn't sleep much. But I'm ready. I need to get up there."

I had my doubts, pretty severe ones, but I'd let Zoey decide for herself. I'd give her a taste of what she could expect, and if she crumbled, we would move on.

"Oliver's going to impeach you right off the bat. That is, he's going to establish you lied to the police, and you did it repeatedly. Kept changing your story. Speaking of which, we need to go over that."

I'd half-expected she'd crumble right there, not wanting to delve into what happened again. But she ran through it all, beginning to end, and didn't complain when I broke in with questions. I tore into her story every which way, pulled every thread I could think of, dissected the details. Throughout it all, Zoey stayed calm, and more than that, she stayed consistent.

"You can't jump around," I said, on our third run through. "If you leave out a detail, forget it. Move on. Jumping back in the story makes you look uncertain—or worse, like you're adding invented details."

Zoey huffed, but she tried again and again. And again. She was persuasive, I'd give her that. But her story was sparse. She hadn't seen much. And some of her choices would be difficult to explain.

"Oliver will go hard on you. He'll ask tough questions. Starting with, why did you flee the scene?"

Zoey just sat there, her lips a tight line. I could see she was tired, but we had to get through this.

"I need you to answer that. Why did you flee the scene?"

"Um…" She coughed. Looked down at her knees. "I don't really know why. I just, I just did."

"Were you scared if you stayed, you'd get arrested?"

"No! I don't know. I just ran. I just *did*. I don't really remember running away. I remember Mom lying there, and her blood everywhere, and then I was running out into the woods."

"So, what you're saying is, you were in shock."

"Yes! Yes, in shock. My brain was, like, fried." She covered her face with both hands. Gulped a deep breath. When she dropped her hands, her eyes had gone haunted. "I wasn't thinking, just running away."

"But you stopped running and took out your phone. You pulled up your Threads app and posted your alibi. You're saying you did that while you were in shock, eight minutes after you saw your parents killed?"

She sat silent, staring at her own knees.

"Why did you post that picture and say you were home bored?"

"Because…because…" She went for her sleeve and started picking, then jerked her hand back and slid it under her thigh. "I took out my phone to call the cops. But then it hit me, they might think *I* did it. Because I already shot Harold Rooney. So I—"

"Stop right there." I held up my hand. "Don't bring up the Rooney case, no matter what."

"But if he asks me—"

"He won't ask about that. As long as we don't bring up Harold Rooney, Oliver can't use his shooting to establish prior pattern. But once you open that door, Rooney's fair game."

"Okay, well, I thought they might think I did it. And the pic was right there when I opened my phone. So I stuck it up without really thinking."

"So you opened your Threads app, tapped on New Thread, uploaded your picture, typed out your caption, then you hit post without really thinking?"

"Um… Yeah? It's not hard. It takes like two seconds."

"Don't get sassy. The jury won't like that."

I ran her through all the ways Oliver might pick away at her, all the threads he might pull to fray her credibility. Then I tackled her texts, and what had led up to them, why she'd said her father was 'gravy-ass butt goo.' Why she'd said her mother should drive off a cliff. She held up better than I had thought she would, answering those questions calmly. Keeping her cool. But this was the easy part. The real test was coming.

"Zoey, were you ever physically abused by your parents?"

She stiffened and swallowed, not answering right away. Her voice was quiet when she finally spoke. "Yes. Yes, I was."

"What form did that abuse take?"

"It, um…it…" She closed her eyes, breathing in deep through her nose. "Is there any chance he won't ask? About abuse?"

"I don't think so," I said. "I know I would in his shoes."

"Do I have to, um…"

"What?"

"I don't know. I'm picturing all of them, the jury, the judge, everyone in the gallery hearing me say this. It feels like betraying them. Disrespecting the dead."

My heart ached for her, but I couldn't protect her here. The second she took that stand, her abuse became fair game. "Once you get up there, you can't change your mind. The judge can and will compel you to answer. If you don't want to do this—"

"No, I do." She took another big breath. "It was for their lawsuits. They didn't, like, hit me. Or...not a lot. Mom slapped me sometimes, but all moms do that, right?"

I wanted to tell her all moms do *not* slap. To hold her and comfort her like hers should've done. But she needed to feel like she would on the stand—alone, on the spot. And I needed to see her deal with that kind of pressure. I needed to gauge how she'd handle the real thing, and if she could do it without tanking our case.

"But the worst thing..." She was picking her sleeve again. "The worst thing was, um, they burned my back. I don't know what they used, but they scarred my whole back up so they could turn around and sue Dr. Karen."

"Do you still have those scars?"

"Yes."

"Do they hurt?"

She dug her nails into the meat of her arm. "Yeah, uh, they pull. Because I was a little kid when it happened. I grew, but the scar tissue isn't as stretchy. It pulls and it hurts."

"And does that make you angry?"

Zoey didn't say anything.

"Does that make you angry?"

"Yes! Yes, okay? It hurts and it looks bad, and I can't go swimming. I can't wear certain shirts, or backless dresses because I don't want people to stare or ask questions. And all so my parents could... Yeah.

I was mad when I found out it was their fault. But I'd known for months. I was going to tell on them."

"But you didn't, did you?"

"No, because—"

"You thought they were trying to do it again, didn't you? When they decided to send you to Utah?"

"Would you quit talking over me?" She shut her mouth with a snap. Hid her face in her hands. "I can't do that, can I? Yell at Mr. Altman?"

"No, you cannot. And he *will* cut you off. He's going to pelt you with yes or no questions, trying to force you to give answers without nuance or context. But that doesn't mean you have to answer that way. You can respond with a narrative that tells the full story."

"And if he cuts me off anyway?"

"I'll come back to those questions on my redirect. You *will* have a chance to explain your side—but losing your cool will be a big strike against you."

"I won't," Zoey said. "I'll breathe like you taught me. But what I keep coming back to is, why would they do that?"

"It's just how it works. How lawyers question witnesses. We want to elicit a particular story, so we ask questions whose answers support what we—"

"No." Zoey stopped picking and smoothed out her sleeve. "I mean, why would my parents…what's *wrong* with me? You'd never hurt Ian to win a settlement. Nobody's parents I know would do that. So what's wrong with *me* that mine didn't love me enough to care more about keeping me safe than getting money? That they would use me, and let me get hurt?" She was crying now, huge, messy tears. "I don't get what I did."

To hell with keeping up the pressure. I couldn't just sit there and watch her cry over this. "You didn't do anything." I whistled the puppies in, and they jumped on the couch. Zoey gathered them to her and kissed all their heads, wiping her eyes on their black and gold scruffs.

"We should break here," I said. "It's time for lunch. Why don't I call Ian, and you can get some pizza?"

She looked up, forlorn. "But did I do okay?"

"Yes. You did well. We still have work to do, but right now, I want you to go and get pizza. And remember, it's not you. This was all them. There's *nothing* you did, or ever could have done, that would make you deserve that from your parents. There is nothing wrong with you. Do you hear me? Nothing." I knew she wouldn't believe me, not yet. It would take years of therapy to close up that wound. But I still needed to say it.

"I hear you," she said. "I wish you were my mom."

It was all I could do not to break down right there. Tonight, I'd go home and hug Ian tightly, and make all his favorites—no. Get Sean to make them. Sean's cooking was better. We'd all eat together, and I wouldn't nag. I wouldn't ask about college or Ian's plans. Did he know I'd still love him if he didn't go to college? He had to know that, but did he? Did he?

I stepped into the hallway to wipe my eyes and to call Ian to pick Zoey up. The two of them left, and I sat with the puppies. I felt like I'd just been hit by a car—aching everywhere, knocked around, winded. I remembered wondering the same thing when Dad hit the bottle: why was I not worth getting clean for? Why didn't he love me enough to be there? But he'd never hurt me like the Conrads hurt Zoey. I couldn't even imagine the depth of her pain.

My phone buzzed, and I sniffed hard and cleared my throat. I answered, still hoarse.

"What's up, Alia?"

"I've got something, and I think you're going to like it! No, I *know* you are. This is huge." Her excitement was palpable, but all I felt was hollow. I pinched my own arm, trying to focus.

"What have you got?"

"Okay, so the traffic cams were a non-starter. No speeders, nothing, all through that night. But you know the Harrogates, out past my dad's place?"

"The ones with the pit bulls and the barbed wire fence?"

"Yeah, that's them. So, my dad's pretty tight with them, and he talked them into talking to me. And I finally convinced them to let me look through their cam footage. I don't mean just a Ring cam. I mean, they've got…man. They've got high-end cameras *all* through their property, and the one on the driveway captured our guy."

My heart leaped. "Hoodie Guy? So, he exists?"

"Yeah! Or, I think so. It's around the right time. This crappy red pickup goes by, and the driver's wearing, that's right, a black hoodie."

"Did you get his license plate?"

"That's the bad news. It rained the night before, and you know how those back roads get. His license plate was covered in mud."

"Still, this is good. This could be something."

"I'm going to see if I can track down that pickup."

"Perfect. Call me the second you find anything."

I went to hang up, but Alia stopped me. "Hold on. Before you go, are you okay? You sounded weird when you answered the phone."

I swallowed. I wasn't okay at all, but now wasn't the time. "I'm all right," I said. "Just a rough start with Zoey."

"Well, get some lunch. I'll talk to you later."

I hung up and sat there. Eating didn't sound very appealing, but I had the defense of a lifetime coming up Monday. I owed it to Zoey to go into that strong.

30

I slept late on Sunday. Well, late for me. I woke around eight, sore and headachey, to discover Sean had brought me breakfast in bed.

"What's the occasion?"

"No occasion," he said. He leaned down and kissed me on top of my head. "Ian's out for the day, if you have work to do later."

I took a bite of my toast, but my stomach felt queasy. Ian was with Zoey, because this might be their last chance. Tomorrow, I'd get up and mount my defense. We'd have a verdict by the end of the week, and the odds were high that would be guilty. The kids were celebrating her freedom while they still could.

I managed one piece of toast and a few bites of eggs, then I headed downstairs to work on my closing. A lot of my argument would depend on Alia, and whether she could track down that old red pickup. Without that pickup, I didn't have much. I had the police investigation, focused solely on Zoey despite her parents having numerous other enemies. I had her lack of injury after the fight. Other than that, I had a wing and a prayer.

I dove in anyway and worked through the morning, so absorbed I barely noticed Sean making lunch. He set a sandwich in front of me.

"Hey. Time to eat."

"Thanks, hon." I went to pull him in for a hug, and as I did, I spotted movement. A human-shaped shadow out on the deck. "Is somebody out there?"

"Yeah, uh, your dad? He's been here all morning."

I rubbed my hip, groaning. "All morning? Why?"

"He's fixing the deck railing."

I bit my tongue on a sharp remark. Sean had said he'd fix that. What was he thinking, springing Dad on me today of all days?

Sean moved behind me and massaged my tense shoulders. He thumbed the kinks out of my stiff, aching neck. "I asked him to do it so I could take care of you. Besides, he owes you."

I leaned into Sean's hands, going limp. Losing focus. My annoyance drained away and I let myself drift. Sean had a point. It felt good to be cared for, good to have family who'd pitch in and help. Maybe it wasn't too late for me and Dad. We'd never get those years back he'd spent in the bottle, but we still had time left to build something new.

"Thank you," I said. "For always being here."

Sean started to say something, but the back door slid open, Dad letting himself in.

"Hope I'm not interrupting."

"No. I'm on lunch." I took a bite of my sandwich, egg, and bacon on pumpernickel. My favorite comfort food.

"How's everything going with the big case?"

"It's going all right," I said, not wanting to get into it. "How's the deck coming?"

"Looking real good. I fixed up your railing, and now I'm straightening that crooked step."

"You don't have to do that."

"Yeah, I do. Can't have you slipping next time it rains." He went to the fridge and got out two Cokes, and passed one to me and took one for himself. "I was thinking next week, if you don't mind—"

My phone buzzed, and I held up one finger. "Hey, Ian. What's happening? You kids need a ride?"

"Mom…"

All the hairs rose on the back of my neck. "Ian, what's wrong?"

"We're at the hospital. Zoey, she's hurt."

I jumped up. "What happened?"

"A hit-and-run." Ian's voice cracked. "They won't tell me anything. You need to come."

I was already hustling for the front door, Sean trailing after me, followed by Dad. "Did you see who hit her?"

"No. I don't know. I…I couldn't focus on anything but her. She wouldn't wake up. Are you on your way?"

I had one shoe on already and was chasing the other. "I'll be there in five—no, ten minutes." I wanted to tell him she'd be okay, but I had no way of knowing if that was true. All I could do was get there ASAP.

"What's happening?" said Sean, as I grabbed for my coat.

"A hit-and-run. Zoey got hurt."

"How about Ian?"

"He's fine. Just scared. Listen, can you drive? My leg is all stiff."

Sean drove us over in record time. Ian was waiting outside the ER. When he saw me, he ran to me like a little kid. I went to hug him, but he latched onto my arm and pulled me forward.

"You have to come quick. They won't talk to me."

I'd called Auntie El on my way over, in case they wouldn't let me in to see Zoey. She was Zoey's legal guardian for now. But I didn't see her, so I headed inside, leaving Sean to grab her when she arrived. I strode up to the charge nurse with a confident smile.

"I'm Maggie Gallagher, Zoey Conrad's lawyer. Can I get an update on her condition?"

The nurse was a big man, but I could see he was nervous. "Are you her guardian?"

"No, but I've called her, and she's on her way. I'd like to be able to give her an update."

"Let me just, uh—I need to check with her doctor." He picked up his desk phone and tapped in an extension. I slid my arm around Ian, who was fidgeting, restless. Behind us, the doors whooshed open and cold air rushed in, along with Sean and Auntie El. I waved at the nurse to catch his attention.

"This is her guardian, Louise O'Brien."

He set down the phone. "Ms. O'Brien can head back, but only her. The rest of you can wait in the seats over there."

Auntie El glanced at Ian before turning back to the nurse. "How is she doing?"

"She's conscious," he said. "She's doing well. They're just getting a cast on her, then she can go home."

Ian slumped against me, lax with relief. I hugged him tighter, breathing easier myself. We made our way to the seats and settled in to wait.

"I thought she was dead at first," Ian said. "That truck came out of nowhere. And she went flying into the ditch."

"A truck?" I sat straighter. "What kind of truck?"

"I don't know, like a pickup?"

"What color?"

"Red."

I grabbed him by the arms. "Red? Are you sure?"

"Yeah, a red pickup. Kind of beat up."

I remembered the clip Alia sent over: a ratty red pickup, patchy with rust. "Did you see the driver?"

"No, just the truck. And just for a second as he sped off. I went straight for Zoey, so…"

"You did the right thing." I hugged him again, tears in my eyes. How close had he come to getting hit too? Knocked into the ditch right beside Zoey?

Auntie El came back out and plopped down across from us. "It's only her wrist that's broken, thank goodness. She's bruised and banged up, and she has a sore head, and the doc said to watch her for a concussion. But as soon as her cast sets, she can come home."

"Did she say if she saw the driver?"

Auntie El glowered at me. "*That's* your first question?"

"He might be her best shot at staying out of jail."

Ian jerked upright. "What?"

"You should talk to Officer Bligh," said Auntie El. "He was just in there getting her statement."

"Without me!" I jumped up, then sat down again. She'd said *was*, past tense. The damage was done. Not that there ought to be too much damage. Zoey was the victim here, not a suspect. Still, I'd have to grill her about that conversation. If Officer Bligh had brought up her murder case, even in passing, that could be grounds for a mistrial.

"But she's really okay?" Ian leaned forward. Auntie El took his hand.

"Yeah, hon. She's fine. Why don't you come back with us when we're done here, and you two kids can watch some TV?"

"She shouldn't watch TV with a concussion," said Sean.

"Okay, then they can play some board games. I'll whip up some comfort food and we'll all do game night."

"I can't," I said. "I need to get to the office."

"Well, the rest of us. You're in, right?" She pointed at Sean.

"Yes, ma'am."

Auntie El turned to Ian. "And how about your grandpa?"

But Ian didn't seem to hear her. He was staring at me, eyes round and shocked. "Mom? Are you saying you know who did this? Was it the killer? The guy in the hoodie?"

I stood up. "I promise, we'll talk once I've figured some things out. But right now, I need to get to the office, and you need to stay here. Zoey needs you."

"She was right." Ian's voice was thick, choked with anger. "She knew if she said anything, he would find out. He must've read in the papers she saw the real killer. Now he's coming to get her, and—"

"Ian. *Ian.*" I crouched down in front of him. "No one's coming to get her. She'll be safe on the farm."

"And Carl will be there," said Auntie El. "Why don't you text Grandpa, and he'll come out too?"

Ian was breathing fast. Sean rubbed his back.

"The dogs'll be up there. They'll bark up a storm if anyone comes."

Ian relaxed a little at that, and pulled out his phone. I stood feeling useless as he sent his text. Useless, and pulled in a dozen directions, none of which left me time to comfort my son. But there was one thing I could say before leaving.

"Ian."

"Yeah, Mom?"

"I'm proud of you."

He smiled just a little, and then his smile broadened—but not for me. They'd wheeled Zoey out. Ian jumped up and ran to her. Auntie El followed, and they both helped her up and steadied her on her feet. She stumbled and laughed, and Ian laughed with her, and then they hugged right there in the lobby.

If this was to be Zoey's last free weekend, at least she was spending it surrounded by family. Not her family, granted, but mine was pretty great.

31

It snowed hard on Monday, and the courthouse was chilly, its rattling old heaters struggling to keep up. Zoey sat shivering at the defendant's table. I took off my jacket, and she put it on.

"Won't you be cold?"

"No. I run hot." Especially on a high-stress day like today, with Zoey's whole future hanging in the balance. I'd noticed the jury checking out her cast, and the bandage on her brow where she'd hit a rock. She was pretty bruised up, and in a way, that worked for me. It gave the jury a notion of how fragile she was. How easily Paul Conrad could have subdued her if she'd been his attacker. When we rose for Judge Yost, she swayed, off-balance. When we sat, she cradled her broken wrist to her chest.

I called my first witness—Dr. Gillies, the forensic expert I'd used to shoot down Oliver's reconstruction. Now, I needed him to do the same for the jury: rip into the evidence and taint it with doubt.

"Dr. Gillies, you've examined the evidence from the Conrads' crime scene?"

"I have, at length."

"And you've reviewed the state's analysis of said evidence?"

"I have." He shifted, impatient, and I moved it along.

"Did you agree with the State's findings?"

"Their findings, yes. Their conclusions, not so much."

I frowned at his pedantry. He was losing the jury. "Could you explain what you mean by that?"

"I mean, they did a fine job documenting the scene. The evidence was well-preserved and well-labeled. Where I have a problem is with their analysis. They drew some conclusions I wouldn't have."

I glanced at the jury. They were glazing over. But I didn't need them on his side. I needed them on *mine*. And the best way to do that was to say what they were thinking, to cut through the jargon.

"So, they were guessing?"

Gillies huffed, put out by my simplification, then seemed to remember he was on my side. "Not guessing, per se. But they made some leaps not supported by evidence."

"Such as?"

Dr. Gillies reached for his notes. "One major conclusion the State drew was that the killer was between five foot four and five foot seven. To reach that conclusion, they'd have studied the same evidence we did: the victims' locations, the trajectories the bullets took through their bodies, then the angles those bullets took into the walls." He had slides to illustrate, and he brought up the first one, a diagram of the shot that took out Paul Conrad. A red line showed the bullet fired nearly straight on, through Paul Conrad's throat and into the wall.

"The State saw the wound trajectory through Mr. Conrad's throat, at a slight upward angle, as though fired from below. From that, they concluded that the shooter was smaller than the victim, estimating their height between five four and five seven. But the bullet passed cleanly through Mr. Conrad's throat without hitting bone, which might have changed its trajectory." He switched to a new slide, a diagram of the bullet's path. "You can see here the slight upward angle, and you might assume he was shot from below. The State also made assumptions based on the angles the bullets took through the wall."

He changed slides again, to a shot of the wall. "I wasn't satisfied with the State's analysis of those angles. You can see in their photo, the drywall had crumbled, making the angles of the gunshots difficult to measure. But I went to the crime scene and did my own analysis, and I found one of the bullets had passed through the drywall." He switched to a new slide of a wooden beam. "It had lodged here, in this crossbeam. The State's expert failed to measure that angle, but I measured it, and it was only seven degrees, which points to a taller shooter.

"From this evidence, I'd conclude the trajectory of the bullet through Paul Conrad's throat had more to do with his position relative to the shooter than their respective heights. He may have crouched. Ducked. Looked up or down. The evidence available, in my opinion, does not point to a small-statured shooter."

"What about Lorraine Conrad, the evidence there?"

"Mrs. Conrad was shot through the back of her skull. From stippling to her scalp—stippling being small burns from gunpowder hitting the skin—we determined the killer stood directly behind her and fired from a distance of under two feet. The State looked at the downward angle of the bullet's path through her brain and assumed she had bent down to unlock the door."

"And you don't agree?"

"Again, there's insufficient evidence to support that conclusion. She *may* have bent down and been shot from above, or she may simply have *looked* down, while standing upright. If she was crouching, the killer would have been smaller. If she was standing, we'd expect someone taller. But the bullet, in this case, didn't exit her head. It didn't lodge in the door, so we don't have that angle. We can't determine the killer's height from this evidence."

Oliver tried to shake Gillies on cross, but this time his ego worked in my favor. He'd anticipated Oliver would revisit his prior blunder, the mislabeled evidence that'd led to a retrial, and had come prepared with a cold retort.

"That was a clerical error, not a procedural one, and in the years since, it has not been repeated. We have more checks now when we handle evidence, and I'd be glad to walk you through those in detail."

"No need," said Oliver, moving on fast. "You said you couldn't determine the shooter's height from the evidence available?"

"I said the evidence didn't support the State's determination."

"Can you say, to a certainty, the shooter's height was *not* between five four and five seven?"

"No."

He left it at that, and I called Hugh Barlow, the lawyer who'd represented the Conrads in most of their suits.

"Mr. Barlow, how long did you work for the Conrads?"

"I've represented them in various matters since 2002."

"What types of matters?"

"Well, they first hired me to draw up their wills. Then, a year later, they had an issue with, ah…" He scratched at his chin. "I've represented them in various civil matters."

"Civil matters, like personal lawsuits?"

"Yes, some lawsuits. Some personal injury, property damage."

"How many lawsuits were there exactly?"

Barlow looked uncomfortable. He shifted in his seat. "Sixty-four claims over two decades."

"In your experience, is that a high number of lawsuits for one set of complainants?"

"It's, yes, quite high for two complainants. But in my view at the time, all the cases had merit. I investigated, of course, looked into each claim. And I saw no reason not to move forward."

I let Barlow keep talking, covering his own ass. He wasn't saying anything of particular value, but the jury was picking up on his discomfort. I wanted them to see that and draw their conclusions, not just about Barlow, but the Conrads as well.

"Did you personally receive any threats from these defendants, or witness any retaliation against the Conrads?"

Barlow cleared his throat again. "Yes, I had threats come into my office. I helped the Conrads file restraining orders, and one of the defendants vandalized their garage. I documented the damage at their request."

"Can you describe the damage?"

"They'd spray-painted a word I'm not comfortable repeating."

"A profanity, then?"

"Yes, a profanity."

"Did you file harassment suits on the Conrads' behalf, against anyone they had recently sued?"

"Yes, twice. The first time was in 2016. The second time was two years after that, and covered both harassment and property damage."

"Property damage?"

"A brick through their window with a note attached. The note contained what the Conrads construed as a death threat."

"What did it say?"

"It said 'rot in hell, f-ers.'"

I let that sit a moment, then I went on. "Mr. Barlow, did any defendant reach out to you directly after being sued by the Conrads?"

"A few times. I told them it wasn't appropriate."

"And what was the tenor of these encounters?"

Barlow shrugged, palms up. "They were…upset."

"Did one of them throw a paperweight into your fish tank?"

Barlow's brows beetled. "A paperweight, yes."

"Why did she do that?"

"Because…" He exhaled, thick with frustration. "The Conrads' young daughter, that is, your client, trespassed on the defendant's property. She fell and hurt herself climbing the fruit trees, and the Conrads sued under the attractive nuisance doctrine. After paying her settlement, the defendant went bankrupt. The bank foreclosed on her home. But she was behind on her mortgage long before that. The suit from the Conrads was—"

"Who was the defendant in this case?"

"Margaret, ah…" He scratched his head. "Sorry, Margaret Lawrence. It's been a while."

"Margaret Lawrence." I paused a moment to let that sink in. I knew a lot of the jurors would know who she was—on-and-off homeless, on-and-off drunk. Angry for sure, and she blamed the Conrads.

"Was she the only one to lose a home or business as a result of the Conrads' lawsuits?"

"No, she was not."

"Was she the only one to respond with anger or violence?"

"No."

I had him go through the rest of the cases, every suit that'd resulted in violence or threats. The jury listened intently; these were people they knew. People they worked with, or saw around town. I could see they were surprised by some of the names.

When I was finished, Oliver rose and set to work. "Mr. Barlow, you mentioned in the attractive nuisance case, the defendant from *this* case was injured in a fall. How long ago was that?"

"Thirteen years ago."

"So, the defendant was three?"

Barlow shifted. His chair creaked. His face had gone red. "Yes, around that."

"And she was injured?"

"She broke her leg."

A couple of jurors glanced Zoey's way, taking in her cast again, and her darkening bruises. Oliver let them. I knew what he wanted—to let them see her pain, and feel it themselves, and then imagine it curdling to anger.

"Was that the only time Miss Conrad was injured, leading the Conrads to file a lawsuit?"

"No."

"How many other times did they sue because of her injuries?"

"On three other occasions. Four lawsuits, total."

Oliver picked through all four, making Barlow detail how Zoey was injured, how much the Conrads won. He never said outright, or even implied, that the Conrads had purposely put Zoey in danger—much less that they ever harmed her themselves—but as he went on, I could see the jury adding up two and two on their own. By the time he stepped down, he'd achieved his objective: casting the Conrads as monsters and Zoey their victim. A victim who, he'd have them believe, finally snapped.

I had time for one last witness, and I called Alia to testify to the threats she'd found to the Conrads online. But Oliver objected on grounds of hearsay, and Judge Yost backed him up.

"Unless you want to subpoena those people directly, I'm ruling this hearsay and inadmissible."

I let Alia go, cursing myself. It had been a gamble bringing her in, but I'd hoped Yost would side with me, and let her speak. Now she'd wasted an hour she could've spent tracking Hoodie Guy, and I was no closer to making my case.

Zoey was subdued on the ride home, smoothing her sleeve out where she'd picked at it during court. She'd plucked the hem loose, and now it hung crooked. "Sometimes, I think I *did* do it," she said.

I choked on thin air. Was she confessing? "I could try for a plea deal," I gasped through coughs.

"No, I mean, I didn't—I know I didn't. But sometimes it feels like it might as well be the truth. Everyone thinks it, like OJ Simpson. He was acquitted, but ask anyone and they'll all say he did it. He killed his wife."

"That's not—" I coughed again. "That's *nothing* like this."

"I know, but I'm so tired of feeling ashamed. Of how they all look at me, like I'm this freak."

"Get a good rest tonight." I pulled up to the farmhouse. "Play with those puppies and eat a good dinner, and get all your frustrations out. Punch a pillow, maybe. Then tomorrow, I need you to come into court and tell your story just like we practiced."

"Like we practiced," she echoed. "I can do that." She zipped up her coat and jumped out of the car, and I yelled out after her to get lots of sleep. As if that would make this any easier.

Tomorrow would be the worst day of Zoey's young life, next to the day she'd lost her parents.

32

Zoey on the stand was like an old Western. Like the lone cowboy up on his horse, lined up against a gauntlet of bristling guns. One sudden move and the bullets would fly.

I banished the image. Drew a deep breath. Zoey wasn't a cowboy, but that didn't mean her life wasn't at stake, in its own way. Oliver would savage her, no stopping that. But if I guided her through this just right, *just* right, she might have a chance yet to carry the day.

"Can you state your name for the record, and tell us why you're here today?"

"I'm Zoey," she said, her voice soft but steady. "Zoey Conrad, and I'm here because…" She looked down and swallowed. Folded her hands. "I want to tell all the truth. Not—not just parts of it."

"What do you mean by 'just parts of it?'"

"I mean, how the witnesses—" She plucked at her sleeve. "They were only able to tell parts of it, the parts they knew. I saw the whole thing. Or, I mean, I heard it."

"So, why don't you tell us, right from the start?" I spoke gently, smiling like it was just us. Holding her gaze to keep her eyes off the jury. Normally, I'd want a witness to connect with the jury, look at them, confide in them. Get them on her side. But Zoey was fragile. I couldn't risk them distracting her. "What time did you go home that night?"

"Around half past nine." She licked her lips and went for her sleeve again, then stilled her hands with a visible effort. "I went to get a few things. My clothes. A few books. I was staying at the RV park—I did that sometimes. People leave their RVs there stored for the winter, and I sometimes hang out there when I need my space."

"What did you find when you got home?"

"I found my parents up in my room. They had my suitcase out on my bed."

"And what were they doing with your suitcase?"

"They were packing my things. They said they were sending me to this school in Utah. Like a reform school. I—I said no. We fought. I mean, we argued. Not a physical fight. But I said some things, and Mom ran out. And that's when Dad said he heard something downstairs." She was shaking already, and hugging herself. Her teeth were chattering, making her hard to hear. This was already rough on her, telling her story. And when Oliver got to her, it would get ten times worse. I could only hope she was ready for that.

"Take a deep breath," I said.

She sucked air through her nose.

"That's good. One more."

Zoey breathed in, then out, and slowly calmed down. I walked her through her testimony as gently as I could, getting her to describe what she'd heard, what she'd seen. The man in the hoodie. She cried through a lot of it, but she didn't shut down the way I'd worried she would.

"Mom ran," she said, with a loud sniff. "Not to escape, but like, to get to Dad. I heard her scream, and I knew he was... Gone. Then she screamed again, and I heard that man run after her. Then gunshots. I couldn't do anything. I..."

"Take your time."

Zoey gulped in a big breath. "I couldn't move. I could still hear him down there, and I thought he'd come up. I thought he would kill me, but he ran out the back instead. I waited a minute, then I ran to Mom. I knew Dad was dead, but I hoped she might..." She scrubbed at her eyes and sat blinking hard. "I saw where he'd shot through the back of her head."

I waited to see if she'd say anything else, and when she didn't, I prodded her on. "What did you do after that?"

"I ran out through the side door and into the woods. I thought he might still be out there, so I kept running. It hit me I maybe should call the police, but when I pulled my phone out, I got scared. So I posted instead, what I wished was true."

"What did you post?"

"That I was home bored. In the RV. If I *had* been, I'd never have seen..." Her face crumpled and she hunched up, hiding her eyes. I glanced at the jury and saw we were losing them. Their sympathy was gone, replaced with confusion. Zoey's "home bored" post just didn't make sense to them. Its content, its timing, that she'd done it at all—everything about it bothered them. It still came across as an attempt at an alibi.

"Zoey, ah..." I paused. I could make this make sense to them. But in order to do so, I'd need to bring in the Rooney case. I'd fought hard to exclude that at our pretrial hearing, and with good reason. Oliver could use it to establish a pattern, to paint Zoey as a habitual violent offender.

"Ms. Gallagher?" Judge Yost was giving me a strange look.

"Sorry," I said. I *had* to explain this. If I didn't, it would hang over deliberations—this thing Zoey did that made no sense. And they all knew, anyway, she'd shot Harold Rooney. The whole county knew. I had to embrace it. "Zoey, why were you scared to call the police?"

She stared at me. I'd warned her over and over, not to bring in the Rooney case. No matter what. Now I nodded, and I heard her swallow hard.

"I got arrested before. When I shot Harold Rooney. It was self-defense, but they said it was murder."

"And what was that like for you, being arrested?"

She sniffed. "It was awful. I went to jail. That was bad, but the worst part was going to court, everyone accusing me of—of something I didn't do. Talking about me like I was this monster. The way people looked at me. I thought, I thought…" Zoey wiped her nose on the back of her hand. "I thought if the cops found out I was there, they'd do it again. Assume I was guilty. So instead of 911, I pulled up my Threads app. I'm sorry. I get it. I know it was dumb. But I knew they'd come after me, and I got scared."

Some members of the jury had softened now, but a few still looked doubtful. One older man was scratching his chin. But I wasn't done yet. I had more still to come.

"Zoey, I'm going to ask you now about something else. Are you okay to keep going?"

She nodded yes.

"I'll need a verbal response on that. Are you okay to keep going?"

"Yes," she said. I wasn't sure she'd ever be okay again, after everything she'd seen, and what she'd been through. But for now, I just had to get her through this.

"Were you injured two days ago in a hit-and-run incident?"

She nodded, then remembered. "Yes. I was hit by a truck."

"Can you describe that incident, as you recall it?"

"I was walking with Ian by Pam's Chicken. We were going for Greek food at that new place. He saw this dog and went over to pet it, and I heard an engine revving. I turned around and this pickup was swerving. I thought he was skidding, like he hit black ice, but when I jumped back, he...he followed. I screamed, then I guess that's when he hit me. I don't remember that part, or him driving off."

"Did you see the driver?"

"No, just the truck."

"And can you describe that truck?"

"Yeah, a red pickup. It looked like a farmer's truck—old, kind of dirty."

I'd called Mr. Harrogate to the stand before Zoey, the owner of the camera that'd caught the red pickup. He'd authenticated the footage, and I'd then called Officer Connor to establish chain of custody. I hadn't shown the evidence to the jury yet. Now I brought up the clip on the projector. "Have you seen this video, marked as Defense's Exhibit 114?"

"Yes."

"And can you tell us what you saw?"

"The same truck that hit me."

"Your Honor, at this time, I'd like to offer this video, marked as Exhibit 114, into evidence. As a reminder, this is home security footage taken by Joel Harrogate, on Rural Route 6 at the forty-mile marker, approximately six miles from the Conrads' home, taken at ten 10:22 p.m. on the night of the Conrads' deaths, approximately twenty minutes after the murders."

"Your Honor, I object to this evidence," said Oliver. "This is clearly a story concocted after the fact, and it's unreliable and highly prejudicial."

"Overruled," said Judge Yost. "The video's in. You may cross on its reliability, counsel."

The jury leaned in as I started the clip. I could sense their curiosity and their burgeoning hope. Juries didn't love slapping kids with life sentences, especially girls. I could feel their wheels spinning: could this give them an out? Could this be their reason to let Zoey go?

The clip was high quality as security feeds went: hi-res, full color, and fairly well-lit. At first, all it showed was Rural Route 6, a ribbon of dirt road flanked by high trees. Then headlights flared, and the picture went white. When it cleared, a red pickup sped into view, mud spraying up as it ran through a puddle. It burst past the camera, which caught a shot of the driver—a hunched, hooded figure gripping the wheel. Then he was gone. I played it back quarter-speed, pausing when I got to the frames with the driver. I turned to Zoey.

"Is this the same vehicle that hit you?"

"Yes. That's the one."

"How do you know?"

"See that rust?" She pointed at a rust patch by the front fender. "I saw that same rust when I tried to jump back. Plus, it's all banged up, like the one that hit me."

A murmur ran through the jury box, drawing a glare from Judge Yost.

"Thank you, Miss Conrad. That's all for this witness."

I sat, knowing I'd done the best job I could. Got the jury on Zoey's side as far as they'd go. Oliver's job now was to undo all that, and I could see from his posture he was confident he could do it. He approached Zoey, smiling, a show for the jury, clearly signaling that *what's about to happen is not an attack*. But it would be, a brutal one, and I felt sad for Zoey. She'd done a brave thing, getting up on the stand. Now she would pay the price for her courage.

"Miss Conrad, the morning after the murders, you spoke to your boyfriend, Ian Gallagher, correct?"

"Yes."

"What did you tell him?"

"I told him, um…" Zoey glanced at me. "I told him I thought I needed a lawyer."

"And what did the two of you decide to tell your lawyer? About where you were and what you were doing?"

Zoey swallowed. "We decided to tell her I was with Ian. That we went to the RV and played Switch."

"Was that true?"

"No."

"And where did you tell Ian you actually were?"

"I told him I had a fight with my parents, then I ran back to the RV."

"Was *that* true?"

"No."

"Did you know Ian would lie for you, to the police?"

Zoey went for her sleeve, then clasped her hands tight. "He said he would, yes. I told him not to at first."

"At first?"

"He said they wouldn't investigate if we told them the truth, and I thought if they looked, they would find the real killer."

"So you agreed to this lie?"

"Yeah, I agreed, but I—"

"When it came out you *had*, in fact, returned to your parents' house, did you come forward about seeing the killer?"

"No. I just stuck to what I first told Ian, that we fought and I ran off before the—the murders."

"Then the Tulleys' Ring cam revealed *that* was a lie, and you're telling us now, you saw the real killer. A killer in black, who drove a red pickup. Miss Conrad, that's also a lie, isn't it?"

Zoey shook her head wildly. "No! No, it's true."

"Or, did you get in an accident and see your chance to spin yet another of your tall tales? You'd have us believe the killer came back for you—in broad daylight, on Main Street, he ran you down?"

She sniffed. "That's what happened."

"Is it? I wonder." Oliver stalked back to loom over Zoey. "Miss Conrad, you first claimed you were home bored. Then you claimed you were there at the scene of the crime, but you left before ten. Now you're saying you *were* there and you saw the killer, and now he's come back to finish the job. That's three lies just about where you were at the time of the murders, and now you expect us to believe this story over your other ones?"

Zoey sat silent.

"Miss Conrad?"

"Yes, because it's true."

"But your other stories weren't?"

"No, because—"

"Miss Conrad, did your parents ever physically abuse you?"

Zoey recoiled at that, with an audible gasp. I'd prepared her for this, and for the grilling to follow, but Oliver's abrupt change of tacks had rattled her too much, and she was struggling to hold herself together. She opened her mouth and closed it again.

"Miss Conrad, were your parents physically abusive?"

"I... I don't..." She pressed her lips shut. Judge Yost tapped his gavel to get her attention.

"The witness will answer the question."

"I'm sorry," said Zoey. "I'm just, I'm not sure... Mom slapped me sometimes."

Oliver pressed his advantage. "Anything else?"

Zoey coughed. "I don't know."

"Remember, you are under oath."

Zoey closed her eyes. Bent over the witness stand. After a long moment, she straightened up again. "She burned me. Mom did. With some kind of chemical."

The courtroom erupted in sudden chatter, incredulous voices, horrified gasps. Judge Yost banged his gavel louder this time.

"Order, please. Order. I'll have order in this court."

The crowd settled down, and Oliver resumed his attack. "When did this happen, and when did you find out it wasn't an accident?"

"It happened when I was six. I had a rash, and we went to the doctor, who gave us a cream for it. Mom swapped out my prescription with something that scarred my whole back up. I found out last summer, when I heard them talking. They were thinking of doing the same thing again, with Dad's omeprazole, to his GI doc."

"How did that feel, to find out what they'd done to you?"

Zoey sniffled. "I didn't want to believe it at first, so I reviewed the court transcripts."

"And what was your reaction based on your review?"

"It was clear to me that my parents intentionally burned me."

"And how did *that* feel, being convinced that your parents intentionally harmed you?"

"It hurt. I felt horrible. I felt like…why? Was that all I was to them, a prop for their lawsuits?"

Oliver leaned in. "Did you confront them?"

"No. Or, well, yes." Zoey squirmed, and I willed her to breathe. We'd been through all this, over and over. All she had to do was stick to the truth. But I could see her coming apart at the seams, losing her grip on her tenuous calm. Sensing her panic, Oliver steamed in.

"When did you confront them?"

"The night…"

"What night?"

"The night of the… The night they were killed."

I coughed to hide a gasp. She hadn't said *that* before, not once in the hundred times we'd been through her story. All she'd told me was that they'd fought about Utah.

"You confronted your parents the night they were killed?"

"They were sending me to reform school so I'd get hurt. So they could sue and get more money. I told them I knew what they were planning—and that I wasn't going to play along this time. I said I was leaving, and I—I yelled at them. My last words to them were yelling." It came spilling out of her, her sadness, her guilt, not for the murders, but the things she had said. But to the jury, it looked just as bad. I saw outrage on every face in the jury box and even though the outrage was *for* Zoey, not *at* her, it would still work against her. The jury was full of anger at what her parents had done to her. Anger, like they'd assume Zoey had felt on that night, after learning how her parents planned to use her again. Like she *had* felt then, like anyone would.

Anger that fit nicely with Oliver's narrative: pushed to her limit, she had finally snapped.

On redirect, I did my best to rehabilitate Zoey. To draw out her hurt in place of her anger. But the damage was done now, despite my best efforts. Turning the tide would depend on my next witness.

"I'd like to call Pam Ackerman to the stand."

Oliver rose. "I object to this witness. She's not on the list the defense provided, and I don't see her relevance to this case. Even if we assume Miss Conrad was intentionally struck, there's no evidence whatsoever suggesting a connection to this case, Your Honor."

"Your Honor, Pam Ackerman runs a business on Main Street, which looks out on the scene of my client's hit-and-run. She witnessed the incident from start to finish, and the jury has a right to hear what she saw."

"I'll allow an hour's recess while the State interviews the witness. But when we come back, she will testify."

I'd have liked to spend that hour comforting Zoey, but instead, I focused on my strategy. My case hung in the hands of Pam Ackerman, fried chicken queen of Kerry, Ohio. She could win the day for me or she could tank me, depending on how she came off to the jury. When I'd interviewed her, she had been chatty. A little *too* chatty. Prone to tangents. I'd need to keep that in check, keep her focused. Concise.

She waved at the jury as she took the stand, and a couple waved back, before remembering where they were and wilting, embarrassed. Everyone knew Pam, and she knew everyone, and I knew I could play that trust in my favor.

"Ms. Ackerman—"

"Oh, Pam, hon. Call me Pam."

"Sure, of course, Pam. Let me start with an easy one: do you run Pam's Chicken on Regis and Main?"

"You know I do, Ms. Double Big Bumper, extra coleslaw."

A snicker went up, and I chuckled too, even as I knew I needed to move things along. This was still a courtroom. I needed less personality now, and more focus. "You make great chicken, Pam, but for the sake of our records, I need you to give me a clear yes or no."

She sobered up. "Yes. I do run Pam's Chicken."

"And were you working two days ago at 1:12 p.m.?"

"Honey, I—sorry. Yes, I was working. I worked all day yesterday, open to close."

"Did you witness an accident during your shift?"

"I saw that girl get run down right after the lunch rush."

"Could you describe for the jury what you saw?"

Pam drew herself up and the jury leaned forward, eager to hear what she had to say. She was a big talker, a big storyteller, and that could be good for me or really bad, depending on how she held up on cross.

"Well, like I said, it was just after the rush, and I was up front helping bus tables. I saw them coming, the defendant"—she nodded at Zoey, who flashed a half-smile—"and her boyfriend. They were coming up Main, and I thought I'd better keep an eye out for them. With her on trial and all, folks can be cruel."

"Yes, yes, they can. So, what happened next?"

"Her boyfriend spotted the Adlers' dang dog, out of the yard again and strolling up Main. So he went to get it, and she crossed the street."

"Who did?"

"The defendant, Miss Conrad. She was standing on the corner of Regis and Main, looking across Regis at that new little Greek place. Then I heard the truck rev, and it came flying—"

"From which direction?"

Pam looked thrown for a second, unused to being interrupted mid-story. Then she recovered herself and went on. "From back down Main. She turned around, the defendant did, and just as she turned, that truck swerved toward her. It came up on the curb and she ran away, but it swerved *again* and struck her sideways. She flew into that drainage ditch up along Regis, and the truck kept on going, never slowed down. I yelled out for Annie to come get the license plate—my waitress. She's young. She's got sharp eyes. But by the time she came running, he'd gotten away."

"What did the truck look like?"

"Red. Beat up. Maybe a Chevy."

"Beat up how?"

"Rusty, paint peeling. Dirty, as well."

Zoey had mentioned rust. These details were good. "Did you see the driver?"

"Only a glimpse. He was sort of hunched over. And he had his hood up, hiding his face."

"His hood?"

"Yeah. The driver was wearing a hoodie."

I grilled her some more on what she had seen, drawing out the details, such as how the truck had swerved twice. How it had kept coming for Zoey when she'd tried to run away. Then Oliver stood and did his best to shake her, picking on her poor eyesight and trying to cast doubt on how much she'd seen.

"Your shop is how far from the scene of the accident?"

"Across the street, so maybe twenty feet?"

"And you couldn't read the license plate from twenty feet?"

"Honey, I'm sixty. I'm in three book clubs. My eyes are *tired*."

The jury snickered again, but Oliver ignored them. "But you did see the truck bouncing up on the curb?"

"Yeah, I saw that, and I saw it swerve into her. I can see a whole truck, hon. It's the size of…a truck." That got a louder laugh, and Oliver frowned. He tried picking instead at what had happened, trying to confuse her on the order of events. But Pam had her story straight, and she stuck to it, bringing the jury along for the ride. She'd done well, but I couldn't tell if she'd done enough. Even if the hit-and-run had been on purpose—which, from her testimony, it seemed like it had—a lot of people in town didn't like Zoey. Friends of the Conrads. Folk from their church. One of them could've come for her and not been the shooter.

I called one last witness: the officer who'd taken Pam's statement that day. He confirmed he'd spoken with Pam and taken her statement, and that he had done so within ten minutes of the accident—before the red truck evidence came into court. This showed that Pam Ackerman hadn't witnessed the accident and jumped to conclusions based on that evidence.

All I had left now was my closing argument, and to stand the slightest chance, it would have to be killer.

33

I woke up sick the day of closing arguments. Headache, sore throat, blocked sinuses.

"It's not an omen," said Sean, passing me a mug of hot tea. "Drink this. It's got honey and chamomile."

I sipped my tea, and it did help somewhat. The steam cleared my stuffy nose, but not as much as I'd hoped. I'd still be "burdering" my way through closing arguments, every M coming out as a B.

Ian came down in his best suit, and I remembered I'd told him he could skip school for this.

"You've got this," he said, and went to sit next to me. I pulled his chair away.

"Not so close. I'm sick."

"You're sick today? So they'll postpone this?"

I hated to kill the light of hope in his eyes, but, no, they wouldn't. "Not for a cold."

"Can't you say it's pneumonia? Buy Alia more time?"

"It wouldn't matter. I've rested my case."

"But if they catch the real killer, won't they dismiss the charges?"

"That's a big 'if.' Go on, eat your breakfast."

We ate in silence as I ran through my closing, making a couple of last-second tweaks. Then we drove in together, me, Sean, and Ian. Zoey was waiting there with Auntie El.

"Do you think they'll come back today? I mean, with the verdict?"

"There's no way of knowing. It could take hours, even days."

"*Days?*" Zoey's face fell.

"It can happen."

We headed into the courtroom, somber and on edge. Zoey seemed listless as she took her seat, like she'd already lost hope. Judge Yost came in, and we rose, then we sat, and then it was time for Oliver's closing.

"Ladies and gentlemen of the jury, your job here today is to determine, beyond a reasonable doubt, whether Zoey Conrad is guilty of her parents' murders. All of the evidence points to her guilt. *All* of the evidence. Not some. Not most. It all points in one direction, and that direction is…" He pointed at Zoey. The jury all looked.

"First we have the Ring cam from the Tulleys' front door. It shows the defendant leaving the home, not before the murders, as she initially claimed, but five minutes *after*, out the side door—stepping over her mother lying dead on the floor.

"We have the 'home bored' post, a clumsy attempt at an alibi, posted only three minutes after Miss Conrad fled the scene—her first lie, one that she admitted to you on the stand. Formulated before her parents' bodies had gone cold.

"We have the testimony of forensic analyst Geri Rice, confirming the defendant's prints on a book used to strike Mr. Conrad. Fiber transfer from her shirt to his. The defendant's footprint on the laundry room floor. And let's look at her claims of a second shooter: if there was such a man, where is the evidence? Where are *his* prints? Fibers off *his* shirt? Where's his DNA? Nowhere, that's where. No evidence exists in this case of some supposed shooter beyond the defendant's word. And from her own testimony, we know that can't be trusted.

"As to this red truck, this hit-and-run—it's a red herring by the defense. They've seized on the defendant's latest tall tale and come up with this footage of a red truck. Is it the same red truck? She claims it is. But her claims have been lies from beginning to end. New evidence comes up; she changes her story. This is what she does. She has an accident, and she thinks, 'I can spin this to my advantage.'

"First, she was home bored. Then she was at the house, but she left early. Now she witnessed the murders, and the killer is after her. So, what's the truth? Who killed the Conrads?" Oliver paused. Turned to the jury. I watched his face fall, his eyes go sad.

"The truth is, the defendant did kill her parents. Her motive is overwhelming: a lifetime of abuse that left her scarred, physically and emotionally. She felt worthless. Rejected. Betrayed by her parents, and that night, she walked in on them betraying her again—setting her up once again to be hurt for their financial gain. She reacted with anger. With lethal violence. With the weapon she knew she'd find in her father's desk—the weapon she'd used to kill once before.

"When you deliberate, I urge you to ask yourself, what's the evidence telling you? *All* of the evidence. Taken together, it paints a clear picture: a picture of an angry young woman. A young woman who came home and fought with her parents, until their argument escalated with tragic results. The evidence in this case establishes the that the Defendant is guilty beyond a reasonable doubt. Her statements on the witness stand about some other suspect are no more credible than the previous lies she indisputably told. For these reasons, you *must* come back with a verdict of guilty."

I stood up next, and I took a deep breath, which was a foolish mistake. My nose tickled mightily. I tried to contain it, but this sneeze was coming. It would not be denied. I caught it in my elbow, an explosive *atchoo*, so loud one juror laughed. Oliver snorted.

"Excuse me," I said.

"Bless you," said Judge Yost.

I sniffed, cleared my throat, and let the silly moment pass. Then I straightened up and faced the jury. There was no point pretending that hadn't just happened, so I figured I might as well lean into it. "Moments of levity can be a relief sometimes, can't they?" I said with a smile. Some jury members smiled back at me. "But this case isn't funny," I continued, letting my smile fade, "and it's not straightforward. My colleague just told you to look at all of the evidence, and that's what I want, too. Because despite what he said, all of the evidence does *not* point to my client.

"The forensics in this case are ambiguous at best. Do they prove beyond a reasonable doubt that my client committed murder? Absolutely not. All they prove is that she lived in the house. She read a book on the shelf and left her prints on it. In the laundry, her shirt picked up fibers from other shirts. Nothing in the forensic report proves my client so much as touched the gun that night, let alone killed anyone with it.

"Per the ME's testimony, Paul Conrad was involved in a physical altercation immediately prior to his death. But the evidence does *not* support my client's involvement. She left no DNA anywhere on her father. Not a shred. The State is asking you to conclude that there was some sort of mutual combat that took place, yet not a hint of Miss Conrad's DNA was found anywhere on Mr. Conrad. Not only that, Miss Conrad didn't have a single injury to her—not a single scratch, not a bruise, nothing—when she was arrested just two days later. You saw the photographs of the scene—broken glass everywhere, furniture overturned, bruises on Mr. Conrad's knuckles that were consistent with striking someone or something with force. Yet Miss Conrad—a sixteen-year-old kid, less than five foot six, walks away completely unscathed? Paul Conrad was a grown man in excellent health. It doesn't add up. That's reasonable doubt. And when you stack it up with the forensic evidence that the State expects you to rely upon, it makes even less sense. The forensic evidence established nothing at all that was definitive. Not a single item of forensic evidence conclusively connected Miss Conrad to the murders. The evidence just isn't there.

"As for the red pickup—my colleague referred to it as a red herring, but it's a lot more than that. That pickup was caught on the night of the murders, speeding away from the Conrads' house. Later, when the news reported my client's claim of having witnessed the actions of the real killer, that same red pickup struck her on the street. Not only did it strike her, but it *swerved* to strike her—not once, but twice. Pam Ackerman described it driving up on the curb, Zoey running to avoid it, then it swerving again. A red, beat-up truck, like Zoey described. What that says to me is, the killer tried to silence her before she could testify. But he failed—and you had a chance to hear her story. To hear the truth of what happened that night."

I couldn't tell if the jury was buying it, if their frowns were the thinking kind or disbelief.

"We have two stories here, laid out in the evidence: one where my client snapped, one where she didn't. One where she killed her parents, one where she loved them and still wanted to have a relationship with them, in spite of their flaws. The evidence supports both to some degree, and that, ladies and gentlemen, is reasonable doubt. Where you find reasonable doubt, you must find not guilty. Guilty means guilty *beyond a reasonable doubt*, and that doubt exists here, so you must find not guilty." I said it one more time, "You *must* find not guilty," and then I stepped down. I'd stirred them, I thought. But had I convinced them? Had I won their hearts?

Oliver wasted his rebuttal, I felt, spending most of it defining reasonable doubt. "The standard isn't *any* doubt, any unanswered question. It's whether a reasonable person in possession of the facts, as presented, would likely conclude the defendant is guilty. The reasonable conclusion here, the right conclusion, is that she's guilty, beyond a reasonable doubt."

After, we all sat outside the courtroom, shoulder to shoulder on a bench in a hall—me, Ian, Zoey, Sean, and Auntie El.

"I can't tell how that went," said Auntie El. "You were great, though." She nudged me. "Apart from the sneeze."

That raised a chuckle, the halfhearted kind. Zoey turned to me.

"So, what now?"

"We wait." I pulled out a Kleenex and wiped my raw nose. "We head back to the office, grab coffee, and wait."

34

We sat through the morning not saying much, constantly checking our watches, our phones.

"What's too long?" said Zoey.

I'd been daydreaming—catastrophizing—but now I snapped back to reality. "What?"

"What's too long for the jury to be out? I mean, I know they *can* be out as long as it takes, but what's the cutoff for, 'uh-oh. This is bad.'"

I laughed without humor. "No cutoff. Sometimes it's quick, sometimes it's slow. It's not a good sign or a bad one. We could speculate all day, but—"

"Hello? Lunch boy!"

I groaned on reflex at Dad's voice through the door, but I reminded myself that at least he was trying. He'd never hit me or burned my back or made me feel like his love hinged on how I did in school. He'd let me down badly in other ways, but he was here now, putting in an effort.

"It's open," I called, and he let himself in, and set out a Greek feast on my cluttered desk. None of us had much appetite, but we picked at it anyway.

"This could be my last meal before I become a convict." Zoey reached for a grape leaf. "I guess I should enjoy it more, but…"

"Don't say that," said Ian.

"But it could, if—"

My phone rang, and everyone froze. I picked up, then listened, and then I hung up.

"They're back," I said.

Zoey went pale. "Does that mean, does that mean…"

"Time to head back." We all scrambled our coats on, and Dad packed our leftovers and stowed them in my mini-fridge. Everyone headed out while Dad straightened up, but I hung back a second.

"Hey, Dad?"

"Yeah, sweetheart? Everything okay?"

I laughed. "Too soon to tell. But what I wanted to say was…keep showing up."

He looked confused for a moment, and then his face lit up. "You mean that?"

"I do. It's been nice, you know, catching up."

He flung out his arms and, before I could dodge him, he had engulfed me in a great, crushing hug. I squirmed to no avail.

"Dad, no, come on!"

"I want you to know, I don't take this for granted," he said, sounding uncharacteristically solemn. I'll do what it takes to earn your trust back."

I felt myself choke up and swallowed hard. I couldn't show up for verdict with my mascara all smeared. "They're waiting. I've got to go."

He stepped back, eyes moist. "I'll always be proud of you. Always have been."

I ran out of there blinking, my heart light as air. Things weren't fully fixed between me and Dad—that would take time and effort on both of our parts—but I could see a path now to him in our lives. To me maybe trusting him someday down the line.

The courtroom was tense as Judge Yost called us to order. I studied the jury, trying to read their expressions. Juror number three had a smile on his face, but was that benevolence or only relief that it was all over? Juror number seven kept licking his teeth. A few of the others glanced at us. The rest of them didn't, keeping their eyes fixed on Judge Yost.

Judge Yost cleared his throat. "Would the foreperson please rise?"

Juror three stood, the man who'd been smiling. He didn't look at us now, and his smile had vanished.

"Have you reached a verdict?"

"We have, Your Honor." He had it in his hands, a folded sheet of paper. Now he held it out, and the bailiff took it. Zoey made a low sound, and I saw she'd gone pale. She was picking the skin on the back of her wrist, scratching in panic. I took her hand to still it.

"Please, *please*," she whispered, loud in the silence. I shushed her as Judge Yost unfolded the verdict.

"The defendant will rise."

Zoey stood, and I stood along with her, my arm around her to hold her steady. Some defendants collapsed when the verdict was read—even when it was "not guilty." The release of tension was too much for them. Judge Yost pushed his glasses up and read aloud.

"We, the jury, having been duly impaneled and sworn in the county Donahoe of the State of Ohio, find the defendant, Zoey Conrad, not guilty on the charge of aggravated murder, in the case of Paul Conrad."

A murmur ran through the court. Zoey gripped my arm. "What?"

Judge Yost banged his gavel, and then he kept reading. "We further find the defendant, Zoey Conrad, not guilty on the charge of aggravated murder, in the case of Lorraine Conrad."

Zoey stood gaping, her jaw hanging slack. "What did he…?"

"This matter is now concluded," said Judge Yost. "Members of the jury, thank you for your service."

The jurors all stood, gathering notebooks and pens. Pulling their jackets on. Chatting amongst themselves. Zoey sagged against me, but kept her feet.

"What did he say? Did he say not guilty?"

"Yeah, hon, he did." I pulled her into a hug. I figured she needed a good, tight mom hug to ground her back in reality. "It's over. You're free now."

"I can just…go?" She looked around her like she was lost. Like she had no idea what to do now. "I didn't plan anything. For what to do next. I thought, I was positive—"

"Zoey!" Ian bumped me aside in his haste to get to her, and he swept her into a fierce hug. Auntie El got in too, squeezing in from behind. They held her and rocked her, and she laughed, then she sobbed.

Auntie El pulled back first. "Don't we need to get out of here?"

Zoey sniffled and wiped her eyes. "I guess so, right?"

"Let's go breathe some free air." Ian took her arm. He walked her out of the courtroom and down the hall, out through the foyer and into the light. We stood on the courthouse steps, cameras flashing, mics coming at us from three different news crews. But if Zoey noticed them, she gave no sign. She tilted her head back and took a deep breath and smiled. It was sad and hesitant—but it was a smile.

"Thank you," she said, looking to me, then Ian, then Auntie El. "All of you. I mean it. I'd never have gotten through this without all of you. Auntie El, I don't know how I'll ever repay you for letting me stay with you. And Ian, Ms. Gallagher…" She sniffled again. "One day, I'm going to have a family like you."

The press shifted over to cluster around Oliver as he came out behind us, and I spotted Dad at the foot of the steps. He beamed up at me, and I felt sad—sad for the times we'd missed after Mom died. Sad for us both having to find our own ways through our crushing grief. But we *had* made it through, and we had a second chance. A family like we had—that didn't sound so bad.

"Come on," said Ian. "Let's go celebrate."

We all marched down the courthouse steps and back to my car. The nightmare was over. We'd won. I had *won*.

35

"I'll be sad to see her go," Auntie El said. We'd come in, just the two of us, to clean up the office now that the trial was done. "It's been nice having a kid around again."

I groaned, my back aching, and grabbed a stack of files, boxing them up to send off to storage. "I'd be glad to get out of here, in Zoey's place. Most folk won't know her out in Tacoma. She might have a chance at a fresh start.

Auntie El smiled. "Yeah, I talked to her aunt. She's a nice lady. Said Zoey can bring a pup, even two if she wants."

I'd gotten the same feeling from my own talk with Zoey's aunt in Tacoma. She was kind. She cared. She would give Zoey the life she deserved.

"You know what gets me," said Auntie El, "is how that lady grew up side by side with Lorraine, and one turned out lovely, the other a monster. You never do know with folks." She reached for the whiteboard eraser, then stopped and stepped back. "Seems almost a shame to erase our hard work."

"Erase it, be done with it." I flopped back in my chair. "I need you to do me a favor. If ever you catch me considering taking another case like this—if you even hear me say the word 'murder'—I need you to slap me upside the head."

Auntie El laughed and got to work on the whiteboard, clearing off our timeline, our theories, our suspect profiles. "He was a good man, you know, Sal Ackers."

I frowned. "Sal Ackers?"

"Leo's dad. The one the Conrads sued for burning their lake house. Dollars to donuts they burned it themselves."

Donuts sounded good. It would be lunchtime soon. Maybe I'd stop home and pick up Ian.

"I used to use Sal for my repairs," said Auntie El. "You wouldn't remember this—you were off in the Army then—but he used to do all his own TV spots. He'd dress up, sing jingles. Oh, he was such a sport." She put her hands on her hips and bumped her hips side to side. "Make all your problems a thing of the past. Call 55-AKERS, we're lightning fast."

I chuckled, because I had seen those ads, long, long ago. Back in high school. "Remember the one where he wore that pigeon head? Where he did that dance, like—" I broke off, thunderstruck.

"Maggie? You all right?"

I grabbed for my laptop.

"What's going on?"

"Just…give me a second…" I pulled up my browser, my heart beating fast.

The Ackers website was gone when I went to check it, but his ads had been popular back in the day. I found one on YouTube and pulled it up. On screen, Sal danced a tango with a broom in a wig. The fast tango beat faded into his jingle, and his logo popped up. I leapt to my feet. "That's it! The lightning bolt! It's Leo Ackers!"

"What?" Aunt Louise peered at the screen. "What's that in the background? Is that...?"

A cold wave rushed through me as I saw what she meant—way in the background, behind Sal Ackers, snuggled up tight to their peeling storefront—

"Red pickup," I croaked, just as my phone rang. I grabbed it without looking. "Maggie Gallagher."

Someone yelled down the line, off in the distance. I heard rustling, another yell, then a loud thump.

"Hello? Who is this?" I checked the screen. "Ian?"

More rustling. Shuffling. My stomach churned with anxiety and mounting dread.

"Ian, talk to me. You hear me? It's Mom."

The line went dead. I tapped to call back, but it went to voicemail.

"Maggie? You all right?" Auntie El asked. "You're white as a sheet."

I went to say something, but my vision grayed out. I grabbed my desk for support. Swallowed back bile. Auntie El steadied me, but I shook her off. That voice, that shouting voice, had it been Leo? Had his voice been hoarse like that the day I met him?

"Maggie?"

"Call 911," I said. "Call Liam. Call everyone. It's Ian. I think he's...I have to get home." I was already running, dialing again as I went. Ian's voicemail picked up, and I cursed. I could already hear Auntie

El on the phone, but would help come soon enough? What was happening?

I flung myself into my car and drove like a maniac through the snow-quiet streets. I should've spun on black ice and wound up in a ditch. But somehow I stayed on the blacktop, tearing down my street. I screamed around the corner and there, there it was, parked sideways on my snow-covered lawn. There, red and brown and covered in rust, an old, ratty pickup, just like Zoey'd described it.

The pickup.

The red pickup.

Leo Ackers.

I should've waited for the police. But I didn't. I couldn't. In my head was just *Ian*. I needed to get to him, throw myself in front of him, do whatever it took to protect him from Leo. So I barged in like a fool and nearly tripped over Sean knocked out on the floor. I couldn't breathe until I'd checked his pulse and found it beating steadily. Then I blundered down the hallway yelling for Ian. He yelled back.

"Mom, no, get out!"

"Ian? *Ian!*" I charged into the living room and my stomach bottomed out. I broke out all over in a cold, clammy sweat. Ian was standing half in front of Zoey, who was staring, frozen, at Leo Ackers. Leo's lips were peeled back in a teeth-baring grin, and in both hands, he was clutching a pistol pointed toward my son.

Somebody whimpered—maybe me, maybe Zoey.

"They killed my old man." Leo widened his stance. "They killed him as sure as if they shot him dead."

"I'm sorry," said Zoey.

"It wrecked him, to lose the business. He was so proud of what he'd built—a business, a legacy. And they took that away. And you knew…" The gun wobbled, still pointed at Zoey. She shrank away. Ian moved to shield her.

"I really am sorry." Zoey edged out from behind Ian. She tried to step in front of him, but he pulled her back.

"I never wanted to kill them." Leo licked his lips. "All I wanted was for them to know what they did. Did you know my dad died of a broken heart? Stress cardiomyopathy was what the doc said, but I looked it up. It's a broken heart. They broke him, and that's all I wanted to tell them. But then your old man went for his gun." Leo adjusted his grip on his pistol, letting go with one hand to wipe his slick brow. "It wasn't my fault. It happened so fast. Why the hell didn't you turn them in? I saw on the news, all that they did to you. How your mom burned you, and you kept your mouth shut? Why would you protect her? Why would you, why?"

Zoey made a small sound, choking, distressed.

"She's only a kid," I said. "She's a victim too."

"She could've said something. Put them in jail. Kept people like my dad safe from them and their schemes. Their *lies*."

Behind Leo, I caught a glimmer of movement, Alia sneaking onto the deck. Auntie El must've sent her, but she didn't barge in like I had. Instead, she sidled up slowly, gun drawn. I took care not to look at her and risk alerting Leo.

"You're right," said Zoey, and her voice cracked. "I should have come forward, but I was scared. I'm sorry you lost your dad, and—"

"It's too late for that." Leo's finger twitched, and my legs turned to jelly. I almost fell, but instead I yelled out.

"Wait! Wait, hold on. This isn't Zoey's fault."

"Then whose is it? Whose?"

My head spun. I couldn't think, but I tried anyway. "There are things you don't know. Have you heard of, uh, hearsay?"

Leo's lips twitched. "Hearsay? Like, lying in court?"

I knew not to tell the man with the gun he was wrong, so I nodded. "Yes. That's it exactly. There are things you can't testify to in court, like things you overheard. Zoey overheard her mother admitting she inflicted the burns. But that was hearsay, so her hands were tied. If she'd come forward, the cops would've told her she had no case, because it was hearsay."

Leo blinked sweat from his eyes. "Is that true?"

I shuffled closer. "You want me to show you? There's a book right behind you up on that shelf, a big, dusty blue one, *Principles of Litigation*."

Leo turned to look for it, and I whacked his arm. The pistol went flying, and he dove after it. But Alia was faster, crashing through the back door. She barreled into him like a ton of bricks, and the next thing I knew, he was flat on his face. I started for Ian, but he ran for Sean, Zoey hot on his heels. They dropped down beside him. Sean sat up, and my relief was so strong my knees buckled, and I went down next to him on the floor. He slid his arm around me and pulled me close.

"Mags, oh my God... Ian, come here."

Ian hugged Sean, then pulled back to look at him. "Your head. You're still bleeding."

"I'll get the first aid kit." Zoey ran off to find it, and I leaned into Sean.

"Baby? You all right?"

"Yeah, I think so." He touched the gash on his forehead and flinched from the pain. "Might need a stitch or two, but yeah. I'm okay."

Outside, sirens rose, the cops arriving. Alia was guarding Leo, sitting on his back. But all the fight had gone out of him and he lay dull-eyed.

"It's over," said Ian. He nudged me. "Right, Mom?"

"That's right."

"They'll leave Zoey alone, now he's confessed?"

I guessed Zoey would be dealing with questions for a while yet. But Leo would be arrested now, tried and convicted. Zoey's name would be cleared for good. "She'll get some peace," I said, believing that one day, she would. Leo would go to prison, maybe death row. The news would move on, and the world along with it. Zoey would have her chance to rebuild her life.

I stood, still shaky, as the cops rushed in. The nightmare was over. Finally.

36

We had a big BBQ to celebrate—Zoey's freedom, my win, the kids' spring break. Everyone came. The whole family. Alia. Even a few kids from Ian's school.

Leo had confessed the second the cops showed up, the truth pouring out of him as they slapped on the cuffs. He'd been taken in, and he'd pleaded guilty. That nightmare was finally, truly over.

Zoey's aunt Joyce had agreed she could stay through the end of the school year. She'd been scared to go face a whole new set of kids, and sad at the thought she'd miss Ian's graduation. The aunties had talked and chosen to let Zoey decide where to live. She'd had few enough choices in her young life, and she deserved the chance to have a say.

Her eyes had gone round when her aunt raised the subject. "You wouldn't be mad at me if I wanted to stay?"

"Oh, honey, no." Aunt Joyce had hugged her. "This is your life, and you're almost grown now. If you want to finish the year with your friends, I'm not going to uproot you."

Zoey had taken the weekend to think before deciding she wasn't ready to go yet, not now the gossip was settling down.

Now, she was helping Sean out on the grill, flipping the burgers while he held forth on cooking times.

"Folks say 'flipping burgers' like it's this easy job, but it's a whole science. The heat, the temperature, even the charcoal all work together to get that right taste."

I rolled my eyes, having heard it a million times, but Zoey seemed to be enjoying herself. She kept asking questions, egging Sean on, so I went over to talk to Alia.

"Enjoying your burger?"

"Mm, yeah. It's good." She took another bite and licked her lips. "Thanks for letting the kids tag along." Alia had brought a few cousins, two boys and two girls, who'd been tearing around all day with Liam and Patrick's kids. I still hadn't sussed out the size of her family, except there were lots of them, and they were loud. I kind of hoped she would bring them around more. Like Auntie El had said, it was nice having kids around.

"Are they two sets of twins, or is one girl older?"

"Actually, they're triplets—the boys and Maureen. And then there's Paula, and she's, yeah, a year older."

The triplets and Paula ran by with a couple of Patrick's kids. They raced through the remnants of winter's last snowbank, and ran in circles screaming "cold, cold." I was just getting wistful, picturing Ian at that age, when I heard a glass clinking and turned to look.

"Mom? Everyone?" Ian was clinking. "I know this is cheesy, but I've got an announcement, and I wanted to get to it before the party gets too wild."

A few laughs went up at that, and Ian beamed.

"As some of you know, I've been applying to colleges, and I just heard back from the Rhode Island School of Design."

We all stood expectant. After a moment, he grinned ear to ear.

"Oh! I got in. Was that not clear?"

Sean rushed him first, spatula dripping. A cheer went up as they shared a big hug. I got in on that, and Zoey did too, though I figured she'd probably already known. Dad tried to squeeze in, but there was no space for him, so he reached over and clapped Ian's back.

"So, you're happy?" said Ian, when I pulled back.

"Happy? I'm ecstatic! You got into college!"

"You don't mind that it's art school?"

"Why would I mind?"

He shrugged. "Well, because, you know. You're a lawyer. And you were in the Army, so…"

"So I can't like art?"

"I didn't mean *that*."

I hugged him again to show I was teasing. "I'm proud of you, kiddo. That's a great school."

Zombie came running by with someone's lost hot dog, Alia's cousins in hot pursuit. Ian yelled "*Bad* dog," and joined the chase. Sean had his phone out, and I bumped our elbows together.

"So, how far is it?"

"Huh?"

"To Rhode Island."

He laughed. "Google says it's about a twelve-hour drive. Seven hundred miles, give or take." He put his phone away and slid his arm around me. "He'll call and text, and he'll come home for holidays. Christmas. Thanksgiving. And we'll have summers."

Zombie bounded up and squeezed between us. The kids ran around us, kicking up dust. They made me feel sad, because the days of Ian being that size were long gone. Soon it'd be just me and Sean again. Well, us and Zombie. At least we'd have that.

The sun went down and the kids broke out the sparklers. They played with Zombie until he passed out. Then, one by one, they conked out as well. Alia half-carried the triplets out, and loaded them into her borrowed SUV. Patrick took his kids home, and Liam packed his up.

"I feel bad," he said, as they pulled on their coats.

I turned to look at him. "Bad? About what?"

"I'm not saying it was my fault that Ackers...y'know." He touched his own forehead, where Sean had a scar from Leo's assault. "But if I'd done more digging, we might've had Ackers in time for the trial."

"You thought you had the killer."

"I did, yeah. But I've been thinking about what you said in court. About the Conrad case being my first homicide. I keep asking myself, was that a factor? *Did* I miss something I should've seen?"

I kissed him on his cheek. "If you did, so did all of us."

"You thought she did it?"

I looked out at Zoey helping Ian clean up. It was hard to imagine her taking a life. But she had—Harold Rooney's, the first night I'd met her. A tiny part of me had wondered, when the jury came back, if Oliver was right. If she'd actually done it. Up till the moment Ackers confessed, I'd still been wondering, had I freed a killer?

"I didn't know what was true," I said. "She told so many stories."

"How's she doing now?"

I smiled. "A lot better. Auntie El says her nightmares have stopped, and she's talking about applying to college next year."

"Good. That's good. She deserves a fresh start."

The kids ran out past him, and Liam followed. I went out too, to help Sean with the tables. We folded them one by one and carried them to the garage, and with the last one put up, we stood catching our breath.

"We're getting old," said Sean.

"Speak for yourself." I smacked him, halfhearted, and he pulled me in for a kiss.

"I'm proud of us." Sean squeezed my hands. "The way Ian's stood by Zoey—not many kids his age would do that. Whatever he does next, he's going to be great."

I leaned into Sean's arms and my heart swelled with pride. We'd done our jobs, raised him up right. Now, he'd be headed off on his next adventure. And Zoey as well, she'd have a future now. She'd had a rough start, but Ian had been right about her. He'd seen her strength all along, and her good heart.

"Look there," said Sean, and pointed out at the yard. Ian was helping Auntie El with the punch bowl. Zoey was packing away the kids' toys. Ian said something and she threw a ball at him, and he caught it and tossed it back. Auntie El wagged her finger, pretending to scold them, and then all three of them headed inside.

"A happy ending." Sean hugged me, and he was right. Somehow, this whole mess had come out all right.

END OF THE BLOODIED CLIENT
MAGGIE GALLAGHER LEGAL THRILLER SERIES BOOK 2

The Midwest Lawyer, April 24, 2025

The Bloodied Client, January 15, 2026

The Wrong Victim, May 21, 2026

PS: Do you enjoy legal thrillers? Then keep reading for exclusive extracts from **The Wrong Victim, Small Town Conviction,** and **Defending Innocence.**

ABOUT PETER KIRKLAND

Loved this book? Share it with a friend!

To be notified of Peter's next book release please sign up to his mailing list, at
www.peterkirklandauthor.com

ABOUT PETER

Peter Kirkland grew up in Beaufort, South Carolina. As a kid, Peter loved history and learning about his area. One year in school, he was given a project to research a few South Carolina law cases and the precedents they set and their effect on people's lives. This research project lit the flame for his passion for law and creating a more equal justice system since. Soon after this, Peter began reading legal thrillers voraciously and enjoyed the legal maneuvering and justice found within. As an adult he has continued researching the law and understanding the system and its effects on individuals. A few years ago, he decided to try writing his own legal thriller.

Now a full-time writer, he uses his research, passion for justice, and real case studies to bring together courtroom dramas with deep, rich characters, and gripping twists and turns. New to the industry, Peter would love to hear from readers and other authors and invites you to connect with him through:

BLURB

In a small town that's already decided the verdict, one lawyer fights for the truth...

When Attorney Maggie Gallagher takes on a volatile new client still reeling from a devastating personal loss, she never expects the case to spiral beyond the courtroom. After Maggie loses the case, her furious client goes viral for a public rant aimed at a ruthless healthcare CEO.

Days later, the CEO and his lawyer are killed in a fiery explosion aboard the CEO's yacht.

The prime suspect? Maggie's grieving client…

After threatening the CEO in public, the distraught woman's motive couldn't be clearer. But when the dead lawyer's fiancé brings Maggie unsettling information about his fiancée's shadowy past, Maggie begins to suspect the CEO may not have been the intended target after all.

As Maggie races to untangle a sinister web of secrets and lies, the pressure of her growing caseload threatens the fragile stability she has fought so hard to build for her family. And in a town hungry for a conviction, every misstep could seal her client's fate.

With the clock ticking, Maggie must uncover the truth before her client is condemned for a crime she didn't commit—while the real killer walks free, ready to strike again.

Get your copy of *The Wrong Victim*
Available May 21, 2026
(Available for pre-order now)
www.peterkirklandauthor.com

EXCERPT

Chapter One

I was on a roll.

I had the jury right where I wanted them, convinced they were experts on contract law. Nodding along with my closing argument, confident in every picky detail. All that was left now was to bring the case home to them. Bring it back to my client and all she had lost.

"This case is about my client, Sara Stephenson, and the contract she had with Vista Insurance. Vista breached that contract by failing to pay when the clear terms of the contract obligated them to do so. Their failure was intentional, and it was fatal."

I paused to let that sink in, and it should've been devastating—every head on the jury turning to Sara. Turning to take in her pain and her loss. Instead, they all jumped as a car horn blared, a rude, sustained blast from the chaos outside. This case had sparked outrage and that had brought protests, including out-of-town activists with banners and signs. With the verdict in sight, their ranks had exploded, blocking off traffic down Kerry's main road. Now the gallery broke out in excited chatter. The jurors sat blinking, their focus shot.

Judge Rabinowicz glowered and reached for his gavel. Sara, behind me, was grinding her teeth. She didn't care for surprises, and I didn't blame her. Not after all she'd already been through. I hurried over to calm her down.

"It's all right," I said, as the judge called for order, pitching my words for Sara alone. "We're through the hard part, just wrapping up."

Judge Rabinowicz waited till I was done with Sara, then he gave me a tense nod. "Ready to proceed?"

"I am, Your Honor." I took a deep breath to quell my own irritation. This interruption wasn't ideal, disrupting my closing in the minds of the jury. Would they remember the arguments I'd spent days constructing, how I'd held their hands through the dense contract law? Or had that stupid horn shattered the impact of my hard work? The best I could do now was a quick recap, then hit them full-force with my emotional payload.

"There's no dispute that Bill Stephenson had stage four follicular lymphoma. We've heard from his oncologist, an expert in her field, that with prompt treatment, his chances were good. We've heard from a parade of experts, both mine and Vista's, and not one has refuted one simple fact: even when it's not caught until stage four, follicular lymphoma has a five-year survival rate of eighty-seven percent. *Eighty-seven percent.* Almost nine out of ten.

"What that means in plain English is nine times out of ten, a patient like Bill lives five more years. He goes into remission. He gets more good days. That's what Sara was told by Bill's cancer team: that she'd have more time with him, quality time. They had a whole scrapbook, their 'second chance guide,' packed full of plans for his new lease on life. They were going to go sailing. Learn to cook. Take the honeymoon they couldn't swing when they married. That scrapbook, I counted, had sixty-two pages, crammed with their hopes for Bill's next chapter."

Sara sniffled behind me. I paused again. The jury watched her throat work as she swallowed her grief. I didn't have to look to know they were seeing her loss graven into every line of her face. Into her dark hair, streaked with new gray. Bill's death had aged her ten years in a day, or so she'd told me in our first meeting. To look at her now, I'd have said more like twenty. Sara was thirty-five, and she looked at least fifty. Her ravaged face was my strongest exhibit, and I stood a long moment as the court drank her in.

"Vista had a duty to act in good faith in processing Bill's claim, and they failed in their duty. They denied his claim with no reasonable justification, and, as a result, Bill's treatment was delayed. Vista acted with malice by dragging their feet on the claim, and as a result of this delay, an infection set in, followed by sepsis, leading to Bill's preventable death. Due to the actions of Vista Insurance, Bill lost his life. And Sara lost Bill. We've heard testimony to her emotional distress, her ongoing struggles with PTSD and depression. These *are not*, as Vista claims, pre-existing conditions.

"We've heard from her therapist, who knows her well—who'd been treating her for workplace stress prior to Bill's death—and the therapist confirmed that she'd been mentally healthy up to that point. Frustrated with work sometimes. Frustrated with life. But Sara Stephenson's mental health was overall good. Only with Bill's death did depression set in. Grief so profound she couldn't work. She lost her job. Couldn't get out of bed.

"Six months of unpaid leave cost Sara her livelihood, but that's nothing to her, stacked against Bill. What Vista cost Sara when they denied treatment was everything in her scrapbook. Her plans with Bill. Their hopes and dreams for the rest of their life."

I felt in my marrow, I had the jury. They were all leaning forward, eyes big and wet. If they had to pick sides right now, they'd tip for the plaintiff.

"Your job as the jury is to look at the evidence, and decide based on everything you've heard and seen in court, is Vista liable? We've proven they are. Vista's evidence in no way refuted that they breached the contract, that they did so in bad faith, and because of Vista's malingering, Bill met an early death. Vista also failed to refute that their bad faith actions caused Sara emotional distress." I stepped to one side, away from Sara, leaving her sitting starkly alone. I wanted the jury to see her that way, hunched and exhausted, all by herself without the man who should've been by her side. I needed them picturing themselves in her place, asking themselves what they'd want from Vista. Pricing out in their heads five years of life, five years with a loved one gone up in smoke.

"I'm confident that when you examine the evidence you'll find in favor of the Plaintiff on each of her claims. I'm also confident that you'll award her just compensation for the damages Defendant caused and that your award for punitive damages will reflect the egregiousness of the Defendant's conduct."

As I sat down, a cheer went up, not from the courtroom, but from the protest outside. It was pure coincidence, but the timing was eerie. An answering ripple ran through the court, a scatter of sudden and startled applause. Judge Rabinowicz went for his gavel, but the hubbub was already ebbing away. Sara sat wide-eyed, hand pressed to her mouth. I leaned in to comfort her.

"Hey, it's all right. You're doing great."

"I wish I still believed in—in God. Or in signs." She was still staring straight ahead like she hadn't heard me. "Because if I did, I'd think we just won."

Get your copy of *The Wrong Victim*
Available May 21, 2026
(Available for pre-order now)
www.peterkirklandauthor.com

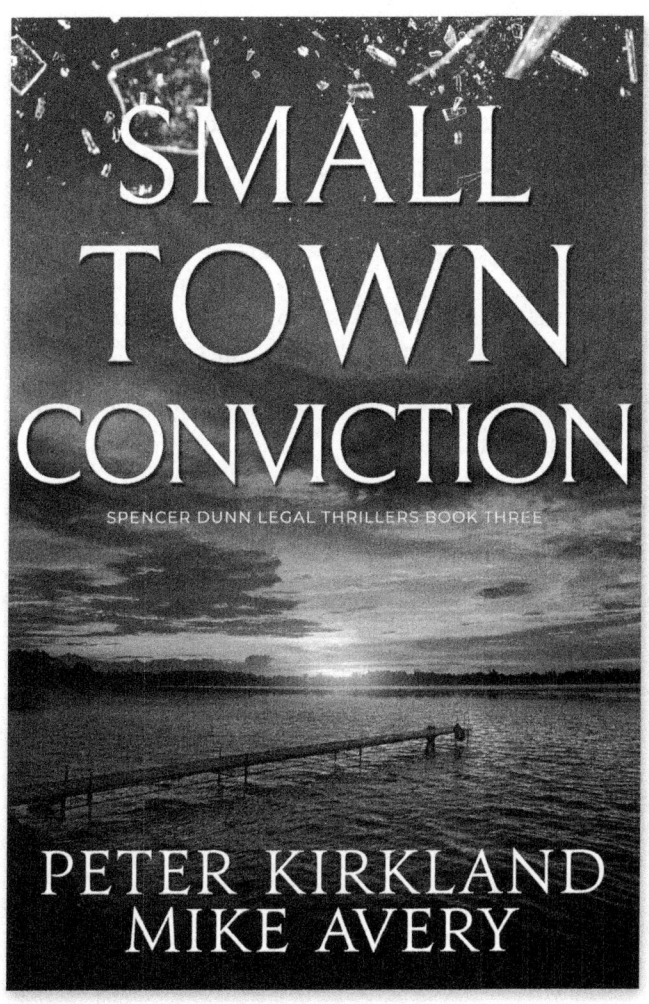

BLURB

One small town. One deadly weekend. Three shocking crimes…

A local business owner is shot and disappears under mysterious circumstances. Another man goes on a hit-and-run rampage. And a horrifying day care incident sends innocent children to the ER. At first glance, the events appear unrelated. But as he investigates, local attorney Spencer Dunn begins to think otherwise.

When Spencer digs beneath Autumn Harbor's idyllic surface, he uncovers a dark thread weaving the cases together—a thread that leads straight to Jack Butcher, the flashy civic leader whose shiny public persona masks a rotten core. For years, Butcher has operated from the shadows, untouchable… and Spencer is determined to change that.

With pressure mounting and his own family under threat, Spencer races to connect the dots before his innocent clients are convicted. But the truth is more twisted than he ever imagined—and Butcher will do anything to keep it buried.

Now, with the impact of past and current cases coming to a head, Spencer must put more than his legal skill to work—or he may become the next casualty.

Get your copy of *Small Town Conviction*
Available February 26, 2026
(Available for pre-order now)
www.peterkirklandauthor.com

EXCERPT

Chapter One

"It's a miracle those kids didn't die." Alastair shook his head in grateful disbelief.

"They would have, if your client hadn't had that Narcan ready and waiting," I said. "Pretty reckless, keeping heroin in the house where you operate a day care."

"She says the drugs weren't hers, that she didn't know anything about them."

"If that's true, why did she have the Narcan?"

It was Monday, and I was eating an early lunch near the courthouse with my boss, who was also my father-in-law. He'd been in court that morning, representing Cathy Silver. Children at her day care center had found packages of heroin in a playroom cupboard and torn them open, ingested some of the powder, and had to be rushed to the hospital after she gave them a dose of Narcan.

It would have been an upsetting story in any case, but my wife and I had a new little girl at home, a four-year-old we were hoping to adopt. To put it bluntly, Alastair's case freaked me out.

"I don't know," Alastair said. "Cathy hasn't told me much, other than to deny any knowledge of the drugs. Even though she's lived in Autumn Harbor her whole life, the judge denied bail on the grounds that she presented a threat to the safety of the community."

I nodded and looked down at the Reuben I'd ordered. I loved sauerkraut. Whenever I was in New York, I'd get a hot dog slathered in it from a street vendor. Thinking about those kids in the hospital, however, made its tangy aroma smell more like rotten eggs. I pushed my plate away.

"I don't know what's going on in our little town," Alastair continued. "Had you heard about Joe Murrell, who runs We Love Your Junk?"

"We Love Your Junk?" I asked. "Please tell me that's a secondhand store and not some sort of adult business."

Alastair gave me the side-eye. "It's the local waste haulage company. Anyhow, the owner's gone missing. Didn't show up for work on Friday or Saturday. Then there's your new client."

Roy Pelletier, an accountant, had been driving through town Saturday night and hit a pedestrian. Rather than stopping, he'd fled the scene and led the police on a high-speed chase before finally slamming into another car. Accountants could be reckless just like anyone else, of course, but Alastair was right—that was a lot of weird incidents in a short period.

"I guess it's all good for us criminal defense lawyers," I said, though my stomach was still uneasy. "I'd better get going," I added. "I need to talk to Roy before the hearing." I didn't know Pelletier well, but I'd been introduced to him at Whiskey Business, my wife's bar and restaurant, and we'd exchanged pleasantries a time or two.

I met him in the lockup next to the courtroom where he was due to be arraigned at two. No other prisoners were present, so we could talk privately through the bars of the cell. He appeared to be wearing the clothes he'd been arrested in. They were filthy.

"Before we go in front of the judge, I need you to tell me what happened Saturday night," I said. "Anything you say while we're talking about your case is covered by the attorney-client privilege." A friend of his had dropped off a check for the retainer at my office that morning. "That means I can't repeat it without your permission, except to others in my firm and anyone else we might hire to work on this with us. You do need to know, however, that if you tell me you did the things you're charged with, I can't put you on the stand to deny them."

He nodded and said he understood.

"I'm jumping ahead a bit, but I can't help wondering," I said, "how'd you get so dirty?"

"I guess I was dizzy after I hit the other car. I opened my door to get out, but I stumbled and fell on the ground. I tried to get up, but I kept falling. Finally, I decided to sit where I was until help came."

"How long did you feel dizzy?"

"A couple of minutes. The cop helped me to my feet after he took care of the other driver, and by then I felt better."

"What did you tell the officer?"

"Nothing. He took a good look at the situation and then read me my rights. I thought the smart thing to do would be to keep my mouth shut."

"Good call. Okay, let's back up to how this all started—before the first collision. Can you walk me through the whole thing?"

Roy wiped sweat from his forehead. "I was out for a drive, and I must have hit something … someone … at the corner of Myrtle and Main. It was dark, and the streetlight was out. I didn't see anyone, but I heard a loud thump on the passenger side. I panicked and hit the gas."

"Why didn't you stop to see what had happened?"

Roy was a few inches shorter than I was and had to look up to meet my eyes. "I know I should have. I can't tell you why I didn't. Maybe it was, like, adrenaline? I wasn't thinking. My foot just stomped on the gas, and I shot out of there."

"Where had you been going before the collision happened?"

He shook his head. "Nowhere. I was just driving around to pass the time."

"Do you have any outstanding tickets or criminal charges that you were afraid would come to light?"

"No."

"Had you been drinking? Was your auto insurance in effect?"

"Of course I have insurance, and no, I hadn't been drinking. There's no question about that. You don't have to take my word for it—the breath test they gave me at the station came back negative."

Many hit-and-run drivers left the scene because they knew things would get worse if they stopped, whether due to preexisting legal issues or their impaired status at the time of the incident. It seemed that Roy simply fell into the category of people for whom shock triggered flight.

"Anyway," Roy said, "right after that, I mean, like, a couple of seconds, I noticed a car coming up fast behind me."

"Did it have lights and a siren on?"

"No. I had no idea it was a cop. It scared the you-know-what out of me, and I kept accelerating, trying to get away. I was flying. It couldn't have been even a minute before I smashed into another car that was pulling out of a parking space. That's when I realized I couldn't just keep going."

"What happened then?"

"Like I said, I fell getting out of my car. The guy who'd been chasing me flashed a badge, told me to stay where I was, and headed over to the other car to check on the driver. I guess he, the driver, was hurt, because after a little while an ambulance arrived, and they put him on a stretcher and took him away. Then the cop came back to me and got me on my feet, read my rights, and arrested me."

Roy told me he was an accountant who worked for a number of people and businesses in town, that he'd lived in Autumn Harbor ever since he'd graduated from college, and that he'd never been arrested or even gotten a parking ticket. That was all good from the standpoint of bail, but it made me wonder if there was more to the accidents and high-speed chase than met the eye. I didn't want to get surprised by whatever that might be in the courtroom, so I made him go through everything one more time, giving me every detail he could. He insisted there was nothing else to the incident and said he had just panicked.

I left Roy in the lockup and waited in the courtroom for his case to be called. After the judge disposed of a few minor matters, the clerk called my case, and the bailiff brought Roy before the bench and released his handcuffs.

"Roy Pelletier," the clerk called out, "charged with violations of Section 2252, hit-and-run, Class C; Section 2413, driving to endanger, Class C; Section 2414, refusing to stop for a law enforcement officer; and Section 751-B, refusing to submit to arrest."

Judge Barbara Robinson was on the bench, wearing her trademark purple rhinestone glasses. She was known for her independence and unpredictability. I'd appeared in front of her several times, usually with decent results but sometimes with a very bad outcome. "Is your client prepared to enter a plea, Mr. Dunn?" she asked.

"Yes, Your Honor."

The clerk read out the charges again, one at a time, and Roy pleaded not guilty to each one.

"I'll hear you on bail," the judge said.

John Stanford, the prosecuting attorney, stood. "We're asking you to set bail in the amount of $100,000, Your Honor. The defendant is charged with a hit-and-run accident that caused injuries, then leading the police on a high-speed chase in an attempt to escape, resisting arrest, and finally a second collision causing a concussion and several broken bones. He poses a flight risk and is a danger to the community, and a significant bail is required."

Roy was as pale as a ghost, and I winced. A hundred thousand was probably quite a bit more than he could raise. I'd had other cases against Stanford. He was a young lawyer with little understanding of human failures. I hoped the judge could see that.

"Mr. Dunn," the judge said.

"Your Honor, I know it's unusual to call a witness at an arraignment, but I notice that Officer McElroy, who arrested my client, is in the courtroom this afternoon, and with the court's indulgence, I'd like to ask him a few questions before you set bail."

"Very well," the judge said, "but keep it brief, Counselor."

The officer took the stand and was sworn in, and I moved to stand in front of him in the witness box. "Officer McElroy, I just have a few questions for you. First, the car in which you chased my client wasn't a police car, was it?"

McElroy looked briefly at the prosecutor, then back to me. "No, it was my private car."

"So it wasn't equipped with lights and a siren or any police department markings, was it?"

"No, sir."

"Where did you find Mr. Pelletier after the second accident?"

"He was sitting on the street next to his vehicle."

I nodded. "Did you give him any instructions?"

"Yes, I told him to remain where he was."

"And he did, didn't he?"

"Yes."

"When you returned to him, you placed him under arrest?"

"Yes, sir."

"He didn't resist in any way, struggle with you, or attempt to flee, did he?"

"Not at that point, sir."

"No further questions."

Stanford stood. "Officer, what car were you in that evening?"

"Like I said, my personal car. It's a bright yellow vintage Ford Mustang. Very distinctive."

"To your knowledge, had Mr. Pelletier ever seen that vehicle?"

"Many times. We know each other. He does my taxes, and he's often complimented me on my car. He knew who was chasing him."

That came as a surprise to me, and I stifled a burst of irritation at my client. Why hadn't he told me that when we spoke before the hearing? I got quickly to my feet. "Objection, Your Honor. The witness can't know what was in someone else's mind."

"Sustained," the judge ruled.

"Nothing further," Stanford said.

I got up again. "Just one or two questions on redirect, if the court please."

The judge looked unhappy about the time this was taking. "Proceed. But just one or two."

"Officer, it was nighttime when this incident occurred, was it not, and the streets were dark?"

"Not completely dark."

"You had your headlights on?"

"Yes."

"So someone in the car ahead of you, looking at your vehicle in his rearview mirror, would mostly just see your headlights? It would've been very difficult, maybe impossible, to see the vehicle itself, wouldn't it?"

McElroy smirked. "As you said, Counselor, I couldn't know what someone else could see."

What they could see wasn't exactly the same thing as what they knew or had been thinking, but I didn't want to test Judge Robinson's patience by pressing the issue. I was confident she had gotten the point, and, grudgingly, I had to admire the officer's wit in trying to turn the tables on me. "No further questions."

"You're excused," the judge told McElroy.

"Your Honor," I said, "before addressing the question of bail, I'll move to dismiss the charges of refusing to stop for a law enforcement officer and resisting arrest, the former on the ground of lack of scienter—the defendant had no reason to know it was a police officer chasing him—and the latter on the basis of the officer's testimony. Once my client knew that McElroy was a law enforcement officer, there was no resistance."

One of Judge Robinson's pet peeves was overcharging by police and prosecutors. She liked to get directly to the nub of the issue. She looked at Stanford. "I think it will sufficiently serve the interests of justice for us to try the defendant for the hit-and-run and driving-to-endanger charges."

Stanford looked like he had something to say about that, but given Judge Robinson's demeanor, he swallowed it. "No objection, Your Honor."

"Very well," the judge said, "the counts for refusing to stop and resisting arrest are dismissed."

"Thank you, Your Honor," I said. "Given that, I suggest that bail in the amount of $5,000 would be sufficient. Mr. Pelletier has lived in this community ever since he finished school. He has no prior record and is well known here. He has an accounting practice and does the taxes of many local citizens. Given his ties to the community, he cannot be considered a flight risk, and given that we're essentially dealing with automobile accidents, I don't think it would be fair to consider him a risk to the community."

Judge Robinson didn't hesitate before saying, "Bail is set in the amount of $10,000, and the defendant is ordered to surrender his driver's license to the clerk's office and to refrain from operating a motor vehicle until this matter is resolved." She set a date for Roy's next court appearance, and the clerk called the next case.

The guard took Roy back to the lockup, and I followed.

"Can you post that?" I asked.

"No problem. Can you call my friend for me? He'll bring cash to the jail."

Roy gave me the friend's name and number, and I agreed to call him.

"If he shows up quickly, you should be out before dinner," I said. "We'll talk again in a couple of days."

Get your copy of Small Town Conviction
Available February 26, 2026
(Available for pre-order now)
www.peterkirklandauthor.com

BLURB

An innocent client harbors dark secrets…

Defense attorney Leland Monroe lost it all: his big-city job, his reputation and, worst of all, his loving wife. Now he's back in his hometown to hit restart and repair the relationship with his troubled son. But the past is always present in a small town.

Leland returns to find his high school sweetheart hasn't had the easiest of lives—especially now that her son faces a death sentence for murdering his father. Yet what appears to be an open and shut case is anything but. As Leland digs deeper to uncover a truth even his client is determined to keep buried, a tangled web of corruption weaves its way throughout his once tranquil hometown.

Leland soon realizes it's not just his innocent young client's life that's at stake—powerful forces surface to threaten the precious few loved ones he has left.

Grab your copy of *Defending Innocence* (Small Town Lawyer Book One)
eBook
Paperback
Audiobook
www.peterkirklandauthor.com

EXCERPT

Chapter One

Judge Callahan was staring at me over the top of his glasses, and I reached up to adjust the volume on my hearing aids. I wasn't used to wearing them yet, and figuring out the correct volume for different situations was a work in progress. Thankfully, the low-level whistling that had been tormenting me since I put them on this morning went away, and my shoulders went down a notch.

With a nod to my client, I dropped my prepared speech onto the counsel table and walked slowly toward the jury box. I stopped a few feet from the railing at the front of the box and waited a moment. My eyes moved slowly from juror to juror. They stared at me impassively. I could read nothing on their faces.

"A prosecution like this is a terrible experience for the Williams children," I began. "At a time when they should be able to rely on their parents for stability and support, intolerance and vindictiveness define their family life. Their father filed criminal charges against their mother. Their private lives have been invaded by a public trial. The possibility of their mother's conviction has imperiled their ability to feel secure and protected. Thank goodness this is finally coming to an end. What that end will be is up to you."

I couldn't believe my client's ex-husband had talked the prosecutor into filing charges for criminal restraint. Maybe he was a major contributor to the DA's reelection campaign. I wasn't yet sufficiently connected in Autumn Harbor to know. I had to hope the jury found the charge as ridiculous as I did.

"Mary Williams was excited to take her children on an adventure in Canada. It was a special trip. Kids love to visit their grandparents. Grandparents let them get away with stuff their parents are strict about—candy, TV, you know what I mean." I looked at the jurors old enough to have grandchildren and smiled.

I gestured in Mary's direction. "Mary planned the trip properly. She got an agreement from the children's father to take the children out of the country. That's the responsible and respectful thing to do, and that's what she did." I was starting to find my rhythm, though I still felt shakier than I liked.

"When Grandpa suggested they spend a couple of days at his cabin in the woods, it promised to make their adventure even more exciting. Mary didn't need her ex-husband's permission for that. She was entitled to change her day-to-day plans in Canada. She had the right, as the custodial parent, to manage the trip as she saw fit." So far, so good.

"Then, suddenly, when they were in northern Ontario, there was an emergency. You can't plan for emergencies. They come out of the blue, and you do the best you can. Sometimes everything goes well. Sometimes it doesn't. When people are stressed and upset, they're not always able to manage things perfectly. But this is life. We have to make allowances when someone's plans are upset by unexpected and frightening events."

Judges generally kept their expressions neutral during arguments by counsel. Judge Callahan, a senior jurist with white hair and a pink complexion, was no exception. I got a little nod, however, from His Honor on the nature of emergencies.

I pursed my lips and cocked my head. "That's what happened here. Grandpa got sick. Very sick. He had to be airlifted to a hospital." I shook my head. "What could be more alarming? Imagine it. The helicopter lifts off, taking Mary's father away." I raised my arm, mimicking the takeoff, and looked past it toward an imaginary sky. "Mary doesn't know if she's about to lose him. She wants to get to his bedside as quickly as possible. Maybe these will be the last few moments she has with her father."

I walked back to the defense table and stood behind my client, my hands on the back of her chair. "In that dire moment, Mary does the best she can for her children. She arranges for them to be looked after by a longtime friend of the family, someone who babysat Mary herself when she was a child. She sends a message to the children's father, explaining the situation. She informs the kids' school and their karate and music teachers that they will be absent, and why. She contacts the parents of her daughter's friends to say her upcoming birthday party will need to be rescheduled. She does everything she can think of to keep the children's life as normal as possible while she's on her way to the hospital."

Shaking my head, I resumed my spot in front of the jury box. "Those are not the actions of someone who is engaged in the criminal restraint of her own children to infringe on their father's rights." A couple of the jurors shook their heads in response, and I felt—though didn't show—a surge of optimism. "As you've heard, Mr. Williams never got Mary's message. There's no evidence that was her fault. As I said, in an emergency, sometimes things go off course. Was Mary trying to deprive her ex-husband of time with the children? Certainly not. In fact, in the message she sent him, she suggested he take an extra weekend with the kids to make up for the time he would be missing." That, too, seemed to get a positive response from the jurors.

"Mr. Williams complained that Mary didn't confirm that he received her message. In an ideal world, where she wasn't worried to death at her father's bedside in the hospital, she might have done that. Her failure to do so under the circumstances here can hardly be considered a criminal act."

I turned and pointed at Mr. Williams. He was the kind of person whose resting face betrayed arrogance. I hoped that the jurors assigned that frame of mind to him. "He didn't do everything perfectly either. He might have checked with the school, the karate and music teachers, or the parents of his children's friends to see if they knew what was going on. If he was as worried as he now claims he was, wouldn't you expect him to reach out to anyone and everyone who might have the slightest bit of information? He called *no one*." I paused to let that sink in. "No one. Not until three days after he missed his weekend—just one day before Mary and the kids arrived home—when he called, again, not the school or other parents, but the police." The idea of going the better part of a week without checking on a child's welfare was so alien to me that I still found it hard to imagine… though I knew all too well that plenty of parents did far worse to their kids.

"The prosecutor has tried to suggest that Mary had a history of keeping the kids with her on their father's scheduled weekends. But in fact that only happened on two occasions. Once, one of the kids had a stomach bug, and Mary thought he wouldn't do well on the hour drive to the father's place. The other time was soon after the divorce, and the child had a meltdown and didn't want to leave home. Two incidents over the whole time the parents have been separated is hardly a pattern. It doesn't demonstrate disregard for the other parent or for the law. Young kids get sick. They throw tantrums. The same things might've happened at the father's house. In his concern for the children's health and feelings, Mr. Williams might well have delayed returning them to their mother until things calmed down."

I paused and gave another small shake of my head. I was glad I didn't handle matrimonial disputes on a regular basis. Too often they ended up as battles between parents in which the children were the principal victims. "Managing visitation issues in a divorce isn't easy. It takes patience and understanding. The parents have to be willing to give each other a break when problems arise—which can be a challenge when emotions run high. But," I emphasized, "the most important thing is the children's welfare. The Williams children were well taken care of in Canada. They were worried about their grandfather, but they were safe and nothing bad happened to them. And hopefully they're fine now, despite the stress and publicity of this trial. But they won't be fine if their father's vendetta against their mother is successful."

I grimaced. "No. A prosecution like this is not the way to resolve minor problems that arise during a divorce. There is no evidence here of the criminal restraint of children. There is no evidence that Mary intended to deprive Mr. Williams of his right to spend time with his children. There is no evidence that she intended to violate any law. A guilty verdict would be a travesty of justice."

Time to wrap this up. I hoped I'd made all my points persuasively.

"It's up to you to set this family back on the right path," I said, trying to press my sincerity into each juror's heart. "The path of mutual respect, understanding, and cooperation. You can do that with a verdict of not guilty. That is the correct verdict under the law and, equally if not more important, the one that will protect the welfare of the Williams children."

I sat down. Mrs. Baynard, juror number four, the gray-haired schoolteacher in the front row, stared at me with an expression so stern, so angry that I wanted to turn away. I waited a second, then looked down and folded my papers into a pile. I couldn't tell what her reaction meant. Was she angry at me? Why? While the prosecutor was getting to his feet for his closing argument, I reviewed everything I could remember. I couldn't imagine what might have set Mrs. Baynard off… unless something had been said during the trial that I missed because of my hearing issues. I didn't think so—I'd been carrying spare batteries every day, just in case I noticed my hearing aids giving the slightest bit of trouble—but if I had, it was too late to do anything about it.

Grab your copy of *Defending Innocence* (Small Town Lawyer Book One)
eBook
Paperback
Audiobook
www.peterkirklandauthor.com

Printed in Dunstable, United Kingdom